T0104028

Avenging Portia

Valerie S Armstrong

Order this book online at www.trafford.com
or email orders@trafford.com

Most Trafford titles are also available at major online book retailers.

© Copyright 2016 Valerie S Armstrong.

All rights reserved. No part of this publication may be reproduced, stored in a
retrieval system, or transmitted, in any form or by any means, electronic, mechanical,
photocopying, recording, or otherwise, without the written prior permission of the author.

Print information available on the last page.

ISBN: 978-1-4907-7313-1 (sc)
ISBN: 978-1-4907-7312-4 (e)

Because of the dynamic nature of the Internet, any web addresses or links contained in
this book may have changed since publication and may no longer be valid. The views
expressed in this work are solely those of the author and do not necessarily reflect the
views of the publisher, and the publisher hereby disclaims any responsibility for them.

Any people depicted in stock imagery provided by Thinkstock are models,
and such images are being used for illustrative purposes only.
Certain stock imagery © Thinkstock.

Trafford rev.   05/12/2016

 www.trafford.com

North America & international
toll-free: 1 888 232 4444 (USA & Canada)
fax: 812 355 4082

Author of: Livvy

No Roses for Abby

Follow the Butterfly

Looking for Lucius

Relative Truths

For my family and friends who supported me through a difficult journey, while writing this story.

Chapter One

I don't remember my mother. She died just before my second birthday. She was skiing in the mountains of Norway, near the town of Lillehammer, the place where she was born, when she lost control and hit a tree, killing her instantly. I didn't need photographs to show me how beautiful she was, although we had albums full of them. I only had to look at my sister, Portia, who everybody said was the spitting image of her. My first memory of Portia was the day I fell out of a tree, onto my back, and looked up to see her running towards me. I think I was about three-years-old and Portia was eight, but she reminded me of my favorite china doll; the one with the pale golden hair that tumbled over her shoulders, and eyes the color of the sky on a bright summer's day.

We lived with my father in Scarsdale, a village located twenty five miles north of New York City. Our house was on Chedworth Road, a five bedroom colonial, built thirty years before I was born. It was a grand house, all brick and stone with vaulted ceilings, casement windows and a huge garden bordered by towering oak trees. My parents moved from the city to Scarsdale right after they were married. My father was a senior marketing manager at J. P. Morgan when he met my mother. He was thirty-six years old and already very successful in business but he had not been as successful in relationships. Among the circles in which he usually traveled, he met many women whom he found to be both attractive and with above average intelligence, but they weren't marriage material. My mother, on the other hand, was exactly what he was looking for. He was on a skiing vacation in Lausanne at the same time that my mother was there, visiting a cousin, and she had stopped in for a cocktail at Château d'Ouchy, the hotel where my father was staying. The way Daddy tells it, he walked into the bar and stopped in his tracks when he noticed my mother. He claims she was the most beautiful woman he'd ever laid eyes on. Two days later, in Villars, he saw her again. He was enjoying an après ski drink at L'Arrivee when she walked through the door and sat at the bar, just a few feet away from him. Once again, he was mesmerized by her beauty. He knew this was the perfect opportunity to introduce himself and, when he approached her and mentioned he had seen her in Lausanne, it turned out to be the beginning of a love affair my father thought would never end.

My mother's name was Ingrid Helberg. Her family moved from Lillehammer to Oslo when she was an infant and her father worked for a major marine transportation company. I never did understand exactly what he did and I only met her parents and brother, Henrik, once, when my father took us to Norway for a visit, years after her death. After a long distance romance that lasted only three months, my father persuaded my mother to move to New York. Immediately after she arrived, she settled into a walk-up in Gramercy Park and got a part- time job as a translator at the United Nations. She had been educated at the University of Oslo and was fluent in English and French. Eighteen months later, my parents were married and they moved into the house in Scarsdale.

I would often sneak into Daddy's home office and look at the photo he kept on his desk. I don't really know why this particular picture was so special to him because we had one whole album dedicated to their wedding. Maybe it was the expression on my mother's face, I'm not really sure, but one thing I am sure of, she looked stunning. Her strapless gown was ivory, a color that complimented her wonderful pale gold hair and my father looked especially handsome in a dark grey suit and silver tie. He had always been an attractive man, just under six feet tall, with thick, dark brown hair, brown eyes and a trim physique. It was easy to understand why my mother had been drawn to him but it was his character that must have really touched her heart. When he talked about my mother, he always told me how kind and thoughtful she was, always thinking about other people but it sounded to me like he was talking about himself. He was the kindest person I ever knew and I wish he was still with us but, sadly, he passed away at the age of sixty-seven from a massive heart attack.

My mother was only twenty-four when Portia was born and Daddy had just celebrated his fortieth birthday. He was overjoyed to finally become a father and was anxious to have more children. Three years later, my mother was pregnant again but, just after the first trimester, she miscarried. This put her in a deep depression and, even with the help of medication; she found it difficult to cope. It was only when Daddy brought home a six-week-old German shepherd puppy that she began to recover and, from that moment on, she lavished attention on him and named him Griffin. Less than a year later she was pregnant again and, this time, there were no complications. Two days before her due date, in March 1983, she gave birth to me, an eight pound six-ounce chubby little girl with a smattering of dark hair and blue eyes, which eventually turned brown. They decided to call me Samantha, but from the very beginning I was always known as Sam. According to Portia, my mother doted on me and she always felt a little left out but I figured that, as I got the short end of the stick in the looks department, it was a fair trade.

Two weeks before my second birthday, my mother flew to Lillehammer to spend some time with her brother, Henrik, who, having just separated from his wife after six years of marriage, was feeling the need to expend some of his frustration on the ski slopes. She had never been away from home before and, after she left, Griffin was constantly roaming the house looking for her. He had no idea he would never see her again. It took almost a month before he stopped pining and it took the same length of time for my father to realize he wasn't able to take care of us, while continuing to work full-time. He had been relying on friends and neighbors to help out but it was only a temporary solution and he finally decided to hire a live-in housekeeper.

Margaret Bristow was forty-five years old when she came to live with us. She had emigrated from a town in the north of England and spoke with a strange accent. Portia and I took to her right away and she insisted we call her Maggie. She was so different from my mother; a little on the plump side with short, mousey brown hair and a round face but she was always smiling and within days, Griffin had found somebody new to pamper him.

I don't remember much about those early days with Maggie but, by the time I was ready for kindergarten, we had formed a strong bond. Daddy had given Maggie the use of my mother's car and, every morning, we would take Portia to classes at Seeley Place Elementary and pick her up again when school was over. During those hours alone together, she would read to me or take me to the park and sometimes, I would help her around the house. I remember the times we spent in the kitchen, when she would try and teach me how to cook. Often, Maggie would make the traditional dishes from the area where she grew up, like Lancashire hotpot, Chester pudding and Eccles cakes. Daddy thought she was a treasure, especially when he arrived home from a busy day and she insisted he relax with a glass of wine before he even thought about listening to us girls prattling on. "You just sit awhile, Mr. Colin," she would say. "You need to take the load off your feet."

Portia no longer thought I was the favored one. Even though Maggie spent a lot more time with me when I was very young, she lavished attention on my sister and, over the years, Portia became more and more self-confident. Meanwhile, by the time I was ready for middle school at the age of eleven, I had managed to get rid of my baby fat and, when I looked in the mirror, I was satisfied with the reflection staring back at me. My hair, still almost as dark as the day I was born was an unruly mass of curls, but I liked it that way and my face wasn't bad either. My brown eyes were fringed with long lashes, my nose was refined just like my father's and I had pale skin with just a few freckles. Portia told me I was going to be ravishing when I grew up but I didn't really know what that meant at the time. She had no idea how extraordinarily beautiful she was when she was seventeen and a senior at Edgemont High. She was so attractive that she would turn heads when she walked into a room and she lost count of the number of boys who asked her out on a date, but she had no interest in any of them.

I was twelve when I first met Emily Flynn. Her family had just moved to Scarsdale from Chicago. Her father worked for a computer software company and had been transferred to New York. When she walked into the cafeteria at lunchtime on her first day at school, I noticed her immediately. Her hair seemed to float in a mass of curls around her face and it was a startling shade of red, almost ginger. She was so tiny that, when she stood in line at the counter, everyone else seemed to tower over her. I watched as she put small amounts of food on her tray and then looked around as though she was lost. I shifted down to the far end of the table where I was sitting and waved my arm in her direction. It took a few seconds before she noticed me and, when she did, she hesitated before walking slowly towards me. I didn't wait for her to reach me, I got up and took a step towards her, "Here," I said, "come and sit with me."

She smiled and I noticed that she had unusual green eyes and skin like porcelain. "Thank you," she replied, as she set her tray on the table and sat down.

"I haven't seen you here before," I said. "What grade are you in?"

"I'm in eighth grade but I just got here an hour ago so I haven't been to any classes yet."

She looked so young I was surprised by her answer, "I'm in eighth grade. How old are you?"

"I'm eleven but I skipped a grade," she replied as she picked up her fork and began picking at the paltry serving of pasta on her plate. "Oh, I see. What school were you in before?" "Hawthorne Elementary in Chicago; we just moved here last week." She looked down and continued to pick at her food while I sat staring at her in silence for a moment or two. Suddenly, she put her fork down and looked across at me. "What's your name and how long have you lived in Scarsdale?"

I told her my name was Samantha Lawrence, but everybody called me Sam, and then I proceeded to tell her all about my family. When I mentioned my mother died when I was just a toddler and I never really knew her, I noticed her eyes fill up with tears and I think it was then that I felt an emotional connection with her. By the time the lunch hour was over, I discovered her father had worked for the same software company since leaving college and her mother was an interior decorator but was taking time off to care for Emily's baby sister. They also had a Norfolk terrier named Sadie and a cat named Copper. I laughed when she told me that, "Does your cat have fur the same color as your hair?"

Emily grinned, "Almost," she said. "Both Sadie and Copper are having trouble adjusting to our new house. Sadie always slept on my bed but now I have to put up with the two of them."

Knowing that Emily loved animals made me like her even more and before we left the cafeteria I was inviting her to come to my house for dinner the following weekend. From that moment on, we became lifelong friends.

Chapter Two

A year after I met Emily, somebody new came into our lives. My father hadn't been involved in a serious relationship in the eleven years since my mother died. I knew he'd dated on occasion but he'd never introduced us to any of the women he went out with. Maggie would shake her head every weekend when he would stay home reading, working on his computer, taking long walks with Griffin, or keeping Portia and me entertained. Often, on a Friday night, she would ask him, "Are you doing anything special this weekend, Mr. Colin?" and Daddy would just grin and reply, "Yes, I'll be here with you and the girls, Maggie."

During the late fall of that year, we noticed that, one or two evenings a week, he began to spend time away from home. Then, one weekend in February, he told us he was going skiing with a colleague. We didn't ask him any questions when he left but we were anxious to hear all about his trip, when he got home on Sunday night. Portia and I were hovering in the hallway, when we heard his car pull into the driveway, and we were all over him when he walked through the door. He embraced us both, asked us to wait while he took off his coat and boots and then ushered us into the family room. I was nervous when he said he needed to talk to us and Portia must have sensed it, because she put her arm around me and pulled me down beside her on the sofa. "What is it, Daddy?" she asked.

He smiled a little sheepishly, "Well, I told you I was going skiing with a colleague, and that was the truth, but I didn't tell you my colleague was female."

I turned to see Portia's reaction and noticed the look of delight on her face as she spoke out. "Oh, that's wonderful. How long have you been seeing her? Tell us all about her."

"Her name's Erica Sherman and she came to work for the company last June. We started dating in September and it's becoming quite serious. I didn't want to say anything up until now because I didn't want to disrupt your lives."

"But, Daddy," Portia said gently, "Mommy's been gone for a long time and you deserve to have someone else in your life. Sam and I won't be here forever and we wouldn't want you to be alone. I'm really happy for you and I can't wait to meet this lady. What else can you tell us about her?"

"Thank you, honey. Well, she's just a few years younger than me. She's been married and divorced but never had any children and she's very, very smart."

"But what does she look like?" I interjected as I began to imagine some evil stepmother encroaching on our lives.

"You can see for yourselves on Saturday. I've asked her here for dinner."

Portia clapped her hands together with excitement, "Oh, can I go and tell Maggie? She'll be so pleased."

My father grinned and waved her out of the room then turned to me. "What are you looking so solemn about, Sam?"

"You're not going to marry her are you?" I asked scowling.

He came over and sat down next to me. "There's a possibility that could happen but we're not rushing into anything. You don't need to worry, Sam, I'll still be here for you just like I've always been."

I leaned my head against his shoulder, "But it won't be the same and what if she doesn't like me?"

He chuckled and ruffled my hair, "What's not to like? She'll think you're adorable and I think you'll find she's pretty special too."

"You still haven't told us what she looks like. Does she look like Mommy?"

With another chuckle, he replied, "No, she doesn't look a bit like your mother and that's all I'm saying. You'll have to wait until Saturday."

Maggie was excited when she heard my father was bringing Erica to dinner. By Tuesday she was already preparing the menu and couldn't keep the smile off her face. We had entertained before, but only for friends and neighbors. Daddy's parents were retired and lived in Florida and they never came to visit, even though they had been invited on several occasions. Then there was my uncle Dave, my father's older brother who married an Indian girl and lived in New Delhi, so we never saw him either. Usually, Maggie served her usual fare, the same type of meal she would feed us every night but this time, for some unknown reason, she seemed to be going overboard.

"What's so special about this woman coming here?" I asked, when I noticed her gathering up a pile of recipe books and putting them on the kitchen table.

She frowned as she sat down and pulled the first book from the pile, "I think you know why it's special, Sam. This will be the first time your father's brought home a young lady since your poor mother passed away."

"Hmmm. She can't be that young. Daddy said she was just a few years younger than he is and he's almost fifty-four so she must be pretty old."

Maggie shook her head, "So I guess that makes me ancient seeing as I'll be sixty in a couple of years?"

I knew I'd put my foot in it and had to redeem myself. "But I don't think of you as old. You look the same as when you first came here."

Maggie chortled, "You know that's a lot of nonsense. I've gained at least twenty pounds and look at these wrinkles."

"I don't see any wrinkles," I lied.

"Go on with you," she said waving her hand at me. "Go and play with Griffin and leave me to look through these recipes."

"Oh, okay," I grumbled and left the room hoping whatever she served to Erica, it made her sick.

When Saturday came, Daddy asked that we wear something nice for dinner and be on our best behavior. Portia was always well behaved and always looked presentable so I think he was really directing his request at me. This didn't make me any more inclined to welcome his new girlfriend but I knew I had to make an effort. Portia helped me pick out a green jersey wool dress, Maggie bought me for my twelfth birthday, and she straightened my hair so that it wasn't quite as unruly as usual. I thought I looked quite presentable until I saw her come out of her room in a white lace blouse and long black skirt, with her hair in loose waves. She looked so sophisticated and I felt like a dormouse in comparison, but I was never ever jealous of my sister. She was like the mother I never knew; always looking out for me and taking the time to listen to me whenever I needed to talk. When we had a sex education class at school, Emily and I giggled about it but when I came home and told Portia, she made me sit down while she explained how serious it was and not to be taken lightly. That's when I asked her if she'd ever done it and she just laughed and said she hadn't even been on a date. I loved having these conversations with her; she was always so patient with me, even if I had trouble understanding some of the things we talked about. I know I didn't need a second mother hovering around the house.

At seven o'clock, Maggie was still busy fussing with the table settings, when I heard a car drive up. I peeked out of my bedroom window and, by the light of the carriage lamps on either side of the front door, I saw a sleek looking silver car stop and then the driver's side door opened. I held my breath as a woman stepped out onto the driveway. From where I was standing, on the second floor, she looked tall and she had on a dark fur coat, matching hat and knee high boots with wedge heels. She paused to look in her purse before she closed the car door and I felt even more animosity towards her because I didn't approve of anyone wearing fur of any description. Then, suddenly, she looked up in my direction and I darted behind the curtain but not before I had a glimpse of her face. There was no doubt that she was striking. I couldn't really see her hair because of the hat but it was obvious she was dark and had milk white skin, dark eyes, and wore a lot of make-up. It was the brilliant red lipstick that reminded me of the wicked queen from Snow White. I just knew I wasn't going to like her. A moment later, I heard the doorbell ring and my father making his way down the hall. I ran to the top of the stairs and peeked through the bannister railings. I couldn't wait to get a closer look. My father opened the door and I heard him say, "Hi there, you're right on time. I thought you might be late after all the snow we had earlier. Here let me take your coat."

As he helped her out of her coat, she said, "It was fine, and I had no problem with your directions."

I noticed her voice was low and kind of raspy but I was more interested in what she really looked like. I was right about her being dark, in fact when she took off the hat, I saw that her hair was black as coal and styled in a short sleek bob. If her hair had been longer she could have been a dead ringer for Morticia from the Addams family, but maybe that's what I wanted to believe. Her clothes didn't help either. She was in black from head to toe and she was wearing tights. She was way too old for tights as far as I was concerned. The moment I knew they were headed for the living room, I ran down the stairs and stationed myself right outside the door. I was just in time to hear my father say, "This is Portia. Portia I'd like you to meet Erica."

They must have shaken hands and Portia said, "Welcome to our home, Mrs. Sherman. I'm so happy to meet you."

Erica responded in her raspy voice, "It's a pleasure to meet you, Portia, and please call me Erica."

There was some talk of the weather while my father got Erica a glass of wine and a club soda for Portia, then I heard him ask, "Where's Sam? She should be here by now." Portia didn't get a chance to answer because I popped my head around the door and called out, "Here I am."

Daddy waved me into the room, took my hand, and then walked me over to where Erica was posed on a wing chair near the fireplace. That's how I saw her anyway, perched on the edge, with one leg crossed over the over. "Erica, I'd like you to meet the youngest member of the family. This is Samantha but she prefers to be called Sam."

Erica didn't get up; she merely cocked her head to one side, smiled, and said, "I've been looking forward to meeting you, Sam."

I was close enough to notice the wrinkles around her eyes and mouth and I paused for a moment before replying, "Nice to meet you too," then I immediately turned on my heel and spoke to Portia. "What are you drinking?"

She obviously recognized my mood and gave me a warning look before she patted the sofa and said, "Come and sit down beside me. Daddy's making you an Apple Julep."

"What's that?" I asked screwing up my face.

"It's got apple and pineapple juice in it, so I'm sure you're going to like it."

I looked around and suddenly realized I hadn't seen Griffin. Whenever, somebody came to the door, he was right there to greet them. I immediately jumped to my feet, "Where's Griffin?" I asked, addressing nobody in particular.

"He's sleeping upstairs," Portia answered. "Sit back down, Sam, he's quite all right."

"No, he can't be," I said as I started to walk towards the door, "he always comes when someone rings the doorbell."

I didn't get very far because my father grabbed my arm, "Leave him, Sam," he said sternly.

I glanced around the room and felt a growing sense of alarm, "What happened to him?" I cried out.

Portia began to get up, and my father was just about to speak, when Erica rose from her perch and said, "He really is all right, Sam. Your father offered to shut Griffin in his room while I'm here because I have a deadly fear of large dogs. I'm so sorry but I'm sure he will be fine."

I looked at her with utter disgust and then turned to my father, "How could you do this. He's not used to being shut up. I'm going upstairs to let him out."

Erica looked at my father helplessly as Portia walked over to me and took my arm. "It's okay, Sam, really. I peeked in on him just before Erica arrived and he was sound asleep. He didn't even hear the doorbell."

I shrugged off her hand and faced my father, "What did you do to him. Did you put something in his food, Daddy?"

I stepped back when I saw the look on my father's face. He was angry. "That's quite enough, young lady. We have a guest and either you behave yourself or you can go to your room."

"Fine, I'll go to my room," I shot back as I flounced out of the door.

Chapter Three

I don't remember what time it was when Portia came to my room but she found me asleep, fully clothed, with Griffin lying beside me. She gently woke me up by stroking the top of my head and then sat down on the edge of the bed. "You need to get undressed, Sam, and put on your pajamas. You must be hungry so Maggie sent me up with some dessert and a mug of cocoa. I'm just going to leave for a bit while I let Griffin out; it's too late for his usual walk and I'll be back in a few minutes."

I just nodded my head as I watched her leave the room with Griffin and then, after changing into my pajamas, I crawled back into bed and began devouring the cheesecake which Portia had left on my bedside table. It was my favorite with caramel and crushed pecans. I guess Maggie decided to serve one of her own specialties. I had just finished drinking the cocoa when Portia returned with Griffin. "Sorry, I was so long but he got covered in snow and needed drying off. He might still be a bit damp so you may not want him on your bed. I gave him some kibble in case he was hungry too."

I didn't get the chance to stop Griffin from jumping up beside me, not that I wanted to. I felt very protective of him knowing Erica didn't want him around. "Has she gone?" I asked.

Portia nodded, "We have to talk about what happened. I know you were upset but you really have to try and control your emotions."

"I don't care, just because she's afraid of dogs, she can't make us shut Griffin away like that. I hope she never comes back."

Portia slowly shook her head, "Oh, Sam, you don't mean that. She's actually quite nice and if she makes Daddy happy, then you're going to have to compromise. Erica isn't afraid of all dogs, she's just afraid of large dogs. Apparently she was badly bitten as a small child and she's never gotten over it."

"Well, she'd better get over it. What if Daddy marries her? What would happen to Griffin? Would we have to get rid of him?"

Portia reached for my hand, "What I'm going to say might upset you even more but you have to face the truth. I'm sure, from the conversation tonight that they aren't thinking of marriage in the near future. It could be two or three years from now and by then Griffin would be close to sixteen years old. German Shepherds don't usually live that long so it may never be an issue."

"No," I protested, throwing myself half on top of Griffin, "he's can't die. Don't say that."

Portia reached over and tried to pull me away, "I'm so sorry, Sam, but you have to face it sooner or later."

I pounded the bed in frustration, "It's not fair. What am I going to do without him?"

"You just go on with life, the same way we did after Mommy had her accident. You know, Sam, maybe you'll get another dog: a small one that Erica can deal with."

"No, I don't want another dog. I don't care what she wants. I hate her and I never want to see her again."

Portia stood up, "Now you're being childish. You can't keep this up. Daddy's very annoyed with you and I can't really blame him."

I slid down in the bed and pulled the covers over my head, then waited. I didn't hear anything for a moment then Portia whispered, "Goodnight, Sam."

I laid there awake for a long time, snuggling up to Griffin, and thought about what she'd said. It hurt that she thought I was being childish, after all I was only twelve years old. It had always been, Daddy, Portia, Maggie, Griffin and me. Why did anything have to change?

The next day being Sunday, I knew my father would be home all day and I wasn't looking forward to it. I deliberately came down late for breakfast and noticed the house seemed very quiet. I found Maggie in the kitchen rolling out some pastry, "Good morning," I said, "Where is everyone?"

She glanced over at me and went back to her rolling, "Your father and sister took Griffin for a walk. I think they went to the park."

I felt a little left out as I walked over to the window, "It's stopped snowing but it still looks cold. I hope they put Griffin's coat on."

Maggie ignored my remark, "Why don't you sit down and I'll make you something to eat; how about some eggs and toast?"

"Yes please, I'm starving."

"I'm not surprised," Maggie said as she put the pastry to one side and took some eggs out of the refrigerator. "You didn't have any dinner last night and you were late getting up. Did you sleep in or were you just avoiding your father?"

I lowered my head as I answered, "I guess he's really mad at me."

"Well, let's say that he's disappointed. I heard what happened and you can't blame him."

"That's what Portia said but locking Griffin up wasn't right."

"Is that really why you're so upset?"

"Yes, but I wouldn't want that Erica person here even if she did love big dogs."

Maggie put two slices of bread in the toaster and chuckled, "Ah! So there's more to it. Don't you want your father to be happy?"

"He was happy enough before she ever came along. I don't like her; she looks like a witch."

Maggie shook her head, "Sam, oh Sam, what are we going to do with you. I actually thought she was quite attractive. A little too much make-up for my taste but that's none of my business."

"How could Daddy like her after being married to Mommy?"

"Well, there's no question that your mother was a natural beauty but looks aren't everything."

I stared at Maggie as she began to whip up the eggs in a bowl. "How come you never got married?" I asked.

She looked over her shoulder at me and grinned, "What brought that on? Believe it or not, I was married once and my husband thought I was pretty but that was a long time ago."

I know my mouth dropped open in astonishment, "What happened to your husband?"

Maggie put the bowl aside and walked over to the table, "He was killed in the Vietnam war. We were only married for three years."

I could see tears beginning to form in her eyes, "Tell me about him. What was his name?"

I heard the toast pop up from the toaster but Maggie didn't notice it. She sat down and took hold of my hand, "His name was Paddy Bristow and he was Irish through and through. I could listen to him talk all day." At that her face lit up and I squeezed her hand. "He was good looking too; tall with coal black hair and the bluest eyes you've ever seen. I'll never forget the first time I met him. I was on vacation in Dublin with my sister, Birdie, and we stopped for a cup of tea in this quaint little restaurant. He was sitting at the next table and he smiled at me. I thought he must be smiling at Birdie, because she was a whole lot prettier, but then he smiled again and I felt my heart give this little flutter."

I was really enjoying listening to Maggie and wanted to hear more, "Did he say anything?"

She grinned, "Yes, he asked us where we were from and a few minutes later he joined us at our table."

"Then what happened?"

Maggie sighed, "Well, we had to go back to Manchester but we kept in touch. We wrote letters and he came to visit me twice then, just over a year later, he asked me to marry him. We were so happy, Sam, but we only had those three years. He was drafted into the army then sent overseas, and he never came back."

"That's so sad. What about babies? Didn't you have any children?"

At that, she got up from the table and moved back to the counter. She had her back to me when she replied in almost a whisper, "I was three months pregnant when they came and told me Paddy wasn't coming home. They said it was the shock that did it, when I lost the baby." I started to get up but she whirled around and stopped me with a wave of her hand, "Enough of this. I just wanted you to know that you don't have to be beautiful like your mother to be loved by somebody else. Relationships are built on trust, respect, good communication, kindness and compassion. Maybe your father has that with Erica."

"But what about Griffin, Maggie, it's not fair to lock him up every time she comes here?"

She shook her head, "I'm not sure what we can do about that but you need to talk to your father about it and try not to get upset."

I nodded but I couldn't help feeling things weren't going to turn out the way I wanted them to.

Chapter Four

When my father and Portia arrived home from their walk, I was in the family room reading. I heard the commotion as they came in the front door and then, a few minutes later, Griffin came bounding in and nuzzled my knees like he always did. Portia appeared looking red faced and rubbing her arms, "Wow, it's freezing out," she said. "There weren't many people out walking their dogs today."

"Why don't you sit by the fire for a while?" I suggested.

"No, I'm going to make a cup of tea. Daddy will be along in a minute, he wants to talk to you."

"Oh, oh, I guess this is about last night."

"Yes, but he's not annoyed, at least not anymore, so just listen to what he has to say."

I nodded as she left the room, with Griffin trailing behind her, and waited for my father with some trepidation. It seemed like ages before he walked through the door and sat down opposite me in his favorite recliner, "How's it going, Sam?" he asked.

"Okay, Daddy," I answered. "I suppose you want to talk to me about yesterday. I'm sorry if I upset you."

He sighed, "Well, it was a bit dramatic but I know how you feel about Griffin. I have to admit, I was not only annoyed, I was embarrassed, but I've had some time to think about it and I agree that it isn't fair to Griffin, or you."

I couldn't help smiling, "Really, Daddy?" Does that mean Erica won't be coming here anymore?"

He grinned as he shook his head, "No, it doesn't mean that but, if she does come, it will only be for an hour or two, at the very most, and you don't have to stay with us the whole time. You can spend however long you like with Griffin, in your room."

I looked at him with skepticism, "How long is that going to last? What if you get married and she moves in here?"

He rolled his eyes, "I'm not getting married, Sam, at least not for a long, long time and anyway there's something else I have to tell you. Erica feels she needs to see someone about her fear of large dogs."

"You mean a shrink, or someone like that?"

My father chuckled, "Yes, a shrink or a therapist. Maybe she'll be able to overcome her fear and then there won't be a problem."

"I guess that would be okay," I said reluctantly, knowing deep down I was never going to like Erica no matter what she did.

A year later, Portia enrolled at Concordia College in Bronxville. It was only four miles from home and Daddy bought her a year-old Toyota Corolla to take her back and forth. The college had a Health Studies program, which incorporated all elements of non-clinical healthcare such as food and nutrition, social problems etc. and Portia was in her element. There were times, I know, when she would have preferred to stay on campus but we were glad she chose Concordia and came home to be with us every night. Although I had a few good friends and Emily and I were very close, I always considered Portia to be my best friend and I couldn't bear to think of her being away from us. Meanwhile, Erica continued to be a presence in my father's life and a thorn in my side. She never did see a shrink as far as I could make out and, whenever she came to visit, I spent as little time with her as possible, always making an excuse to join Griffin in my room, or take him for a walk. I never did figure out what Daddy saw in the woman but, I guess he eventually saw her the way I did and gave her the boot. When he told me their relationship was over, I tried very hard not to look smug but I couldn't help it. Good riddance to bad rubbish.

I was fourteen when I transferred from middle school to Edgemont High. Emily and I ended up in the same class, and while she was a whiz at math, I was top of the class in English, both literature and grammar. Daddy always said I should take up journalism or some other form of writing. He even suggested I could become a famous author and keep him in the lap of luxury when he was an old man. I didn't like to think of Daddy as ever being old. He had just celebrated his fifty-fifth birthday and he still looked almost as young and handsome as when I was little. I did notice he was having a problem with his back but he just laughed it off and said it was arthritis. I always expected him to be in my life forever and I never wanted to think about death. My mother dying was enough but, of course, we couldn't avoid the inevitable. Eventually, it was Griffin who was taken away from us, just like Portia said, and I don't think I ever felt so sad. He didn't suffer though; he just went to sleep one night and didn't wake up. Thankfully he was lying right beside me and I hope he drifted off knowing just how much I loved him.

It was a bright sunny day in May, when we buried Griffin in the pet cemetery in Hartsdale, just a few miles away from our home. Emily was with me, along with my family, and she brought me a lot of comfort. She had lost her own dog, Sadie, just a few months earlier and I'd been the one standing by her side, in almost the same spot. After we said our tearful goodbyes, she suggested I get another dog but it was too early for me to think about that. Emily was lucky, she still had Copper and I considered adopting a kitten after I got over the loss of Griffin, but I needed time to grieve.

My father had a surprise for us when we arrived home. He called Maggie into the family room and made us all sit down. "I think we need a break from all this sadness," he said.

He was standing near the fireplace with a large envelope in his hand, "What's in the envelope, Daddy?" I asked with some apprehension.

He smiled, "We're all going on vacation," he said.

I looked at Maggie and back at my father, "Maggie too?"

"Yes, Maggie too," he replied.

"Yippee! Where are we going?" I cried out excitedly as Portia reached over in an attempt to quieten me.

"How does Alaska sound? You always talked about wanting to go on a cruise, Portia, and I thought this would be the perfect opportunity."

Portia gasped, "Oh, Daddy, it sounds wonderful. Tell us more about it. When would we be going?"

My father sat down and placed the envelope on the table beside him, "We'll be leaving on July 15th. We fly directly to Anchorage and then take the cruise on the Coral Princess all the way south, to Vancouver."

"That's in Canada. Whoopee, we're going to Canada," I yelled.

Daddy chuckled, "That's right and we'll be seeing glaciers, and icebergs, and maybe even whales. I've booked three cabins so you two girls will have to share. I'll leave the brochure here for you to look at."

Maggie looked stunned, "I don't know what to say, Mr. Colin," she said. "This is so generous of you."

At that, my father got up and started to leave the room, "You deserve a break just as much as the rest of us, Maggie," he said.

I'll never forget the trip to Alaska. It was like a whole different world to me. I always thought it was freezing there, no matter whether it was summer or winter, but when we arrived in Anchorage it was sixty seven degrees. The ship was amazing and I loved our cabin with its own balcony. Daddy was right; we saw glaciers and icebergs, two humpback whales and even a grizzly bear, and several eagles flying overhead. If I wasn't gaping at the scenery, I was stuffing my face with all the food available. It's a wonder I didn't get sick. Best of all was watching Maggie enjoying herself, especially when she met up with a group of people from near her home town. It was the best thing Daddy could have done to cheer us all up but I wondered if it would be the last trip we would be sharing together. I tried to put the thought out of my mind and, by the time we got home, I was ready to seriously think about getting that kitten.

Two weeks later, Portia and I drove to the animal sanctuary in Westchester. There weren't any kittens for adoption but we both fell in love with an adorable two-year-old cat named Molly. When we first saw her, she was all rolled up, looking like a ginger ball of fluff and then, when we tapped on her cage, she stretched out onto her back as though she was inviting us to tickle her tummy. "Oh, Portia, she's so sweet," I whispered. "Can we take her home?"

Portia put her arm around me, "Yes, let's," she said. "We'll probably have to fill out a lot of papers and we need to get supplies, like food and litter."

I was jumping up and down with excitement and couldn't wait to take Molly home so that my father and Maggie could see her. That was one of the best days and I knew Griffin wouldn't have been jealous. Maybe if we'd gotten a dog, he wouldn't have been so pleased. I never regretted our decision to adopt Molly and I knew she'd be around for a long, long time.

Chapter Five

By the time I transferred to Concordia, the same college Portia had attended, I'd decided I wanted to concentrate on writing. I enrolled in the English program specializing in creative writing and journalism while Emily immersed herself in business administration, which sounded very dull to me, but I didn't tell her that.

Portia was no longer living at home and I missed her terribly although we saw each other as often as we could. She had moved to the city and was sharing an apartment on the Upper East Side with three other girls. She'd lost interest in a career in health care after she'd taken several courses at Concordia in fiction, drama and poetry, which involved British and American literature from the Middle Ages to the present. She had visions of acting on Broadway and planned to enroll at the American Academy of Dramatic Art, after she had saved enough to afford the tuition fees. Daddy said it would take her forever to come up with the amount needed and offered to pay but Portia refused. She intended to stand on her own two feet. In the meantime, she was working at a high end clothing boutique in the West Village, owned by a rather eccentric French woman named Veronique. I loved hearing stories about the customers, or clients, as Veronique insisted on calling them. Most of them were wealthy women, who had no problem spending thousands of dollars on a single dress with a coveted French label. Occasionally, somebody famous would drop in and Portia would have difficulty trying to maintain her composure, but she had been instructed to be professional at all times. When she wasn't working, she hung out with her roommates and, on weekends, she would often take the bus back home to spend the weekend with Daddy and me. When she moved to the city, she no longer needed her car and so she generously passed it on to me so that I could drive back and forth to college. I always wondered what she did on weekends when she didn't come home and, one day, she confessed she'd met someone she thought she could have a real relationship with, even though they'd just started dating. His name was, Hayden, twenty-three years old, originally from Philadelphia, and a graphic designer for a travel agency. Naturally, I wanted to know all about him, what he looked like, when could I meet him and when was she bringing him home to meet Daddy. Portia told me that if I wanted to come into the city the next weekend, we could have lunch together and, if I approved, she would invite him to come to Scarsdale. "Are you serious?" I asked, "You want me to approve of him?"

She chuckled, "Just kidding."

I frowned and then it hit me, "Oh, I get it. You're thinking of Erica. Well, he doesn't have to worry unless he has an aversion to cats."

At that, Portia roared with laughter, "You are something else, Sam. Don't worry; I'm pretty sure he told me his mom has a cat."

Later that day, I told Daddy about Portia's new friend and he seemed really pleased. That gave him the opening he needed to tell me he'd met someone at the International Auto Show the week before. He'd been admiring a 1932 Packard owned by Franklin D. Roosevelt when a woman turned to him and remarked, "Don't you ever wonder what it would have been like to have lived back then?" After that they just started chatting and ended up having coffee together.

"Are you going to see her again?" I asked, holding my breath.

Daddy nodded, "Yes, I'm taking her to see a revival of the play, The Best Man, on Saturday."

"I see," I responded slowly nodding my head.

Daddy looked at me and frowned, "I hope we aren't going to have a repeat of the Erica incident."

"That's what Portia said after she told me about Hayden. That was a long time ago, Daddy. Are you ever going to let me forget it?"

"Not as long as it doesn't happen again," he shot back with a big grin on his face.

"What's she like?"

"Her name's Elizabeth, but she likes to be called Beth, and she's a widow. Her husband died two years ago after a lengthy illness. Apparently he was passionate about old cars and they went to all the auto shows. She said she felt closer to him when she went there alone after his death."

"I think I like her already," I interjected.

Daddy smiled, "She's nothing like Erica. She's fair and a little bit overweight and she gave up working full-time several years ago. She used to be a paralegal so she helps out at her old law firm occasionally."

"Does she have any children?"

"Yes, she has two sons, both married. One lives in Queens and the other is in the military and was recently deployed to Saudi Arabia."

"Oh, dear, that must really worry her."

"It does, especially now that his wife is pregnant with their first child. She's just hoping he's able to get back home when the baby is born."

"When can I meet her, Daddy?"

He put his arm around my shoulder, "Soon, honey. Maybe we'll invite her and Portia's friend to dinner at the same time and Maggie can make one of her favorite recipes."

"What a good idea. What about next week?"

Daddy grinned, "Hold your horses. I need to talk to Beth to see when she's available and I also have to talk to Portia. Don't worry it won't be too long."

That night as I lay in my bed with Molly curled up beside me, I felt a little left out. I was wondering when I would meet somebody new.

The following Saturday, I met Portia and Hayden for lunch at the Elim Deli which, according to Portia, was a hidden little gem of a place on Lexington with great food and reasonable prices. I was relieved she hadn't suggested anywhere more formal, especially as I'd arrived fifteen minutes early, and only felt a little conspicuous as I waited while sipping on a glass of wine. When Portia came through the door, she saw me immediately and came rushing over to plant a kiss on the top of my head. "I see you started without us," she said.

I looked up at her and couldn't help noticing how happy she looked and just as gorgeous as always, in a brown leather jacket with a leopard print scarf draped around her neck. "I didn't want to be late," I replied, "so I left home in plenty of time."

Portia remained standing and turned to the young man standing behind her. She took hold of his hand and motioned him forward, "This is Hayden," she said glancing at me and then back at him, "and this is my little sister, Sam."

Hayden took a step forward and extended his hand, "I'm happy to meet you at last, Sam," he said, as I looked up into the most remarkable green eyes.

After we'd settled at the table and ordered lunch, I got a really good look at my sister's new friend and I wasn't disappointed. He was tall, with a mop of light brown hair, attractive, in a boyish sort of way, and casually dressed in a tan corduroy jacket and blue jeans. On top of that, he was not only interesting to talk to but he was funny too. I liked him immensely. Portia kept watching for my reaction and when we both made an excuse to visit the restroom, before parting ways, she couldn't wait to ask me what I thought. "He's lovely," I remarked.

She grinned, "So you approve and I can bring him home?" I laughed and gave her a hug. "Yes, I know Daddy will like him too. Let's try and arrange something for next weekend, if you're not busy, and maybe we can meet Daddy's new lady friend at the same time."

We weren't all able to meet the following weekend because Maggie had come down with the flu. I suggested we all go out somewhere but my father wouldn't hear of it. As it turned out, it was another two weeks before we were all sitting around the dining room table feasting on a cress and avocado salad, beef wellington with creamy scalloped potatoes, and apple crumble for dessert. Maggie had fully recovered and really outdid herself but, when she kept flitting in and out of the room making sure everyone's wineglass was full, I began to wonder what she was up to. It didn't take me long to figure out she'd taken a fancy to Hayden, and I couldn't blame her. He was such a likeable young man and kept us amused with stories about some of his experiences in college. I know my father was impressed. As for Beth, I wasn't sure at first. She seemed really shy but, as the evening progressed, she appeared to relax and began to interact with the rest of us. Daddy explained later, he was the first person she'd gone out with since her husband died and visiting the family was a big step. Physically, she was as Daddy had described her, fair and a little overweight, but while I'd expected someone rather dull and dowdy looking, I was way off the mark. Her hair was short but styled in almost a pixie cut and she reminded me a little of the actress, Shirley Jones. She was wearing a simple black dress with a pearl choker necklace, but I got the impression her outfit was expensive and wondered if she was like one of those wealthy women who frequented the boutique where Portia worked. I meant to ask Daddy about that later.

I never really got the chance to talk to Beth until after dinner was over and we were moving into the living room for coffee and liqueurs. We were walking through the hallway when, suddenly, she spied Molly perched on the stairs leading up to the second floor. She stopped and put one hand on her chest, "Oh, my goodness," she said. "I adore cats." "Really?" I responded. "Her name's Molly. You can stroke her if you like, she's very sweet." Beth didn't hesitate. She moved forward quickly, ran up two or three stairs, and scooped Molly up into her arms. I immediately called out, "You're going to get hair all over your dress."

She just shook her head and descended the stairs, "It doesn't matter. Look how precious she is. She looks just like our Pru."

"Pru? Do you have a cat named Pru?"

I saw tears start to form, "Not any more. She died right after my husband passed away but she was almost nineteen, so she had a good long life."

I placed a hand on her arm, "I'm so sorry."

She looked at me and smiled, "Thank you, Sam. You know, I'm so happy I came here tonight. You and your sister are both lovely."

"I'm glad you came too," I said, and I genuinely meant it.

Chapter Six

Daddy and Beth got married almost two years to the day after they first met. Neither one of them wanted anything fancy so they opted for a civil ceremony, and a reception at our house in Scarsdale. We had invited my grandparents but they were in their early eighties and didn't want to travel up from Florida. I was disappointed, as I hadn't seen them for several years and I felt badly for my father, because I know he wanted them to meet Beth. I'd been introduced to her son, Ross, and wife Beverly, almost a year earlier, when we were invited to attend the baptism of Beth's granddaughter, Caroline. Luckily for Ross, he was able to be in attendance at the birth of his first child and had returned from overseas for a second time for the baptism. At the same time, I met Beth's other son, Neil, and his wife Lisa, and I was pleased to see the interaction between her family and my father. They seemed really happy that their mother had found somebody to spend the rest of her life with.

The weather was ideal on the day of the wedding. It was early September and close to seventy degrees, with the sun streaming down and just a slight breeze. Beth's closest friend, Cheryl, was there to support her, and she looked amazing in rose chiffon, but the belle of the ball was Beth herself, in a soft grey gown covered in tiny seed pearls. I don't think I'd ever seen her look so happy. Among the other guests were two of Daddy's golfing buddies and their wives, a colleague from J. P. Morgan, my best friend Emily and her boyfriend, Portia's three roommates, and Hayden. And there was one more guest, Aaron Reynolds who I'd met six months earlier. He'd just graduated from Columbia University and was interning in the legal department at Goldman Sachs. It was Emily's boyfriend, Larry, who introduced me to him. I'd dated three or four boys from Concordia but the relationships were casual and I didn't expect to get involved with anyone seriously for a long time, after all I was only eighteen. My first encounter with Aaron gave me no reason to think any differently. I had always been drawn to the tall, dark, athletic type but Aaron was none of those things. He was of average height, very slim, with tousled blond hair, blue eyes, and fairly nice looking, but nothing to write home about. I wasn't sure I even wanted to go out with him again, after that first meeting, but Emily convinced me I needed to give him another chance. When I'd had time to think about it, we'd spent most of the evening sitting in a movie theater and afterwards, at the coffee shop, Larry had monopolized the conversation, so I didn't really get to talk to him at all. On our second date, we went into the city and visited the Natural History Museum. I'd been there twice before, but Aaron made the experience a lot more enjoyable. His passion for animals was evident as we toured all the exhibits and he mentioned, on two occasions, that he was determined to go on safari one day. After the museum, he took me to dinner at a nice little Italian restaurant in the West Village and we got to know a lot more about each other. I discovered he lived alone in a two room rental on the east side and was an only child. His parents were divorced and he hadn't seen his father since he was five years old. His mother had worked two jobs to take care of him and put him through college then, after he left home, she went to live with her sister in Santa Ana, just south of Los Angeles. It was another three weeks before I brought him home to meet my family and both Daddy and Portia liked him right away, while Maggie thought he was the cat's whiskers, whatever that meant. I never did understand some of the expressions she came out with. Speaking of cats, Molly was sitting on his lap, less than fifteen minutes after he first entered the house, and I knew then that he was somebody special.

I'd been to Aaron's apartment on two occasions, once while I waited for him to change clothes after he'd come from the office, so that we could go to Central Park and sit on the grass to watch a concert. And, another time, when he made me a lovely shrimp fettuccini dinner and we watched some amateur videos he and his friends had made in college. He'd never pressured me to go any further than kissing and, five weeks into our relationship, I was beginning to wonder if he was gay. In some ways, I almost hoped he was because I was nervous and didn't really know what to expect. I thought about talking to Portia about it but I didn't want to embarrass her because I was almost certain she'd slept with Hayden by this time. On my third visit to his apartment, I decided to make the first move and, after three glasses of wine, I was ready. We were sitting on the couch, when I sidled up close to him and started licking the side of his neck. He began to chuckle and said, "What are you up to, Sam?"

"What do you think?" I answered as coyly as I could manage.

He turned to me and took both of my hands. "Do you really want to do this?" he asked. Not sure how to reply, I just nodded and he took my face in his hands and kissed me lightly on the lips. "You're a virgin, aren't you?" he said.

I couldn't look him in the eye and felt myself blushing, "Yes, but I'm eighteen and I want to know what it's like."

Looking very serious, he stood up and led me slowly into the bedroom, "In that case, come with me and I'll show you."

Everything after that was a bit of a blur but I know I enjoyed it and I wasn't even shy about lying there afterwards, naked as a jaybird, with Aaron beside me wearing only his socks. I do remember snuggling up to him and remarking, "I was beginning to think you were gay." He roared with laughter, "No one's ever told me that before. I hope I've convinced you I'm not." Since that night we'd been intimate several times and each time it got more and more passionate. It wasn't long before I realized I'd fallen in love with him.

After dating for a few months, Aaron told me he'd like us to build a future together, but he thought we were too young to get engaged. He wanted to finish his internship and thought I should graduate from Concordia and pursue a career for myself, before we made any plans. He didn't want us living in a two room apartment for more than a couple of years because, eventually, he wanted a house of his own. Portia admired him for his practical nature, meanwhile, she was still struggling to come up with enough to attend acting academy and didn't feel fulfilled working at the boutique, but she still refused Daddy's help. She had settled into a comfortable relationship with Hayden but there seemed to be something missing. I rarely saw them holding hands and, when I asked her if they'd thought about getting married, she told me they'd talked about it, but she wasn't ready. She still wanted to pursue an acting career before she settled down. I began to wonder if I would be the first to walk down the aisle.

Chapter Seven

Six months later, just after my nineteenth birthday, I discovered I was pregnant. I don't know how it happened because I'd finally had the courage to talk to Portia about being intimate with Aaron and she'd accompanied me to the doctor, who promptly put me on the pill. The moment I had any suspicion, I bought a home pregnancy test and, when it showed a positive result, I panicked and immediately called Portia at the boutique. Less than an hour later, she was beside me holding my hand, while I tried to keep my composure. "What am I going to do?" I asked.

"Well, first of all you have to make sure the test is correct. That will mean a doctor's visit. Then, if you are pregnant, you'll have to tell Aaron. He has the right to know. I still think you're too young to get married but if that's what you want, and he agrees, then I'll support you. If, on the other hand, you decide not to keep the baby, then you have to decide whether you want to terminate the pregnancy or go through with it and put the baby up for adoption."

"What if I want to keep the baby and Aaron doesn't want to marry me?"

"Then we'll look after you. Daddy's not going to abandon you, Sam."

I sighed and shook my head, "But Daddy's only been married for a while and he and Beth aren't going to want a baby here."

Portia slipped her arm around my shoulder, "It's not going to be easy, but I know they'll both be there for you and I think Maggie would actually be thrilled."

I smiled when she said that, "She does love babies, doesn't she?"

Portia smiled back, "Yes, she does, and she'll spoil this one rotten."

We decided I shouldn't tell anyone about the pregnancy until I'd been to the doctor and was absolutely sure. Keeping it to myself for almost a week, before my appointment, was one of the hardest things I had to do and, if I hadn't had Portia to talk to, I think I would have blown it. I even made an excuse not to see Aaron, because I didn't think I could keep the secret from him. I was sure he'd know something was up because I was so edgy. Even Beth asked me if anything was bothering me and I had to lie and say I was worried about an essay I was working on. Finally, on a Friday afternoon, Portia and I walked out of the doctor's office and crossed the parking lot in silence then, just as we reached the car she turned to me and said, "I guess I'm going to be an aunt."

I gave a weak smile and nodded, "I'll call Aaron when we get home and tell him I need to see him, the sooner the better."

I arrived at Aaron's place at six o'clock that night. I could tell right away that he was nervous about my telephone call. He was anxious to know what was so urgent and I suddenly realized he might be thinking I wanted to break up with him. When I walked through the door, he'd already poured me a glass of wine and handed it to me before I sat down but I just placed it on the coffee table and said, "I don't want the wine, Aaron."

He frowned and sat down beside me. "What is it, Sam, are you ill?"

I took a deep breath and replied, "No, I'm not ill, I'm four weeks pregnant."

I watched as he gasped and then reached for my hand. "Oh my god; how long have you known? Are you absolutely sure?" I nodded, "I took the test on Monday at home and had it confirmed by the doctor this afternoon."

He released my hand and stood up, "How could this have happened, Sam, you told me you were on the pill?"

"I am on the pill; at least I was until Monday. Not all contraceptives are one hundred percent effective."

He sat down beside me again, "What do you want to do about it?" he asked in almost a whisper.

"I'm not sure. I think it depends on what you want to do."

He was quiet for a moment, "I always said we were too young to get married but I don't want any child of mine to go through what I went through, and I don't want to see the mother of my children struggle, the way my mother did."

"So what are you really saying, Aaron?"

"I think we should get married before the baby is born. I don't quite know how we'll manage but I'll get some extra work if I have to."

I got up and walked towards the window. I had my back to him when I said, "What about love, where does that come in?"

The next moment I felt his arms slip around my waist, "You know I love you, Sam. All I ever wanted was for us to be together but I've never had much to offer you. I wanted to wait until I had a good paying job so that we could live somewhere decent and then think about starting a family."

I turned and looked him directly in the eyes, "We could still do that."

He frowned, "What do you mean?"

I wanted to see his reaction, "I could have an abortion and then we could go on just like nothing happened."

He backed away from me and, for a moment, I think he looked angry, "No way. You're not aborting any child of mine."

I stepped forward and drew him into my arms, "Thank you. You don't know how happy it makes me to hear that. I love you so much."

Chapter Eight

Victoria Ingrid Reynolds was born on November 14th, 2002. Victoria was a name I'd always loved and Ingrid was, of course, my mother's name. When we found out we were having a girl, I was overjoyed because I hadn't had too much experience with boys growing up.

My pregnancy had gone well. I'd only had a few days of morning sickness and the delivery itself was a lot easier than I'd imagined, thanks to the epidural I demanded the minute I decided I'd had enough agony. Aaron and Portia were both in the room with me and they couldn't wait to hold the baby. I remember smiling at Portia when I saw the look on Aaron's face as he held his daughter in his arms for the first time. He looked so proud.

The very next day, I was released from the hospital and returned home. Not to the two bedroom apartment in the city, but to my childhood home in Scarsdale. When I managed to face my father and tell him I was pregnant and Aaron and I were getting married, he was disappointed but insisted we come and live with him and Beth. At first, Aaron was totally opposed to the idea but, the more my father tried to convince him it would give us the initial time we needed to get on our feet and get a place of our own, he slowly came around. Beth was very supportive and Maggie was over the moon about the baby, although she wasn't sure I needed to get married right away. Beth wanted us to have a grand wedding with all the trimmings but Aaron wouldn't hear of it and nobody could persuade him otherwise. In the end we had a civil ceremony and a celebration dinner at The Russian Tearoom with just immediate family, Emily and Larry, and Aaron's mother, Jane, in attendance. Jane had flown up from California and was staying at the house for a few days. She was quite a bit older than I'd expected, even though I'd seen several photographs of her, but it was obvious she doted on Aaron and I liked her immediately. I think she was a little uncomfortable, when she first arrived, because she hadn't expected me to come from such an affluent neighborhood but Beth was the perfect hostess, and went out of her way to make her welcome. When she finally left to return home she promised to come back as soon as the baby was born but, unfortunately, just a week before the big event, her sister fell and broke her hip so she had to stay and take care of her.

The decision to take Daddy up on his offer and live at the house was a godsend. I had no idea what looking after a newborn entailed and I needed all the help I could get. Not that Vicky was a difficult baby; in fact, she rarely cried and slept right through the night after just two short weeks. She was a very pretty child with the cutest button nose and fine hair, almost exactly the color of Aaron's. I'm not sure who she really resembled at that particular time but, I was hoping it wasn't me. I had put on over forty pounds during my pregnancy and even though I'd lost a good deal of the weight, I still felt fat and unattractive. Portia tried to convince me I'd soon be back to my old slim self and, after listening to me complain over and over again, she urged me to join a health club and to take a little more care with my diet. I hated exercising and made every excuse not to go and Aaron was no help. He kept telling me I was beautiful and I was being too critical of myself. In the end, with Portia supporting me, I was back to my former self and had a lot more energy. By this time, Vicky was six months old.

When I was close to my due date, I'd dropped out of college with no intention of going back. My aspiration to begin a career working for a major newspaper or magazine had to be put on the back burner. Daddy tried to encourage me to continue my education while insisting that, between Maggie and Beth, Vicky would be well taken care of during the day but I wouldn't hear of it. I had grown up without a mother and I wasn't prepared to put my child through that. At first, I missed college life and enjoying all the fun times with my friends. It took me some time to settle into the routine of looking after an infant but I loved to cuddle up with my daughter and, the more time I spent with her, the more my love for her grew.

Most weekday evenings, after Aaron got home, we would have dinner with Daddy and Beth and then go to our own part of the house to spend time alone with Vicky. We had our own huge bedroom that had been sectioned off, so that we had an area for a comfortable couch, a large screen television, an ensuite bathroom, and an adjoining nursery. It was perfect and Maggie had no problem with us invading her kitchen for snacks. Meanwhile, Molly had decided she preferred our company and had taken up residence in our room. The only time she left was to eat or use the litter box which remained where it had always been, in a small hallway at the back of the house. At first I was worried, like all new mothers, she would smother the baby but my fears were unfounded and Vicky loved to snuggle up with her. Aaron was so patient and kind, and such an adoring father, that I grew more in love with him as each day passed. He encouraged me to give myself some space and spend time with Emily and, occasionally, we would go to a movie or out for a bite to eat. I loved hearing about her life but I didn't envy her. I was quite content with being a wife and mother. He also urged me to spend more time with Portia and, when he wasn't using the car to commute to the city, I would often drive in to see her.

The following summer, when Vicky was almost nine months old, we took advantage of the garden. It was a special place with all of the towering trees and colorful flowers. She loved being outside with Molly and was already attempting to take her first step. Her hair had lightened and she was beginning to look more and more like Portia. Her eyes were the same color and she was tall for her age, just the same way my sister had been. Daddy doted on her and I caught him spoiling her on many occasions. I would catch him giving her candy after I'd mentioned, several times, that I didn't want her eating a lot of sugar. I was really into a health kick after I'd gotten down to my normal weight and was even considering becoming a vegetarian. Maggie was not impressed when she heard this. Coming from the north of England, she was used to hearty food, like Lancashire hotpot and fish pie. Over the years, she'd adapted her cooking to feed us lighter and more healthy food but the idea of accommodating my desire for, what she called, all that green stuff, was met with disdain. In the end I decided to placate her and settle for anything, as long as it didn't include pork, beef or lamb.

On a Sunday in early August, Aaron and I were stretched out on lawn chairs in the garden. It was hot and somewhat humid and the perfect day for a swim but Daddy had never wanted a pool. There'd been a drowning at a neighbor's house, at the time he was negotiating to buy the property, and he worried about the safety issues with small children. Vicky was sleeping in her stroller in the shade, while Daddy and Beth were on their knees weeding the huge expanse of lawn. I had no idea why they bothered because we had a professional gardener, on a regular basis, who took care of the grass and the flowers and I couldn't see any weeds. I think they just liked to get their hands dirty.

I was engrossed in a book by Jodi Picout, one of my favorite authors, when I thought I heard voices coming from the house, I couldn't imagine who Maggie was talking to and then, suddenly, Portia came into the garden and called out, "Hi, everybody. It's only me."

I jumped up to embrace her and then stepped back to get a good look at her. She looked as cool as a cucumber in white shorts, a mint green tank top, a pair of canvas espadrilles and aviator sunglasses. "We didn't expect you today," I said, just as Daddy and Beth reached us.

There were more hugs and then Portia responded, "I thought I'd surprise you. I figured you'd all be out here on such a lovely day."

"Where's Hayden?" I asked.

She didn't reply but, instead, glanced over at Aaron, "I think Aaron's ignoring me," she remarked,

I looked back and realized he'd fallen asleep and was already beginning to show signs of sunburn, "Poor baby," I said, "Vicky was fussy last night for some reason and he got up to see to her. I'd better wake him up and make sure he moves out of the sun."

"Where's Vicky?" Portia asked.

"She's over there under the tree. I think she's asleep but go and take a peek."

After she'd made her way over to the stroller, I said to my father, "I wonder where Hayden is. She didn't answer me when I asked her."

Daddy shrugged, "Maybe they had a lover's quarrel. It happens now and again. Ask her again later, after she gets comfortable. I'll get her another lawn chair."

While Portia was cooing over Vicky, who was now awake and cooing back, Maggie came out into the garden with iced tea and lemonade for everyone. At the same time, she asked Portia if she was staying for dinner but she declined, claiming to have had a large lunch and wanting to be back in the city by seven. Now I was even more curious as to what she was up to but decided to wait until I got the chance to spend a few moments alone with her.

Less than a half hour later, I happened to go into the house to get Vicky some papaya Maggie was cutting up for her. She seemed to really enjoy sucking all the juice out. I was about to go back outside when Portia came in and intercepted me, "Can you come back inside," she said, "I'd like to talk to you."

I frowned but nodded and then stepped out into the garden. After I parked Vicky's stroller next to Beth, who was now relaxing with a magazine, I announced, "I'm going to show Portia a new dress I bought. We won't be too long." Everyone just muttered without looking up and I went back inside where Portia was leaning against the kitchen counter talking to Maggie, "Come on upstairs," I said, "I want to show you my new dress."

Once we got to my room, I wasted no time. "Okay, what's going on? Why aren't you with Hayden? You always see him on the weekends."

She walked over to the couch, sat down, and patted the seat beside her. "Come," she said.

I was concerned now and, after I'd settled beside her, I took one of her hands in mine, "What is it, Portia, you're scaring me?"

She smiled, "There's nothing for you to worry about, Sam. I just wanted to tell you what was going on before I told Daddy and Beth."

I shook my head, trying to imagine what she was going to say, "What is it?"

Her face lit up, "I've fallen hopelessly in love," she said.

I know my mouth dropped open, "Who with? What about Hayden?"

"I told Hayden last week I couldn't see him anymore. It was dreadful, Sam. He was pretty upset and couldn't understand why I'd break up with him after we'd been together for so long. I tried to tell him our relationship wasn't going anywhere but he wouldn't buy it and I finally had to tell him the truth."

"Which is?" I interjected.

"That I'd met somebody else. He still wasn't convinced and even suggested I'd come back to him after I'd had my little fling, as he called it. I felt so bad because he's such a great guy and I wish we could remain friends but that's not going to happen. We both ended up shedding a few tears. It was one of the hardest things I've ever had to do."

"But who's this other man you met? Tell me all about him."

Portia's face lit up again, "His name's Philip Barrington and he's well known in financial circles."

"Wait a minute," I interrupted excitedly, "Isn't he the son of John J. Barrington?"

Portia smiled and then nodded, "Yes, you're right. His father was in the news a lot before he died last year. He made a fortune in the stock market and left most of it to his two children, Philip and Serena."

"What about his wife, didn't she inherit anything?"

"Helen Barrington died of breast cancer almost seven years ago and Philip's father never remarried."

"So where did you meet him?"

"He came into the boutique to buy a birthday gift for his sister."

I frowned, "I thought someone with that much money would send their assistant."

"Not in this case. He's really close to Serena and wanted to pick something out personally."

"So what did he end up buying?"

"A very expensive Marc Jacobs crocodile handbag."

"And were you the one who waited on him?"

"Yes. I noticed this white convertible pull up to the curb. I found out later, it was a Bentley, just one of three cars he owns and, when he hopped out, he almost took my breath away."

"Really? Why, what did he look like?"

Portia sighed, "He was all in white, white jeans, white tee, white sneakers and one of the most handsome men I think I've ever seen. When he came through the door and glanced around I had a chance to really look at him. It was hard to tell his age but, as he got closer, I could see a slight smattering of grey in his hair, which was almost black. He was very tanned and had the darkest eyes and, when he noticed me coming towards him, he extended his hand and said, 'Good morning, I'm Philip Barrington. Perhaps you can help me find a birthday gift for my sister.' He kept hold of my hand, as I stood almost mesmerized, but I finally managed to say, "Of course, sir, I would be happy to assist you."

I was breathless with anticipation as I asked, "What happened next?"

"He just stared at me and said, 'And what's your name?' When I told him, he said, 'Ah, like the car?' I laughed and answered, 'No, like a character in The Merchant of Venice.' He smiled, the most incredible smile, 'I knew that,' he said. He finally let go of my hand and I asked him what type of gift he was looking for. He really had no idea so I showed him some lovely Hermes scarves and some rather expensive costume jewelry but, he finally settled on the bag."

"Then did he ask you for a date, or what?"

Portia nodded, he suggested that, as I was named after one of Shakespeare's characters, I might like to go with him to see Cymbeline, which was playing on Broadway. I hesitated before I agreed to go out with him; after all we'd only just met. Then I saw Veronique descending on us with a sour look on her face and I quickly scribbled my phone number on a scrap of paper and asked him to call me. He grinned as he took the paper and stuffed it in his pocket. Then he turned to Veronique and said, 'Good morning, Madame. You have a wonderful boutique and this young lady has done a remarkable job of helping me select a gift for my sister.' Well, I thought she was going to melt into the floor, like the Wicked Witch of the West."

I giggled, "So when did he call you?"

"The very next day and that's not all. He sent three dozen red roses to the shop. I found it all a bit overwhelming."

"Did you go to the theater with him?"

"Yes, the following Friday. I didn't want him picking me up at home because the girls would have gone gaga and embarrassed him. I agreed to meet him for dinner first, at Barbetta's."

"Oh, wow, I've heard of it. It's supposed to be really swanky. What on earth did you wear?"

"Well, I think I tried on every single thing in my closet but I ended up wearing my black, sleeveless dress with the high neck and lace insert."

"I don't think you could have chosen anything better. You always looked so elegant in that dress and it really sets off your blond hair."

"Well, I have to admit, I felt really comfortable and Philip complimented me several times."

"That doesn't surprise me. Did he look as good as the first time you saw him?"

Portia got a far-away look in her eyes, "Oh, Sam, he's so handsome. He had on a black suit with a pale blue shirt, open at the neck. I could hardly take my eyes off him."

"He obviously felt the same way about you. What did you two talk about?"

"Family, mostly but, I have to be honest, I'd already googled him so I knew a lot about his background. I discovered he was thirty-four and he'd been married but his wife drowned in a boating accident three years ago, in the Mediterranean."

I gasped, "Are you sure it was an accident?"

Portia frowned at me and shook her head, "You have a suspicious mind, Sam. From what I read, Philip wasn't even with her at the time. He was back at the hotel in Marseilles, having lunch with a friend."

"What kind of boat was it? Who was she with when it happened?"

"It was what they call a daysailer and she was alone. Philip actually told me all about it. I didn't mention I'd checked him out on the internet. Apparently, his wife, her name was Leanne, loved to sail alone. She always said it was a lot more fun than travelling on their yacht."

"Are you telling me he owns a yacht?"

"Yes, I think he said it was seventy feet and has three cabins."

"Oh my, where does he keep it?"

Portia chuckled, "Somewhere on the French coast, I can't remember."

"Did they ever find out how his wife drowned? How did they find her?"

"Some fisherman discovered the boat drifting with nobody in it. Then they noticed a rope trailing from the back of the boat and started hauling it in. Leanne was on the other end."

"How awful; that must have been a shock."

"The autopsy showed she had an aneurism. The theory is she went for a swim and tied herself to the boat with a length of rope for safety. They figured she'd only been in the water for about two hours."

"How long had they been married?"

"Just two years and thankfully there weren't any children. Philip was devastated and admitted that, after a three month spell when he cut himself off from people, he just let loose and started drinking and partying. His father and sister finally intervened and he threw his energy back into his work."

"What happened after dinner? Did you go to the theater?"

Portia nodded, "It was a great play and we had a private box so we were really close to the stage. In the intermission, we were having a quick drink and ran into some friends of Philip's. They suggested we meet them afterwards at the Rooftop Terrace in the Marriott. Normally I would be tired out on a Friday night and not too keen on being out until all hours, but I was so pumped up, Sam. I think I could have stayed up all night; Philip had that kind of effect on me."

I hesitated for a moment but couldn't stop myself from asking, "Did you sleep with him?"

Portia shook her head, "No. We've only dated three times and I would never invite him back to the apartment. I thought he was going to take me to his place, after we had lunch today, but he said he had some tennis match lined up with a friend this afternoon."

"What about tonight? Are you seeing him? Is that why you can't stay for dinner?"

"No, it's Caroline's birthday so the girls are taking her out. You may remember meeting her, she moved into the apartment when Renee moved out."

"I vaguely remember her. So when are you seeing Philip again?"

Portia lowered her head and then looked up again, "That's the thing, Sam, he's asked me to go to Cabo San Lucas with him next weekend."

"But that's in Mexico, isn't it? How can you go so far just for a weekend?"

"Actually it's for four days and we'll be flying there on his private jet. I can hardly breathe just thinking about it."

Just at that moment there was a knock on the door and Beth poked her head in, "Sorry, Sam," she said, "but Vicky's getting very fussy and we can't seem to settle her down. Would you mind seeing to her?"

I immediately jumped up, "Of course, I'll be right there," then I turned to Portia. "Let's go to the garden, we can talk later. Call me tomorrow when you break for lunch."

She followed me downstairs and whispered in my ear, "Don't say anything yet."

I nodded as I reached back and squeezed her hand.

Chapter Nine

That evening, after we'd put Vicky down for the night, I went online to see what else I could find out about Philip Barrington, but I was most curious to see what he looked like. It only took me a moment to understand why Portia found him so attractive. There were several images of him in all types of situations; playing tennis, sailing, at the theater, and in each one of them he was immaculately dressed and more handsome than any movie star I could think of. Now, I was really intrigued to read all about him and started researching every website I could find. His family background was well documented and I learned that his sister, Serena, was forty-two, unmarried, and had lived with her female partner in West Palm Beach for the past ten years. I was surprised to learn she was gay and even more surprised when I saw her photo. I expected her to be as attractive as her brother but she was rather plain, with short, light brown hair, extremely tall and extremely thin.

There were many accounts about the death of Philip's wife and I read them all. It seems that, at no time, was there any suspicion about the cause of her drowning and I felt a great sense of relief. I'm not sure why I immediately suspected foul play when Portia told me what had happened. I guess I'd been watching too much television. It was obvious Philip's father had been a very wealthy man and both his son and daughter had inherited a great deal of money, as well as some valuable real estate. Philip owned a five room apartment on Central Park West, a townhouse in the Mayfair area of London, a villa in Cabo San Lucas and some property in Menton, in France. He also owned a private jet and the seventy-foot yacht named, Justice, which I discovered was the second name of his father, John J. Barrington. I wondered if he'd been in any serious relationships since his wife died but photos, and the odd report, only showed casual dates with models or actresses. That led me to research Leanne Barrington and find out more about her. There was no doubt she'd been a beautiful woman, but totally different from my sister. Her hair reminded me of a Renoir painting I was familiar with, The Girl with Auburn Hair, and she had the most amazing green eyes. Far from being a model or actress, she had been wealthy in her own right and an advertising executive with Young & Rubicam. Discovering his wife had come from a very affluent family and had an important career caused me to think about Portia. We had certainly had a comfortable upbringing but, we were as poor as church mice in comparison to the Barringtons' and Portia had no career to speak of. I know she planned to go to drama school but I often wished she'd pursued her interest in medicine. I loved my sister so much and I didn't want to see her get hurt. I just wondered how long it would take before Philip got tired of her and broke her heart. I was so concerned that I decided to confide in Aaron, but he wasn't too helpful. He was the kind of person who felt everyone should be free to choose their own lives and nobody else had the right to interfere. In principle, I agreed with him but it was my sister we were talking about and, even though she was five years older than me, I was worried about what she was getting into. I guess my mothering instincts were beginning to surface.

The next day, Portia telephoned just as I was helping Maggie prepare lunch. She said she'd given a lot of thought to going away with Philip and just couldn't pass it up. She then asked me if I'd tell Daddy about Philip, but not to make a big deal of it. I said I'd do my best and made her promise to call me before she left the city. The thought of her flying on a private jet made me especially nervous, never mind being thousands of miles away with someone I'd never even met. I waited until we'd finished lunch before I broke the news to my father and Beth. Maggie had just finished serving coffee when I blurted out, "Portia's not seeing Hayden any more. She met someone else."

Daddy frowned while Beth almost dropped her cup, "Are you serious? When did you find this out?"

"Yesterday, but she didn't want me to say anything until now. His name's Philip Barrington and he's worth a fortune. He......"

I didn't get any further because Daddy interrupted me, "Is he related to John J. Barrington who passed away recently?"

I nodded, "That's him. Philip and his sister inherited everything and now he's taking Portia away for the weekend."

Daddy frowned again, "Would you mind repeating that, young lady?"

"He's taking her to Cabo San Lucas on his private jet. He owns a villa there."

"Where did she meet this person?" Beth asked.

"At the boutique, a couple of weeks ago; he was shopping for a birthday gift for his sister."

"And she plans to spend a weekend with him so soon?" Daddy said.

I looked at Aaron for support and he actually smiled then looked at my father and remarked, "Things aren't quite the same as they were in your day. Life's become a little faster-paced."

Daddy shook his head, "Yes, I'm well aware of all this new technology and everything having to be instantaneous but I didn't think people just hopped into bed with each other right after they'd just met."

I had to chuckle, "Oh, Daddy, you're so naïve. Anyway, I didn't say Portia was sleeping with him."

"Now you're being naïve," Aaron said.

On Thursday afternoon, Portia called me in a state of panic, "Sam," she said, "I thought I should call you now because I won't have time this evening. All my spare time's been spent shopping for clothes for this trip and I still need to buy another bathing suit. If I don't find one I like, I don't know what I'm going to do."

My sister had always had a flair for fashion but this seemed a bit excessive. "You already have at least three bathing suits; isn't that enough?"

"Two of them are really ancient so I only have the black bikini left. The minute I get off work, I'm getting a pedicure and then I have to run over to this new beachwear shop on Third Avenue. I just hope I can get something there."

"Sounds like a lot of hassle to me just for a weekend. What time are you leaving tomorrow?"

"A limo is picking me up at noon and I'm meeting Philip at Teterboro airport. It takes about five and a half hours to fly to Cabo San Lucas."

"I've never heard of Teteboro airport. Where is it?"

"I looked it up. It's only about twelve miles from here. Apparently that's where most of the private jets are kept."

"Aren't you nervous?"

"I'm not nervous about flying but I'm freaking out about spending a whole four days with Philip. He's so smart, Sam, I'm not sure I can keep up with him intellectually."

"What are you talking about? You're one of the smartest people I know."

Portia sighed, "I'm not so sure. I just hope he doesn't regret asking me."

I hesitated, then chuckled, "I'm sure you can keep him occupied."

Portia hesitated before replying, "That's another thing, Sam, I've only ever slept with Hayden. The more I think about sleeping with Philip, the more anxious I get."

It didn't surprise me to learn that Hayden had been the first man my sister had been intimate with and I could empathize with the way she was feeling, "Try not to obsess about it, Portia, just let things happen naturally."

"When did my little sister get so wise?"

"Since I met Aaron and became a mother. I guess you could say I grew up."

"I'm so proud of you, Sam. I never thought you'd get married and have a baby before I did but, seeing the way you've matured and been able to handle everything just amazes me."

"It will happen for you too one of these days, Portia. Who knows, maybe Philip's the one and you'll be set for the rest of your life. I can hardly imagine what that would be like."

"Whoa! We only just met, who knows what will happen in the future."

"Well, you never know. In the meantime, you have a fabulous weekend and good luck finding that bathing suit. Make sure it's a bikini that shows a lot of skin."

Portia giggled, "You're terrible, Sam, but I love you."

"I love you too. Take care and have a safe flight."

Chapter Ten

Even though Beth offered to look after Vicky while Aaron and I spent the weekend at Montauk, on Long island, I spent a lot of time thinking about Portia and wondering what she was doing. I knew she wouldn't be arriving back in the city until late on Tuesday evening, so I didn't expect her to call me until sometime on Wednesday. I assumed she'd be working, so it would probably be lunch time before I heard from her. When Wednesday came, I was fidgety all morning and Vicky seemed to pick up on my mood because she was irritable and I finally lost my patience. I think it was the first time I'd ever raised my voice to her and it even scared Molly, who scampered away and hid under the couch. My father and Aaron were both at work and Beth had a dental appointment, so that left me alone with Maggie. She suggested I sit down and relax with a nice cup of coffee and a couple of her homemade shortbreads and, when that didn't help, she shooed me out of the house so that I could work off whatever was bothering me while she took care of Vicky.

I decided to go for a walk and ended up at the Midway Shopping Center. I wasn't too fond of shopping but soon found myself browsing through racks of dresses at Marshalls.

I ended up buying a lightweight, emerald green sheath, with a rather revealing neckline. I had no idea when and where I'd wear it, but it lifted my spirits. Then, rather than going straight home, I went to the supermarket and bought six chocolate croissants and decided to sit outside the mall on one of the benches. It was a beautiful day, not too hot, and I just sat there and people watched, while I nibbled on one of the croissants. I knew it was getting close to lunch time and Maggie would be annoyed at me for spoiling my appetite but this was one of those days when I needed to indulge myself. Hopefully, by the time I got home, I would soon be hearing from Portia.

Maggie was waiting for me when I got to the house. She'd made me a grilled chicken sandwich along with a small garden salad and I didn't have the heart to tell her I wasn't hungry. Vicky had settled down right after I left and had been asleep for the last half hour. I was relieved, because I didn't think I could cope with her until after I'd spoken to my sister. I was just about to ask Maggie if there'd been any calls when she told me Portia had phoned and left a message for me. She was too busy at the boutique to chat and would call back after dinner. I was disappointed, to say the least, but at the same time, it eased my anxiety knowing she was back in the city safe and sound.

I was wondering what to do all afternoon when, suddenly, there was a knock at the door and, when I opened it, the only thing I could see was a huge bunch of flowers. Then, to my delight, Emily lowered the flowers and cried out, "Surprise!"

I was so pleased to see her; I almost crushed the bouquet when I threw my arms around her, "Emily! How lovely to see you. Come on in."

She followed me to the kitchen, where Maggie was clearing up the lunch dishes, and while they exchanged hugs, I managed to find a vase big enough to contain the wonderful arrangement of lilies, carnations and daisies. I was so happy to see my best friend and couldn't wait to hear all her latest news so, I grabbed a bottle of white wine and two glasses and ushered her out into the garden. "I hope you've eaten," I said, "Otherwise I'll ask Maggie to make you something."

She grinned, "I shared half a large pizza with Larry before I came here."

"How do you get away with it?" I asked, staring at her tiny frame. "You eat like a horse and don't gain an ounce."

She shrugged, "I take after Mom. You know what a string bean she is."

I nodded, "How are the studies going?"

"Well, right now, as you know, we're on summer break so I'm glad to have some time to relax. Larry and I just got back from a week in the Adirondacks. We were camping with another couple at Lake Placid. It was so nice there, Sam, I wish you could have been with us."

I sighed, "I wish I could have been with you too. It's not easy getting away with a baby although Beth took care of Vicky while Aaron and I were in Montauk over the weekend."

"Oh, that must have been a wonderful break for you. How is Aaron doing at Goldman Sachs?"

"He finishes his internship in a couple of months and he'll be eligible for a position as a paralegal. He's excited because then he'll feel like he's really pulling his weight instead of having to rely on Daddy."

"That's great; I'm really happy for him. What about you? Are you happy, Sam?"

I hesitated but Emily was my best friend and she deserved to know the truth. "I have to be honest, I thought I'd be content staying home and being a wife and mother but it isn't very fulfilling. I couldn't have wished for a better husband and I adore Vicky but something's missing. If we weren't living here with my father and Beth, I might feel differently. Don't get me wrong, they've been amazing and Maggie's been such a big help with Vicky but, maybe that's the real issue, I don't really feel needed. Most of the time, especially when Vicky's sleeping, I have very little to do. Maggie does all the cooking and cleaning and she doesn't always like me getting in the way. I'm not sure how long it will be before we can afford a place of our own."

"It sounds like that could be a long way off. What about getting a part-time job? Perhaps between Maggie and Beth, they could look after the baby while you're at work."

"I've thought about that but they've done so much for us already, I just feel I'd be taking advantage. I didn't tell you this before, Emily, but Daddy wanted to put a substantial down payment on a house for us as a wedding present but Aaron wouldn't hear of it. At the time, I agreed with him, but now I wish I'd talked him into accepting Daddy's offer."

Just as I finished speaking, Maggie came out into the garden, "Vicky's awake; I can hear her whimpering. Do you want me to see to her?"

Emily intervened before I could answer, "Oh, I'd love to see her. Can we bring her out into the garden?"

For the next hour Vicky was the center of attention and I was a little miffed because I was enjoying having a meaningful conversation with my best friend. Then again, I knew I wasn't in the best frame of mind, worrying about Portia, and I began to feel a little guilty. When the time came for Emily to leave, it was still only four o'clock, so I decided to go for a drive and take Vicky with me. We ended up at the Greenburgh Nature Centre where they had an outdoor animal display which included prairie dogs, rabbits, chickens, sheep, goats, turkeys, honeybee hives and even a birds of prey aviary. I'd been there several times but this was the first time I really got to see it through the eyes of a small child. Vicky was fascinated, especially by the rabbits and, when I finally decided it was time to leave, she got very upset and screamed her head off until I managed to get her strapped into her car seat and we were on our way home.

Beth was already at the house when we arrived. She hadn't been able to resist the lure of the 5th Avenue shops, after her dental appointment, and was anxious to show me her new fall outfit and the sweet little pink dress, embroidered with rosebuds, she bought for Vicky. I couldn't help thinking how lucky Daddy was to have found her. She was always so kind and had the patience of a saint.

Chapter Eleven

It was almost eight o'clock when I finally heard from Portia. Thankfully, Vicky was already tucked up for the night and Aaron was with Daddy in the family room, watching a baseball game between the Yankees and the Texas Rangers. I was alone, playing solitaire on the computer, when the phone rang and I raced over to snatch up the receiver. I just assumed it was my sister, "Portia, is that you?" I asked, holding my breath in anticipation.

"Yes, it's me. Sorry, I'm calling so late but Veronique decided today was the day to take inventory. I think she did it deliberately just because I took a couple of days off. Anyway, I can talk now. Is this a good time for you?"

"Are you kidding? I've been waiting all day to hear about your trip. I want to know everything so start at the beginning."

"Well, I'm afraid the beginning didn't go too well. When I got to the airport, Philip wasn't there. The pilot of the plane intercepted me, before I even boarded, and told me Mr. Barrington had been held up on important business and I was to go ahead and he'd meet me at the villa."

"Are you serious? He expected you to go all that way by yourself. I would have turned right around and gone back home."

"Believe me, I considered it but the pilot convinced me I had nothing to worry about and there would be a car and driver at the other end. I decided to take a chance and, before I knew it, we were in the air and there was no turning back."

"What was it like, the plane, I mean?"

Portia sighed, "Luxurious, all soft cream leather and it even had a small bar. The attendant, his name was Manuel, was very sweet. He served me a wonderful lobster salad for lunch and a rather large glass of champagne. I felt very decadent."

"So, what happened when you arrived?"

"Cabo San Lucas is a couple of hours behind us, so it was about four o'clock when we touched down. A car was waiting for me and we drove for almost an hour before turning through a stone archway and approaching a villa, which literally took my breath away. It looked like there were several buildings all in the Spanish style with red tile roofs and surrounded by palm trees. When I stepped out of the car, a tiny woman with a dark complexion, and coal black hair, was waiting to greet me. She welcomed me and told me she was the housekeeper and her name was Carlotta. She then insisted on taking my suitcase and led me inside. Oh, Sam, when I looked around, I couldn't wait to explore but she took me straight to my room. It was completely furnished in heavy dark furniture, set off by brilliant colors everywhere; in the paintings on the walls, the bedspread, and this enormous couch covered in piles of cushions. There was also a terrace which faced the ocean and, below me, I could see an infinity pool and what looked like two or three guest houses. Carlotta suggested I might want to relax for a while after my journey but I told her I wanted to see the rest of the villa and didn't even want to bother unpacking until later. She said she understood and took me downstairs to this magnificent kitchen where she introduced me to Roberto. He was not only the chef but he was also Carlotta's husband. They'd been employed by the

Barrington family for almost eight years and lived in one of the guest houses. I learned that Philip's parents often spent time there, before his mother died, and his sister vacationed there for two weeks every year. Carlotta thought I might like to explore the villa and grounds on my own and then perhaps I would like something to eat. I thanked her and started to wander around then I soon realized I could easily get lost. There seemed to be so many rooms, all decorated in bright colors and, what I assumed, were Mexican artifacts scattered everywhere, on shelves, on table tops and mounted on the walls. Oh, Sam, I could go on all day about the place but it was when I walked outside that impressed me the most. There was a courtyard with a wonderful stone fountain and there was the infinity pool overlooking an ocean, the color of turquoise, and miles of beach with incredible rock formations."

"It sounds fabulous. I hope you took lots of photos."

"I did, but not until later, I was too occupied just taking everything in. I could have kept wandering around but I was worried I wouldn't be able to find my way back. Anyway, after a few anxious moments, I found the kitchen and Roberto was preparing a marvelous vegetable enchilada for me. He suggested I might like to eat out by the pool and asked if I'd like some wine with my food. I settled on a glass of Merlot and had just sat down at one of the poolside tables, when Carlotta came out and told me Philip had telephoned and he wouldn't be there until noon the next day. I asked if he'd given any explanation for the delay but she said he hadn't. I have to admit, I was disappointed and a little annoyed. Here I was in the most beautiful surroundings and nobody to share it all with. I felt pretty lonely right then, Sam."

"I would have been mad as a hatter. What did you do for the rest of the day?"

"I went back to my room and started to unpack and that's when I noticed the armoire was empty. Then, I walked into the en-suite bathroom, which was huge, and there were all kinds of lotions and creams obviously meant for a woman. I realized I had to be in one of the guest rooms."

"I bet you thought you'd be taken to the master bedroom."

Portia nodded, "Yes I did and, although I'd been really nervous thinking about it, now I was really confused. I sat down on the bed and thought a lot about Philip and how little I'd actually learned about him in the few times we'd dated. I knew all about his family and business background, and about his wife's death of course, but that was all. He hadn't talked much about himself, in fact I'd found him a little aloof at times."

"Really; didn't that bother you?"

"It did a little but I thought he may have been preoccupied with business. Don't forget, Sam, he has a sizeable fortune and is involved with several companies. He must have a lot on his mind."

I nodded, "That's true, but you'd think he'd have enough people working for him who could take over when he wanted a few days off. As for putting you in a guest room; that's a bit strange." I hesitated for a moment then continued, "Maybe he's gay."

Portia chuckled, "No he's not gay; I can tell you that for sure."

Suddenly a light came on in my head, "Ah ha! So you did sleep with him. When? What happened? When did he arrive?"

"Slow down, Sam, I thought you wanted to hear everything."

"I do. What did you do that night?"

"After I unpacked, I took a walk on the beach and then I went for a swim in the pool. Later Roberto brought me these amazing crunchy fritters sprinkled with chocolate and a raspberry margarita. It was pleasant sitting by the pool and it was a beautiful evening but I felt so lonesome and decided to go to bed early. I went looking for Roberto and Carlotta to say goodnight and then went up to my room but I knew I'd have trouble falling asleep, so I decided to read the book I'd started on the plane. I actually got so engrossed in it that, when I glanced at my watch, I saw it was almost midnight."

"What book were you reading?"

"A John Grisham novel; A Painted House. I'll give it to you as soon as I've finished it."

"So, carry on. Did Philip arrive the next day?"

"Yes, he arrived almost exactly at noon. He was so apologetic for not being able to fly down with me and leaving me alone all night that it was easy to put any bad feelings aside. I was so happy to see him, Sam."

"So now tell me what happened after that. I'm waiting to hear all the juicy parts."

I heard Portia sigh before she replied, "You're incorrigible, you know that don't you?"

I giggled, "Yes, but you love me anyway. Now don't keep me in suspense."

"Well, the first thing he did was to ask Carlotta to move all my belongings into the master suite. I was kind of taken aback but Carlotta didn't bat an eye. After she left to go upstairs, he asked me if I had a problem with changing rooms. All I could think about was having a complete stranger sorting through my things but, I just stood there like a dummy and shook my head."

"Wow, he sounds like someone who likes to take charge."

"That's for sure and I felt a little uncomfortable the way he ordered Carlotta and Robert about. He wasn't ever mean but he was very direct and they always addressed him as, sir. He also insisted they refer to me as Miss Lawrence. I felt so embarrassed but I suppose he was brought up in that environment and so its second nature to him. Anyway, after lunch, we went for a swim and then we went back inside and this couple arrived for, what Philip referred to as, the afternoon happy hour. The woman, Linda, was about Beth's age but her husband, his name was Henry, seemed quite a bit older and they were obviously neighbors. They came from Chicago and had known Philip's father for several years. They talked about him quite a lot. Henry was very amusing and kept flirting with me but his wife took no notice, except to say he was harmless. They invited us to go to their villa the next night and Philip accepted. Then he suggested the four of us go into town and have dinner at a place called Sunset Da Mona Lisa. It sounded very elegant and I was still in shorts and a tank top and not sure what to wear. Linda suggested I just change into something casual as where we were going wasn't particularly fancy."

"And was it fancy?"

"No, and I managed to pick out the perfect outfit. You must remember the white cotton dress you always liked. I'm so glad I decided to take it with me. I just added my silver pendant and some earrings and I fit right in. The restaurant was fabulous, Sam. It overlooked the ocean and, when the sun went down, it was so romantic. I had the most delicious scampi dish I think I've ever tasted. We'd already had quite a bit to drink back at the villa, but Henry kept ordering more wine and tequila shots. By the time we were ready to leave, he was as drunk as a skunk and Philip had to prop him up on the way to the car. When we dropped them off at their villa, which looked equally as imposing as Philip's, Linda wanted us to come in for coffee but we declined. It had been a long day and I know I was beginning to feel weary and just a little tipsy."

"Don't tell me he took advantage of you when you were drunk."

"I wasn't drunk, I was in full possession of all my faculties and, when we got in the house, he suggested we have coffee before calling it a night. I knew it would keep me awake but I felt silly asking for decaf. Carlotta and Roberto had already finished up for the day, so we ended up in the kitchen and Philip made the coffee. That surprised me because I didn't think he'd even know how, after being waited on hand and foot all his life. We sat outside near the pool and talked for a while and then he suggested I might want to turn in and he'd join me later. I wasn't sure what to make of that, but when he kissed me rather passionately before I headed upstairs, I figured he just had something to take care of and would be up shortly. It was only when I got to the top of the staircase when I realized I had no idea where the master suite was. Thank goodness there was no one else staying over, because I had to peek into two or three rooms before I found it. It was pretty obvious it was the master suite because it had to be four times as large as the guest room I'd been in. It even had a completely separate sitting area with a couch and two armchairs. Once again, color dominated everywhere, the floor, the walls, the bedding, and the bed itself had an enormous carved wooden headboard. Just to be sure I had the right room; I peeked in one of the armoires and saw my clothes had been hung up and my shoes were lined up beneath them. I found my nightgown in one of the drawers and raced into the bathroom to take a quick shower. Oh, my god, Sam, I wish you could have seen the bathroom. The tub was big enough for four people and I swear all the faucets were gold plated. I was in such a panic, I didn't want Philip to catch me in the shower, so I was in and out in minutes and safely under the covers. I'm telling you my heart was pounding."

"Why, Portia? Were you scared?"

"Not really; just nervous. I'd only ever been with Hayden and I didn't know what to expect. I think Hayden was almost as naïve as I was. I knew Philip was a lot older and I was sure he'd been involved in several relationships, as well as having been married. However, as it turned out, I didn't need to be nervous at all."

"Well, I don't expect you to tell me exactly what happened, but were you disappointed?"

"There's actually nothing to tell."

"What do you mean?"

"I was awake for what seemed like forever waiting for him. I must have dozed off for a while because, when I looked at the clock, it was almost three in the morning. I thought about getting up and going to look for him and all sorts of stupid things were going through my head."

"Such as?"

"Like, maybe he had a lot more to drink and fell in the pool. Then I got a little annoyed. This was the third time he hadn't shown up when he was supposed to. I thought he may have been toying with me and that's when I decided to stay where I was and to hell with him."

"Good for you. Best thing to do with someone like that is, let them think you couldn't care less. So I gather he never came to bed all night?"

"That's right and I think I only got a couple of hours sleep."

"What excuse did he have when you saw him in the morning?"

"You won't believe this but, when I went downstairs at just after eight, he was being served breakfast by Carlotta in the dining area just off the kitchen. Roberto intercepted me and asked if I'd like some scrambled eggs, Mexican style. I had no idea what that meant but I told him I'd love to try them and then I started to walk towards Philip. When he saw me, he stood up, waved me over, and said, 'Beunos dias', then he pulled out a chair and asked me how I'd slept. I was absolutely dumbfounded but I didn't want to make a big fuss in front of Carlotta, who was still close by, waiting to fill my coffee cup. I waited until she was far enough away and then I asked him where on earth he'd been all night. He apologized and said he'd fallen sound asleep on the lounge chair, near the pool, and didn't wake up until the sun came up. When I asked how he managed to shower and change his clothes without coming back to the room, he explained that he didn't want to disturb me, so he used one of the guest houses where he kept some extra clothes. I didn't know what to make of it and I was still annoyed, but he acted as though it was no big deal and I didn't want to spoil the rest of the weekend."

"Did you ever get to sleep with him?"

Portia hesitated then sighed, "Yes, and it was worth waiting for."

I was longing to hear more but Aaron came into the room and interrupted our conversation. The baseball game was over and he thought I might like a glass of wine and watch a movie with him. I could hardly ask him to go away while I finished talking to Portia so I suggested she call me back the next day. After I hung up the phone, I felt a little envious of her. It all sounded so exciting, even if a little puzzling.

Naturally, Aaron asked me about Portia's trip and, the next morning at breakfast, Daddy and Beth wanted to hear all about it too. I decided not to give them any details and merely said she had a great time and would probably be coming by soon with lots of pictures. I didn't hear from her again until just before dinner. She said she was meeting Philip and was in a bit of a rush with no time to chat. I was a bit disappointed but, when she promised to drop in on Sunday, I decided to stop speculating about the rest of her trip.

Chapter Twelve

On Sunday morning, it was raining and the sky was an ominous shade of grey. When I noticed Molly cleverly prying open the closet door in our room and creeping inside, I knew we were in for a storm. I was just hoping it wouldn't stop Portia from paying us a visit. Just before lunch, as I was putting Vicky down for a nap, she called Maggie and said she hoped to arrive at around three but could only stay for a short while, as she was having dinner with Philip and his sister. I was hoping she'd stay and eat with us and I'd be able to spend a little private time with her but, by a quarter after three, when she still hadn't shown up, I was getting a little fidgety. Daddy kept telling me not to worry, even though a storm was now raging and they were expecting some flooding in the area. I just couldn't help imagining her stuck somewhere or in an accident. At three thirty, she finally telephoned and apologized for not calling earlier but she'd left her cell phone in another purse and had to borrow someone else's. The rain had caused a pile up near Mt. Vernon and there was no way she could get through. Eventually, she managed to get off the highway and was sitting in a coffee shop waiting to make her way back into the city. I was relieved to hear she was all right but upset we wouldn't be seeing her and I made her promise to visit one evening during the week. Unfortunately that didn't happen, but I did eventually get to see her and meet Philip for the first time.

On Tuesday, Portia dropped in on my father at his office and he managed to take some time out to have lunch with her. From what I gathered, she only gave him a few details about her trip but made quite an impression with photos of the villa and the Cabo San Lucas area. Daddy also commented that he thought Philip was a rather handsome young man and he and Portia made a very attractive couple. I was really envious that he'd seen all the photos and I hadn't even seen a single one but then he announced, Philip had invited us all to dinner on Friday at Daniel's. I was astounded because Daniel's was one of the most exclusive restaurants in New York and it probably cost a fortune to eat there. I was anxious to know if Daddy had accepted and when he said he had, I was all in a dither about what I was going to wear. Beth suggested I call Portia and find out just how formal it was because we didn't want to feel out of place. Meanwhile, Aaron, being very practical, suggested we just google it and, when we did, we were relieved to see, even though the place itself looked luxurious, some men were without jackets or ties and there didn't appear to be any dress code. "It's certainly a lot different than when I was younger," Daddy remarked.

By Friday, I was a bundle of nerves. The day before, Aaron had insisted I go out and buy a new dress to wear to the dinner. I asked Beth if she'd come with me, as I knew she had good taste and would make sure I was getting a bargain. We traveled into the city and shopped at Nordstroms and, after trying on at least five dresses, I finally found what I was looking for; a navy, sleeveless sheath in a lacy material which was perfect for an evening in late summer. However, despite being pleased with my purchase and enjoying a wonderful lunch with Beth at Le Grainne Café, I was still anxious about meeting Philip for the first time, especially in such an upscale restaurant.

I felt particularly sad that Maggie couldn't come with us. I'd always considered her family but, as we weren't footing the bill, I didn't think it was appropriate for her to join us. In any case, somebody had to take care of Vicky. I was so lucky to have a built-in baby sitter and sometimes I'd think about working part-time just to get out of the house and meet other people. I still enjoyed being a mother but it was hard having a grown-up conversation, when my whole life seemed to be consumed with bottles and diapers. Maybe that's why I was feeling a little inadequate about socializing with someone like Philip. Unlike, the people he usually associated with, he might find me rather tame. I was mulling this over during the afternoon, when I took Vicky out in her stroller and walked through our neighborhood. Looking around me at all of the wonderful houses with their beautifully manicured lawns, I began to realize we were just as rich as the Barrington's in our own way and I wouldn't have traded my family for all of their money. The further I walked, the more resolute I became and, by the time I got home, I was beginning to look forward to the evening.

Chapter Thirteen

We decided to drive to my father's office on Park Avenue, leave the car there, and then grab a taxi over to East 65th Street. As expected, getting a taxi on a Friday evening wasn't that simple and I was sure we were going to be late. As Aaron stood curbside, frantically waving at every cab that went by, I thought he looked rather handsome. He was wearing a pair of dark grey slacks, black jacket and a crisp white open neck shirt while Daddy wore a navy business suit, with the requisite striped tie he put on every morning before leaving for work. Meanwhile, Beth, with her usual flair for fashion, wore a lovely lilac, jersey wool dress which was cut on the bias and accentuated her waistline. Before leaving the house, she'd talked about going on a diet but I assured her she looked amazing. Actually, I think we all looked pretty good and I was feeling more and more confident about meeting Philip.

We arrived at Daniel's, just a few minutes after seven and, the moment I stepped out of the taxi, I was impressed. The exterior had a marquee and several potted plants framed the entranceway. Then, when we walked through the doors, I was dazzled by the elegance; there were soaring columns forming archways, subdued lighting, round tables with pristine white tablecloths and wonderful elaborate place settings. This was exactly what I had imagined; a place where the rich and famous came to eat. I was so engrossed in my surroundings, I didn't even hear Daddy giving our name to the maître d' and, it was only when Aaron nudged me and I started following along behind Beth that my heart started to beat a little faster. Suddenly, I saw Portia coming towards us and I could feel myself begin to relax. She was smiling at Daddy and looked amazing. Her hair appeared to be even lighter than usual and fell in loose waves about her shoulders. She was wearing a powder blue chiffon dress which accentuated the color of her eyes and I think every man in the room must have been staring at her. She hugged all of us and then grabbed Beth's hand, "Come," she said, "I want you to meet Philip."

Finally, I caught sight of the man who I believed had captured my sister's heart and he literally took my breath away. He was much more handsome than any photo I'd seen of him. He rose from the table as we approached and I waited while Portia introduced my father, Beth, and Aaron. He greeted all three of them graciously and then, before Portia could say another word, he turned to me, took my hand in his, and said, "You must be Samantha. What a pleasure it is to meet you at last."

I was struck dumb for a moment. His eyes were mesmerizing and I had trouble gathering my thoughts. I slowly withdrew my hand and responded, "I've been looking forward to meeting you too. Thank you for inviting us here tonight."

"It's my pleasure," he said, still looking at me intently.

I felt uncomfortable and had to turn away and that's when he suggested we all sit down and have an aperitif. I looked at Aaron and he rolled his eyes. I knew exactly what he was thinking. Once seated, I decided to speak up, "I'd like a glass of Riesling, please."

Beth ordered the same while Daddy asked for a vodka martini and Aaron, bless his heart, asked if they had any beer. I looked across at Portia who grinned and said, "You can have anything you want."

"Yes, please be my guest," Philip said. "All of the food here is excellent and so I am not even going to attempt to recommend any of the dishes."

"This is a remarkable place," Daddy commented. "I've heard a lot about it but I've never been here."

Philip nodded, "It's one of my favorite places to eat. Actually I do a lot of business in the area so it gives me an excuse to drop in here fairly often."

I couldn't help myself when I chimed in, "My idea of dropping in somewhere for a meal would be McDonalds for a big mac."

Daddy gave me a sour look but Philip just grinned, "I can understand that, Samantha. Even I enjoy McDonalds now and again."

"It's, Sam," I said.

He looked puzzled for a moment and then said, "Ah, I see, you prefer to be called Sam; my apologies."

At that moment, our drinks arrived and we sat silently as the waiter poured about an inch of wine into Beth's glass and she was obliged to nod her approval. I tried to appear as though I'd observed this ritual several times before but, I was actually feeling a little awkward. I looked over at Philip and noticed he was being served a cocktail which I didn't recognize. "What are you drinking, Philip?" I asked.

He picked up his glass and replied, "It's a Manhattan; a mixture of whiskey, sweet vermouth and bitters." Then he raised the glass and said, "Here's to a pleasant evening. Thank you for accepting my invitation."

After that, all of us, except Philip, studied the menu, which was difficult to understand because we'd never heard of some of the foods and there were no prices. Aaron asked Philip if he could explain some of the dishes and it was obvious he was familiar with all of them but still declined to recommend anything. After we placed our orders, Beth wanted to hear all about Cabo San Lucas and I got to hear about some of the tourist spots and all of the wonderful restaurants, serving traditional Mexican food. By the time our appetizers arrived, I was famished and tucked right into a delicious concoction made with tiny scallops and ingredients I'd never tasted before. Once finished, I could hardly wait for the entrée and I wasn't disappointed. The veal was as soft as butter and the asparagus and caramelized onions were perfectly cooked. Everyone commented on the presentation and the wonderful taste. Afterwards, none of us could even look at the dessert menu, even though I nearly succumbed to the temptation of a chocolate marzipan mousse.

Philip and my father had one thing in common; they both liked to play tennis. When Portia pointed out that Daddy hadn't played in years, Philip suggested he join him at his club one day for a match. I immediately suspected he was attempting to gain my father's approval. At one point, I decided to just sit back and observe what was going on and it was easy to see Portia was hanging onto Philip's every word. She had hardly spoken the whole evening and I was making an effort to see Philip through her eyes. There was no doubt he had movie star looks and impeccable manners but, there was something about him that bothered me. I really wanted to get Portia alone for a few minutes as we'd never been able to finish our telephone conversation so, after coffee was served along with Drambuie and apricot brandy liqueurs, I excused myself to visit the ladies room and signaled Portia to follow me. After at least five minutes had gone by, I wasn't sure she was going to join me. I was still fussing with my hair when she walked through the door. "What kept you?" I asked.

She shook her head, "I didn't want to make it too obvious. You know how it looks when two women go to the ladies room together."

"No I don't. How does it look?"

"Come on, Sam, don't be naïve. You obviously want to talk to me in private about what you think of Philip."

"That's true but I also want to know why you never called me back after we last talked."

Portia sighed, "I'm sorry but I've just been so busy and I have to admit, after I got off the phone, I began to feel a little guilty about discussing what happened with Philip."

"So you slept with him after all. I knew it."

Portia started to turn away, "Let's not do this now."

I reached out and grabbed her arm, "Portia, don't leave. I'm sorry. It's evident you care a great deal about Philip and I'm happy for you."

She turned and looked at me intently, "Are you really, Sam, because I get the feeling that Philip makes you uncomfortable."

I squirmed a little because there was some truth in what she was saying, "I'm just not used to being wined and dined in a place like this. I feel a little out of my depth. Philip seems perfectly nice and he's certainly very attractive."

Portia slipped her arm around my shoulder, "If you're sure that's all that's bothering you, let's go back to the table and we can talk tomorrow or sometime next week."

I nodded and said, "Let me just touch up my lipstick."

She smiled and remarked, "By the way, you look fabulous tonight in that dress. It really suits you."

"And you look gorgeous in that color blue. You remind me of a photo I saw of Mommy that was taken with Daddy on vacation in Norway."

Portia looked pensive for a moment, "I wish she was here with us tonight."

When we got back to the table, Philip was talking about his house in Menton, on the French-Italian border. He said he was planning to go there before Christmas and was hoping Portia could go with him. As he was talking, I began to study him and couldn't help noticing how dark his skin was. I didn't think it was just a result of the weekend in Cabo, or even exposure to the sun during the exceptional summer we'd been experiencing in New York. My curiosity finally got the better of me and I interrupted him to ask, "Where did your family originate from? My guess is that they were from Italy or Spain."

Daddy glanced across at me and frowned, as though I'd said something out of place, and Philip obviously noticed this and said, "It's quite all right, Mr. Lawrence, I don't mind answering Samantha's question."

"It's Sam," I said rather abruptly.

Daddy frowned again while Philip smiled and bowed his head slightly, "Again, my apologies. Now where were we? Ah, yes; you are absolutely correct. My father's side of the family was English through and through but my mother's side came from Torremolinos, when it was a sleepy little village and not the popular tourist spot it is today. My grandmother, Nona, was the daughter of a fisherman and my grandfather was in the Royal Navy. Apparently, he was serving in the Mediterranean when there was a problem with the ship he was on and they had to dock in Malaga for repairs. He met my grandmother while on a few days curfew, waiting for repairs to be completed. He, along with a shipmate, was exploring the coastline, south of Malaga, and came across the village where my grandmother lived. They got talking to some fishermen and, from what I've been told; when Nona brought her father his lunch that's when my grandfather first laid eyes on her. They struck up a conversation and the rest is history, as they say."

"If your grandfather was in the Royal Navy, then he must have been English too," Aaron remarked."

Philip nodded, "Actually, he was from Scotland. Eventually, Nona moved to Edinburgh, where they were married, and then they immigrated to the States and settled in Boston. My mother was born a year later."

"I want to hear about your father's father," I said. "Was he born with a silver spoon in his mouth or did he work for his money?"

Aaron kicked me under the table and Daddy almost gasped, "Sam," he said, "don't you think that's a little inappropriate?"

"Why? It's a perfectly legitimate question?" I protested.

Philip chimed in, "I agree. It's a perfectly legitimate question," and then he stared at me intently as he continued. "My grandfather, Henry Barrington, grew up in a middle class family in London. At the age of thirteen, when he wasn't at school, he began helping his uncle in the construction business. By the age of eighteen he'd saved enough money to put down on his first house, which he renovated and then sold at a handsome profit. From then on he got heavily into real estate and later got involved in the stock market. He made his first million by the time he was twenty-eight. In those days, that was a lot of money. Does that answer your question, Sam?"

I had a feeling he was mocking me and I wasn't going to let him get away with it. "So, you just inherited all this wealth. It must be nice."

Daddy, who'd been clutching his napkin, threw it down on the table and said, "That's enough, young lady," then turned to Philip. "I must apologize for my daughter's rudeness and I think we should call it a night. We still have to drive back to Scarsdale."

"There's nothing for you to apologize for, Mr. Lawrence," Philip responded.

"Nevertheless, I think we should be leaving," Daddy said, turning to Beth. "Come along, my dear."

Everybody started to get up from the table except for Portia and me. Philip glanced at her and said, "Portia?"

She looked up and replied, "I'd just like a word with my sister alone, if you don't mind."

Philip nodded while Daddy, Beth and Aaron wished her goodnight and then they all moved away from the table.

I figured she was annoyed with me. "Is there something you wish to say?" I asked almost defiantly.

"What's the matter with you?" she said. "You've been behaving like a spoiled child. I've never seen you like this before, except when you decided you didn't like Erica."

I was quiet for a moment. I hated Portia being upset with me. "I'm sorry," I whispered, "I didn't mean to be rude."

Portia shook her head, "Well you were; very rude. You embarrassed the whole family. I'd really like to know the reason for all this. Philip went out of his way to see we had an enjoyable evening and you spoilt it."

I began to feel a little defensive and started to get up. "I said I was sorry."

"Not half as sorry as I am. We'll talk about this later."

I walked around the table to say goodnight and kiss her on the cheek, but she turned her head away. I figured the best thing I could do was leave, so I made my way to the exit, where the family was gathered and I could hear my father thanking Philip for his hospitality. Aaron, noticing me coming towards them, suggested they were ready to go, and they began to make their way out. I was just about to follow them when Philip stopped me, "Sam," he said, "I hope to see you again very soon. I enjoyed your company."

I still wasn't sure if he was mocking me or not, but I thought I'd done enough damage so I thanked him for a lovely evening and walked outside to join my family. In the taxi, on the way to pick up the car, there was dead silence. Nobody uttered a word but I could feel the tension. I figured everyone was waiting until we were out of earshot of the driver, however, I was wrong. Once we were back in our own car and on the highway, with my father driving and Aaron and me in the back seat, Beth said, "What did you think of the restaurant, Colin?"

Daddy kept his eyes straight ahead as he responded, "I don't think this is a good time to have a post mortem on the evening, Beth. I think we should all sleep on it."

Aaron looked at me and shrugged and I could see Beth glancing in the mirror to see if she could catch our reaction. It was all so awkward.

Chapter Fourteen

As soon as we arrived back at the house, I ran inside and up the stairs calling out goodnight, and tiptoed into Vicky's room. I could see she was sound asleep. I didn't want to wake her, so I backed away very slowly and bumped into Aaron. "Oops," I whispered, "I didn't hear you come in."

He glanced over at the crib, "I see she's out like a light, let's hope she sleeps through the night."

Once back in our room, Aaron let me get ready for bed without saying a word, while he sat watching the late news. It was inevitable; he was waiting for the right time to ask me why I'd behaved the way I did. I attempted to drag out my nightly ritual of removing my make-up and brushing my hair but Aaron was a patient man. It was only after I'd slipped into bed and picked up the book I was reading, from the bedside table, that he turned off the television and got up from the couch. He walked over and stood looking at me with his arms crossed against his chest, "What happened back there, Sam?" he asked.

I put my book down and looked up at him, "You really want to know?" I answered.

"Of course I want to know. I've never known you to act like that before. It sounded to me like you were trying to humiliate the man."

I nodded, "That's because I don't like him. I don't trust him and I don't want to see Portia get mixed up with him."

Aaron sat down heavily on the edge of the bed, "Wow! You came to a lot of conclusions in such a short space of time. We were only in his company for a couple of hours."

"Maybe that's one thing you don't know about me. I'm good at figuring out what makes people tick. That's why I married you."

Aaron smiled, "Oh, no you don't. Complimenting me isn't going to throw me off the subject. You have absolutely no reason to make a snap judgment like that. I found Philip to be intelligent, and exceedingly generous. I think he'd be a good catch for Portia."

"Well, I don't. He may be intelligent, but I bet he had the best education money can buy and he can afford to be generous. That doesn't impress me."

"What does, Sam?"

"Integrity, honesty, loyalty, patience; all the things you stand for, Aaron," I replied reaching for his hand.

He took my hand and stretched out, fully clothed, on the bed beside me, "I think you're changing the subject again. How do you know Philip doesn't fit your concept of an ideal partner?"

"I just feel it in my bones. Women are much more intuitive than men about these things."

"In that case, you'd expect Portia to feel the same way."

I scooted closer and laid my head on his shoulder, "Portia can be naïve sometimes. She's much too trusting."

Aaron sighed, "Sometimes I wonder who's older out of the two of you. How old is Portia, by the way?"

"She's twenty-five."

"And how old is Philip?"

"He's much, much older."

"How much older, Sam?"

"He's thirty-five."

Aaron chuckled, "Oh dear, he's almost old enough to be her father. Really, Sam, ten years is nothing."

I snuggled up even closer and nibbled on his ear. "Why don't you take those clothes off and come to bed."

He chuckled even louder, "I gather you've had enough of this conversation and I'm getting these slacks all wrinkled."

Less than five minutes later, he was lying naked on top of me, after having peeled off my nightgown and trailing a bunch of kisses all the way down my body. It didn't take me long to forget all about Philip Barrington.

The next morning, I was up early taking care of Vicky and I heard my father going downstairs. I was hoping he was going into his office, which he did occasionally on a Saturday morning. I thought that maybe, if he got engrossed in his work, he would have more time to cool down. It was obvious he was very annoyed with me and sooner or later we would have to have our little talk. Thankfully, he left the house a few minutes later and I crept downstairs only to be confronted by Maggie, who had picked up on Daddy's mood. "What's with your father this morning," she asked," he wouldn't even stop for breakfast."

"He's annoyed with me," I replied.

Maggie put her hands on her hips and shook her head, "What did you do now?"

"Well, apparently I was rude to Portia's boyfriend."

"And why is that? Didn't you like him?"

"Not particularly."

"I see. No one could ever call you two-faced, Sam. I remember how you acted up when your father was dating Erica. Anyway, other than that, how was the restaurant?"

"Lovely and the food was delicious. There weren't even any prices on the menu."

"Well, you have to admit, it was very generous of Portia's young man to treat you all."

"Why? He has pots of money and he can afford to spend it just to impress people."

"Now you're being very unfair."

I began to feel defensive again, "Don't you lecture me too, Maggie. I've already heard enough from Portia and Aaron and I still have to deal with Daddy."

I was pleasantly surprised, later that day, when my father returned from his office. I happened to be leaving the house with Vicky, just to take a short walk and get some fresh air, when he pulled into the driveway. He stepped out of the car, greeted me with a hug, and then peered into the stroller, "How's my sweet girl?" he asked.

I put my hand on his arm and gently asked, "Are you referring to me or Vicky?"

He looked at me rather solemnly, "I was referring to Vicky, but don't worry, Sam, I'm not going to reprimand you about last night. I was angry and disappointed but I think you're well aware your behavior was not acceptable. We'll say no more about it."

I had to bite my tongue because I didn't agree, but I hated it when I was at odds with him, so I kissed him on the cheek and said "Thank you, Daddy. We're just going for a stroll. I'll see you at dinner."

He merely nodded and I watched him as he disappeared through the front door, then I breathed a sigh of relief.

Chapter Fifteen

The next time I spoke to Portia, she didn't mention our evening at Daniel's but, I got the distinct impression she was avoiding the subject of Philip altogether. She mentioned Veronique was having a sale and that I should check it out if I planned on coming into the city, and she also talked about one of her roommates, who was severely depressed after losing her mother in a car accident. When I finally got to ask her what she'd been doing in her spare time, she confessed that she'd been to the theater to see Man of La Mancha and had attended a cocktail party, where she met Philip's sister, Serena, and her partner Lotti. "What was she like?" I asked, full of curiosity.

"Very tall, very thin, and not too attractive; it's hard to believe she's even related to Philip."

"Did you have a conversation with her?"

"Not really. We exchanged the usual pleasantries but I found her to be rather aloof, as though she didn't approve of me."

"What about the girlfriend?"

"Lotti? It's pretty obvious she's the more feminine of the two. She seems quite a bit younger and has long fair hair, and is very pretty. She was wearing a stylish wrap-dress in a lovely rose shade, while Serena wore black slacks and the standard white shirt. Lotti has a rather heavy accent and I couldn't quite place where she was from. I later discovered she came here from Hungary when she was in her early twenties. She was married to a doctor in Budapest but they separated soon after she met Serena. She divorced her husband within a year and Serena persuaded her to move here."

"It sounds like you must have been chatting for quite a while."

Portia hesitated, "Oh no, Lotti didn't tell me all this. Philip did."

"Does he get along with Serena?"

"Yes, as far as I know. They don't see each other so often now, because she lives in Florida. She happened to be in New York with Lotti, visiting some mutual friends of the family. I believe they have some connection to the theater."

"I see. Speaking of that, what's happening with acting school? It seems like it's taking forever. Do you think you'll ever save enough to afford the tuition? I'm sure Daddy will still be willing to help if you ask him."

There was a long pause before Portia answered. "To be honest, Sam, I've given up the idea."

I was surprised and immediately suspicious, "You can't be serious. Don't tell me you're going to keep on working at the boutique? What kind of a career is that?"

Portia paused again, "Maybe we should talk about this later."

Now I was really anxious to know what was going on, "Why can't we talk about it now? You've dreamed about being an actress for so long. What made you change your mind?"

I waited, and for a moment thought we'd lost contact, then I heard her say, "I'm quitting my job because Veronique won't allow me the time off to go to Menton with Philip in November, and he wants me to spend the Christmas holidays with him in London."

I literally gasped, "Are you out of your mind? How are you going to support yourself if you don't have a job and how can you even think about going away at Christmas? The family has always been together for the holiday. I can't believe you're even considering this."

Portia's voice rose slightly as she responded, "I'm not really interested in your opinion, Sam. This is my life and I can live it whichever way I choose."

I was just about to answer when I heard an ominous click. She had actually hung up on me. I sat there for a moment with the phone still in my hand. We had always been so close and never fought, except for the odd childish squabble when we were younger. I felt as though I was losing my sister and it was all because of Philip. Something wasn't right but there wasn't anything I could do about it.

I didn't know whether I should tell my father what was going on. I thought about discussing my dilemma with Aaron, but he didn't really know Daddy well enough to be sure how he'd react. I realized the best person to talk to was Maggie. She had been with us since the beginning, when my father was still grieving for my mother.

I was helping her clear away the dishes for dinner when I mentioned I wanted to speak to her privately. She was always very discreet and just nodded and whispered, "Come and see me in my room later." It was almost nine o'clock when I managed to slip away from everyone and make my way to Maggie's. She had just put on a comfortable robe and was making a pot of tea when I arrived. After she let me in, I noticed Molly curled up on the couch. Every so often, she decided she wanted a change of scenery and would end up in Maggie's room. I settled down beside her while Maggie continued fussing with the tea and then offered me a cup, which I declined. "So what did you want to talk to me about, Sam?" she asked as she sat down in the chair opposite me. I proceeded to tell her about my conversation with Portia and needed to know whether I should tell my father. She didn't hesitate to inform me that it was not my place to tell him and it was entirely up to my sister. I have to admit, I breathed a sigh of relief but I still wanted to know what she thought about the whole situation. We talked for quite a while but Maggie felt it was too soon to come to any conclusion about the nature of Portia's relationship with Philip. She agreed that it seemed to be moving forward rather quickly and we would just have to wait and see. When I again voiced my concerns about Philip, she suggested I reconsider the basis for my negative attitude and if, by any chance, the relationship was serious, how I would deal with it.

By the time I left, it was after ten o'clock and I was feeling, not only weary, but a little disheartened. I figured, once my father heard what was going on, maybe at least one person in the family would support me. Aaron was watching the news when I finally reached our room. He was curious to know where I'd been and, with a chuckle, remarked that he was ready to send out a search party. I told him I'd spent some time with Maggie but didn't mention Portia; I didn't want to get into it with him. I just wanted to relax and cuddle up on the couch. It didn't take too much persuasion on my part before we were soon making out. I knew I could always rely on my husband to take my mind off of anything that was bothering me.

Chapter Sixteen

Soon after my conversation with Portia, I discovered she'd invited Daddy to have lunch with her. Since she'd been living in the city, and with Daddy's office not too far from the boutique, they usually tried to get together every three or four weeks. Beth was the one who told me Portia had phoned my father and mentioned she really needed to talk to him. I was certain she'd finally decided to tell him about quitting the boutique and spending the holidays in London but Beth didn't have a clue. I was hoping her curiosity would get the better of her and she would call Daddy to find out what it was all about but, unlike me, she had the patience of a saint and wanted to wait until he got home that evening.

Aaron was working late at his office, when my father drove up at just after six. I watched him from the living room window, as he stepped out of the car, and noticed he looked tired and seemed reluctant to come into the house. When a neighbor walked by with his dog, he retreated to the end of the driveway and started chatting with him, while I hopped from one foot to the other mumbling to myself. I was dying to know what Portia had told him. Finally, he began to walk back and, as he approached the front door, I couldn't help myself, I ran to open it and called out, "Daddy, there you are."

He glanced at his watch and then back up at me, standing on the top step, "Hi, Sam, what's going on? It's only a few minutes after six."

I felt a little silly, "Oh, nothing's going on. I thought it was later than that."

I held the door open for him and, as he passed me, he asked, "Where's everybody?"

I closed the door and followed him down the hallway, "Beth and Maggie are in the kitchen and Vicky's having a nap."

"What about Aaron?"

"He's working late. Why, Daddy, did you want to see him?"

He hung up his coat, put his briefcase on the hall table, and then turned to face me, "We might as well all get together in the kitchen right now."

I nodded but didn't say anything as I made my way to the kitchen. Standing in the doorway, I looked at Beth and Maggie standing at the counter preparing dinner, and announced, "Daddy's here."

It got a little tense when he suggested we all sit down as he had something to tell us. Of course, Maggie knew what it was all about but Beth had no idea and I watched her face as my father repeated what Portia had already told me. Then, before anyone could comment, he turned to me and said, "I know you were aware of all this, Sam, and I know you didn't hold back, telling your sister what you thought. Now, I think I should give you my opinion." I started to speak but he held up his hand to stop me. "Portia is a grown woman and entitled to live her life without any interference from any member of this family. I'm concerned about her giving up her job but she has sufficient savings to allow her to take some time off. We may be disappointed that she no longer wants to go to acting school but, let's face it, she's a little too old now to consider a career in the theater. She has the opportunity to travel and spend time with a man she obviously has deep feelings for. We haven't had time to get to know Philip but he seems like a decent young man and I suspect things might be getting a little serious between them. If, down the road, this leads to marriage, then I'm not opposed to the idea. Portia would be well taken care of financially and may never have to work again."

Beth interjected, "Do you really think things are getting that serious between them, Colin?"

My father nodded, "Yes, I do and Portia tells me Philip would very much like to meet with the family again. I proposed that he come here for dinner on Saturday."

I gasped, "You're kidding? He's coming here?"

"Well, Portia's calling me tonight after she speaks to him. She has to make sure he doesn't have a previous engagement and, if he's able to accept my invitation, Sam, I don't want a repeat of the Erica fiasco."

I made a face and hissed, "I was all of about twelve at the time."

Maggie chuckled, "Yes, but I sure do remember what a little missy you were."

Beth frowned, "What happened?"

Daddy shook his head, "Long story. Let's just say, if Sam doesn't like someone, she doesn't hesitate to let them know it."

I shrugged my shoulders, "I can't help it. I can't be all sweet as sugar when I don't like someone."

Beth frowned again, "Are you saying you really don't like Philip?"

Daddy intervened, "I think she's already made that perfectly clear and if there's any chance we're going to have another incident, then I suggest," he continued turning to me, "you stay upstairs or go out for dinner on Saturday."

"Now you're treating me like a child," I responded angrily. "I wouldn't miss this for the world."

Daddy finally grinned, "That's what I'm afraid of."

The next morning, I discovered that Philip was delighted to receive the invitation and looked forward to seeing us all again. Now, I had three days to anticipate how the evening would turn out and, although I was nervous, I could hardly wait. Meanwhile, after I filled Aaron in on the whole situation, it bugged me when he commented that it would be nice to have another man close to his own age in the family. I told him he was really jumping the gun.

Maggie thought about making a traditional English dinner. She was aware Philip spent a lot of time in London and thought he might enjoy it. Once she'd decided on a menu of rib roast, roast potatoes, Yorkshire pudding and Brussel sprouts with peas and pearl onions, along with chocolate Bundt cake for dessert, she was in her element, shopping, chopping, mixing, and shooing everyone out of her way. In the meantime, Daddy was researching the most appropriate wine to serve and finally settled on a Bordeaux. Personally, I thought it was all much ado about nothing but, I have to admit, I was obsessing a bit about what to wear. Beth mentioned she was going to wear one of her long jersey skirts with a simple black top and suggested I pick out something similar, so that I'd be comfortable. The year before, Portia had given me a lovely royal blue maxi dress, with long sleeves and a scoop neck and, at the time, I was still struggling with a bit of baby weight but now it fitted me perfectly. All it needed was the silver pendant in the shape of a heart that had once belonged to my mother.

Chapter Seventeen

Saturday came much sooner than expected and I was busy most of the day helping Maggie clean house and complete the preparations for dinner. Although she had already done most of the work, over the previous two days, there was still a lot to do and she insisted the dining room table was set with our best china, and the glassware had to be sparkling. I was beginning to wonder if she was expecting a member of the royal family, the way she was carrying on. Meanwhile, Beth stayed well away from the kitchen and was only allowed to take care of the floral arrangements for the table. Once, when I ran into her in the hallway, she whispered, "Can't I do anything else to help?"

I put one finger to my lips and whispered back, "She's having the time of her life. I think I'll have to run into town and get her a maid's outfit so that she can serve dinner in it."

Beth tried to suppress a laugh just as Maggie appeared at the kitchen door looking very serious. "Did you manage to get those flowers yet, missus?" she asked.

"Just going to get them now, Maggie," Beth replied and headed for the front door.

I fed Vicky a little earlier than usual, hoping she'd be settled in her crib no later than six-thirty. Of course, she had to pick that particular day to act up and it was almost seven by the time I'd tucked her in, sang her favorite lullaby twice over, and finally saw her eyes begin to close. I had showered earlier in the day, so I only needed to change clothes and touch up my make-up, but I needed to hurry because I wanted to be downstairs when Portia arrived. I hadn't spoken to her since she'd hung up on me and I had no idea how she'd react when she saw me. I preferred to be with the rest of the family when she walked through the door.

I'd just slipped my shoes on, when Aaron called upstairs to tell me there was a Bentley pulling into the driveway. I felt my heart start to race a little, so I took a few deep breaths and then ran down to the bottom of the stairs, where Aaron was waiting. He took my hand and said, "You look lovely, Sam."

I smiled and the doorbell rang just as my father and Beth came out of the living room. The three of us stood back as Daddy answered the door and greeted Portia, "Hi, honey, good to see you. Where's Philip?"

I heard her answer, "He's just getting a couple of things out of the car." Daddy stood aside and suddenly there she was, looking as beautiful as always in a long black cape with her blonde hair tumbling around her shoulders. She came towards me with her arms outstretched, "Hi, Sam," she said.

I stepped forward and we gave each other a hug, then she hugged Beth and Aaron and slipped off her cape. She was wearing a figure hugging burgundy dress and a gold necklace with an antique locket, I'd never seen before. It looked expensive and I wondered if Philip had given it to her. A moment later, I heard Philip talking to my father and I stepped to one side so that I could get a clear view of him. He was handing Daddy a bottle of wine and carrying, what looked like, two bouquets of flowers. He looked even more handsome than the last time I'd seen him at Daniel's, when he'd been wearing a formal, dark grey suit. This night, he had on a navy blazer and a dove grey polo neck sweater. There was no question, he had great dress sense but my next thought was that he could well afford it. He approached Beth first and handed her one of the bouquets; a vibrant mixture of crimson roses and red dahlia's. Then, he turned to me and handed me the other bouquet of bright yellow chrysanthemums, "Hello, Sam" he said, "it's nice to see you again."

Before I had a chance to respond he was shaking Aaron's hand and I stood back feeling a little awkward until Beth tapped me on the shoulder, "I'll take the flowers and put them in water. You go on into the living room and join the others."

I passed over the bouquet and, as I wandered into the living room, I heard Daddy say, "This looks like a rather special bottle of Chardonnay, Philip. I believe I read somewhere that your father was a connoisseur of wines."

Philip was settling down beside Portia on the couch and nodded, "Yes, sir. I inherited a rather impressive collection of vintage wines. The majority of them are stored at the house in Mayfair, but I do have a number of bottles here in New York."

They continued to discuss wines as Daddy served cocktails and then Beth came into the room and announced dinner would be ready in about half an hour.

I caught Portia's eye a number of times, hoping she would add to the conversation and finally she asked, "How's Vicky? Is there any chance we'll get to see her tonight?"

Aaron cut in, "I don't think so, unless you'd like to peek in on her after dinner. We don't want to wake her up. Sam will go with you."

I got the feeling my husband was paving the way for Portia to spend some time alone with me. He knew I was upset that we hadn't talked to each other for a while. I looked at him, smiled, and slipped my hand into his, "That's a good idea, honey. We'll go up later."

Just then, Molly appeared in the doorway. She looked a little nervous and I wondered if she was wary of Philip but I was wrong. I was surprised when he got up and walked over to her, then bent down to stroke her, "Who do we have here?" he asked.

Portia replied, "That's Molly, but be careful otherwise you'll get hair all over your jacket."

He continued to scratch her behind the ears and she rolled onto her back purring loud enough for me to hear. "I didn't think you were the type that liked animals," I said.

I heard my father draw in a breath but Philip didn't seem to notice and he stood up and looked at me with, what I perceived to be, a challenging stare, "Our family has always had pets, Sam. We've had bull terriers going back three or four generations and Serena and I always had cats and rabbits when we were children. Serena owns a horse and takes care of my two dogs, Max and Buddy, at her place in West Palm."

"Why don't you look after them yourself?" I asked, staring right back at him.

He grinned, "Because, I spend so much time traveling, it's better that they stay with my sister. I try to get down and see them two or three times a year." I merely nodded and he slowly walked away and sat down again, leaving Molly still stretched out on her back, waiting for more attention.

I was relieved when Maggie came into the room to announce dinner was ready. I couldn't help chuckling to myself when I saw she had on a rather severe black dress and a row of pearls, and she even had lipstick on. Who was she trying to impress? It didn't take me long to find out because she was all over Philip, once we were seated at the dining room table. She fussed over him like a mother hen until my father finally said, "I think we have everything we need, thank you, Maggie."

I have to admit, the meal she cooked up was superb and, when she crept into the room with a pot of coffee and placed it on the sideboard, Philip looked over his shoulder and said, "Maggie, I hope I may call you that; dinner was perfect. I haven't had a good English meal like it in quite a while."

Maggie blushed, bright red, almost did a little curtsy as she thanked him, and then scurried out of the room. Portia looked across at me and rolled her eyes and we both started to laugh. Suddenly all the tension I'd been feeling drained away.

After dinner, we went back to the living room for more coffee and liqueurs and Philip brought up the subject of Christmas. He mentioned he would be spending the holidays in London and would like Portia to accompany him. He understood we were disappointed about the family not being together and invited us to join him, as his guests. I know my mouth dropped open, and Aaron immediately reached over and put his hand on my arm, to stop me from saying a word. Before my father had a chance to respond, Portia spoke up, "I really would like to go with Philip, Daddy, but I would absolutely love it if everyone could come along too."

My father paused for a moment and then said, "That's very generous of you, Philip, but I think it would be better if we stayed here. Vicky is so young and needs a lot of attention. It would be difficult for Sam to enjoy herself under those circumstances. Then there's our Maggie; we wouldn't dream of leaving her here alone over the holidays."

"Maggie is welcome to come along too," Philip said.

Daddy shook his head, "No, I've made up my mind; we'll stay here." He then turned to Portia and continued. "You go ahead with your plans. We'll miss you, honey, but I know it's an opportunity you can't pass up."

Portia nodded, "Thank you, Daddy, for being so understanding."

"I'm sure you'll have a wonderful time. London is a marvelous place to be at Christmas," Beth remarked.

I sat there feeling like a bump on a log. Nobody even asked my opinion and it looked like my father had made up my mind for me. I would have jumped at the chance of going to London, especially if I had Maggie along to help me with Vicky. Aaron noticed I'd gotten really quiet and said, "Why don't you and Portia pop in on Vicky now. Just make sure you don't wake her up."

Portia stood up, "Yes, let's go up now, Sam, because we're going to be leaving soon. It's getting a bit late."

Molly followed us up the stairs to Vicky's room and settled on a chair near her crib. My sweet daughter was lying on her side, hugging her favorite teddy bear and sucking her thumb. She looked so content and I felt a great sense of pride when Portia looked down at her and said, "She's so beautiful, Sam. She reminds me a lot of those photos we have of Mommy when she was a baby."

I put my hand on her shoulder and said, "I think she's going to look like you, Portia." She started to shake her head but, before she could say anything, I asked, "How are you? Are you really happy?"

She smiled and put her arm around me, "I am now that we aren't fighting any more. I missed you, Sam."

"I missed you too, but I was talking about you and Philip. Is it getting serious between you?"

"I think so. He didn't mention it tonight, but I told you the last time we talked that he wants me to go with him to his place in France before the holidays, and he's already made arrangements. He hasn't told me he loves me or anything like that but I've been seeing a lot of him and I think he really cares for me."

"Have you quit the boutique yet?"

"I have one more week to go. Veronique wasn't too happy when I gave her my notice but she's such a romantic, she said she understood."

We continued talking for a few more minutes and then Vicky began to stir, so we tiptoed out of the room and made our way back downstairs. When we walked into the living room, Philip looked up and said, "Ah, there you are. I think we should be on our way, Portia."

Once again, as we said our farewells, Philip looked me in the eyes and said, "Sam, I hope to see you again, very soon." And, once again, I doubted his sincerity particularly as he held onto my hand a little longer than necessary.

Chapter Eighteen

On November 24th, while we celebrated Vicky's first birthday, Portia left to spend ten days in Menton and she called me soon after she arrived. Philip had arranged to meet her there, after a business trip which had taken him to Amsterdam and Paris. This time she flew by commercial airliner, but it was first class all the way. We heard from her the day after she reached the villa, the same day that Philip was due to arrive. I couldn't help commenting that it seemed like she was always having to wait for him. She ignored my remark and was anxious to tell me all about Menton. On the drive in from the airport, in Nice, she said she was awestruck by the scenery. Apparently Menton was known as the prettiest town in France and was perched on a hill, overlooking the Mediterranean. The villa itself, was almost five hundred years old and built on four levels. She added that nothing could have prepared her for the interior, furnished in the French country style, rustic yet elegant at the same time. She'd been greeted by the housekeeper, a rather elderly woman named Colette, who had worked for the Barringtons' since she was in her twenties. She lived with her daughter in a small house, near the center of town, and took care of maintaining the villa, on a regular basis. When, any

member of the Barrington family was in residence, she moved
into one of the bedrooms and, in addition to cleaning up and
taking care of the laundry, she managed to cook whatever
meals were requested, although Philip was fond of eating in
the local restaurants on most days. I was surprised Portia had
learned so much about the housekeeper, in such a short time,
but apparently Collette liked to talk and her command of the
English language was excellent. She had known Philip since
he was a small boy and was very fond of him but, when Portia
asked about Serena, she was less enthusiastic. I suspected, she
may have been old school and didn't approve of her lifestyle,
but maybe Serena wasn't a particularly nice person. I'd already
made up my mind that I wasn't going to like her. Eventually,
after chatting for quite some time, Portia told me she was
disappointed about missing Vicky's birthday and hadn't yet got
her a gift, because she was hoping to find something unique
in France. I suggested an antique music box. I had seen one in
the shape of a bird cage and it was the type of gift I was sure
Vicky would treasure as she grew up. I was reluctant to finish
our conversation because I knew it was getting close to the
time when Philip was expected. Once he arrived, I assumed
Portia would be too wrapped up in him to even think about
calling home again. As we said our goodbyes I felt really sad, as
though I was losing my sister. It wasn't jealousy or even envy; it
was something else I couldn't quite put my finger on.

Four days later, we celebrated Thanksgiving. We really
missed Portia but, two days after she returned from France, on
a rainy Sunday afternoon, she came for a visit. We all gathered
in the family room while she told us all about her trip. The
day after Philip arrived, they had driven across the border to
Ventimiglia, a small Italian town famous for its market. It was
there that she found the perfect gift for Vicky, not a music box,
but an antique doll dressed as Marie Antoinette; it was perfect.
A few days later, they made an impromptu tour along the coast
to Monte Carlo, where Philip's yacht, Justice, was moored, but
he decided against taking her out as he preferred to have at
least one other crew member on board. Portia said the interior

was luxurious, all gleaming wood paneling with a lounge and dining area, and three cabins, beautifully furnished with damask coverings on queen-size beds. In Menton, she met a friend of Philip's, Henri Vanier and his wife, Jeanne, and they ate out together on several occasions. Apparently, Henri's favorite restaurant was Mirazur and Portia said the view and the food were to die for but, after ten days of eating out every night, and enjoying the lavish brunches Colette served up, she was sure she'd gained five pounds and was reluctant to get on the scales. When I asked her if she planned to go on a diet before she left for London, she sighed and said, "We leave in less than two weeks. I'm beginning to wonder if I should even go."

"Why?" I asked. "Because you're afraid of all the heavy food those Brits dish out, or are you feeling guilty now about not being with the rest of the family?"

Portia didn't get a chance to answer because my father spoke up, "Now, Sam, let's not go there; we've already been through this. I'm sure your sister's just feeling a little overwhelmed having just come back from being away for ten days. She's not used to all this traveling."

Portia nodded, "Thank you, Daddy, that's exactly how I feel."

"I still think you should go," Beth said, "and maybe we can all do something together for New Year's Eve."

My father shook his head, "I'm not sure these young people want to spend New Year with us old fogeys."

Beth grinned, "You speak for yourself. I can still keep up with the young ones, even if you can't."

Everyone began to chuckle and, once again, the tension in the room evaporated.

After Portia's visit, I only got a chance to speak to her once, before she left for England. It was a rather tearful conversation because I knew I would miss her terribly. This would be the first time we hadn't spent the holidays together. Beth tried to cheer me up by offering to take care of Vicky, and insisting Aaron and I go into the city for dinner and a movie. I jumped at the chance because, although we went to the movies fairly often in Scarsdale, we didn't often eat out. The city was so much more exciting and sometimes I wished Aaron and I could afford to live there. We took Beth up on her offer and decided to eat at Ellen's Stardust Diner in Times Square, home of the singing waiters and lots of fun. Then Aaron suggested we see Spiderman and, at first, I was totally opposed to the idea but my husband is such a sweet talker that I finally gave in. I must admit, I enjoyed it, but it was even more enjoyable cuddling up in the back row.

The Monday following our night out, Maggie and I were already decorating the house for the holidays and Beth was in town, shopping for more ornaments to put on the tree. I loved this time of year and I was anxious to see how Vicky reacted to all the lights and the colors. I was just hoping we'd have a white Christmas because everything looked so much prettier with snow on the ground and on the trees.

Beth had invited her son, Neil, and his wife, Lisa, for the holidays. They arrived at just after eleven on Christmas Eve, and I began to feel the next few days without my sister might not be so difficult after all. Lisa was just a couple of years older than me and had a great sense of humor, and I knew she was somebody whose company I would enjoy. She reminded me a little of Emily, with her red hair and white skin. Then, in the late afternoon, there was a knock at the front door and when I opened it, there was Aaron's mother standing there, suitcase in hand and grinning like a Cheshire cat. "Oh my goodness, Jane," I said, "What a wonderful surprise. Come in, come in. Nobody told me they were expecting you."

She chuckled as she stepped inside, "That's because I didn't tell anyone I was coming. I was visiting Jackie, an old friend of mine in Queens, and decided to stay over for a day or two. Then I thought I'd pop over here, because I couldn't resist seeing the look on Aaron's face when I showed up."

I helped her take off her coat and boots, "Beth's family's here for the holiday. We've put them up in the guest room but Portia's room is vacant and you can stay as long as you like."

"I didn't mean to impose on you, dear. I'm booked on a flight back to Sacramento tomorrow and I can always stay at a hotel for one night."

"Nonsense, I wouldn't hear of it. Aaron will be so happy to see you and Maggie's cooking enough food for an army, so one extra guest isn't going to make a bit of difference. Now, let's go and surprise everyone," I said, taking her arm and leading her down the hall to the family room.

We were almost there when she said, "You mentioned Portia's room was vacant. Where is she?"

"Believe it or not, she's in London. Aaron must have told you about the boyfriend. Well, he's got pots of money and he's already taken her to France and Mexico."

"Lucky girl," she remarked just as Aaron walked out into the hall. He stopped dead in his tracks and his mouth dropped open. Jane chuckled, "What's the matter, son; cat got your tongue?"

He stepped forward to embrace her, "Mom, this is the best surprise. I can't believe you're here. How did you get here and why didn't you tell me you were coming?"

"I was in the city visiting Jackie and I took a taxi over here. I didn't tell you because I knew you'd make a fuss. I'm going back home tomorrow but I'll be staying here tonight. Sam said I could have Portia's room. If you want to make yourself useful, you can drive me to the airport in the morning. My flight leaves at three."

"But tomorrow's Christmas day. Why would you go home then?"

"Because I knew not too many people would be traveling and I wouldn't have to deal with all the crowds."

Aaron looked at me and remarked, "Now you know how I got to be so smart. I take after Mom." With that he, grabbed her hand and pulled her into the family room, "Look who's here everyone," he called out, with a huge smile on his face.

Chapter Nineteen

The holiday seemed to go by in a flash and the house suddenly felt empty. Christmas morning had been chaotic with everybody around the tree opening up gifts, while Vicky crawled amongst the wrappings and Molly insisted on dragging all of the discarded ribbons out into the hallway. Maggie made a wonderful brunch and we sat around the table sipping on cranberry mimosas and peach Bellini's. Then Aaron left to take his mother to the airport and things settled down until dinner, when we were treated to a traditional meal of turkey and all the trimmings.

Neil and Lisa stayed for two more days and then my thoughts turned to Portia. Daddy kept telling me that, more than likely, she was very busy and hadn't had time to call. I didn't think it was much of an excuse considering it only takes a few minutes to pick up a phone and connect with the family. The very next day, I understood why she hadn't called. She had no idea what to say to us.

My father had picked up a copy of the New York Times and was sitting in the family room reading the business and sports pages, while Beth was glancing casually through the other sections. I'd just walked into the room when I heard her say, "Oh, my goodness, Colin, look at this."

"What is it?" I asked.

She looked up at me and sighed, "Sam, I didn't realize you were there. I'm sorry but you're not going to like this."

My father put down his paper as I walked across to peer over Beth's shoulder. When I looked down, I could hardly believe my eyes. There was a photo of Portia with Philip holding onto her arm. She was attempting to cover her face and I immediately noticed the huge ring on her left hand. Then I read the words that literally made me gasp, "Philip Barrington celebrates his engagement to Portia Lawrence in London." Beth looked up at me and asked, "Shall I read it out loud?" I nodded and she continued, "Philip Barrington, 37, heir to the Barrington fortune, was seen at Annabel's last night celebrating his engagement. His future bride, Portia Lawrence, 26, is a native of New York. The couple spent the holiday at Philip's Mayfair home along with Philip's sister, Serena and her partner, Lotti Herczeg. This will be the first marriage for Miss Lawrence, and the second for Philip Barrington. His first wife, Leanne, drowned in a boating accident several years ago. Since that time, he has been linked with a number of high profile women, including the actress, Helena Waring. When asked what attracted him to his fiancé, he claimed that, apart from her obvious beauty, she had an innocent way about her he had not encountered before. He concluded that not having been in the public eye was an added bonus".

Beth finished reading and looked at me to see my reaction but, at that moment, Aaron walked into the room and must have sensed something had happened, "What's going on?" he asked.

I turned and took a step towards him, then threw my arms around him as the tears started to fall. He held me tightly against his chest, while Beth stayed sitting and my father stood up and said, "I'm afraid there's an announcement in the paper that's upset her."

Aaron frowned, "What announcement?"

I tried to tell him as I continued to sob, "Portia got engaged and she didn't even let us know."

Beth got up and handed Aaron the paper, "Here, you'd both better sit down and you can read it for yourself, Aaron."

He led me over to the couch and kept on holding my hand as he silently looked at the photo and read the caption underneath. Then he looked up at my father who was pacing the floor, "Colin, what do you make of all this?"

My father stopped pacing and sat down opposite us, "I think it was a complete surprise to Portia and it probably all happened so quickly, she was caught up in the moment. I believe her feelings for Philip were a lot stronger than we realized and when he proposed, she was caught off guard. I'm sure she didn't expect to see her picture in the New York Times, and was probably hoping to let us know before we found out for ourselves. This is all speculation, of course, but I know my daughter and she wouldn't deliberately keep something like this from us."

I had only been half listening, because I was trying to recall what the time difference was between New York and London. "Isn't London way ahead of us, time wise?"

Aaron nodded, "Yes, five or six hours I believe."

I got up and felt myself growing angry, "So it must be afternoon there now and there's no excuse for her not calling."

"Maybe she's scared or embarrassed," Beth said.

"That's ridiculous," I responded. "We're her family. I'm going to find Philip's number and call his house."

Aaron put his hand on my arm, "Don't do that, Sam. Give your sister a little longer to contact us. There may be a legitimate reason why she hasn't phoned."

I hesitated and then answered grudgingly, "All right, I'll give her until six o'clock, it will be about midnight there, and if we haven't heard from her by then, I'm calling the house and I don't care if I wake everybody up."

Aaron shrugged, "Okay, I guess there's no sense in trying to change your mind?"

I stood up, "No sense at all and now I'm going to break the news to Maggie."

Vicky had just learned how to maneuver herself along the downstairs hallway by staying close to the wall. She looked so cute wobbling along on her little legs with a big smile on her face. We were concerned she'd find her way into the kitchen where all kinds of accidents could happen so, later that day, I was sitting on the bottom step watching her, and ready to grab her if she made the wrong turn. I didn't expect Molly to get in her way and trip her over, causing her to bump her head so severely that I was worried she might have a concussion. Aaron tried to convince me she was okay but I insisted on taking her to emergency to be sure. We drove to White Plains Hospital and waited for two hours before we managed to see a doctor. In the meantime, Vicky fell asleep in my arms even though I tried to keep her awake, because that's what I heard you should do. The doctor proclaimed her to be perfectly all right but, just to be sure, he suggested we wake her up every two or three hours, even during the night.

By the time we got back home, I was exhausted and Aaron suggested I have a little nap before dinner. I went up to our room, taking the page from the New York Times with me, and I sat on the edge of the bed staring at the photo of Portia. Although her face was partially covered, she looked frightened, like a deer caught in the headlights. Her hair was piled on top of her head in a style I'd never seen before and she was wearing a form fitting lace dress with long sleeves and a high collar. I couldn't tell what color it was because it was a black and white photo, but it looked white. All she needed was a veil to make her look like a bride. I didn't want to think about her marrying Philip so; I put the paper down and lay down on the bed in an attempt to get a few minutes sleep. I closed my eyes and tried to stop my mind from thinking about Portia but, it was no use. Even when I picked up the book I'd been reading from the bedside table, the words just swam before my eyes. Why hadn't she called me?

Chapter Twenty

After discarding the book and just lying there staring at the ceiling, for what seemed like an eternity, I thought I heard a light knock at the door. I waited for a moment and then heard it again so I called out, "Come in."

My father poked his head in, "Hi, honey, sorry to disturb you," he whispered. "I hope I didn't wake you."

"I swung my legs over the side of the bed and sat up, "No, Daddy, I haven't even been asleep. Is it dinner time?"

He came further into the room, "No, not quite. I just wanted to come and get you. Portia's on the phone." I jumped up and started towards the door but he grasped my arm. "You don't have to hurry; she's talking to Beth at the moment."

"Have you spoken to her?" I asked.

He nodded, "I happened to answer when she called."

"What did she say? I'm dying to know."

"I think it would be best if you speak to her yourself, Sam."

"I don't like the sound of that," I remarked, as I exited the room and went downstairs with my father following behind me.

I could hear Beth's voice coming from the family room, so I ran down the hallway and stopped in the doorway. Beth looked up and signaled me to come in, then said into the phone, "Portia, Sam's here now so I'm going to let you speak to her. I'll just say bye-bye for now and once again, congratulations. Have a safe journey back and come and visit as soon as you can." She hesitated for a moment and then continued, "Thank you, dear. Now, here's Sam," and she handed me the phone.

I felt the tension begin to build as I took the phone from her but she smiled at me then left the room. I took a deep breath and said, "Hi, Portia."

"Sam," she answered, "it's so good to hear your voice. I know you must be angry with me. Daddy told me you already know about the engagement. I certainly didn't intend for you to find out that way. I'm so sorry."

"Why have you waited so long to call? Even if it was a total surprise to you, you've had plenty of time to call before now. We're your family, Portia, perhaps we're not important to you."

"Of course you're important. I meant to phone you earlier, I really did but I didn't know how to tell you. It took me all day to summon up the courage and all the time you already knew. I had no idea there was a photo in the paper and that you'd see it."

"I see. Who do you think all those reporters were with their cameras taking pictures?" I asked sarcastically.

"I didn't think, Sam. I'm still having trouble getting used to the idea that Philip is a public figure. This is all new to me."

"Is this what you really want, Portia, or was Philip so persuasive that you just couldn't say no to him?"

"I agreed to marry him because I love him and I wish you could be happy for me. Daddy and Beth both seem pleased, although they would have liked to have joined us in the celebration."

"Well, maybe you can invite us all to the wedding to make up for it."

Portia sighed, "Please, don't do this, Sam, you're my sister and I love you. I would never get married without you being there."

"Have you decided on a date?" I asked, holding my breath.

"No, but we don't want to wait too long so it will probably be this summer and it will be in New York."

"Well that's a blessing; I expected it to be thousands of miles away."

"Neither of us wanted that. Most of Philips friends and business acquaintances are in New York, as well as you and the rest of the family."

"Will you be back before New Year? We talked about getting together."

"I don't think we will. I'm so sorry, Sam, but I heard Philip talking to Serena about a party at her place in West Palm. She invited us and I know Philip wants to go."

"So, his sister comes before your sister. That's really nice, Portia. I get the feeling this future husband of yours is rather controlling. I just hope you're doing the right thing."

There was silence on the line for a moment and then Portia whispered, "I think I'll say goodbye now. Take care of yourself and kiss Vicky for me."

I started to say goodbye but it was too late, Portia had already hung up.

When Aaron found me sitting with the phone still in my hand and tears running down my face, he was annoyed. The only thing was, he wasn't annoyed with Portia, he was annoyed with me. "You have to let go, Sam," he said. "Your sister's engaged now and living her own life. My god, what's going to happen when Vicky grows up and wants to move away?"

"Well, I hope she won't abandon her family," I shot back.

"Portia isn't abandoning you; she just has different priorities right now. She's in love with Philip and you can't blame her for wanting to be with him. You're upset because she won't be spending New Year with us, but it's only one day. There'll be plenty of other days when you can get together."

"That's not the only reason I'm upset. You know how I feel about Philip. I think she's making a mistake."

"You have no justification for the way you feel about him, Sam. He's going to be part of this family now and you're going to have to accept that, or you're just going to alienate Portia even more than you have already."

"Is that what you think I've done?" I asked rather indignantly.

Aaron nodded, "Yes, I do. I think you need to think long and hard about what you're doing. I know you think Philip is controlling but I think you're the one who's trying to control your sister's relationship with him. It's time you changed your attitude."

I sat with my head bowed for a moment and then wiped away my tears, "I'll try, I really will but it's not going to be easy."

Aaron tilted my head up so that he could look me in the eyes, "That's my girl," he said. "Now let's talk about what we're going to do at New Year."

At dinner later, nobody mentioned Portia and I got the feeling Aaron had suggested to my father and Beth that we not talk about her, otherwise I might get upset again. When I brought up the subject of New Year, Daddy said a colleague, John Brigham, had invited him and Beth to a party at the Sunningdale Country Club and he had just been on the phone to see if it was possible to bring two guests. Apparently two members of the club had been called out of town on a family emergency and John told Daddy we'd be more than welcome. I'd never been to Sunningdale but I knew Daddy had played golf there a few times, as John's guest, and had even dined there once or twice. He suggested the party would be an elegant affair so we'd better get our glad rags on. That immediately got me thinking about what I was going to wear and all thoughts of Portia flew out the window.

Later, I wondered if Maggie might have wanted to take New Year's Eve off instead of baby-sitting Vicky but she was more than happy to stay home. She claimed she'd been to enough New Year parties, when she was younger, to last her a lifetime. Now that I didn't have to worry about Vicky, I could concentrate on my wardrobe and I considered buying a new dress but Aaron thought my little black velvet number with the long sleeves and scoop neck would be perfect. I thought I'd better try it on to make sure it still fitted and I must admit it looked perfect, with my strappy sandals and a long row of pearls that had belonged to my mother.

On the night itself, I applied mauve eye shadow, lots of mascara and crimson lipstick, piled my hair casually on top of my head and added a pair of drop pearl earrings. Aaron commented that I looked absolutely smashing. He didn't look too bad himself in his best navy suit with a snow white shirt and sky blue tie.

We'd just finished getting ready and were about to go downstairs when Daddy called up to me, "Sam, Portia's on the phone. She wants to wish you a happy New Year."

I looked at Aaron and sighed but he put his hand on my shoulder and said, "You'd better go and talk to her."

I walked slowly downstairs, trying to think what I could say, and found Daddy waiting for me. "Take it in the family room," he said.

When I picked up the phone all I could say was, "Hello."

Portia immediately answered, "Hi, Sam, I just wanted to wish you a Happy New Year. I understand you're going to Sunningdale. I'm sure you're all going to have a lovely time."

"Where are you calling from?" I asked.

"From West Palm; we're at Serena's place. We just arrived here. We came straight from London. She's having this lavish party with about fifty or more guests and it's all being catered by one of the top chefs in Miami. Honestly, Sam, I can't get over the way these people throw money around. The house is absolutely gorgeous, and it's got five bedrooms and goodness knows how many bathrooms. I've no idea why Serena and Lotti need such a big place although, from what I hear, they do a lot of entertaining."

I got the distinct feeling Portia was rattling on because she wasn't sure what else to say and I was having trouble too so I decided to keep it light, "What time does the party start?"

Portia giggled, "Not until ten, I'll be starving by then. We just got here about two hours ago and only had a small meal on the plane."

"Didn't you use the private jet?"

"No we were on a commercial airliner and it took almost ten hours. I think I've had enough traveling for a while."

"I hope that doesn't mean you'll be staying there after the holiday is over?"

"No, of course not; Philip needs to get back to New York and I really want to come home to see you all. I really miss you, Sam."

I began to feel teary eyed but I tried to be upbeat, "Well then, I expect to see you the minute you get back. Maybe we can all go out to dinner."

"I'd like that. I can't wait to see you."

"Me too; happy New Year, Portia, enjoy yourself tonight."

"I'll try. I love you, Sam."

"Love you too, bye bye."

I hung up the phone and that's when my emotions got the better of me and the tears began to fall. I felt a hand on my shoulder and turned to see Aaron, "You're going to spoil your makeup, honey," he whispered as he took out his handkerchief and began to wipe my tears away.

I grasped his wrist, "You're going to get mascara all over it."

He shrugged, "Lot's more where this came from," he said. "Now, go and repair your face, or whatever it is you have to do, because it's almost time to leave."

"Yes, sir," I replied and flounced out of the room.

The party at Sunningdale was wonderful. Daddy was right, it was elegant and I knew I had worn the perfect outfit for the occasion. Beth looked especially lovely in a plum coloured chiffon dress and, at midnight after Aaron and I shared a rather passionate kiss, I couldn't help noticing the loving looks between Beth and my father. I was so glad she had come into our lives, I couldn't have wished for a better stepmother. The whole evening had been a great success and we were so grateful to John for inviting us. I just wish Portia had been there too.

Chapter Twenty-One

Two days later, the holidays were over and everyone was getting back to their normal routine. Aaron and my father had both gone off to work, Beth had gone shopping with a neighbor, Maggie was at the supermarket, and I was just exiting the front door with Vicky in her stroller. There had been a few inches of snow over the last few days, so I knew it would be heavy going but I was too restless to stay in the house. I was attempting to drag the stroller down the steps when, suddenly, a racy looking red car came speeding along the road and pulled into the driveway. I didn't know much about cars but it looked expensive and I wondered who an earth it could be. Suddenly the driver's door opened and out stepped Portia looking like a million dollars in a military style, dove grey coat and knee high black boots. She grinned when she saw me, "Sam, thank goodness I caught you."

I was so surprised to see her, "Portia, why didn't you tell me you were coming? A couple of more minutes and nobody would have been home."

She slammed the car door and came up the driveway, "I just suddenly had an impulse. I had to see you. Where is everybody?"

I smiled as I hugged her, "Some people have to work," I said, "and Beth and Maggie are out shopping."

"Well that will give us a chance to talk. And how's my little angel?" she asked peering into the stroller where Vicky was sleeping peacefully.

"Hardly a little angel," I answered, "I think she's into her terrible twos early."

Portia laughed, "Were you going for a walk in all this snow?"

"Not any more. Come on in and I'll make some coffee."

She helped me get the stroller back inside and we left Vicky in the hallway while we went into the kitchen. "It's so good to be here, Sam."

"Well, you should come more often. By the way, whose car is that you're driving?"

She looked a little sheepish, "It's mine; Philip gave it to me for Christmas."

"Wow, that's some present. What is it, a Porsche?"

"No, it's a Ferrari. I'll let you drive it sometime, you'll love it."

I suddenly remembered I hadn't seen her ring but, when I glanced down at her left hand, I noticed it was bare, "Where's your engagement ring? I've been dying to see it."

"To tell you the truth," she replied, "I'm almost scared to wear it when I go out anywhere. I just forgot to put it on this morning."

I poured the water into the coffee maker and took two mugs from the cupboard, "Do you think you'll ever get used to it, Portia?"

"You mean all the big houses, the fancy cars and traveling to all these exotic places? It's all a bit overwhelming but it's exciting, Sam. I just wonder when the time will come when I'll feel the need to do something more constructive."

"You mean like going back to work?"

"Perhaps, I'm not really sure."

"What about children? You always said you'd like a family someday."

She looked pensive, "I have to be honest; we haven't really discussed it. I get the impression Philip isn't too keen on the idea."

"Well that doesn't surprise me," I said and immediately wished I could take it back.

"What makes you say that?"

I paused for a moment and replied, "Well, with all his business ventures, he must be a very busy man. When would he have time to spend on his kids? Anyway I think you need to discuss having children before you get married. What if he doesn't want any? Would that be a deal breaker?"

Portia sighed, "I don't know, Sam."

I poured out the coffee, brought it to the table, and sat down. "This is serious. You need to think about what you'll be giving up if you marry him and he doesn't want children. Sure, you're madly in love with him now, but that won't last, Portia. You also have to think about him being ten years older than you. You'll probably be a widow by the time you're sixty and then you'll be all alone."

She shook her head, "My goodness, you've got this all worked out haven't you?"

"Just saying, that's all."

"I'm sure he'll want someone to carry on the family name eventually; after all Serena isn't going to be any help there."

"Well, let's hope it's in the next few years because the longer you wait, the harder it might be to get pregnant."

"I'm only twenty-six."

"I know. I'm just concerned that you know exactly what you're letting yourself in for."

Portia hesitated and then looked me straight in the eye, "You don't like Philip do you?"

I lowered my eyes and took a sip of coffee, "I didn't say I didn't like him. I don't even know him."

"Precisely, so I wish you'd give him a chance. He wants to arrange another celebration of our engagement here. Perhaps then you can get to know him better."

I was a little startled, "You mean, here at the house?"

"No. It will probably be at his place in the city. You will come won't you, Sam?"

I reached over and grasped her hand, "Of course I'll come. I want to see how the other half lives."

Portia chuckled, "I figured you'd say something like that."

She stayed for the rest of the day and the whole family sat down to dinner together. It was just like old times and I kept glancing at my sister, sitting opposite me at the table, thinking how great it would be if she never left. Aaron was pleased to see I was in such a great mood but his main focus was on taking a test drive in Portia's Ferrari.

One week later, we received an invitation to attend the party, formally announcing the engagement of Philip to Portia. I was a bit peeved when I first opened the envelope, after all we were family and I expected something a little more personal but, within an hour of having picked up the mail, Portia called to ask if we'd received the invitation. She said, she meant to call me to let me know it was coming and then it completely slipped her mind. She just wanted me to see what the invitation looked like and I had to admit, it was very elegant, printed on heavy cream colored paper and embossed with gold lettering. The party was to take place on the last Saturday in January, at Philip's apartment on Central Park West and I realized I still had to find a suitable gift. What on earth do you give someone who has pots and pots of money?

That evening at dinner, my father thought we should consider pooling whatever we could afford and just buy one gift between us. We spent an hour trying to come up with ideas but, in the end, Beth remarked that she thought we were overthinking it. She was certain Portia wouldn't expect anything extravagant and suggested we have a family portrait taken, including Vicky and Maggie, and frame it in an antique wood or silver frame. I thought it was a wonderful idea and it didn't take any effort to convince Aaron and Daddy. Beth agreed to make an appointment with a professional photographer and also agreed to accompany me on a shopping expedition for a new dress. Despite my reservation regarding the whole affair, I was beginning to feel just a glimmer of excitement and I could hardly wait to set foot in Philip's apartment, which I had just discovered was a penthouse suite with a private elevator and a view of Central Park.

The following week we all assembled in the living room, waiting for the arrival of the portrait photographer. It was a lot simpler than driving to the studio with Vicky, and we felt a lot more comfortable in our own home. We decided not to be too formal and were all dressed in our very best casual outfits, except for Maggie who insisted on wearing a navy suit and the requisite pearl necklace. I had considered asking her to change her clothes but convincing her to be included in the photo had been difficult enough. When the photographer arrived, he asked for a tour of the house before setting up his equipment in the family room. By this time, Vicky was beginning to fuss and I was getting anxious, but Aaron managed to calm her down and, less than an hour later, it was all over.

The very next day, Beth and I went shopping for dresses. We parked the car at Daddy's office and took a cab to Macy's, hoping we'd find something suitable and not too expensive. This was the time of year when all of the stores were promoting their post-holiday sales and we had to fight our way through hordes of women ploughing through mountains of clothes piled on tables. After twenty minutes, we'd both had enough and exited the store feeling a little defeated, then Beth suggested we try Bloomingdales. I wasn't too optimistic and expected to encounter the same unruly crowd of people but I was pleasantly surprised. Although busy, we had no problem finding our way to the racks of dresses and we spent the next half hour trying on several different styles. Beth was the first one to find something she was really happy with and I had to admit, the royal blue wrap with cap sleeves made her look at least ten pounds slimmer and brought out the color of her eyes. I was having a much more difficult time and then, suddenly, Beth held up a silver sequined sheath with a boat neck and three quarter sleeves and I just couldn't resist trying it on. When I came out of the dressing room, she smiled and said, "It's absolutely perfect, Sam. You look like a movie star."

"Yes, but look at the back," I responded and turned around to show her the dress was practically backless. "How on earth am I going to wear this? Aaron will have a fit."

"Well, we'll have to go to the lingerie department and find a suitable bra, unless you want to go without one altogether. As for Aaron, he's going to love it."

I sighed as I looked back at myself in the mirror and then realized I hadn't even checked the price tag. "Take a look at the tag, Beth. How much is it?"

She took a look and then grimaced, "It's a little pricey, Sam, even though it's on sale."

"How much?"

"Two-fifty and that's before tax."

I shook my head, "I can't spend that much on a dress. I can just imagine Aaron's reaction if I bought it."

"Then don't tell him. Just say it was a bargain and leave it at that. Look, it's a special occasion and it's time you treated yourself to a new outfit. You've got those strappy silver shoes that will go perfectly with the dress and I have a clutch I can lend you. You'll look amazing, Sam, and I know Aaron will be as proud as punch when he sees you."

I looked back in the mirror again, "What about my hair, Beth? Do you think I should get it cut?"

"No, I like it long like that. You are so lucky to have such thick curly hair. Just leave it the way it is."

I glanced at Beth's pixie cut which framed her face perfectly, "You shouldn't complain. I always wished I could wear my hair short like you. Ever since I first saw Mia Farrow, I wanted to cut my hair."

Beth chuckled, "We always want what we don't have, don't we?"

I nodded and stood silently thinking for a moment, "I'm taking the dress. I'll get changed and then we can look for the lingerie department."

After we managed to find the perfect bra, Beth was beginning to feel tired so I suggested we go to Bloomingdale's, David Burke restaurant for lunch. We both had the Cobb salad and a glass of white wine and just enjoyed having the time to relax. I think we had both been feeling the effect of being confined to the house during the winter months and spring was still over two months away. Getting back to the usual routine was always such a letdown after the holidays but, at least, we now had the party to look forward to.

Chapter Twenty-Two

On the night of the party, we drove into the city and parked in a private area on a cul-de-sac adjacent to Philip's building. Parking was always a problem in New York but Portia had made sure we were well taken care of and I had to wonder how all the other guests were managing. I remarked to Aaron that they probably all had chauffeur driven limousines and just got dropped off at the front door. When I stepped out of the car and looked up, I wasn't very impressed with the architecture. Daddy told me it was neo-renaissance style, whatever that meant, and I'd better wait until I got inside before I passed judgment. He also mentioned the building was close to the Dakota Apartments where John Lennon lived, when he was shot. I wasn't too impressed by that bit of information either, after all, I wasn't even born when that happened and I was more into the Back Street Boys than the Beatles.

We had experienced a major snowfall the day before and there was a lot of snow on the streets. There was no way Beth and I could walk to the main entrance in our flimsy sandals so I had to convince Aaron to start the car up again and drop us off. He grumbled and suggested we should have brought our boots but I gave him such a scathing look that, seconds later, we were back on Central Park West and pulling up to the entrance of the building. "We'll wait for you in the lobby," I called out as Beth and I maneuvered the few steps up to the main door.

When we got inside, I thought I was in a hotel. The marble floors were a wonderful pale apricot color and there were soaring marble columns and several groups of velvet covered wing chairs. The concierge was dressed in an immaculate dark brown uniform and treated us as though we were royalty. He took our names and, after checking in a rather ornate looking register he advised us that, as soon as the gentlemen arrived, he would take us to the private elevator. In the meantime, we were to please take a seat. I grinned at Beth and we made our way over to the first set of wing chairs and sat down. "What do you think of this place?" I whispered.

"It's pretty fancy," she whispered back. "I can't wait to see inside the apartment."

We noticed the concierge looking in our direction and we weren't sure if he could hear us so we didn't say another word until my father and Aaron entered through the front door. I couldn't help thinking what good looking men they both were and tonight they had gone all out to look their very best. After much indecision about what to put on, Aaron had finally decided to wear a dark grey suit with a crisp white shirt and silver tie. The silver tie was actually my suggestion because it would match my dress. Speaking of the dress, when Aaron first saw me in it he was speechless, especially when I turned around and he saw my whole back was exposed. "My god, Sam," he said, "a couple of inches lower and you'd see the crack in your bum."

I turned back and made a face, "So you don't like it?"

He took a step towards me and took hold of my hands, "Like it? I love it! Wow, you look so sexy. I've never seen you in anything like this before."

I let go of his hands and tugged at the hem which came just above my knees, "Do you think it's too short?"

He stooped down and ran a hand up under my skirt, "Are you kidding? All the better for what I have in mind."

I pushed his hand away, "Stop it, or we'll be late for the party."

"See if I care," he answered.

I had almost been tempted to let my husband make love to me right then and there but it would have meant ruining my makeup and my hair, and having to listen to my father complaining because we were running late. Now as I looked at Aaron and remembered that moment, I wished I'd been impulsive and just gone for it. As Beth and I got up to meet them, the concierge came out from behind his desk and led us to a small elevator which was almost hidden behind one of the columns. He stepped in with us, turned a key in a lock, then stepped out and we were immediately ascending but I had no idea how many floors we passed before we suddenly came to a stop and the doors opened.

We emerged from the semi-darkness and silence of the elevator, to find ourselves amidst the bright lights and hubbub of a party in full swing. Our coats, and the gift I was carrying, were immediately retrieved by a rather stern looking man, dressed in a conservative suit and tie, who introduced himself as Bennett. He knew exactly who we were, no doubt having been advised by the concierge, and informed us that Miss Lawrence had asked him to let her know as soon as we arrived. With that, he left us waiting near the elevator and we weren't sure whether we were to stay where we were, or proceed in the direction of the throngs of people we could see and hear at the end of a rather long hallway.

Beth looked around then walked over to a painting, one of many adorning the walls. "My goodness," she said, "this looks like a Monet."

My father stepped up behind her and peered over her shoulder, "It does, but I doubt if it's authentic, it would be worth millions."

Just then we heard Portia call out, "Daddy, Beth, you're here," and we watched as she came towards us down the hallway. She looked like she was almost floating in a turquoise chiffon, one-shouldered dress and gold high-heeled sandals. Her hair was loose, falling straight and sleek and adorned with a single white orchid. I don't think I'd ever seen her look more beautiful. She embraced my father and then Beth and then threw her arms around Aaron and me, "I can't believe you're all here," she said and then stepped back. "Sam, you look amazing. I love your dress. Turn around I want to see the back."

I glanced at Aaron and he shrugged as I spun around as quickly as I could without falling over on my four-inch heels. "Wow," Portia remarked, "that's the sexiest outfit I've ever seen you wear. You're going to have all the men drooling over you."

I chuckled, "I've had enough drooling from Aaron. Never mind me, you look gorgeous. What did you do to your hair?"

"I just made it straight for a change."

"I really like it," Beth remarked.

Portia turned to her, "Thank you, Beth. You look very elegant; that color blue suits you. I'm so glad you came tonight and I hope you enjoy the party."

My father stepped forward, "Shall we go in now?"

I put my hand on his arm, "Wait, Daddy, I want to see the ring."

Beth's face lit up, "Oh, yes, let's see it, Portia."

My sister extended her left hand and I gasped when I saw the huge emerald cut diamond on her finger, "Heavens, it's enormous. How many carats is it?"

"I think it's five carats," she answered.

"You're a lucky young lady," Daddy remarked.

"I know. Philip's very generous," Portia responded as she lowered her hand.

I have to admit, I was feeling a little envious, especially when I looked down at my own engagement ring. I usually just wore my wedding band and only put the ring on when we went out to dinner, or on a special occasion. It was a pretty pear shaped diamond, and I loved it when Aaron proposed to me, but now it looked so miniscule compared to Portia's. The next instant, I felt guilty, after all I had the most wonderful husband in the world and I still had the ominous feeling that Portia's marriage to Philip would be a mistake.

Aaron broke into my thoughts, "Come on, Sam, we're going in now," and with his hand on my shoulder, he guided me down the hallway, behind the others.

We stepped through the open doorway into a room filled with people chattering in groups, or milling about, all with drinks in their hands. I spotted Philip right away because he stood out in the crowd, not only because he was taller than most but because he was exceptionally handsome and there was something magnetic about him. Suddenly, he looked across to where we were standing, caught my eye and smiled, then gave a slight nod of his head. I think I was the only one who noticed because, in the next instant, Portia said, "Serena's here and I want you to meet her." We all followed her but were intercepted by a young man carrying a tray of champagne. I certainly needed a drink and was grateful to have something to do with my hands, other than carrying the silver beaded clutch Beth had let me borrow.

We approached a group of four or five people and it was easy to spot Serena after Portia's description of her. She was as tall as her brother, but reed thin and very masculine looking. The white wool slacks and black shirt she was wearing left no doubt, she had no interest in men. Portia tapped her lightly on the shoulder and said, "Excuse me, Serena, I'd like you to meet my family." When she turned around, Portia introduced each of us in turn. Serena merely nodded without offering her hand, even though my father extended his and was obliged to withdraw it, rather awkwardly.

When Portia stopped speaking, Serena said in a haughty voice, "It's very good of you to come. I hear it's still snowing."

I was thinking what a snooty cow, and replied, "Well, it usually snows in New York at this time of the year."

Aaron, who was holding my hand, squeezed it and I assumed he was sending me a message, but Serena seemed unfazed and looked me up and down, as though I'd just crawled out of the woodwork, then responded, "How interesting, I had no idea."

I knew, immediately, this could turn into a battle of wits but I didn't get the chance to prove I was smarter because this rather slight, pretty woman with long fair hair, and wearing a lovely white lace dress put her hand on mine and said, in the gentlest voice, "I'm Lotti and I'm so pleased to meet you. Portia has told me so much about you and the rest of your family."

I covered her hand with my own and couldn't help wondering what on earth this sweet woman was doing hooked up with Serena, "Thank you," I answered, "we're pleased to be here."

Lotti was about to say something else when Serena scowled at me and grabbed her arm, "Come on", she demanded. "I want to say hello to the Hoffmans'."

Lotti, looking a little upset as she was being led away, glanced back over her shoulder and called out, "I hope to talk to you again later,"

I shook my head in disgust and whispered, "So that's Serena, what a bitch."

Beth rolled her eyes and said, "She did seem a bit crusty."

Portia shrugged, "I'm sorry, she's not usually that rude."

Aaron slipped his arm around my shoulders and chuckled, "Well Sam sure knew how to intimidate her."

"Yes, she's pretty good at stirring the pot," Daddy remarked.

I just grinned and said, "I'm starving. Isn't there anything to eat around here?"

Portia led us through the room which I was beginning to notice for the first time. The walls looked like they were covered in the palest green, raw silk and the carpet, which felt an inch thick, was a slightly darker shade of green. Various chairs and couches, amber and peach in color, had been moved back against the walls, to allow people to move freely about the room and, as we approached the impressive buffet table, I found myself facing floor to ceiling windows which ran the width of one wall. We all stopped to admire the view overlooking Central Park, completely covered in snow and with dozens of trees glimmering with fairy lights.

A moment later, Portia announced she wanted to introduce Daddy and Beth to one of Philip's business acquaintances and Aaron announced he was going to see if he could find something to drink, other than champagne. Suddenly, I found myself alone, staring at platters of shrimp, smoked salmon, tiny crab cakes and every other kind of seafood I could think of. I felt my tummy start to rumble as I reached for one of the gold rimmed plates and a napkin at the end of the table when, suddenly, I had the creepy feeling somebody was standing directly behind me. I froze in my tracks then recognized Philip's voice as he remarked, "What an interesting dress, Sam. I believe you're the most stunning looking woman here tonight."

I whipped around and meeting his gaze, responded, "Good evening, Philip. That's a nice compliment but hardly sincere, after all Portia's obviously the most stunning person here and, the rather extravagant ring she's wearing makes her even more memorable."

Philip smiled, "Why, Sam, I'm surprised to hear you describe Portia's ring as extravagant, I would have expected you to call it ostentatious."

"And why would you say something like that?"

He shrugged, "Simply because, I get the feeling you don't exactly approve of me."

"Really?" I responded. "I don't know you well enough to express how I feel about you. As a matter of fact, I'm completely indifferent towards you right now."

I watched closely as his eyes widened in surprise, "Well, you certainly know how to put a person in their place. I was hoping we could become friends, after all I'm marrying your sister."

"The truth is, Philip, I have no choice but to accept you as my brother-in-law, when and if the time comes."

"I see, well that's a step in the right direction and make no mistake, there will be a wedding."

I was just about to open my mouth again, when Aaron arrived holding a rather large glass of beer. "Hi there, Philip," he said extending his free hand. "Congratulations on your engagement. Good to see you again."

Philip shook his hand, "Aaron, good to see you too. I gather you aren't too fond of champagne?"

Aaron raised his glass, "This is my beverage of choice. There's nothing better than a Heineken and I didn't have too much trouble finding it either."

Philip chuckled, "We have everything here tonight, wine, hard liquor, beer, whatever you heart desires."

Aaron glanced at the buffet table. "The food looks pretty appetizing too. Have you eaten yet, Sam?" he asked.

I shook my head and Philip said, "I think I interrupted your lovely wife before she had a chance to even take a bite. Maybe I'd better leave you both to indulge while I get back to mingling with some of the guests." He bowed his head slightly and then looked up again, "Sam, Aaron, I hope to speak to you again later."

I just gave a weak smile while my husband shook hands with Philip for the second time and said, "Sure thing; by the way, nice party."

As it turned out, we didn't speak to Philip again for the rest of the evening and we were only able to spend a few more moments with Portia. About an hour after we arrived, the music, which had been playing very softly, suddenly stopped and Philip asked for everyone's attention. He was holding Portia's hand while he announced the party was to celebrate their engagement and they were planning a wedding for some time in late summer. He continued to say he hadn't expected to find true happiness again, after suffering such a devastating loss, and was grateful to have found such a wonderful partner in Portia. He droned on and on and I still got the feeling he wasn't being totally sincere. Meanwhile, Portia stood motionless, most of the time, looking a little uncomfortable. While he was speaking, champagne was served to all of the guests and when he finally finished with, "Please let's all make a toast to my beautiful wife to be", everyone raised there glass and yelled out, "Here, here!"

I whispered to Beth, "What happened to all of the gifts? I haven't seen a gift table set up."

She whispered back, "I'm not sure but I expect they probably plan to open them all later in private."

"But I wanted to see Portia's face when she saw the photo of all of us."

Aaron, who was standing close by, said, "Are you sure it wasn't Philip's face you wanted to see?"

"Why, honey; what made you even think such a thing?" I responded with a grin.

By eleven o'clock, my father suggested it was probably time to leave, as it was now snowing pretty heavily and it would probably take quite a while to get home. I was actually relieved because I wasn't especially interested in making small talk with people I'd never met before and I was getting a little irritated, having spent so little time with Portia. We finally managed to make our way through the crowd to let her know we were leaving and to thank Philip for inviting us, but he was nowhere to be seen. Portia said he was making sure one of the rooms had been made up for the business acquaintance Daddy had been introduced to earlier, as he'd flown in from Atlanta and was staying the night. When I remarked I hadn't seen any of her roommates at the party, she looked a little sheepish and said they were all on vacation together in the Bahamas and she'd actually moved out just after Christmas. Daddy looked surprised and innocently asked, "Why didn't you tell us you were moving, Portia? Where are you living now?"

She hesitated, so I chimed in, "She's living here now, obviously."

Daddy looked at me and then back at Portia, "Is this true?"

She nodded and then in a very low voice said, "I know you don't approve but it's what Philip wanted and I'm not working so I can't really afford to pay rent."

"What happened to all the money you saved to go to acting school?" I asked.

"I still have it. I'm saving it for a rainy day."

Daddy frowned, "I hope you don't have too many of those and I suggest you make sure you have a good prenuptial agreement in place before you get married."

Beth put her hand on my father's arm, "I don't think this is the time or place to discuss this, Colin."

Aaron spoke up, "I think Beth's right and maybe we should just say goodnight and be on our way."

After a lot of hugging and what seemed like an eternity while we waited for our coats, we were finally back in the elevator and descending to the lobby. Aaron went to get the car while we stood at the front door gazing out at the snow. It was now falling in large flakes and we could see the wind had picked up. When Aaron got back he told us he'd heard on the car radio that there was a traffic accident on the parkway near Eastchester, but they hoped to have it cleared within the next half-hour. We all groaned although we were used to traffic delays because of the weather but I begged Aaron to drive slowly because of the road conditions. I think we were all too tired to discuss the party and I noticed Daddy nodding off well before we got home. Thankfully there weren't any holdups on the way but it was slow going and it was close to one o'clock when we pulled into the driveway. I was looking forward to climbing into bed and snuggling up with Aaron. If I was lucky, maybe he'd let me sleep in and take care of Vicky when she woke up at the crack of dawn.

Chapter Twenty-Three

The next morning, I woke up a little after seven but, noticing Aaron was no longer in bed, I rolled over and went back to sleep until almost nine. I felt a little guilty but I was the one who usually took care of Vicky all week long when Aaron left for work. I had just stepped out of the shower and was wrapped in a towel, when he walked into the bathroom. "Ah, there you are," he said. "Good morning, pretty lady."

I grinned and pulled him towards me. "Perfect timing," I said.

He smiled and asked, "What did you have in mind?"

I pulled him even closer and then tugged the towel away from my body. Perhaps this will help you figure it out," I answered.

He shook his head and picked the towel up from the floor, "No can do, honey, your daughter is asking for her Mommy."

I made a face, "Can't she wait for a few minutes?"

He chuckled, "Since when was I a few minutes man? When I make love to my woman, I like to take my time."

I sighed, stepped over the towel and ran past him through the doorway, buck naked, "Too late. You've lost your chance."

"I'd like to take a rain check," he called out.

I giggled, "Then you'll have a long wait because, right now, it's snowing and they don't expect it to stop for about another eight weeks."

"You're incorrigible, Sam," he remarked.

"I know, but you love me," I answered as I picked up a robe and slipped it on. "Why don't you go on downstairs and tell Vicky I'll be there as soon as I've put on some clothes and brushed my hair."

Aaron started to exit the room and then stopped, "I think Maggie's planning something special for Sunday lunch. She's already fussing about in the kitchen."

"Why, what's the occasion?"

"I have no idea. Maybe you can ask her," he answered and then he was gone.

When I eventually went downstairs, I found Vicky in the family room with Beth. She was sitting on the carpet, perfectly happy, playing with a pile of blocks and when I went to kiss her on the top of her head, she mumbled something unintelligible but clear enough to tell me she was busy. I spoke to Beth for a few minutes and discovered Aaron and my father were in the garage fiddling about with one of the cars, so I decided to make myself some breakfast and headed for the kitchen. Molly was perched on one of the kitchen chairs and Maggie was standing at the counter rolling out some pastry. She looked up when I walked in and smiled, "I was wondering when you'd show your face," she said.

I walked past her to raid the bread bin and see if there was any coffee brewing. "I know, I just didn't want to get up, we had such a late night."

"So I heard from your father. Did you enjoy the party?"

I shrugged as I put the bread in the toaster, "It was okay, but not really my kind of crowd."

"Too rich for your blood, eh?"

"I suppose you could say that. I met Philip's sister; she's a right snooty one. I can't figure out why that Lotti ever got tied up with her."

"What kind of food did they serve?"

"Ah well, that part I really enjoyed. They had this huge buffet table covered in all kinds of seafood and then one section for desserts. They even had trifle like the one you sometimes make, Maggie. By the way, what's this I hear about a special lunch today?"

"Who told you such a thing?"

"Aaron told me. Did he imagine it?"

She shook her head, "No, I'm making a chicken pot pie with a nice fresh garden salad."

"But we don't usually have a big lunch on Sunday; what's the occasion?"

I watched her stop rolling the pastry as I buttered the toast. I noticed she hesitated, as though she wasn't sure whether to answer me, and then she said, "You'll just have to wait and see."

Needless to say, I was really curious but decided not to pressure her. One thing was for sure, it took my mind off of Portia and the night before.

Shortly after noon, Beth announced lunch was ready and, when I walked into the dining room, I noticed there was an extra table setting. Naturally, I immediately thought of Portia and wondered if we were having our own little engagement party but, before I even got a chance to ask, my father revealed that Maggie would be joining us. It was so unusual for Maggie to eat with the family, she always liked to eat by herself in the kitchen or take her meals in her room where she could sit and watch TV at the same time. She had already put a large bowl of salad on the table, along with a basket of home-made bread, and we were sitting chattering among ourselves about what was going on, except for Daddy who was obviously not about to enlighten us.

When Maggie arrived with a tray full of wonderful looking pot pies, we all looked up expectantly but she just grinned, served the pies, and exited the room again. Moments later, she was back with a very large bottle of Chardonnay and five glasses, which she placed next to my father. "I guess you're all wondering what this is all about," she said, "but you need to eat up before your lunch gets cold and then I'll tell you."

"Hell no, Maggie," I said, "I won't be able to eat a bite until I know what you're up to."

She shook her head and sat down in the vacant chair beside me, then looked around the table at everyone. "Very well, I'll tell you but I don't want my pot pies to go to waste."

I took her hand, "They won't, Maggie, believe me. Now what is it? Your birthday isn't until April so we can't be celebrating it today."

She smiled and squeezed my hand, "No, it's not my birthday today but I'll be sixty-five in April and it's time for me to retire."

I knew she was getting a little arthritic and her hands had been bothering her but this news was a shock, "Oh no, Maggie, you can't retire." I said beginning to feel a bit panicky, "If it's too much work for you, we'll help out with the chores. Beth and I can do more in the kitchen and we can get someone in to do the heavy work."

She squeezed my hand again, "You don't understand, Sam, I'm going back home and I'm planning to leave in two weeks."

"This is your home," Beth said, "for as long as you want to stay. We'll hire someone else to come in and do the cooking and cleaning. You won't have to do anything."

Maggie shook her head, "Thank you, that's so kind of you but my sister's not well. She may only have a few more months and I'm going back to be with her. She doesn't have any other family so she's leaving me her house. I've never been there but I've seen the photos and it looks lovely. I think I'll be happy there."

The tears started streaming down my face, "But you could be happy here, Maggie, please don't go."

My father finally spoke up, "Sam, try not to make it harder for everyone. Maggie needs to be with her sister. You have a sister of your own so surely you can understand why this is important to her."

Aaron reached over and started rubbing my back, "Come on, Sam, this is supposed to be a retirement party."

"I know but I can't help it. I'm going to miss you so much, Maggie, and Molly will wonder what happened to you."

Maggie smiled, "I'll miss you too, every one of you, and that crazy cat. Maybe I'll get one of my own to keep me company in my old age."

My father picked up the bottle of wine and said, "Okay everyone, we're supposed to be celebrating so let's all have some wine and then let's dig into this delicious looking pie."

"Good idea." Aaron remarked picking up his fork.

Later that afternoon, Beth and I decided we would take on the job of cooking meals for the family and bring in someone to take care of the cleaning and laundry. To be honest, I wasn't thrilled with the idea but I should have realized Maggie couldn't go on working forever. I knew her leaving would be a great loss to all of us, but especially to Daddy and me. She'd been with us for so long and we never ever thought of her as a servant. When Daddy had been struggling to look after two young children, after my mother died, Maggie was the one who enabled us to live a relatively normal life again. She had been my confidant on many occasions and I loved her bawdy sense of humor. Not only that, but her absence would put an extra burden on me and probably affect the likelihood of me going back to work, when Vicky was in pre-school.

That evening, Aaron suggested we have a proper going away party for Maggie and, rather than have it at the house, we should take her somewhere fancy for dinner. My father thought it was an excellent idea and asked us to think about what we would give her as a retirement gift. Beth proposed we sit for another family portrait, and include Molly, and my father agreed but he also thought she might like a nice new watch, as she'd had the same one since he'd known her. "It still doesn't sound like much after all the years she's devoted to us," I remarked.

"Don't worry, Sam," Daddy responded, "I'm going to give her a few dollars. She hasn't got a good pension to fall back on and she won't be entitled to one when she goes back to England."

"How much were you thinking of giving her, Colin?" Beth asked.

"Well, she's been with us for almost twenty years, so I was considering a thousand dollars for each year."

"Wow, that's very generous, Daddy."

"Not really, Sam. I'm not sure what I would have done without her. She's worth every penny."

"We'll have to get a move on if we're going to have another portrait taken," Beth said, "and we can't do it here because Maggie never leaves the house except on the spur of the moment."

"Mmmm.. that could be a problem because we'll have to take Molly with us and you know how she hates being put in her carrier; plus Maggie will wonder where we're taking her."

Aaron chuckled, "We'll just sneak her out of the house. Maggie won't even notice she's gone. By the way, Sam, you need to get hold of Portia. She'll want to be included in the photo and the dinner."

I nodded, "Yes, I know. She's supposed to call me later tonight. If I don't hear from her, I'll try and get hold of her first thing in the morning."

Chapter Twenty-Four

I didn't hear from Portia that night and, although I was disappointed, I wasn't surprised. On Monday, after my father and Aaron left for work, I called the photographer to set up an appointment and then started to punch in Portia's number. I listened to the ring tone and then heard the inevitable robot voice asking me to leave a message and I ended the call in frustration. I decided to try again later in the afternoon hoping that, by then, I would have heard from her.

Right after lunch, as I was helping Maggie with the dishes, my cell phone which was on the kitchen counter, started to vibrate. I picked it up and began walking down the hall towards the family room. When I answered it, I heard Portia's voice, "Sam, it's me," she said, sounding rather breathless, "I'm sorry I didn't call you last night. We had people here and by the time they left, it was too late."

"It's okay," I answered, even though I was feeling somewhat miffed.

"How did you enjoy the party?" she asked.

I hesitated, "It was very nice, especially the food. You know how I like to eat."

"Philip was sorry he couldn't spend more time with the family but I told him you'd understand."

"No problem. Listen, Portia, I hate to change the subject but I have something to tell you."

"Oh, oh, you're not pregnant again are you?"

"No, nothing like that." I proceeded to tell her about Maggie's decision to retire and move back to England and, as I suspected, she was shocked and upset by the news. "I've made an appointment at the photographers and we need you to be there for the family portrait. We want to give it to her as a gift as well as a new watch, plus Daddy's giving her quite a bit of money."

"When's the appointment?"

"This coming Saturday morning, in Scarsdale, and the following Friday night, just before she leaves, we're taking her to dinner at the Fig and Olive."

There was silence on the other end of the line and, for a moment I thought we'd been cut off then Portia said, "Oh, goodness I'm not going to be able to make the photographers or the dinner. What day is Maggie actually leaving?"

"Two weeks today and don't tell me you won't even have time to say good-bye to her. I can't believe this, Portia, what's so important that you can't find the time?"

I heard her sigh, "We're leaving for Florida with Serena and Lotti in the morning and we'll be gone for three weeks. Philip wants me to stay with them while he takes care of some business in Miami."

I was getting really annoyed and trying to hold my temper, "Well tell him you can't go. Surely he'll understand how important this is to you."

"I can't do that, Sam, it's already been arranged and I don't want to disappoint him."

"Oh, my god, what's come over you? Are you scared he's going to break off the engagement if you don't go? How can you do this to Maggie?"

"I'm really sorry, Sam. I......"

I cut in before she could say another word, "Not as sorry as I am. This is inexcusable and I don't know how you can be so selfish after all the years Maggie devoted to looking after us. I'm ashamed to call you my sister right now," and I abruptly ended the call. I expected her to call me back but she didn't. What was I going to tell the family? I was annoyed, to put it mildly, and decided not to tell my father and Beth until I'd calmed down but, when Beth asked if I'd spoken to Portia, I just couldn't lie. I repeated the conversation I had with her and then told Beth exactly what I thought of the whole situation. She said she didn't blame me for being upset, to which I responded, "I'm not upset; I'm damn mad. How can she just brush Maggie off like that; she's been almost like a mother to us?"

"Maybe she feels obligated to go to Serena's now that the arrangements have been made."

"What arrangements? Getting there? She can go any time. She can hop on Philip's private jet or take a first class flight on any one of a dozen airlines. No, Beth, she's completely under his control and I don't like it. I bet if she mentioned staying behind, even for a day or two for Maggie, he'd probably have trouble understanding why a housekeeper is more important than his sister. He has no idea how much Maggie means to us."

Beth took both my hands in hers, "Sam, I think you're being a little harsh, after all you have no idea how Philip would react."

"Then why didn't Portia even suggest she'd talk it over with him and try to change her plans? He wouldn't have to stay in New York; he could go off to his sister's or to Timbuktu as far as I'm concerned."

"Maybe she'll speak to him, after she's thought it over. Let's just give her a chance and wait a couple of days to see if we hear back from her."

I shook my head, "If she doesn't call back later today, it will be too late. She's leaving tomorrow for three weeks."

Beth and I continued to talk for a while and she did her best to defend Portia, but I wasn't having any of it. She then suggested she would tell my father, because I was too emotional, and it was up to me to tell Aaron.

By the time we all sat down to dinner everyone knew about my telephone conversation with Portia but, because Maggie was flitting in and out serving dinner, we avoided the subject entirely. Later, in the family room, my father made it very clear he didn't want to discuss it but he intended to tell Portia how disappointed he was in her actions, or lack of them, when she got back from Florida. I knew from many years of experience, when Daddy said he didn't want to talk about something, he really meant it, so I was forced to keep my opinions to myself until Aaron and I were alone. As soon as I'd tucked Vicky in bed for the night and read her favorite bedtime story, Goodnight Moon, with all the appropriate animal voices, I returned to our room to find Aaron engrossed in a hockey game between New Jersey and Boston. He didn't even look up when I suggested I needed to talk to him. He just mumbled, "Not now, Sam, I want to watch this." I knew he didn't really want to talk about Portia and he'd probably try to justify her actions to pacify me, so I decided not to bother him and went back to Vicky's room to make sure she was asleep. When I got there, I found Molly curled up on the chair beside her crib. I sat down cross legged on the rug and just stared at the ceiling where dozens of star shaped lights were being projected from the table lamp. After a few moments, I'm not sure whether I was just exhausted or being hypnotized by the images, I must have fallen asleep and that's where Aaron found me, two hours later.

The week went by with no word from Portia and on Saturday, we left the house early for our appointment with the photographer. Aaron and my father made an excuse that they had to go into the office for an hour or two and Beth and I claimed we were hitching a ride with them to go shopping. Sneaking Molly out was a whole different problem, especially when Aaron tried to nudge her inside her carrier and she protested loudly enough for Maggie to hear. We thought she'd come running to see what was going on but she was too busy in the kitchen. Eventually, after a bit of coxing with some treats, she got far enough inside that Aaron was able to close the door and latch it. Now he had to bring her out to the car without letting the cat out of the bag, as it were, with her incessant meowing. Covering the carrier with a blanket seemed to do the trick and we were on our way.

The photo session went quite well, despite having to control Molly who insisted on trying to escape from anyone who attempted to hang on to her. I couldn't blame her for being a little confused; being in a strange place and with all the bright lights. I was feeling a little confused myself and, when I looked around, I knew it was because someone was missing. Where was my sister?

Chapter Twenty-Five

The day my father and I drove Maggie to the airport was one of the saddest days I can remember. I had no doubt I would see her again because, come what may, I was determined to pay her a visit sometime in the future, especially if we happened to be invited to Philip's home in London. Maggie said I could hop the train to Manchester and be there in about three hours. Nevertheless, I couldn't stop crying when the boarding call was announced and I was an emotional mess on the drive back home. We hadn't heard another word from Portia but she'd telephoned Maggie and sent her a gift. It was a beautiful gold bracelet with an inscription which read, 'Thank you for always being there, love Portia'. I know it meant a lot to Maggie but she was overwhelmed when Daddy presented her with the watch, the family photo, and an envelope containing several British, hundred pound notes.

In the days that followed, Vicky couldn't understand where Maggie was and she called out for her often. I didn't want to tell her Maggie was never coming back, so I told her she'd gone away for a little while to get some rest, hoping that eventually she'd get used to her not being there. Molly also seemed a little lost and would wander from room to room looking for her, but I think Beth and I missed her most of all. It was now up to us to take up the slack and we did our best until we found someone to come in and help out with the cooking and cleaning.

Anisha was a young Indian woman who'd previously worked for one of our neighbors, and she came highly recommended. She arrived every weekday at one o'clock and left around seven in the evening, after we'd finished eating. During that time she'd take care of the cleaning and the laundry and cook dinner for the family. The rest of the time, it was left to Beth and me to take care of the meals and Beth was a great help in taking over from Maggie when it came to baby-sitting. It took a few weeks to get used to the change in routine but eventually things settled down and I resigned myself to the fact that, any thought I had of doing anything constructive with my life, would have to be put on hold.

When Portia finally showed up unexpectedly, just as we were sitting down to dinner, she was surprised when Anisha opened the door. According to Portia, Anisha remarked, "Ah you must be Miss Sam's sister. I recognize you from your photo. Would you like to come in?" Portia responded by asking her who she was and Anisha extended her hand and said, "I am Anisha. Your father hired me to help out around the house. I have just served dinner if you would like to join the family." Portia told her she'd already eaten and Anisha directed her to the dining room.

We looked up when Portia came through the door, rolled her eyes and said, "Hi, everyone. The new housekeeper is something else."

"What do you mean?" I asked.

She repeated the brief conversation she'd with Anisha and then commented on her appearance. "She's very pretty, what a lovely face and such long thick hair. How old is she?"

Daddy spoke up, "She's the same age as Sam. Her family came here from Bombay when she was very young. She's a very good cook; why don't you sit down and eat with us."

Portia shook her head, "I'll sit down but I don't want anything. I just popped in to see how everyone was."

After that, it was just like old times with all of us sitting around the table and Portia hardly mentioned Philip at all, except to say they'd already started on plans for the wedding. Knowing how I felt about the idea of Portia marrying Philip, Beth didn't press for any details and, of course, Daddy and Aaron weren't in the least bit interested.

Over the next few months, Portia came to the house a few times when we were all there and I got the feeling she was avoiding spending one-on-one time with me. I suggested coming into the city for lunch but she always had an excuse and, when my father mentioned inviting her and Philip to dinner again, she said he was much too busy.

Maggie had written telling us all about the house she'd be inheriting and she even sent photos. Her sister was now in a hospice, not expected to live more than a few weeks, and she was having a hard time accepting the fact she would be left without a single living relative. My father wrote back asking her to consider returning to Scarsdale and living with us. She would no longer be our housekeeper and she would be with the people who loved her most in the world. When I read what Daddy had written I cried, because I desperately wanted to see her again. Our house wasn't the same without her.

Three weeks later, in the middle of June, we received the wedding invitation. Portia had already spoken to Daddy about giving her away so we knew exactly where and when the ceremony would take place. She had also asked me to be her maid of honor but I'd procrastinated and had not yet given her an answer. The wedding was being held at Gotham Hall, on September 25th and, after I looked up the venue online, it looked so amazing that I got nervous just thinking about being in the wedding party. It was Aaron who convinced me I had to support my sister and, when I finally told her I'd be pleased to be her maid of honor, she was delighted.

At the end of June, my father received a reply from Maggie and it made us all very sad. Her sister had died, just a few days earlier, and she was busy sorting out all her personal papers and belongings. She said she was overwhelmed by my father's offer but wanted to stay in England. She'd already made friends with some neighbors and thought she'd be happy there. She also mentioned that she'd received a wedding invitation, but would not be attending. I finally had to accept the fact that, other than the occasional letter and a possible visit with her, if I ever got to England, Maggie was out of our lives forever.

Before I knew it, I was involved in wedding plans. I think Portia believed I'd now come to terms with her marriage and she began spending time alone with me again. She had asked her four former roommates to be bridesmaids and we had very little time to decide on the dresses. Meanwhile Portia was having her bridal gown designed by a well-known designer in Manhattan. Eventually we decided on peach silk for the bridesmaids and my dress was to be the same style but in a lighter shade. It was all very stressful running back and forth into the city to get fitted, not only for the dress but we also had to have matching shoes. When I thought about the civil ceremony and dinner at the Russian Tearoom, where Aaron and I celebrated our marriage, I began to wish Portia had met someone with a lot less money than Philip. At least, he had insisted on paying for everything, even though my father had offered to contribute a generous amount of money. As far as I was concerned, it really was over the top. There were going to be three hundred guests, and dinner alone was over two hundred dollars a plate. I didn't even want to think about how much Portia's dress was going to cost. Not only was it custom designed but the strapless top was covered in tiny seed pearls. I was certain she would be one of the most beautiful brides anyone had ever seen.

Chapter Twenty-Six

On the day of the wedding, the skies were clear and the temperature was in the mid-sixties. Portia wanted me to stay in the city with her the night before, but I didn't feel comfortable with the idea and told her I'd be at Gotham Hall first thing in the morning. I drove in with Aaron and, while he went off to spend a few hours at the office, I met Portia and the other girls in a room specially set up for us to dress and prepare ourselves for the wedding. The ceremony was to take place at four o'clock, followed by a photograph session, a cocktail hour and then the dinner.

Portia's dress was exquisite and I could hardly take my eyes off of her. Even Aaron remarked, after the ceremony, that he'd never seen a more beautiful bride, except for me of course. I just giggled and stuck my tongue out at him. Daddy looked marvelous in his best black suit and silver tie and I was so proud of him when he walked slowly and deliberately ahead of me with Portia on his arm. I was so busy looking at them, I was oblivious of all the people staring at me and the other girls. It was just as well because I think I would have fainted on the spot. Philip was smiling as Portia approached and he looked incredible. It galled me to see just how handsome he was dressed up in a snow white jacket and black slacks. Every time I saw him, I just felt uneasy and I still couldn't really put my finger on it.

I had never met the best man, a close friend of Philip's and almost as handsome, or any of the four ushers, who were all cousins. I was hoping I'd get to know more about Philip from them later, when there would be dancing until the early hours of the morning. I noticed Serena was sitting in the front row and she actually managed to wear a dress, although it was a hideous shade of green and didn't do a thing to hide her bony frame. Lotti sat beside her looking almost ethereal in ivory lace and, once again, I was intrigued by the odd relationship. The ceremony was very brief and we were soon being ushered into one of the most elaborate rooms I'd ever seen, for the photo session. I think both my father and Aaron were relieved the ceremony was over because they had the strange idea I might disrupt the wedding. It had actually crossed my mind but I never really considered going that far to stop my sister from marrying Philip.

The photo session seemed to go on forever and, by the time I was able to join the family, I was tired and really needed a cocktail. Then, an hour later, I was ready for dinner. Dinner was held in the grand ballroom; a huge oval shaped space with a gilded and stained glass ceiling, marble floors and granite walls. Whoever had planned the table settings had done a magnificent job and, with all of the wonderful lighting, it looked like fairyland. I was a bit upset that I had to sit at the head table with the wedding party because I'd have preferred to have been with Aaron but, then I realized it might give me a chance to learn more about Philip. He hadn't acknowledged me during the ceremony or during the photo session but, when I was being shown to my place at the table, he quickly came over and pulled out my chair for me, "Sam, you look beautiful," he said, "I'm so glad you decided to be Portia's maid-of-honor."

I sat down and then looked up at him, "I didn't want to let her down," I responded.

He nodded and then, with what I perceived to be a smirk, said, "I guess you and I are family now."

I lowered my gaze and answered, "I guess you could say that, seeing as you married my sister."

He put his hand on my shoulder and I literally flinched, "Enjoy your dinner, Sam, and save a dance for me."

At that moment, the best man arrived at the table and slapped Philip on the back, "Well, old chap, what does it feel like being an old married man again?"

I noticed Philip's face darken, for just a second, and then he grinned and said, "Dan, I'd like to formally introduce you to my new sister-in-law, Sam."

Dan smiled at me, "Yes, we chatted briefly after the ceremony. So what do you think about your sister marrying this character, Sam?"

I was at a loss for words for a second and then managed to blurt out, "As long as Portia's happy that's all that concerns me."

Philip laughed, "I don't think Sam approves of me too much."

Fortunately I didn't have to respond because there was quite a commotion as Portia came floating through the room with all four bridesmaids following her.

I'd already taken note that I'd be sitting next to Portia, and not next to Philip. Having looked up proper etiquette online and discovering the maid-of-honor usually sits next to the groom, while the best man sits next to the bride, I breathed a sigh of relief. I wondered why they'd changed the usual seating arrangement but I certainly wasn't complaining. One of the ushers, Philip's cousin, Raymond, was on the other side of me and I found him quite charming, and very entertaining. He was the eldest son of John J. Barrington's only brother, Stephen, and lived in San Antonio so he didn't see Philip very often and was not a very reliable source of information. I figured I'd have to find someone else to interrogate.

Dinner was unbelievable; there was a wonderful light salad with blue cheese, bacon and red onion, followed by a second appetizer of tuna tartare, then lobster Newberg and finally a vanilla crème brulee. This was all accompanied by a continuous flow of wine and the inevitable serving of the wedding cake which, after cutting, was presented in small silver boxes for everyone to take home. My father was the first one to make a toast to the bride and groom and he gave a wonderful speech that left me teary eyed. He talked about the way Portia had been so protective of me after our mother died and what a loving and generous woman she had turned out to be. He said he regretted the fact that none of her grandparents were able to attend the wedding, mostly because of advanced age and health issues and, although he had not yet got to really know his new son-in-law, he hoped to develop a close relationship with him in the future. Finally he raised his glass and said, "Please join me today in wishing Portia and Philip every happiness possible and a long and joyful life together as husband and wife."

After that, Dan spoke and had everyone in stitches. He'd known Philip since third grade and had a number of humorous tales to tell about their antics growing up. It showed me a side of Philip I hadn't yet seen, someone who was carefree, impulsive, and sometimes reckless. Finally, Philip himself rose and thanked everyone for being there and he specifically thanked my father for his kind words and wishes. Then he went on to thank all the members of the wedding party and particularly Dan, the best man, and me, Portia's extraordinarily beautiful sister. When he said that I think I turned a deep shade of red and I glanced over at Aaron. He grinned and gave me thumbs up, so that made me feel better. Philip finished by saying he was a very lucky man to have met such a gorgeous, smart, sensitive and selfless woman and he would do his best to make her happy.

The head table had been positioned in the centre of the room and all of the other tables around the perimeter so, as soon as dinner was over, the wedding party could either move to another location or opt to just mingle with the other guests. Naturally, I made a beeline for the table where my family was sitting and breathed a sigh of relief as I settled down next to Aaron. "Oh boy," I said, "I'm glad that's over."

Aaron patted my knee, "Now you can relax until the dancing begins and then maybe we can shake this place up a bit."

I chuckled, "I can hardly wait but, since when did you suddenly want to show your best moves on a dance floor?"

"Since noticing a lot of guys around here have been giving my wife the eye."

Beth nodded, "You do look lovely in that shade of peach, Sam."

"Thanks, Beth, I have to say you look really elegant tonight. What do you think, Daddy?"

"I've already told her she should be on the cover of Vogue."

Beth roared with laughter, "Oh, Colin, let's not overdo it."

My father suddenly got very serious, "I hope we did the right thing making a donation on Philip and Portia's behalf instead of giving them a gift."

Aaron spoke up, "It was the perfect gift. As I understand it, Philip's mother died of breast cancer and I'm sure Portia would really appreciate it too. Funding for research is really important."

"Aaron's right," I said, "it's much more meaningful than giving them another piece of crystal or china that they don't need."

Just then a six-piece band, set up at one end of the room, began to play very softly. I was about to comment on how nice it was to have live music when it suddenly stopped and Dan, holding a microphone, announced, "Ladies and gentlemen, for the first time as husband and wife, I'd like to introduce Mr. and Mrs. Barrington. Let's give them a standing ovation." We all stood up and applauded as Philip and Portia swept into the room holding hands. Portia was smiling broadly and waving to everyone while Philip had a slight grin on his face. Portia had changed out of her wedding gown and was wearing a short, off-the-shoulder-white lace dress. Her hair, which had been swept back into a loose chignon for the ceremony, now cascaded down her back and she looked stunning. Philip had changed too; he was no longer wearing the formal white jacket but was wearing a beige, linen suit.

"He looks pretty casual," Aaron whispered in my ear.

"That's because they're taking off for the Seychelles right after the reception."

"Where on earth is that?"

"Somewhere near Madagascar in the Indian Ocean; I'll show you on the map tomorrow."

A moment later, Portia and Philip sailed onto the dance floor to Elton John's, Can You Feel the Love Tonight? I couldn't help noticing Philip was an excellent dancer but he also seemed a little remote and, instead of looking at my sister, he was scanning the room as though he was looking for somebody else. After they had circled the floor twice, they broke away from each other and both headed for our table. My father rose from his seat, hugged Portia, and swept her towards the middle of the room, while all of the guests applauded. I was left staring up at Philip, who had extended his hand in my direction. I think he must have recognized the puzzled expression on my face and he chuckled and said, "It's traditional for the groom to dance with the maid-of-honor."

I glanced at Beth and was about to say I thought he should be asking her instead of me but she shook her head and whispered, "Go ahead, enjoy yourself."

I rose, reluctantly, and allowed Philip to take me in his arms. There was more applause as we glided around the room but, as soon as the clapping died down, he loosened his hold on me so that he could see my face, "Well, we're finally related, Sam, so I hope you've now accepted me into the family."

"As I already said, as long as you make Portia happy, that's all that concerns me."

"I see. I assume that means you'll try to be civil to me?" he responded with a hint of sarcasm.

I nodded, "I'll do my best."

He grinned, "What is it about me that bugs you so much? I've sensed from the first time we met, you wanted to keep your distance. Did I say something to offend you?"

I shrugged, "Not specifically."

"Then what's the problem?"

I sighed, "Look, Philip, this is neither the time nor the place to discuss this."

"Then let's get together sometime when it's more convenient, and we can talk about it in private."

"I think, perhaps, we should ask Portia to join us," I answered, beginning to feel annoyed.

He actually laughed out loud, "You think I want to seduce you, don't you? It appears you might even be a little afraid of me."

At that moment I felt a sense of outrage, "Fat chance of that. Take me back to my table," I demanded.

"No problem," he replied and, a minute later, he was smiling and motioning for me to sit down, "Thank you, Sam, that was delightful." He then nodded at Beth and Aaron and chatted with them briefly while I sat there seething. By the time he walked away, the music had stopped and my father was making his way back to the table.

I didn't get a chance to stay annoyed for long because the next dance was a cha cha and Aaron didn't give me any opportunity to refuse him. He grabbed my hand and dragged me onto the floor, where he got right into the mood and goaded me to keep up with him. "Come on, honey," he shouted over the noise of the music, "shake those hips." I couldn't help laughing and, as I swung around, I caught Philip's eye. He was standing next to Portia but staring at me. I kept my attention on Aaron after that, except for the time when I noticed Serena dancing cheek to cheek with Lotti. They made such a strange couple.

I danced with Aaron over and over again, and twice with Daddy. I was actually beginning to feel exhausted and would like to have sat down, but I was trying to avoid Philip. I had no idea what I'd say to him if he asked me to dance again. Obviously I didn't want to make a scene and I didn't want Aaron to suspect Philip might be interested in me. The more I thought about it the more paranoid I became. Maybe I was kidding myself; after all, he'd just married my sister, who was not only gorgeous but a beautiful person. I'd been told I was attractive, sometimes even pretty, but compared to Portia, it was like comparing a BMW to a Rolls-Royce.

As the evening began to draw to a close, an incredible dessert table was set up at one end of the room. Having a sweet tooth, I was in my element and it gave me a chance to take a break and enjoy some wonderful pastries and a much needed cup of coffee. Once back at the table, Daddy suggested that we should think about leaving as we still had to drive back to Scarsdale. "Aren't we supposed to wait until the bride and groom make their exit?" I asked.

Beth replied, "Not all couples leave before the end of the reception. I think your father's right; we should be making a move soon."

I knew this meant we'd have to say goodnight to Philip and I was hoping to steer clear of him. "Okay, we'll leave as soon as we've finished our coffee but first we have to let Portia know we're going."

"Yes, we need to say goodnight to your sister and Philip and wish them the best of luck," Daddy remarked.

Everyone sat waiting while I finished my coffee. I knew I was putting off the inevitable but, the moment I took my last sip; Aaron was surveying the room looking for Portia. Thankfully she was close by talking to a group of people and, as we approached her, she turned towards us and said, "Ah, here's my wonderful family. Don't tell me you're leaving?"

My father reminded her we had to drive home and we were all getting a little weary and she didn't attempt to persuade us to stay. I think she was beginning to feel a little stressed herself after the excitement of the day and I could see shadows under her eyes. When Beth asked where Philip was so that we could say goodnight, she told us he was having a conversation with Serena in another room and didn't want to be disturbed. I thought this was very strange, but I breathed a sigh of relief. I didn't have to see him again, at least not that night.

Chapter Twenty-Seven

During the year following Portia's marriage, we hardly ever saw her. Philip seemed to be traveling most of the time and, when she wasn't with him, she was either at the London house, or in West Palm at Serina's. On the odd occasion, like Thanksgiving, when she came to visit for a day or two, I expressed my disappointment at the way she appeared to have almost abandoned the family, but she always had an excuse. When, I suggested it was Philip who was influencing her behavior, she always got very quiet and I knew, in my heart, I was right. As for Philip, he only showed up at the house once, and that was just before Christmas. He came alone, loaded down with gifts, and explained that Portia wasn't feeling well. He was very vague, until my father pushed him for more information, and he finally admitted she had bronchitis and had been confined to bed for a few days. I was furious when I heard this and demanded to know why he hadn't called to let us know so that we could, at least, visit her and maybe be of some help. His reaction was just what I expected. He claimed she was perfectly all right and had a maid to take good care of her as well as the attention of the family doctor. I tried to explain that it would probably help her recovery if she had a visit from me or her father but, he just shrugged it off. Then, when I asked if they would join us on Christmas Day for dinner, he announced they were going to Cabo San Lucas for the holiday. At that point, I was too upset to even attempt to change his mind and excused myself. I didn't think I would be able to contain my temper if I stayed. Later, Beth told me he was sorry he wasn't able to say goodbye to me but he'd enjoyed seeing the family again, especially Vicky. Naturally, I didn't believe a word of it.

Aaron warned me I would alienate my sister altogether if I kept reacting the way I did towards Philip. It was then, I decided to try and keep my thoughts to myself, but I still wasn't sure if I could ever be more than just civil towards him. As it happens, I had a lot more to concern me in the months to come.

In October, 2005, Vicky celebrated her third birthday. Once again Portia was absent but Aaron's mother had flown up to stay with us for a few days and my dearest friend, Emily, drove up from Philadelphia. We hadn't seen each other since she moved there with Larry and was now working as a manager in a video production company. She hadn't changed one bit; she still had the wild red hair and was as tiny as ever. It was lovely to have guests at the house and Anisha was a godsend. Not only did she put in extra hours just to ensure the guest rooms were made up and kept tidy but, she excelled when it came to cooking. She made a veritable feast one evening with dishes of curried lamb, butter chicken and wonderful basmati rice with saffron, garlic and almonds. She also helped us get ready for Vicky's party, decorating the family room, and wrapping gifts. I was feeling really happy, even though I was missing Portia, but the day after the party, everything changed.

We'd decided to give Vicky a special treat and take her to the Bronx Zoo. Aaron and I thought she was now old enough to enjoy the animals. We'd visited the Central Park Zoo, when she was a lot smaller, but the only exhibit that seemed to attract her attention was the sea lions. The Bronx Zoo was much larger and I was looking forward to going there just as much as she was. Emily had to get back to Philadelphia, so we figured the rest of us could fit into my father's car for the drive to the city. Then, about a half hour before we were due to leave, Beth announced that Daddy wasn't feeling well and had decided not to come. It was unusual for him to be sick, and I was concerned, but Beth said she thought he was just tired and that she'd stay behind with him.

We had a wonderful morning touring all the animal exhibits and Vicky was in her element. This time, it was the gorillas that fascinated her and it was difficult pulling her away from them. I began to lose my patience but Aaron's mom came to the rescue and I began to see where my husband got all his positive traits from.

By noon everyone was getting hungry, so we decided to head to the café for something to eat. I was ambling along, talking to Jane, when my cell phone rang and I was a bit alarmed when I saw it was Beth calling. I'll never forget what she said, after I answered hello. "Sam, it's Beth, I'm sorry to upset your day, dear, but your father's here at Phelps Memorial. He's had a heart attack and it doesn't look good. Please come." Her voice began to break and I felt my heart begin to race. I told her we were on our way and then turned to Aaron and collapsed into his arms.

Daddy didn't make it. He was only sixty seven and his heart suddenly just gave up. The doctors did everything they could to save him but it was no use and I didn't even get the chance to say goodbye. If it wasn't for Aaron, I don't know how Beth and I would have got through the next few days and Jane completely took control of Vicky, with a little help from Anisha. Aaron took care of making all the funeral arrangements and he was the one who called Portia right after we left the hospital, but he wasn't able to reach her. It was the day before the funeral itself when he finally made contact with her and discovered they'd been cruising in the Mediterranean and had lost all telephone connection. Of course, she was devastated, and was on the private jet flying out of Nice that very night. With the time difference, she arrived at La Guardia at eleven o'clock and Aaron was there to pick her up. It was midnight when they got back to the house and I was up pacing the floor, while Beth was curled up on the family room couch. I heard the car drive up and raced to the front door, then ran down the steps, throwing myself into Portia's arms the minute she stepped out of the car. It was pouring with rain but I don't think either one of us cared; we needed each other so badly at that moment.

Aaron gently shepherded us into the house and took Portia's coat and suitcase then, Beth came out of the family room into the hallway. She took one look at the two of us and spread her arms just waiting for us to fall into them. I don't know how long the three of us stood embracing each other and quietly sobbing but it seemed like an eternity. It was too much to bear; Portia and I had lost a precious father, a man who had brought us up and loved us forever and Beth, for the second time in her life, had lost a wonderful, kind and generous husband. Life just didn't seem fair.

On the day of the funeral, we attended a brief service at the Congregational Church. My father wasn't a very religious person and we had never talked about what kind of service, if any, he would want in the event of his death. I did know he was adamant about being cremated and having his ashes scattered on Long Island Sound, near Fairfield, which is where my mother's ashes were scattered.

I didn't expect so many people to be at the church. Several of his colleagues from his office were there and at least a dozen neighbors. Even Emily came back from Philadelphia with Larry, and both of Beth's sons arrived with their wives. The sad thing was, none of my grandparents were there. My father's parents were now both in their early nineties and were not able to travel all the way from Florida, and we had completely lost touch with my mother's family. Then there was Philip, the most obvious absentee. I would have thought he would have been there to support Portia but, according to her, he had an extremely important business negotiation he was dealing with in Tokyo and sent his regrets. How I managed not to make a derogatory comment regarding his absence, I'll never know.

After the service, we watched as the hearse took Daddy on his last journey to the crematorium. That's when it really hit me and I collapsed in Aaron's arms. I thanked heaven for my adoring husband who was always there for me but, at the same time, I felt almost guilty because my darling sister was left sobbing quietly, all alone with nobody's shoulder to cry on.

Everyone went back to the house afterwards, where both Anisha and Jane had prepared enough sandwiches, salads, and pastries to feed an army. It was comforting having so many people in the house and I could have listened all day to the wonderful things that were said about my father. There was no doubt, he was a very special man and losing him would leave a huge void in my life.

After the funeral, Portia only stayed for another full day and then Aaron drove her back into the city and she flew to Hawaii, where she was meeting Philip. He had concluded his business in Tokyo and had decided he needed a few days in the sun. Again, I think he could have been a little more considerate and suggest she spend more time with her family but I got the impression that, when Philip said jump, Portia asked how high.

It was ironic that Thanksgiving was just a week away and Aaron thought we should skip the big family dinner and go out for a quiet meal. That way, Anisha would be able to spend the whole day with her own family. Jane had already returned home and, with Portia gone, it just left Beth, Aaron, Vicky and me. The house seemed awfully quiet even though Vicky, who had just got past the terrible twos stage, was still acting up and recently exhibited two rather disrupting temper tantrums. Fortunately, Aaron had the patience of a saint and always managed to calm her down.

After Thanksgiving, we had to drive into the city to meet with my father's lawyer for the reading of his will. We had no idea what to expect as he had just left a letter, mixed in with his papers, to say the lawyer had the only copy. This didn't surprise me as Daddy never liked keeping confidential papers in the house. Naturally, we expected Portia to be there but she was back in Florida at Serena's house. When I called her about the appointment, I was certain she would want to be there but, again, she had another excuse. It was Serena's birthday and Philip had arranged a surprise party for her at The Breakers Hotel. She was helping Lotti organize everything and just couldn't make it. This time, I wasn't so successful at biting my tongue and our conversation ended on a sour note. As it happens, Daddy only left a token amount to Portia. The will clearly indicated that, after he'd confirmed she an airtight prenuptial agreement, one that his own lawyer had reviewed, with a very generous settlement in the event of divorce, he thought she would be well taken care of. He also made it very clear that, in no way, did the division of his estate imply that he loved or valued her any less. I have to admit I was shocked when I heard this and wondered if Portia already knew the content of the will. Later, I felt she must have done if my father had been involved with the execution of her prenuptial agreement.

The rest of the will shocked me even more because Daddy left me the house, its contents, and all of his investment holdings, valued at close to four hundred thousand dollars, while Beth was to receive a one-time sum of one hundred thousand and his monthly pension. When the reading was over, I was overcome with emotion. Aaron and I had often discussed moving out of the house and making our own way and we knew it would be a struggle. Now we didn't have a worry in the world. Nevertheless, it was a bitter sweet thought.

After leaving the lawyer's office, we decided to go for lunch before driving back to Scarsdale but the three of us were rather subdued. I mentioned I was concerned about Daddy leaving Portia such a small amount but, both Aaron and Beth convinced me, it was my father's decision. Aaron agreed she probably already knew and, if she didn't and felt she was being unfairly treated, then she could always contest the will. I shook my head vehemently when I heard this and told Aaron in no uncertain terms that, if Portia really felt that way, I would sign over half the house to her and give her half of the money. Knowing me as well as he did, he didn't even attempt to talk me out of it. As it happened, I learned later, my father had taken Portia into his confidence and she'd even encouraged him to leave me the house and his investments. I should have known my sister had never been motivated by money. How ironic that she'd met a man who would take care of her for the rest of her life, even if the marriage didn't last.

By the end of November, we were beginning to get used to my father's absence but, every now and then, particularly when I looked at the last photos we had of him, I would break down in tears. Meanwhile, Beth was a tower of strength and I realized she had been through this before and had already developed a coping mechanism. She loved to read and spent a lot of time absorbed in a book, and she enjoyed playing with Vicky. I was so grateful for her company when Aaron was at work all day and hoped she would always stay with us. Then, just three weeks before the Christmas holiday, she got a call from her daughter-in-law, Lisa, to say Neil had just been diagnosed with pancreatic cancer and was in the hospital. The very next day, Aaron took her to the airport and she flew to Boston to be at his side. I had a feeling she would not be coming back.

Aaron commented he'd be glad when the year was over, the way things were going, but he didn't count on the next piece of bad news we received a week later. My grandfather had passed away and we had another funeral to attend. I was sad, but there had been little contact with either of my grandparents for many years and he'd lived a good long life. This time Portia came to our rescue and persuaded Philip to let us use the corporate jet to fly to Fort Lauderdale and she came with us. It was quite an experience, not only because we'd never had the luxury of traveling this way before, but because we were able to jet in and out within two days without any hassle. The service for my grandfather was very brief and my grandmother held up quite well until we were standing at the gravesite. It was then when she broke down and had to be supported by Aaron and one of her neighbors. She looked so frail dressed all in black and I knew it was just a matter of time before we would be coming back again. We stayed overnight with her and, during the evening, Portia and I listened while she told us stories about our father when he was small. I learned things about him I never knew before and it was such a joy to be able to share our memories with each other.

I was upset at leaving my grandmother and even considered asking her to come and live with us but Aaron dissuaded me and so, I left with a heavy heart but I was anxious to get back to Vicky. Anisha had agreed to stay and look after her and I know she was more than capable but I knew Vicky could be a bit of a handful if things weren't to her liking. Little did I know what was to come when we arrived back home.

Chapter Twenty-Eight

When Portia dropped us off at Aaron's office, where we had parked the car, I was reluctant to say goodbye and not sure what to suggest about the upcoming holiday. I think I expected a rejection but she surprised me when she said she was going to speak to Philip about inviting us to Cabo San Lucas and asked if we would we be interested. Aaron immediately said, "Hell, yes. We'll be glad to get out of this damn weather," while I just nodded, not quite sure what I was feeling. Then, moments later, we took our departure and headed for home.

I didn't think, for a moment, that anything else could go wrong but, this time, the 'it always happens in threes', rule didn't seem to apply because number four was awaiting us. It was mid-afternoon when we pulled into the driveway and Anisha was waiting on the front steps. I sensed immediately that something was wrong and went rushing forward, "What is it? Has something happened to Vicky?" I called out in a panic.

She came forward to greet me and shook her head, "No, Vicky's absolutely fine, she's having her nap. It's Molly."

I breathed a sigh of relief as Aaron came up behind me, "What happened to Molly? Is she all right?"

I noticed a tear in the corner of Anisha's eye as she answered, "I'm afraid not. When I took Vicky out yesterday, she must have snuck out before I closed the door and I didn't notice her. When we got back, I couldn't find her. I was getting a bit frantic then Mr. Parks, from next door, came to tell me she'd been run over. He said there was nothing he could do for her and she must have died instantly. He brought her to me in a box and helped me bury her in the garden underneath the big oak tree near the back fence. I'm so sorry." And then she broke down sobbing.

I glanced back at Aaron and bit my lip, to stop from breaking down too, then gave poor Anisha a hug, "It's okay, don't blame yourself. Does Vicky know?"

She nodded, "Yes, Mr. Parks was very kind. He explained to her what happened and even brought over a picture book about animals going to heaven. I don't know how much she understood but she only cried for a minute when she knew Molly wasn't coming back."

I placed my hand on Aaron's arm, "Oh, my god," I said, "I don't know how much more of this I can take."

We never did manage to go away for the holiday because Vicky came down with chicken pox. Both Aaron and I had already had it, so we were immune but Anisha hadn't and, because we were afraid she might catch it and pass it on to her own family, we suggested that she not come to the house until Vicky was better. I don't think I can remember a more miserable holiday. Beth was still in Boston, preparing herself for the inevitable. Her son was now in the terminal stage of his illness and not expected to survive until New Year and, in addition to this terrible news, she had decided she would not be coming back to Scarsdale but would be staying in Boston with a cousin. Meanwhile, Portia had left for Cabo San Lucas and the house felt completely empty.

Aaron did his best to cheer me up and even cooked a turkey on Christmas Day. He also bought me the most beautiful amethyst pendant I knew would look wonderful with my black velvet dress, that is, if I ever got to wear it again. I had to admit I really had little to complain about when I saw how much Vicky was suffering. I felt so sorry for her. The day after she started to feel sick, she developed a fever but we decided to wait one more day to see if she felt better and that's when the rash appeared. After telephoning our doctor and describing the rash, he diagnosed her with chicken pox. I think the rash bothered her more than anything because it was so itchy and even after the spots blistered and then dried over, more spots would appear. She only fully recovered a couple of days into the new year when the holidays were over.

The fact that Anisha had been away for almost two weeks really got me thinking. Now that there was only Aaron, Vicky and me, there really wasn't the need for any help and, although the idea of doing all the cooking and cleaning myself was a rather daunting idea, I realized both Portia and I had been thoroughly spoiled. When I approached Aaron about it, he surprised me when he suggested the house was much too big for us now and perhaps we should sell up and buy something smaller. My first reaction was completely negative. The house had been my childhood home and held so many memories, especially of Daddy, and I couldn't bear the idea of giving it up. Later though, when I'd had more time to think about it, I had to agree that it was certainly something to consider, especially as Vicky would be attending pre-school later that year and, if we were going to move, we needed to make a decision soon.

I wasn't happy telling Anisha we no longer needed her services, except perhaps for baby-sitting now and again, and I had to convince her it had nothing to do with the incident with Molly. The same day we let her go, we got a call from Beth telling us Neil had died that morning and was being buried the very next day. I hadn't known, up until then, that Lisa was Jewish and Neal had converted to Judaism but I had always felt the tradition of burial so soon after death made a lot more sense. It just didn't give Aaron and me the opportunity to go to Boston.

When I spoke to Portia about selling the house, she agreed it was much too big for a small family and, unless I was thinking of having more children, it would be the perfect time to make a move. I was pleased to hear she wasn't upset about selling our childhood home and told her so. She responded that it was just bricks and mortar and leaving it behind wouldn't erase all the wonderful memories she had of growing up there. After our conversation, I thought about her comment about having more children. I realized, Aaron and I had never discussed it but I'd already made up my mind, one child was enough. I always doubted I was a good mother because I didn't have the maternal instinct. I loved Vicky dearly and would protect her with my life if necessary, but looking after a small child didn't really fulfill me and I longed to do something constructive. Later that day, I relayed my feelings to Aaron and, although he was disappointed because he would liked to have had a son, he supported me one hundred percent and suggested that, as soon as we moved and settled Vicky in pre-school, I should get myself a job.

Chapter Twenty-Nine

In the spring, Aaron and I spent a lot of our spare time researching the best places to live. We wanted to be closer to the city; not only to cut down on Aaron's commute back and forth every day, but because we wanted to take advantage of everything the city had to offer. Now that we were on our own and didn't have to pinch pennies, we decided we would spend more time going to the movies, eating out, and even attending some of the wonderful musicals that were playing. The more places we looked at, the more we found ourselves zeroing in on one place, New Rochelle, about twenty minutes from Scarsdale and that much closer to Manhattan. It had a population of about seventy-three thousand and a vibrant downtown area, but it was mostly comprised of single family homes.

Once we'd decided on New Rochelle, we put the house up for sale and began an all-out effort to find a home that would be perfect for our little family. It didn't take too long; in fact, we had only viewed seven properties before we found what we were looking for, on Davenport Avenue, just a stone's throw from Davenport Park, and overlooking Long Island Sound. It was a lovely two-story, with an open floor plan, paneled dining room, hardwood floors throughout and a modern kitchen with a bay window. It had three bedrooms, two full bathrooms, and a wonderful sunroom opening up onto a porch, which overlooked the landscaped back garden. Not only did we love the house, but it was minutes away from Long Island Sound in one direction, New Rochelle Harbor in the other, and most important of all, a transitional learning center, right on our street, for children aged eighteen months to seven.

Selling the house meant we had to get rid of a lot of the furniture and I was reluctant to part with many of the items. Beth came down from Boston to help us with a garage sale. We got rid of a lot of the smaller items, and were lucky enough to find a buyer for almost all of the larger pieces. Beth also helped me shop for the new house. We didn't need any new furniture but we needed new rugs and blinds and I was grateful she took the time out to visit and give me some input. It was so lovely seeing her again and I hoped we would never lose touch. Sadly, she was still grieving over the loss of Neil, but she enjoyed living in Boston and her sister was great company for her.

The day we turned the key in the lock to the house on Chedworth Road, I cried. It was so bitter sweet. I felt like I was leaving Daddy behind but I remembered what Portia said about not being able to erase all the wonderful memories. Then, as we drove away for the last time, and began the journey towards our new home, I began to feel a glimmer of excitement. I was twenty-three years old and finally becoming independent.

It took a while to settle into the new house but, once I had everything organized, I felt pretty proud of myself and couldn't wait for Portia to come and visit. She had driven up, before we moved in, to look at the property and thought it would be the perfect place for us, especially as we were so close to the school. When she eventually returned, after we were all settled, she thought I'd done a marvelous job of arranging the furniture and adding all the little details that made it a home but I found her to be rather subdued. She'd only planned to stay for lunch, and I was anxious to know what was going on, so I finally asked her if there was a problem. She bowed her head and avoided looking me in the eye when she answered, "Philip's going to be conducting most of his business from the U.K. for the next couple of years so he wants us to make London our home base."

I sat for a moment trying to take it in, "When is this happening?" I asked, in almost a whisper.

That's when she looked up and replied, "I'm leaving New York in two weeks."

I felt a little lump in my chest, "Everyone seems to be leaving. First Maggie, then Daddy, then Beth, even Molly, and now you."

She reached over and took my hand, "I'll only be a few hours away, Sam. I'll try to come back often and you can come and visit me any time. I think youd really like London."

I nodded, "I'm sure I would but I'm going to miss you so much. Will you have time before you leave to come back and see us again?"

"I'll certainly try but I know we have a number of engagements before we leave, plus any packing I need to do."

I hesitated and then asked, "Why is it you never bring Philip with you when you visit with us? The last time I remember seeing him was when he dropped by to pick you up after our lunch date, a few months ago. Even then, he only had time to say hello and then rush you out of the restaurant."

Portia sighed, "I know, I'm sorry, Sam, but he's a very busy man. That's why we're moving to London because most of his business is conducted in Europe now."

"Hmmm…. I don't think it's much of an excuse, not having time for your wife's family. You always seem to be at one social event or another; it's not like he doesn't have a life outside of business."

"Well, if you come and visit us in London, maybe the four of us can spend more time together."

I scoffed, "I doubt that. If and when we do come, he's bound to be off somewhere else."

Portia looked a little annoyed, "That's not fair. I know you don't approve of him, that's pretty obvious, but you haven't given him a chance."

"How can I give him a chance when we never see the man? I'm sorry but it all seems a bit odd to me. I know you've been to his sister's two or three times so it's not like he doesn't have some sense of family but where yours is concerned, he doesn't seem to get it. I'm your sister, Portia, the only family you've got left. Don't let him alienate you from us."

Portia stood up, "Now you're being ridiculous," she said. "I've told you, you can come and visit and I'll try to come back as often as I can. I don't know what more you want from me. I think maybe it's time for me to leave."

I looked up at her, "Please sit down. I don't want you to leave like this."

She shook her head, "No, Sam, I think I should go and I'll call you tomorrow. Right now I'm too upset with you to stay."

I stood up and took a step towards her, "Do I get a hug before you go?"

"Yes, of course," she answered and took me in her arms but I could feel how rigid she was.

She left right after that without even looking in on Vicky, who was having her afternoon nap. I knew she wouldn't call the next day and it was almost a week before I heard from her again. She called to say she wouldn't have time to come back again, before leaving for London, but she'd call me the day before she left. When the day came, I never left the house and tried to keep busy just waiting to hear from her but, by eleven o'clock that night, I went to bed feeling terribly sad and feeling a deep sense of abandonment. Even with Aaron snuggled up beside me; I couldn't help thinking, "Where has everybody gone?"

Chapter Thirty

After we enrolled Vicky in the transitional learning center, in the fall of that year, I realized I had a lot of time on my hands and I began to feel restless. I had no friends to speak of, other than Emily who now lived in Philadelphia, and I hadn't had much interaction with our neighbors since we moved in. Aaron suggested I get a part-time job and, while I would have preferred to continue with my education and pursue a career in journalism, I was conflicted because I wanted to be there for Vicky. Growing up without a mother was not an option for our daughter.

I finally found employment at a clinic specializing in the treatment of eating disorders, problems with speech, and various other issues affecting youngsters under the age of eighteen. I spent four hours every day on the reception desk, greeting patients, making appointments, and trying to keep a smile on my face even though, at times it was difficult, witnessing the struggle some of these young people were going through. Bette, who worked full time, helped me to keep my emotions in check. She was a forty-year-old single woman with a bawdy sense of humor and an appearance to match. With bleached blond hair and a decidedly voluptuous figure, which was on display when she removed the white coat we were obliged to wear, she would often entertain me with stories about her successes, or failures, on the dating scene. I couldn't have wished for a more generous individual to work alongside of. She encouraged me every step of the way and helped me cope with the dark side of dealing with mental health issues. If it hadn't been for Bette, I think I would have gone home every day feeling depressed.

Taking Vicky back and forth to school and having a job kept me occupied during the day but at night, if Aaron was working late, my thoughts always turned to Portia. I talked to her briefly, soon after she settled in London, and she mentioned she wanted to find a job but Philip wouldn't go along with the idea. He reminded her that he traveled a great deal and expected her to be available if he wanted her to accompany him. When I asked her if she was satisfied with just sitting around being at his beck and call, I incited another touchy exchange between us and that's when she suggested we email each other in future, rather than telephone. I wasn't sure why she thought this was a better way to communicate until Aaron told me he thought I would have the opportunity to read over my email, before I hit the send button, rather than just blurting out my thoughts. "Am I really that impulsive?" I asked him.

He smiled and nodded, "You don't usually stop and think about what you're going to say, Sam. The words just come tumbling out and you can easily offend people."

I looked contrite, "I'm not like that with you am I?"

He chuckled, "No, because I'm the perfect husband. What could you possibly say to me that would offend me?"

I put my arms around his neck and pulled him towards me, "Absolutely nothing. I don't deserve you. You're the kindest, sweetest man I've ever known."

"You forgot sexiest."

"That too," I responded as I pulled him down onto the carpet in the family room and began to tug at his belt.

Over the next year, I settled into the day to day routine of living in New Rochelle. Portia and I e-mailed each other every couple of weeks but she didn't have too much to say, except that she was getting involved in some charity work and Philip was still traveling a lot. Meanwhile, Vicky was enjoying school and interacting with the other children and, sometimes, I thought I should have reconsidered my decision about not having another child but I knew, deep down, it just wasn't something I could deal with. I had enough issues with the youngsters who came into the clinic for treatment but gradually I became more and more confident and Bette was especially impressed with how I handled the parents. Most of them were patient and understanding but if any of them became difficult, I was able to pacify them with a kind word and a smile. Aaron was surprised, to say the least, when he heard first hand that I didn't react in my usual manner. One day, after leaving the office early, he came to the clinic to pick me up and Bette filled him in on how well I was coping. I think he was very impressed and I knew Bette was impressed with Aaron. The very next day, as soon as I walked through the door, she remarked, "Wow, that husband of yours is a keeper. You didn't tell me he was so good looking and he seems real sweet too."

I chuckled, "Oh yes, well you keep your hands off him. No flashing those boobs of yours when he comes in here."

She roared with laughter, "Don't worry, he's not going to look at an old broad like me."

All in all, life was good but I missed Daddy so much. Beth and I would phone each other often and, one weekend, she drove down from Boston for a visit. It was so lovely to see her again and, before she left to go home, we decided to call Maggie and surprise her. We got a bit teary eyed talking about all the years we'd spent together in Scarsdale and I promised her that, one day, I would definitely travel to England and spend some time with her. It was when she asked about Portia that things got a little quiet. She was hoping, now Portia was living in London, she would have contacted her. I wasn't sure what to tell her except that she was probably traveling a lot with Philip. After I hung up the phone, Beth and I had a long conversation about Portia and, although I know she was empathetic to some degree, I was certain she had no real insight as to how much I missed my sister and how much I worried about her. Ironically, the day after Beth left, I had even more reason to worry.

I was standing in line at the supermarket check-out counter when the cover of one of the weekly tabloids caught my eye. In the bottom left corner was a small photograph of a dark-haired woman being helped out of a car by a man, who looked exactly like Philip. I didn't have time to read the caption so I grabbed a copy, piled it on top of my groceries and proceeded through the check-out. I was anxious to see what it was all about but I was already running late and still had to pick up Vicky from school. Once I finally got home, I settled Vicky down at the kitchen table with a jig-saw puzzle, quickly put the groceries away and, although I needed to start preparing dinner, I just couldn't concentrate. I had to examine the photo and read the article inside. I sat down opposite Vicky, with the tabloid in front of me, when she suddenly looked across at me and said, "What's that, Mommy?"

"Oh, it's just a magazine I picked up. I think there's a picture of your uncle in it."

"Can I see please?" she asked, starting to get down from her chair.

I shook my head and told her to sit back down and I'd show it to her later. At that, she decided she was hungry and, in order to keep her occupied and leave me in peace for a few minutes, I gave her two chocolate chip cookies. I watched her for a moment as she nibbled away and picked at the puzzle pieces then, satisfied she was not going to interrupt me again for a while; I looked at the cover photo again. There was no doubt it was Philip and the caption read, 'Tycoon steps out in Rome with mystery brunette.' I quickly flipped through the pages until I came to an article showing another photograph of Philip with the same woman, exiting the Hassler Hotel. The article was very brief but stated, whoever the woman was,

Philip had been seen with her on two or three occasions while his wife remained behind in London. The implication was obvious; he was cheating on my sister. My immediate reaction was anger but I knew I had to give him the benefit of the doubt. The woman could be a business associate or an old friend but, then again, maybe not. I studied the larger photo and although the woman was attractive, she didn't hold a candle to Portia. Where my sister had light- blonde long hair, and the face of an angel, this woman was olive skinned with shoulder-length dark hair and there was a certain harshness about her. She was wearing a black wrap dress on her pencil thin frame and high-heeled strappy sandals, exposing bright red toenails which matched the color of her lipstick. She was small in stature and gazing up at Philip but his head was turned away from her. I really didn't know what to think so I decided to wait and ask Aaron his opinion after dinner. Maybe he would put it all in perspective and put my suspicions to rest.

I hadn't intended to talk to Aaron until after dinner, when Vicky was already in bed, but he arrived home a little earlier than usual. He breezed through the kitchen door with a big smile, "How are my two favorite girls today?" he asked, as Vicky jumped off her chair and wrapped her arms around his legs. I turned around from the counter, where I was peeling potatoes, and immediately noticed the tabloid still sitting on the table. I only had an instant to distract him but it wasn't enough; he'd already noticed it. "Since when have you been reading these trashy magazines, Sam?"

I didn't get a chance to respond because Vicky piped up, "Uncle's on the cover, Daddy."

Aaron lifted her back onto the chair and then proceeded to check out the photo. "Mmm, it sure looks like your uncle," he said, glancing over at me with a frown.

"It is him," I answered, "and there's more inside. I'm not sure what to make of it but I think we should talk about it later."

Always the diplomat, Aaron merely nodded and left to change his clothes and relax with a Budweiser before dinner.

Chapter Thirty-One

My conversation with my husband didn't exactly allay my suspicions and, although he attempted to discourage me from getting involved, I was too concerned about Portia not to dig a little further. I decided to call her, despite our agreement about e-mailing, but there was no response on her cell phone and I wasn't able to leave a message. I then called the land line number at the Mayfair house and a man, with what I imagined to be an upper class English accent, answered. He informed me that Mrs. Barrington was not at home and he did not expect her return for a few days. When I tried to get more information, he seemed evasive and couldn't tell me where she'd gone or who she was with. I then asked if Philip was there and he was just as vague. I finally gave up and asked him to pass on a message then rang off, feeling frustrated and more concerned than ever. Aaron suggested, she could be with Philip but I wasn't convinced and I considered getting in touch with Serena to see if I could locate her. I knew her main residence was in West Palm and, as she had never been married, I assumed she still went under the name of Barrington. Being a rather public person, I assumed she would have an unlisted telephone and was surprised when I hit the jackpot after contacting information service. As I dialed the number in Florida, I realized she might not be there and could even be in London, but I had to take the chance. Lotti answered the phone and seemed genuinely pleased to hear from me. She had no idea where Portia was but suggested Serena might know and said she'd ask her to come and speak to me. I waited with baited breath expecting a very negative response from Serena and I got exactly what I bargained for; she was almost rude in the way she reacted to my questions and I found it hard to keep my temper. If she knew anything at all, she wasn't talking.

I realized there was nothing more I could do, other than to keep calling Portia on her cell phone and e-mailing, but it appeared as though her phone was switched off and the e-mails kept bouncing back at me with the message, she wasn't available and would respond on her return. That was it, no dates, no explanations, nothing at all. After a few days, I became very worried and a little angry and I was determined to do something about it. I didn't have Philip's private number so I called the Barrington head office in New York and after a run-around I managed to get through to his personal assistant, Pamela Lessing. She was extremely gracious and listened attentively while I explained exactly who I was and my concern regarding Portia. She then surprised me by saying we'd actually met at my sister's wedding and I probably wouldn't remember her, but I'd remarked on the necklace she'd been wearing. I suddenly recalled the attractive middle-aged woman with white hair, swept up in a chignon, with the most unusual necklace made of copper and ivory. She had obviously been introduced to me and, if I'd been told she was Philip's assistant at the time, I failed to absorb that piece of information. As it turned out, she was unable to give me Philip's number, as it was strictly against corporate policy, and she had no idea where Portia was except that she wasn't with him. Apparently, he'd concluded his business in Rome and had continued on to Bejing. He wasn't expected back in London for another week but she said she would be speaking to him within the next two days and would ask him to contact me directly. I felt she was being sincere and the only thing I could do was pray that I'd hear from Philip as soon as he got the message. Maybe then I would find out where Portia was.

I didn't expect, for one minute, Philip would call me back after receiving my message and so, after three more days passed without any word, I telephoned his assistant again. She said she was sorry Philip hadn't contacted me directly but was pleased I'd followed up with her as she'd just learned, my sister was in Menton. When I asked her if she could give me the telephone number there she was very obliging and, as soon as I hung up the phone, I was back on the line again trying to get through to Portia. I was surprised to hear she was in France and couldn't imagine why she hadn't contacted me. I was even more surprised when I expected to hear someone with a French accent answer the phone and actually heard Portia's voice, although she sounded very subdued. "Bonjour," she said, "who's calling, please?"

"Portia, it's me, I've been trying to get hold of you for over a week. Why haven't you been answering your phone or my e-mails?" There was silence for a few seconds and I thought we'd been disconnected, "Portia, are you there?" I called out feeling my heart start to race.

"I'm here, Sam," she replied, almost in a whisper. "I'm sorry I haven't been in touch."

I waited for an explanation and, when I didn't get one, I was a bit annoyed, "That's it?" I asked. "That's all you have to say? I've been worried sick about you. I had to call Philip's New York office to find out where you were and, if it wasn't for Mrs. Lessing, I still wouldn't know. Philip didn't even bother to reply to my message."

There was a moment of silence again and then Portia's voice began to break up, "I had a miscarriage, Sam. Philip thought I would recover a lot faster if I was here."

I gasped, "Oh, my god, why on earth didn't you tell me? When did this happen? How far along were you?"

"It was almost two weeks ago and I was close to six weeks. I didn't want to tell anyone until after the first trimester."

I immediately felt sick to my stomach. "Oh Portia, I'm so sorry. What caused the miscarriage? Do the doctor's know?"

"I fell down some stairs and lost the baby later that day."

"Oh no, you must have been devastated. How did Philip react?" Again, the odd silence and my instinct started to kick in again that something wasn't quite right. "Did you hear me, Portia? I asked you how Philip reacted."

"He was upset and thought, while he was away, I should come here to recuperate."

"I see. How are you feeling now? I noticed you answered the phone, isn't anyone there with you?"

"Yes, Colette, the housekeeper is here but she's just gone to the market. She's been a real comfort to me and I feel a lot better. She should be back very soon."

"How long will you be staying there?"

"I'm not sure but I'll probably go back to London when Philip gets back from China."

I hesitated but just had to ask, "Are you sure everything's okay between you and Philip?"

"Yes, everything's fine," she answered in a low voice. "Please don't worry about me, Sam."

"How can I stop worrying when I don't hear from you? Promise me you'll answer my calls and e-mails from now on."

"I promise, Sam. I miss you so much."

I felt the tears start to roll down my cheeks, "I miss you too, Portia. Why don't you come home for a while? I'll look after you."

"My home's in London now, Sam, with Philip."

"But he's hardly ever around. I see he was just in Rome and you weren't with him."

"He has to travel a lot for business purposes. I understood that when we got married."

I decided not to mention the photo in the tabloid. "Maybe if you eventually have a family, he'll be around a lot more."

"I don't think there'll be any more children."

I was shocked, "Oh no, don't tell me you can't carry a baby to term."

"It isn't that. Philip never wanted a child in the first place."

"What? I thought you said he was upset about the miscarriage."

"No, he was upset that I was sick."

"Is that because he didn't like seeing you suffer or because you disrupted his plans?" I shot back.

"Please, Sam, don't do this again. I don't want to fall out with you but I don't want to listen to you criticizing Philip, every time we talk. Maybe that's why I never took your phone calls or answered your e-mails. You're my sister and I love you but you have to understand, Philip's my husband and you have to accept that."

"I have accepted it but I don't have to like it. You know me, Portia, I say exactly what I think and it's hard for me to be any other way. Sometimes I wonder how Aaron puts up with me, although I have little to complain about where he's concerned. I wish you'd found someone just like him."

"See, there you go again. I know Aaron's a saint but you have no idea what Philip's really like. You've never even given him a chance."

"How can I give him a chance when we never see him, and now that you're over three thousand miles away, that's not likely to change?"

"I don't know what to say to that, Sam, except that I'm sorry we had to move to London, but it won't be forever. I know it's been hard on you losing the whole family. I wish Daddy was still alive and maybe, if Beth had stayed, you'd feel a lot more content."

We continued to talk and I assured her I was perfectly content, although I missed our father terribly. I wanted to tell her what a lovely little girl Vicky was becoming, but I didn't feel the timing was appropriate so I focused more on my work at the clinic. By the time we finished our conversation, I think she was over being upset about my issues with Philip and she promised to call me as soon as she returned to London.

A week later, I picked up a copy of the New York Times and Aaron noticed an article in the business section. It mentioned Philip Barrington's return from Bejing after successfully sealing a deal with one of the foremost technology companies in China. I listened with half an ear, not really interested in the details, only concerned with how long he'd been back in London. Aaron couldn't enlighten me but I expected to hear from Portia within a day or two.

By the following Monday, when I hadn't heard from her, I called her cell phone but she wasn't available and I had to leave a message. I tried twice more over the next two days and finally managed to get hold of her, only to learn she was still in Menton. She said she'd developed a very bad cold and Philip insisted she stay where she was, rather than return to England where it was cold and raining nearly every day. I thought this was rather strange as it was early September and I didn't think the weather could be that bad. When I got off the phone, I went on the internet to check the weather in London and discovered it had been exceptionally warm for the past week and there hadn't been any rain to speak of. Obviously Philip was lying and wanted to keep her out of the way. What was he up to that he didn't want her around?

Already on the internet, I decided to do a little more investigating and googled all the tabloids to see if any more photos of Philip had been published, but I was out of luck. I still figured there had to be another woman in the equation and I was worried about Portia. So much so, I suggested to Aaron I fly out to Menton to see her, and I didn't want to wait. He was shocked that I'd consider going all the way to France when, according to my sister, she only had a cold. It took a great deal of persuasion to convince him I needed to go and he eventually gave in, and even assured me Vicky would be fine without me for a few days. Before I called Bette, at the clinic, to tell her my plans, I decided I should let Portia know I was going to book a flight and expected to be there in two days. Again, I had trouble getting hold of her but I suspect the message I left must have prompted her to call me back right away. "You can't come all this way, Sam," she said.

"Watch me," I fired back, "I'm going to hang up and call the airline. Once I have all the details, you'll have to tell me how I get to you from Nice."

"But, Sam…" she started to say, but I interrupted, telling her I'd call her back and then hung up. Nothing was going to deter me.

Ten minutes later, I was still checking flight times and fares on the computer when my telephone rang. It was Portia. "There's no sense in you coming here, Sam." she said. "I'm going back to London tomorrow."

I was stunned for a moment, "Why didn't you tell me this earlier?" I asked.

She hesitated, "Well, I thought I should let Philip know you were coming to Menton so I left a message with his assistant. She called me back a few minutes later to say Philip was sending the private jet to bring me home. I was really surprised, Sam, I don't know what else to tell you. I hope you haven't already booked your flight."

"Something's really fishy here, Portia. Perhaps I should come to London."

"No, please don't do that," she cried out and it was almost as though I could hear desperation in her voice. "Philip doesn't like surprises and he doesn't like having guests unless they've been invited."

"I'm not just a guest," I responded indignantly, "I'm your sister."

"Please, Sam. You'll just get me in trouble."

I could hardly believe what I was hearing. My sister sounded like a scared little rabbit and I knew I had to do something but decided to step back for the moment. "All right, please calm down. Just make sure you call me once you arrive back in London. I'd like to come and see you; that's if Philip approves."

Portia's voice dropped to almost a whisper, "I'll speak to him, Sam."

I was at a loss as to how to respond to this so I made an excuse there was somebody at the front door, and hurriedly said good-bye.

Chapter Thirty-Two

Later, when I told Aaron about the conversation, he was relieved I wasn't impulsively jetting off to France but agreed Portia sounded a little odd. When I suggested visiting her in London for a few days, he thought I should wait until I got an invitation. I knew he was being sensible but I was impatient and too concerned about my sister to just bide my time. The following day, I telephoned Pamela Lessing at Philip's New York office and asked if she could tell me how I could get in touch with him directly. She was kind enough to give me the telephone number of his London office but said I would have to go through his assistant there, Delphine Stamos. She also reminded me of the time difference and said the best time to find Philip in his office would be early in morning. I thanked her and then pondered on the information she'd given me. Delphine Stamos, what kind of a name was that? It sounded Greek and, out of curiosity, I googled it and then clicked on images and several pictures popped up; all of the same woman. I inhaled sharply when I recognized the face. It was the same woman I'd seen in the photo, stepping out of a car in Rome.

After a moment or two, I began to think about Philip's possible relationship with Delphine. As she was his assistant, maybe she had good reason to accompany him on business trips and perhaps her duties included attending social events, when they involved people Philip was negotiating with. Still, it all looked a little too convenient and I was curious to hear what she sounded like. As it was already early afternoon and hours later in London, I had to wait until the next morning. The very idea of actually talking to Philip kept me awake half the night and at breakfast, Aaron commented on how restless I'd been. I almost told him what I was up to and then decided to wait and see what transpired from my call.

After Aaron left for the office and I'd dropped Vicky off at school, I drove back home, settled comfortably in a chair in the family room, then took a deep breath and punched in the number Pamela Lessing had given me. I listened to the odd double ring tone and then a mechanical voice announced Barrington Multinational and requested I enter the extension number of the party I wanted to speak to. A moment later, I heard the voice of Delphine Stamos and was surprised when she spoke in a distinct English accent. "Philip Barrington's office, Delphine Stamos speaking" she said. "How may I help you?"

I asked to speak to Philip directly but she wasn't going to put me through until she knew exactly who I was, and what business I had with him. I decided to play her little game and told her it was strictly personal, at which she informed me he was out of the office and, if I would give her my name and number, he would call me back. Obviously I wasn't getting anywhere, so I gave my name as Samantha and my telephone number at home. I knew that would get her piqued and she immediately asked for my last name, to which I responded, "Oh, he'll know exactly who I am," and then rang off. After that I sat there all by myself grinning like a Cheshire cat imagining what was going through her mind. I guess it didn't take long before her curiosity got the better of her because, less than ten minutes later, my phone rang and I could see from the call display, it was an overseas number. I didn't even get a chance to speak before hearing Philip's voice, "Samantha," he said, with a chuckle, "what a pleasant surprise. I know you were speaking to Portia recently so I'm intrigued as to why you tracked me down at my office. Is there something you don't want your sister to know?"

"Actually there is," I said, coming right to the point. "I don't really want her to know I have to go around her to get your approval."

Philip cut in, "Approval for what? I don't understand."

"Well, you already made sure I didn't get the chance to visit my sister in France so now I'd like to come to London. Is that going to be a problem too?"

I noticed the slight hesitation before he replied, "No problem at all, Sam, except this isn't really a good time. Portia hasn't been well since she lost the baby and I think she just needs to rest. Maybe it would be a good idea if you waited for a few weeks."

I was getting annoyed again, "You just don't get it do you? Portia needs me now, not weeks from now."

"Why? Did she ask you to come?"

It was my turn to hesitate, "Not exactly but I can tell she's depressed and I think I can help. I know she misses her family and my visit could make all the difference."

Philip sighed, "Look, Sam, I know you mean well but I can't allow it right now. I'll contact you in a couple of weeks and let you know when it will be convenient for you to come here. In the meantime, Portia is in very capable hands and there's no need for your concern."

Now I was really mad, "Screw you," I spat out. "You can't stop me from seeing my sister and I'll be taking the first flight out available. Just don't think you can spirit her off somewhere else before I get there because, if you do, I'll know something's going on you don't want me to know about."

Philip's voice rose in anger, "Suit yourself, Sam, but don't expect a warm welcome." Then the phone went dead.

By the time Aaron got home that evening, I had already booked my flight to London. I would be leaving JFK on

American Airlines at 9.30 the following morning. Naturally, Aaron was a little upset that I'd been so impulsive and hadn't given him any time to make arrangements for transporting Vicky to and from school. It would mean he'd have to change his office hours to accommodate her schedule. I assured him I would only be staying in London until Sunday and, as it was already Wednesday, he only had a couple of days to deal with. Nevertheless, the tension was obvious and, when I went to bed early and suggested he come with me, he said he was busy watching a ball game on TV. It was one of the very few times in our marriage I felt rejected by him.

I had to get up at an ungodly hour to be at the airport, well in time to check in and go through customs. I'd decided to take a taxi to JFK as it was only half-an-hour away, although at that time in the morning traffic would probably be heavy with all the commuters driving into the city. As I was throwing a few clothes into an over-night bag, Aaron woke up and suggested he drive me but it would mean getting Vicky up and I didn't think she'd be too happy. Just before leaving, I crept into her room, kissed her very lightly on the top of her head and then tip-toed out into the hallway. Aaron was waiting for me, dressed only in his pajama pants, and I was tempted to drag him back into the bedroom for a long good-bye, but there wasn't time. Instead, I draped my arms around his neck and asked, "You're not mad at me for going, are you?"

He shook his head, "No, honey. I understand that you're worried about your sister. I just wish I was coming with you."

"I wish you were too but it's better this way and I'll be back home before you know it."

Chapter Thirty-Three

By the time I walked out of the arrivals lounge at Heathrow, it was 8.30 p.m. It had been a long flight but I was still on New York time and I was too excited to feel even remotely tired. As we had been coming in to land, I recognized the Thames below us and Tower Bridge and wished I was here with Aaron on vacation instead of here checking on my sister. Maybe, one day, I'd come back again under different circumstances.

I had no idea how to get to Mayfair, so I had no choice but to take a taxi. I learned later, I could have taken the Heathrow Express to Paddington Station, where I would have been minutes from my final destination and it would have cost a fraction of the price. To add to my dilemma, I was not familiar with British currency and I was worried that I could be taken advantage of. By the time I got to Charles Street, I was a bit of a wreck and wasn't even sure we were at the right place. I stepped out of the taxi and stared up at the house, which was nestled between a row of houses all built of pure white stone, with tall bay windows, a small flight of stairs going up to the front door and an area surrounded by black railings which contained a perfectly pruned miniature tree. Taking a deep breath, I climbed the stairs, rang the doorbell, and stood waiting while I could feel my heart begin to race. After what seemed like an eternity, the door opened and a man, who appeared to be in his sixties, dressed in black trousers and a white shirt, opened at the neck, stared at me and then frowned, "Yes, madam, what can I do for you?" he asked.

I thought I recognized the same voice I'd heard a while ago when I'd called the house, "I'm here to visit my sister." I replied.

He frowned again, "I'm sorry, madam, but you must have the wrong address."

I shook my head, "No, I don't. My name is Samantha Reynolds and my sister is Portia Barrington. She may not be expecting me but Mr. Barrington was aware I would be arriving."

I expected him to welcome me inside but he took a step forward and said, "I'm sorry, Miss Reynolds, but Mrs. Barrington isn't here."

"That's impossible," I responded with my voice beginning to rise, "and it's Mrs. Reynolds, by the way."

I was about to continue when he cut in, "My apologies, Mrs. Reynolds, but I assure you, your sister is not in residence."

"But she told me her husband was sending his jet to pick her up from Menton and bring her back to London. If she's not here, where is she?"

"I'm sorry, but I have no idea. Perhaps you should telephone Mr. Barrington and perhaps he can help you."

Suddenly I got my nerve back, "Look, I've just flown all the way from New York. I have nowhere to go. I would suggest you let me stay here, at least for tonight. My sister would be extremely annoyed if you just turned me away. Incidentally, I'd like to know your name."

He took a step back and opened the door wider, "It's Winston, madam, and perhaps you should step inside for a moment."

I hesitated then walked past him. I found myself in an area, two stories high, with a marble floor, partially covered by a beautiful multi-colored carpet. I heard the door close behind me and turned around, "So, my sister is here," I said.

"No, madam," he responded, pointing to a champagne leather sofa against one wall, "but if you will take a seat, I'll have Mrs. Harte come and speak with you."

I started to walk over to the sofa, then stopped, "Who's Mrs. Harte?" I called out, glancing back over my shoulder. But, Winston had already disappeared so I dropped my bag on the floor and sat down. It was then I noticed the curving staircase at the far end of the room and the portrait taking up a good portion of the wall above the first landing. Even from where I was sitting, I could see it was a life-like painting of an older man and I assumed it was Philip's father, John J. Barrington. I was about to get up so that I could get a better look when I heard footsteps and saw a woman enter through a door off to my right. She looked to be in her sixties, rather matronly, with short gray hair and dressed in a dark robe and, as she got closer, I could see she had the most extraordinary blue eyes. I stood up and was about to speak when she extended her hand and said, "Mrs. Reynolds, please excuse my state of dress but we weren't expecting any visitors. I was just about to turn in for the night. Mr. Harte suggested it would be better if I took care of you."

I frowned, "Mr. Harte?"

She smiled, "Allow me to introduce myself. I'm Rosemary Harte and Winston is my husband. We take care of the house."

I nodded, "I see. Well, as you are aware Mrs. Harte, I've come a long way to see my sister and I expected her to be here. Is that not the case?"

She sighed, "I'm afraid you've been misinformed but we can't let you go wandering off when you have nowhere to stay so, if you'll follow me, we can put you in one of the guest rooms."

She started to turn away but I grabbed her arm, "But where is my sister?"

She looked back at me and put a finger to her lips, "I think we should go upstairs and then we can talk."

I looked around me, not sure what I was looking for but I had an eerie feeling. I followed her up the long flight of stairs into a room that was at least three times the size of our bedroom at home. A four-poster bed was the dominating feature and it was covered in a wonderful damask quilt and, what looked like, a half dozen gigantic pillows. "This is an amazing room," I remarked.

"Oh, this is just one of three guest rooms. The others are just as impressive. Why don't you get comfortable while I go and get you something to eat and drink? You must be very tired after travelling all that way."

"That's very kind of you. I am a bit hungry and I'd love a cup of tea. I hope it won't be too much trouble."

"Not in the least, it will be my pleasure. I won't be too long and then we can have a little chat. By the way, the bathroom's right through that door."

I thanked her as she left the room and started to unpack my clothes. Fortunately I'd thrown in a thin cotton robe but then realized how little I'd actually brought with me. My next thought was, maybe it wouldn't matter because, if I couldn't track Portia down, I might be on a flight back to New York sooner than I thought. I really wanted to have a shower, especially after I saw the bathroom. It was all pale apricot marble, with gold faucets, and the tub could have accommodated three or four people. When I looked around the room again, I noticed there was a telephone on the bedside table and suddenly remembered I should have called Aaron to tell him I'd arrived safely. I was just trying to figure out what the time was back home when Mrs. Harte knocked on the door and came in holding a tray. I raced forward to take it from her but she shook her head and placed it on a small round table near the window. "I thought you might like my special grilled cheese sandwich. I always add tomatoes and mushrooms. Now you sit right down and eat up. I'll pour the tea in a minute once it's steeped enough."

I sat down and noticed there were two cups, "I hope this means you're going to join me. I need you to tell me what's going on."

She sat down opposite me and her expression changed. She suddenly seemed very serious. "Your sister's still in France, Mrs. Reynolds."

"But how can that be? I was preparing to go to France but when I told her I was coming she told me Philip was bringing her back to London."

"I'm afraid no arrangements were made for her to come here at this time. Mr. Harte and I are always apprised of Mr. and Mrs. Barrington's schedules so that we can get the house ready."

"I just don't understand this. I even spoke to Philip about coming here."

"Yes, Mr. Harte mentioned you believed Mr. Barrington was expecting you."

I shook my head, "Something isn't right here. I feel like my sister's being held hostage and I can't get to see her."

Rosemary Harte lowered her head, "I'm going to tell you something but it could mean my job and my husband's too."

My heart started to race, "What is it? You have to tell me."

I waited while she poured me a cup of tea, "Mr. Philip is not like his father. We worked for John J. Barrington for over twenty years and he was always kind and extremely generous. His son is neither of those things and he runs his companies and his households with an iron hand. I'm sorry to say, your sister has come to see that side of him and he controls her every move."

"What about her pregnancy? How did he react when she had the miscarriage?"

I heard her take in a breath, "He never wanted any children and I think he was relieved when she lost the baby." She hesitated for a moment and then continued, "I just hope he wasn't the cause of the miscarriage."

I practically dropped the cup I'd just picked up, "What are you saying?"

"I'm not saying anything but the same thing happened to the first Mrs. Barrington and, just before she was rushed to the hospital, I heard a terrible argument going on."

I gasped, "You're talking about Leanne Barrington, who drowned in a boating accident?"

I noticed her getting teary eyed when she replied, "Yes, the poor, dear soul."

"Do you think it was really an accident?"

She paused and slowly shook her head, "I can't believe I'm telling you this but I've always wondered what really happened to her."

"What was she like?"

"She was one of the nicest people I ever met and beautiful too, just like your sister. She always treated Winston and me like equals and it didn't go over too well with Mr. Barrington. I never heard her say an unkind word about anyone, not even Serena Barrington even though it was obvious there was no love lost between them."

"Mmmm.....I've met Serena. She's not exactly the warm and fuzzy type and I can't understand how Lotti puts up with her."

"I know exactly what you mean." She hesitated before continuing, "You know I shouldn't be telling you any of this. If Mr. Barrington knew we were having this conversation, he'd probably fire me on the spot."

I reached out and touched her hand, "Oh, dear. I didn't mean to put you in this position. Where is Philip, by the way?"

"He's in Amsterdam and not expected back in London until Sunday so he won't even know you've been here."

"Boy, he sure gets around. Anyway, I can't thank you enough for letting me stay for the night. I'm not sure where I would have gone. I've never been to London before, in fact I've done very little traveling."

"I know you lost your mother when you were very young and then your father passed away recently."

I nodded, "Yes, it was hard but Daddy married again and I really like my step-mother. After he died, she moved to Boston, to stay with her sister, and my husband and I sold the house I was brought up in and bought a smaller place a few miles away."

"Mrs. Barrington told me you have a daughter."

I smiled, "Yes, Vicky, she goes to pre-school. She'll probably be wondering where I am but I know her father will take good care of her. Do you have any children, Mrs. Harte?"

"No, I'm afraid Winston and I weren't able to have children. We thought about adopting once but then the years seemed to slip away and now here we are, just two old people with only each other. Anyway, my dear, I'd better let you get some rest and maybe in the morning you can decide what you want to do."

We both stood up and I took both of her hands in mine, "Thank you so much. Goodnight, Mrs. Harte."

"Goodnight, dear, and please call me Rosemary. Just come down in the morning when you're ready and I'll make you a nice English breakfast."

Chapter Thirty-Four

After Mrs. Harte left, I decided to have a bath after all and spent almost an hour luxuriating in the enormous tub, filled with a mountain of bubbles. By the time I'd dried off and slipped into my nightgown, it was well after midnight but early enough in New York for me to call Aaron. I wasn't surprised when he expressed his relief at hearing from me. He'd considered trying to contact me but things were a little tense when I left home so he decided to wait a little longer. When I told him Portia was not in London and I was considering going to France, he wasn't happy. He felt I was going off on a wild goose chase and shouldn't be interfering in my sister's life. We had already had this discussion before and I didn't want to get into it again. I tried to divert the conversation by asking about Vicky and discovered she'd asked about me but didn't seem too disturbed by my absence. This made me a little upset but I tried to look on the positive side, knowing Aaron was obviously taking good care of her. Just before I rang off, I promised him I'd still be home on Sunday, if not before, and would call him again the next day.

I had a restless night because I was still pondering what to do. If I decided to go to Menton, it would mean flying to Nice and continuing on from there. It would be a whole new experience traveling alone in a country where they didn't speak English, and I didn't think the French I learnt at school would help much. I finally fell into a deep sleep at about four o'clock and, when I woke up, it was just after eight. Dressing in the only other outfit suitable for traveling that I'd brought with me, I went downstairs and found myself back in the huge reception area. I had no idea where to go next and was looking around when Winston suddenly appeared, "Good morning, Mrs. Reynolds," he said. "If you would like to follow me, Mrs. Harte has your breakfast ready."

I felt like a special guest as I traipsed after him down a hallway and then into a room which literally took my breath away. It was obviously a small dining area but very informal. There was a round wicker table with four matching chairs, upholstered in an avocado green material and the carpet was the same shade of green interwoven with flowers the color of tea roses, but it was the windows that gave the room its unique effect. One whole wall was taken up with three, floor to ceiling, windows draped with a pure white, chiffon fabric, facing out onto a glorious garden, beautifully landscaped with sweeping lawns and bed upon bed of brilliantly colored flowers.

The table was laid for one, with delicate bone china and rather ornate silverware. I sat down beginning to feel very special and looked up at Mr. Harte, "Thank you. This is a lovely room and the view is wonderful."

He smiled, "It's Mrs. Barrington's favorite room in the whole house," he said.

Just then, Mrs. Harte appeared carrying what looked like enough food for two people. "Good morning," she said chuckling, "I hope you slept well and you're ready for your breakfast. I made you, what we call, a full English."

She put the tray down opposite me and then deposited a plate in front of me. I looked down and gasped when I saw what she expected me to eat, eggs, bacon, sausage, grilled tomatoes and mushrooms, plus a side of order of toast. "Oh, my goodness," I remarked, "this is so much. I'm not sure I can manage all that."

She shook her head as she poured some coffee into a china cup, "Now, now, you need to put a little meat on those bones. Breakfast should be the biggest meal of the day."

I picked up a piece of toast, "We don't have time to eat a big breakfast at home. We're too busy getting ready for work and getting Vicky off to school."

She paused, "Hmmmm. What about on weekends? You have to treat yourself once in a while. Anyway, I'll leave you to it and afterwards maybe you'll tell me what you've decided to do. Just ring that little bell when you've finished and I'll come back and get you."

I looked to see where she was pointing and noticed a tiny silver bell sitting on a small table near the window. "Thank you, I'd like to talk with you some more." At that, she picked up the tray, nodded to Mr. Harte who'd been standing silently just inside the door and then they were gone. I sat picking at my food and gazing out at the garden, feeling nervous about my decision to continue on to Menton, but I couldn't just turn around and go back home. When I'd eaten about as much as I could, I poured myself a second cup of coffee and decided I should try calling Portia before I even considered my next move. If I couldn't get hold of her, I wasn't sure what I would do.

I felt utterly stupid ringing the tiny bell and then standing there waiting for Mrs. Harte to show up but, moments later she was bustling through the door. She glanced at my plate, which was still half full, "Well, I can see you did your best," she said. "Why don't we go to the library where it's comfortable unless you're in a hurry to leave?"

"No, I'm not in a hurry but I think I should try and call my sister before I make any decision about what I'm going to do."

"Of course, there's a telephone in the library you can use. I'll just show you the way and you can make your call and I'll come back in a few minutes."

'Oh, that's very kind of you but it's a long distance call."

She waved her hand in the air, "Nonsense, you just go ahead."

I followed her down a hallway and, when she opened a door at the far end, I stepped through it into a room with two walls completely covered with shelving, filled with leather bound books. It was the kind of place I'd seen in a number of movies, all heavy tan leather furniture, inch thick carpeting and wood paneling. It didn't take me long to find the telephone. It was sitting on a side table and I picked it up with rather a shaky hand because I wasn't even sure what I was going to say. I really shouldn't have been concerned because, despite hanging on for what seemed like forever listening to the ring tone over and over, nobody answered, not even Colette. Now I was even more confused about what I should do. For a brief moment I considered calling Philip again but I was almost certain he would just brush me off. After a moment or two, I decided just to wait for Mrs. Harte to come back and see if she had any suggestions.

I took a walk around and noticed a number of photographs on a bureau at the far end of the room. There was one of Philip's father with a woman, who I presumed to be his mother, leaning against a fence in a wooded area and another of Serena mounted on a horse, looking just as masculine as ever. The other photographs were of Philip casually dressed, all in white, standing on the deck of a yacht and another of Max and Buddy, Philips bull-terriers. I'm not sure why their names stuck in my head but I'd always been a softie when it came to animals and it made me think of Molly and how much I missed her. I was wondering why there wasn't a photo of Portia when I heard the door open and Mrs. Harte entered the room. "Did you manage to get hold of your sister?" she asked.

I shook my head, "No, nobody's answering the phone and I decided not to leave a message until I figured out what to do next. Do you think she's still in France?"

"I would think so, but I can't be sure. Why don't you try calling her again later?"

I paused for a moment, "I could do that but then, if she is there, it will probably be too late for me to get a flight out. If only I could be sure she's all right, but my instinct tells me something's wrong."

Mrs. Harte walked over and laid a hand on my arm, "Try again later, dear, and if it's late you can always stay here again and leave in the morning."

I put my hand over hers, "I couldn't possibly impose on you like that; you've already been so kind."

"Nonsense, and while you're here I suggest you do a little sightseeing."

I contemplated the idea for a moment and sighed, "I'd love to do that. I've always dreamed of seeing London but my heart just wouldn't be in it. Maybe one day I'll come back with my husband and Vicky."

"I understand but you might get a little bored rattling around in this old house all day. Why don't you take a walk; I think you'll be surprised. We're close to Green Park and the Mall which leads right to Buckingham Palace. I can find you a map and mark it so that you won't get lost."

I suddenly felt a glimmer of excitement, "Really, we're close to the palace?"

"Yes, and it's a beautiful day; just perfect for walking, as long as you have some decent shoes."

"I have my sneakers, they're really comfortable. Thank you so much for your suggestion. Maybe it will take my mind off Portia for a little while."

I went back upstairs to get my jacket while Mrs. Harte went looking for a map, then I went back to the library to try calling Portia once more but, again, there was no answer. When I finally walked out of the house, map in hand, and strict instructions to telephone if I got lost, I began to walk past the row of houses which all looked identical and were obviously well maintained. When I turned a corner, I could see the park ahead of me and I was looking forward to spending some time in the open air. It really was a beautiful day with not a cloud in the sky and only a slight breeze and, as I got closer to the Mall, for the first time since I left New York, I felt calm. I continued my walk up the Mall towards the Victoria Memorial and, just a few steps further on, there was Buckingham Palace. There were a lot of people milling around the front gates and many had cameras around their necks. I wanted to get a picture of myself with one of the guards and asked an elderly couple if they could take a shot with my cell phone. That done, we chatted for a while and I discovered they were from Philadelphia and traveling on to Barcelona after spending a week in London. When they eventually left me still standing at the gates, I felt a little sad; I was desperately missing Aaron. That's when I decided to forward the photo to him and text him a message to tell him where I was. I thought he'd be surprised to see me outside the palace.

The elderly couple had mentioned I was in half-an-hour walking distance from Westminster Abbey and then just another few steps to Big Ben, and I couldn't resist. I wasn't disappointed; the atmosphere in the Abbey was so peaceful and I was amazed at the number of famous people buried there like Charles Dickens, Rudyard Kipling and several kings and queens. After an hour, I was feeling thirsty so I visited the Abbey café, had a cup of coffee, then decided to continue on to Big Ben. Again there were a lot of tourists and several of them were strolling along the walkway by the River Thames. I was hoping to see Tower Bridge but it wasn't visible from where I was standing and a little too far for me to walk to, considering how long I'd been on my feet.

I decided to take a taxi back to Charles Street and, as we approached the house, I could see Mrs. Harte standing on the front steps. She waved to me frantically as we pulled up and then dashed forward to open the door, "Oh, I'm so glad you're back," she said, sounding flustered, "I should have taken your phone number and I would have rung you."

I paid the driver and stepped out of the cab, "Has something happened? What is it?" I asked, suddenly feeling anxious.

She raced up the steps with me behind her. "Mr. Barrington's on his way here. He's going to be arriving at the

City Airport in less than an hour and it's only a short distance from here"

I tried keeping up with her as she continued through the front door and then shut it with a bang. "Is that Heathrow?" I asked.

She shook her head, "No, it's for private jets. I was so surprised when I heard his voice. He had a change of plans and wanted Winston to pick him up. He's already left for the airport in case they land early. Mr. Barrington doesn't like to be kept waiting."

"I guess I should leave right away," I said. "I don't want to get you in trouble."

"I think that would be best, dear. I'm not too concerned about him being furious with me, after all there isn't much sense in him firing us now. Winston and I will be retiring at the beginning of next year."

"Oh, I didn't realize you were close to retirement age."

"That's very sweet of you," she responded chuckling, "but we're both in our seventies and it's time to stop and smell the roses. Anyway, if you don't mind, I suggest you gather up your things and find somewhere to stay for tonight and then decide what you want to do. I know a nice bed and breakfast place on White Horse Street, just a short way away. You won't find anything less expensive in this area and I wouldn't suggest you try finding anywhere else, you could end up in a seedy part of London."

I frowned, "I can't imagine any seedy places, everything I've seen looks so wonderful but thank you again for the tip. I'll go and grab my things right now and get out of your hair before Philip gets here. I could stay and confront him but I know it won't do any good and, if he's really angry, I don't want him taking it out on Portia."

After I left the house, I walked to the address on White Horse Street. Fortunately I hadn't much luggage with me, otherwise I would have had to take another taxi and I was getting a little concerned about how much money I was spending. I was sorry I missed saying goodbye to Winston but

Mrs. Harte gave me a big hug and made me promise to keep in touch. She also promised to telephone me right away if she found out where Portia was.

Once I was settled in my room at the small hotel, I decided to take a nap because I was exhausted from all the walking and the anxiety from worrying about my sister. I slept for just over an hour and woke up feeling ravenous. I also felt I needed a good soak and spent the next half-hour luxuriating in a bubble bath. By the time I'd dried myself off and was dressed again, it was close to five o'clock and I wanted to find a place to eat before it started getting dark. The owners of the hotel were very helpful and directed me to the Spaghetti House on Duke Street, because it was more of a family restaurant and inexpensive. Once again, it was only a short walk and, when I entered the restaurant, it felt almost like I was back in New York. The food was typically Italian, all kinds of pasta and several different kinds of pizza. I ended up sitting at a table near a family of three and ordered a glass of Merlot, a Caesar salad and one of their most popular dishes, Spaghetti Bolognese. While I was sipping on the wine and waiting for my food to be served, I studied the family at the next table. The man was talking softly to the little girl, who appeared to be about four-years-old, while the woman gazed at them with a loving smile on her face. At that moment, I missed Aaron and Vicky so much, I considered flying home to New York as soon as I could get a flight. Later, after I'd eaten, I knew I couldn't leave without finding out what had happened to Portia. For the second time, I thought about confronting Philip but I still wasn't sure if it would have repercussions and my sister would suffer. I eventually decided to go back to the hotel and phone Aaron to tell him I was going to France in the morning.

Once back in my room, I sat down on the bed and was just about to call home when I felt my phone vibrate. It startled me for a moment but I guessed it must be Aaron beating me to it. It turned out, I was wrong. I didn't recognize the number but I answered it anyway and was surprised when I realized it was Mrs. Harte. "Mrs. Reynolds," she said, "this is Rosemary Harte.

I'm glad I caught you, I was afraid you may have gone out to dinner"

"I was out; in fact I just this minute got back. Have you got any news about Portia?"

"Yes, I casually asked if Mrs. Barrington would be coming back to London from France and I was informed that she was staying with his sister in Florida."

"Oh, my god," I remarked, "what next? I get the feeling he's lying and I really need to find out the truth."

"Why don't you call Serena and see if she's there. I can get her number for you if you don't have it."

"I do have the number but I think I'll try calling Portia again first. If she's all right, I'll just go on back home but if she doesn't answer and I don't get a satisfactory answer from Serena, I'll get a flight out to Florida in the morning."

"I'm so sorry you have to go through all this. I know it must be terribly worrying."

"Yes, it is worrying and I won't rest until I speak to Portia directly and she convinces me I have nothing to worry about."

"Well, dear, I hope everything turns out well. I'll give you my husband's cell phone number so that, if you ever come back to London, you'll be able to get in touch, even though we may not be at the house anymore."

"I would like that. Thank you so much for everything you've done for me."

"It was my pleasure. Bye bye, dear."

"Goodbye, Mrs. Harte," I whispered back, beginning to feel a little teary eyed.

Chapter Thirty-Five

With some trepidation, I telephoned Aaron to tell him I was going to the airport first thing in the morning, to change my tickets. I didn't think he would be very happy and so I tried to ease into it gently. I asked how well he was coping without me and, of course, we talked about Vicky. I then told him about the places I'd seen in London and when I confessed that I really missed him, he said he was hoping I'd given up on chasing my sister all over the globe and would be on the next flight home. "I expect to arrive back in New York tomorrow," I responded, "but it will only be a stopover because I'm getting a connecting flight to West Palm."

There was a moment of silence before I heard him sigh in desperation, "Why don't you just take a direct flight, although I'm sure you've already looked into that? You're going to be a seasoned traveler by the time you're through."

"Actually it's more expensive to go direct and you really don't have to be sarcastic."

"What else do you expect, Sam? First you're off to London, then you're going to some god-forsaken place in the south of France, and now you're off to Florida. Are you sure Portia's even there? Have you tried to get in touch with her?"

"Yes, of course, but she isn't answering her phone."

"I assume you've called Serena or that Lotti person?"

"No, I haven't because I know I'll just get the run around. I have to do this, Aaron. I have to make sure Portia's all right."

"I must admit, I'm getting a little tired of this. You have absolutely no evidence there's a single thing to be concerned about. This intuition of yours is costing us a great deal of money."

"I'm sorry you feel that way but I'm sure Daddy wouldn't mind me spending some of the money he left me to look for my sister."

Again there was a moment of silence and then, in a very low voice, Aaron answered, "That was a bit of a low blow, even for you. Anyway, it must be getting late there, so I think I'll say goodnight. Call me when you get wherever you end up."

I started to speak but realized he had ended the call. For a brief second, I was annoyed and then, I was terribly sad. Aaron and I rarely argued. Normally he had the patience of a saint and there were times when I know I really backed him up against a wall, but he never raised his voice and we never, ever, went to bed angry. I couldn't blame him for feeling the way he did. He was right, I didn't have any logical explanation for being concerned about Portia but, I would never forgive myself if she was in some kind of trouble and I didn't try to help her. I thought about calling him back but decided to let things cool down for a while. In the meantime, I placed a call to Portia, hoping and praying she'd answer, but no luck. By the time I'd changed into my nightgown and crawled into bed, even though it wasn't really that late, I'd made up my mind. I was definitely going to be on a flight back to the States the next day, come hell or high water.

The next morning, I was at Heathrow early and managed to get a seat on a United Airlines flight to Newark and a connecting flight to West Palm. All in all, it would take about eleven hours and, because of the time difference, it would be around dinner time when I finally reached my destination. I had always had trouble sleeping while traveling long distances, whether by plane, car, or train so I purchased a couple of magazines and a John Grisham paperback and hoped there would be a decent movie showing to keep me occupied. I was fortunate enough to get an aisle seat and, thankfully, the person seated next to me happened to be an elderly gentleman who slept most of the way and only spoke to me occasionally. When we arrived in Newark, I had only forty minutes to spare before boarding the plane to West Palm but this time, I wasn't so lucky. My seat-mate was a middle-aged woman who insisted on telling me her life story and, for just a shade over two hours, I was forced to listen to her chattering away. I was relieved when we finally landed and I was on my way by taxi to the address on Winding Bay Lane but, it didn't take long before I realized I hadn't done my homework. I had no idea the house was so far from the airport and it took over thirty minutes to get there and cost a lot more than I'd anticipated. When we finally turned onto Winding Bay Lane, I was awestruck by the magnificent homes and, when the taxi stopped outside Serena's house, I stepped out onto the sidewalk and just stood there for a moment, taking it all in. Surrounded by palm trees, the size of the house alone was enough to take one's breath away and I loved the way it appeared to incorporate two different styles, with a Spanish red tile roof and soaring columns at the entryway. It was so imposing that I felt nervous as I approached the front gate, which led to a set of double doors inset with glass panels. It was extremely hot, without a breath of wind, and so quiet that the closer I got, the more anxious I became. I finally got up enough courage to ring the doorbell and the silence was immediately broken by the sound of dogs barking. I suddenly remembered Philip's two bull terriers lived with Serena and, although I usually had no fear of dogs, for some reason, my heart began to race. Suddenly the door was opened by a young woman with dark skin, wearing a formal black dress. When she spoke, she had an accent and I assumed she was Cuban as I was aware there were thousands of Cubans in Miami, and the surrounding area. She didn't get the chance to ask me who I was before the two dogs bounded through the door and began running around me. I realized they were just playing and bent down to pat one of them on the head, "Are you Max, or Buddy?" I asked.

The young woman grabbed one dog by the collar and pushed him back inside the house, then she reached for the other one but he tried to escape from her grip, "Max, stop this," she said, "inside right now." At the sound of her voice he settled down and she was easily able to push him inside, "You stay now," she said motioning for both dogs to sit just inside the door, and then she turned back to me. "I'm sorry miss, but they won't hurt you. How can I help you?"

"I'm Samantha Reynolds," I replied, "Portia Barrington's sister. I was hoping to see her."

She looked puzzled for a moment, "Mrs. Barrington's not here," she replied, "was she expecting you?"

I decided to lie, "Yes, I've just flown all the way from England to visit her."

She frowned, "I'm so sorry but she hasn't been here for a long time. When did you last speak to her?"

I ignored her question, "Please ask Serena to come to the door, maybe she knows where my sister is."

She shook her head, "Miss Serena's not here either."

I was getting more and more frustrated, "What about Lotti, is she in?"

She shook her head again, "Both Miss Serena and Miss Lotti are in New York at Mr. Philip's and I don't expect them back for another week. I don't think your sister is with them."

I could feel the tears starting to well up, "Could I possibly come inside for a moment to call a taxi, I need to go back to the airport."

She hesitated and then stepped aside to let me into the main hallway while the two dogs ran ahead of me. "You can use the telephone on the table there," she said, "I can get you the number for the taxi if you will just wait here."

I stood waiting in the center of the hallway, which was more like an atrium with a glass ceiling and towering plants everywhere, with the dogs sitting at my feet. I looked down at them and patted their heads but I was too distraught to give them any more attention. I knew I had no alternative but to go back to New York.

While I waited for the taxi, I learned the young woman's name was Benita and she came from Santa Clara. Her family had fled Cuba when the second wave of refugees had landed in Miami in the early sixties. She had worked for Serena for the last three years as a personal assistant and looked after the dogs when they were away. She couldn't remember the last time she'd seen Portia but she knew it was several months earlier and Philip hadn't been at the house recently. I didn't feel it was appropriate to push for more information especially as I was almost certain she really had no idea where Portia was. When the taxi arrived, I thanked her for her help and began my journey back to the airport with no idea whether I would even get a flight out that evening.

I managed to catch an America Airlines flight which departed just before seven o'clock and would arrive at La Guardia at nine-thirty. By the time we were about to land, I'd already made up my mind that, despite the hour, I was going directly to Central Park West to see if Portia was there. When a taxi finally deposited me outside the building, it was closer to ten-thirty and I didn't expect a favorable reception. As I opened the main door and stepped inside the magnificent lobby, the concierge looked up from his desk in surprise. "Yes, madam," he said, "may I assist you?"

I dropped my bag on the marble floor and sighed, "Yes, please tell Mrs. Barrington that I'm here to see her."

"May I give her your name?" he asked.

"Yes, it's Samantha Reynolds."

I walked away from the desk, while he called upstairs to announce my arrival, and was surprised when he called me over to tell me Miss Herczeg was coming down to meet with me and would I please take a seat. I waited impatiently for Lotti to appear and then I heard, what sounded like, elevator doors opening at the far end of the lobby and suddenly she was walking towards me. She looked exactly as I remembered her, a slight pretty woman with long fair hair, and beautifully dressed. As she got closer, I stood up and she held out her hand, "Samantha," she said smiling, "how lovely to see you. What are you doing in the city so late?"

I clasped her hand for a moment and then stepped back, "I'm looking for my sister; is she here?"

"Portia?" she answered shaking her head. "I think she's in London."

"I've just come from London and West Palm," I said, my voice starting to rise. "She's not in either place."

Lotti frowned, "I don't understand. Why haven't you just tried to contact her by telephone?"

"I have, over and over again but she doesn't answer. I'm getting desperate. Somebody must know where she is."

"Did you speak to Philip?"

"No and I don't want to. I don't trust him. I'd like to speak to Serena though, perhaps she knows something."

"I'm afraid Serena is asleep and I don't want to wake her. She has a bad case of the flu and needs all the rest she can get."

I was just about to make a sarcastic remark when something caught my eye. I suddenly recognized the necklace Lotti was wearing; it was the same one Portia had on when she first brought Philip to dinner at the house in Scarsdale. I took a step forward and reached for the antique gold locket, "Where did you get this?" I asked.

Lotti looked down, "It's lovely isn't it? Serena gave it to me."

"It's Portia's, I remember it. How did Serena get hold of it? What has she done with my sister," I demanded as I started to shake.

She grasped my arm and pulled me further away from the concierge's desk, "Sam, calm down. Nobody's done anything to Portia. Maybe this looks like the same necklace but it isn't, I assure you. There has to be dozens like it. Where did she get hers?"

I paused for a moment while I thought back, "I think Philp gave it to her."

She grinned, "Well, there you are then. Maybe Serena got mine through Philip too."

I breathed a big sigh, "Maybe you're right but where can Portia be?"

She shook her head, "I really don't know but I do think you should call Philip."

I bent down to pick up my bag, "I must go, I'm catching the bus back to New Rochelle tonight."

Lotti glanced at her watch, "It's getting awfully late. What time do you expect to be home?"

"I'm not sure but it really doesn't matter, I'm beyond tired at this point. It doesn't mean I've given up because I'm determined to find my sister. I'll give you my cell phone number so that you can call me if you find out anything."

After I scribbled my number on a scrap of paper, I walked out onto Central Park West and flagged down a cab to take me to the bus station. I had no idea what I was going to do the next day.

Chapter Thirty-Six

By the time I got to the bus station and waited almost an hour for the bus, I realized I should have stayed in the cab and taken it all the way home. It was just under thirty minutes from the station but it had taken me almost two hours, from the time I left Central Park West. I crept into the house, hoping not to wake Aaron, but I'd only just closed the front door when I heard him coming down the stairs, "Sam, is that you?" he called out.

"Yes," I answered, dropping my bag on the floor, "I'm sorry, I was trying to be quiet."

He came towards me and wrapped his arms around me, "It's okay, I'm just glad you're here safe and sound. I missed you."

I felt my body relax as I leaned against him, "I missed you too, honey. It's good to be home."

He took me by the shoulders and held me at arm's length so that he could see my face, "I hope this means you've stopped gallivanting all over the planet looking for your sister. Did you manage to contact her?"

I shook my head, "No, I'm no wiser now than when I left here and I'm exhausted, but I can't stop now, Aaron."

He dropped his arms and stepped back, "Maybe this isn't a good time to discuss this. I think you need to get some rest and then we can talk about it in the morning."

I nodded, "I think that's probably a good idea but first I need to look in on Vicky. How has she been?"

He smiled, "The perfect little angel, but she asked for you a lot. Just try not to wake her up because she'll never go back to sleep."

"Don't worry, I'll just peep in and then I'm coming to bed myself," I said, taking off my jacket.

Aaron grinned, "I can hardly wait," he said, rolling his eyes.

When I woke up the next morning, I realized it was Sunday and I was grateful I didn't have to think about going to work, or getting Vicky to school. I glanced at the clock and saw it was almost nine o'clock. I was surprised I'd slept so late and was just about to get up when Vicky crept into the room and jumped onto the bed. "Mommy, mommy," she cried out planting kisses all over my face.

I giggled, "Hi, honey, I missed you," I said, pulling her under the covers.

We snuggled down together and she tried to tell me what she'd been doing while I was away. Then Aaron came in and announced breakfast was ready and it was time for two lazybones to get up. It all seemed so normal but I knew it couldn't last.

After breakfast, Aaron decided we should spend the day doing fun stuff with Vicky, so we drove into the city and visited the Brooklyn Children's Museum and then spent some time at the Central Park zoo. It seemed obvious to me that Aaron was avoiding talking about Portia and, after dinner that evening, I was just about to bring up the subject when he remembered Beth had called on Saturday night and wanted me to call her back. "Was everything all right?" I asked.

He shrugged, "Seemed to be. We only talked for a couple of minutes because I was just putting Vicky to bed. I told her you were visiting a neighbor; I didn't want to get into what you were really up to. She mentioned something about meeting her for lunch and to get in touch as soon as possible."

"I guess I'd better phone her now. She must be coming to New York, although I'm not sure when I'll be able to meet her."

I hadn't spoken to Beth for three or four weeks and I always enjoyed catching up so, settling in my favorite chair in the family room, I punched in her number on my cell phone. It only rang twice and then I heard her familiar voice, "Hello, this is Beth."

"Hi," I answered "it's Sam. How are you?"

"Oh, Sam, I'm so glad you called. I thought we could get together for lunch in the next day or two."

I was a little surprised she didn't ask me where I'd been or how Vicky was. "Is everything okay, Beth?"

There was a pause and then she replied, "Yes, everything's fine. I'd just like us to get together, that's all."

Something told me there was something she wasn't telling me and I was curious, but I still didn't know how I could make it to lunch without taking more days off from my job. "What about dinner? When are you going to be in New York?" I asked, "If I can get Aaron to leave his office early and pick Vicky up, I can come into the city straight from work."

I heard her sigh, as though in relief, "I'll be there tomorrow; if you can make it then, it would be perfect. Why don't we meet at Tommy Bahama's on Fifth Avenue? What time do you think you could be there?"

I thought for a moment, "I think we'd better say between five and five-thirty because I have no idea what the traffic will be like in rush hour, but I still have to check with Aaron."

"Can you go and ask him now?"

It was obvious she was anxious to see me and I was more curious than ever, so I told her to hang on while I went to find Aaron. I thought he might give me a hard time, especially as he'd had to look after Vicky for the last few days, but he said it was fine and to go and enjoy myself. Sometimes I wondered how I got so lucky in the husband department.

At just after five the next day, I walked into the restaurant and noticed Beth sitting at one of the tables, right under one of the decorative palm trees. She looked right at home wearing a colorful top with a chunky beaded necklace and sipping on, what looked like, a rather exotic drink. When she saw me approaching, she got up and wrapped her arms around me, "Sam," she said, "I'm so glad you came and you made it in good time."

I kissed her on the cheek and pulled out my chair, "Yes, I got lucky, the traffic wasn't too bad but it was a busy day at the clinic and I could use a drink. What's that you're sipping on?"

"This? Oh, it's a Mai Tai. I like to imagine I'm actually in the Bahamas when I come here."

I chuckled, "I think I'll stick with some wine," and I motioned to a waiter, who was just passing by. After ordering a glass of Riesling, I was anxious to find out why Beth was so eager to see me. "I got the feeling you really needed to meet me. Is something wrong, Beth?" I asked.

"Why don't we take a look at the menu and place our order and then we can talk," she responded.

It felt like a donkey's age by the time the waiter came back with my wine and I'd placed my order. I was feeling so edgy, I hardly looked at the menu and ended up having what Beth was having, tiger shrimp pasta and a classic Caesar. Finally I was able to relax a little and took a deep breath before asking again, "Please, Beth, I need to know if anything's wrong. I hope you're not going to tell me you're sick."

She shook her head, "No, Sam, I wanted to talk to you about Portia."

I felt a sudden sense of alarm, "Portia? What about her?"

"You haven't heard from her, have you?"

"No, and I'm worried sick. I know Aaron didn't tell you where I was but I just came back from Florida last night. I went to Serena's to see if she was there and, before that, I was in London looking for her."

Beth's hand flew to her throat, "Oh, my god, I had no idea; you must have been frantic."

"I still am. I have to find her and if you know anything at all, you have to tell me."

"That's why I asked you to meet me here; I do know where Portia is."

The glass I was holding almost slipped out of my fingers, "You do? Where is she? Is she all right?"

"She's okay but she's had a difficult time."

"What do you mean? Where is she?"

She reached across the table to hold my hand, "Please try to stay calm, dear, and I'll tell you everything I know." I nodded and she continued, "Your sister is staying with Maggie and it's probably only a matter of time before Philip catches up with her." I opened my mouth to interrupt but she held up her hand to silence me. "Let me finish, Sam. Portia contacted me because she was too scared to get in touch with you. Philip has the resources to keep tabs on people and I'm sure he's well aware you've been looking for her. Her marriage has been a complete sham. I can't go into all the details, I'll let Portia do that, but she actually fears for her life. I don't know how you're going to manage it but she needs to talk to you. The only safe way to do that is to use a phone Philip can't connect to you. I wouldn't even call from your workplace, if I were you. I know it all sounds a bit paranoid but, according to Portia, Philip has so much money he can buy anyone off and that includes the people you work with. Please don't tell anyone there anything about this, Sam."

I know I'd been holding my breath and finally felt I was able to let it out, "What if someone followed you here?" I asked, looking around me.

"I don't think he knows I'm involved and, in any case, they'd have trouble following me," Beth replied chuckling, "unless they've been traipsing after me in Sack's and Bloomingdale's all day."

"I don't understand," I said, "what happened to make her so fearful that she's gone into hiding. Can't you tell me anything?"

"All I can say is, there's been both mental and physical abuse and there's an issue with infidelity."

"Oh, my god, what if I just go and see her? I could get a flight out late tonight."

"No, you can't do that; Philip may have people watching you."

"Not if I'm really careful. Portia's managed to elude him up until now. He has no idea where Maggie lives and he doesn't even know her last name. Please, Beth, support me in this and let Portia know I'm coming."

At that moment our waiter appeared back at the table with our meals and, after he was satisfied we had everything we needed, we continued to talk while I picked at my food. Suddenly, I'd lost my appetite and, less than an hour later, I was on my way back home. Now I had to deal with Aaron.

Chapter Thirty-Seven

When I walked through the front door at seven o'clock, I heard footsteps on the upstairs landing, "Is that you, Sam?" Aaron called out.

"Yes," I answered, "is Vicky in bed already?"

He came to the top of the stairs, "Just tucking her in. You're just in time to say goodnight."

I took off my jacket, threw it on a small bench in the hallway, and went up to Vicky's room. Aaron was gathering up her clothes to take down to the laundry room when I got there. "I can do that, honey," I said.

"It's okay, I've got them," he replied and then looked at his watch. "I didn't expect you home this early. How was dinner?"

"I'll tell you all about it when I come downstairs," I answered, rubbing his shoulder lightly as I walked over to the bed. Vicky looked up at me with a big smile on her face and I bent down to kiss her on the top of her head. "How's my sweet girl, have you been good for Daddy?"

She nodded, "Yes, Mommy. Daddy let me watch Bugs Bunny and we had ice cream with camels."

I laughed, "I think you mean caramels."

"Uh huh, that's what I said."

"Okay, well I think you'd better say nighty night because you have to get up for school again in the morning."

"All right, Mommy, luv you."

I kissed her again, on the cheek, "I love you too, sweetie. Go to sleep now and sweet dreams."

After I made my way downstairs, I found Aaron in the kitchen pouring coffee into a mug. "Would you like some?" he asked.

"Yes, I'd love some," I answered, "and then I need you to sit down; I have something to tell you."

"I gather this is about Beth," he remarked as he poured coffee into another mug and placed it in front of me.

"Sit down." I said tapping the table, "this is really important."

He frowned and lowered himself onto a chair, "What is it, Sam?"

I proceeded to tell him everything Beth had told me and he sat quietly listening to every word. It was only when I told him I'd decided to go and see Portia that he reacted. "I hope you're not serious. Why don't you just call her like Beth suggested."

I shook my head, "No, I have to see her for myself and I'm thinking of trying to get an overnight flight."

He looked dumbfounded, "Now you're being ridiculous. I think I've been pretty patient so far but this is asking a little too much. I know she's your sister and you're worried about her but you have a family here. You just got home, from heaven only knows where, and now you want to take off again. I may be able to put up with your absence, but your daughter misses you and you're not being fair to her. I think it's time you made up your mind where your priorities are."

"Have you quite finished," I said, my voice rising an octave. "I'm not going away forever and Vicky always has you to look after her. Who has Portia got? I have to go, Aaron, I have to make sure she's all right and hopefully I can persuade her to come home with me."

Aaron shook his head in frustration, "This makes no sense but then who am I to voice an opinion."

"Please don't be angry, honey," I pleaded, reaching across the table for his hand.

"I'm not angry, Sam, I'm worried about what you're getting yourself into."

"Then I can leave tonight and you'll look after things while I'm gone?"

"No, you need to think this through. If Philip is watching your every move in order to track Portia down, you can't just drive off to the airport tonight and hope to catch a flight out. I suggest you wait until morning and, meanwhile, we'll figure out how to get you out of New York without anyone seeing you."

I hesitated for a moment and then nodded, "Okay that sounds like a good idea but first I need to find Maggie's address. I'll make sure I have it and then let's go and sit in the family room and see what we can come up with."

The next morning at seven-thirty, I was in the back seat of Aaron's car and hunkered down so that nobody could see me. Vicky was beside me strapped into her car seat, obviously thinking whatever game I was playing, it was great fun. "Are you all right back there?" Aaron asked as he backed out of the driveway.

"Fine," I answered, even though I was hardly comfortable in the small space I was crammed into.

We dropped Vicky off at school and then proceeded on into the city, to Aaron's place of work on West Street. The plan was for him to go into his office, stay for thirty minutes, and then drive me to Newark Airport in New Jersey. In the meantime, I was to remain in the car and pray that nobody discovered me. Those thirty minutes felt like a lifetime and every time I heard a car pull into a space nearby, I held my breath. Finally Aaron showed up, quickly slid into the driver's seat, and drove out onto the street. "Still okay?" he called out.

"Yes, but I thought you'd never come back. I was beginning to get cramps in my legs."

He glanced back over his shoulder, "Another ten minutes or so and I'll pull over, then you can come and sit in the front."

"Are you sure it's safe?"

He chuckled, "I'm beginning to feel like we're a couple of fugitives on the run."

"Not funny," I remarked.

After Aaron dropped me off at Newark Airport, which we assumed would be a much less obvious departure point than La Guardia, I hurried inside to the American Airlines counter to book a flight to Manchester, only to discover that the next flight out was at seven-thirty that evening. They suggested I check with United so I raced over to the United counter and found that their next flight left at the same time. I hesitated, not sure what to do. It looked like I had no choice but to wait almost ten hours before I could leave Newark, but first I had to make sure I could get a ticket. Luckily, the plane was only three quarters full and I managed to get an aisle seat. I knew it was going to be a very long day, followed by a seven hour flight, and I was almost tempted to call Aaron and ask him to come and get me and take me home, but my concern for Portia was more important than any inconvenience I was about to put up with.

I arrived in Manchester at seven-thirty the next morning which, to me, was about six hours earlier and I was bone tired. I then took a taxi to Victoria station and waited for the train taking me to my final destination, just thirty minutes away. At the station, I picked up a map of the area and a brochure which told me that Hebden Bridge was nestled in a steep valley. There was so little flat land; some houses were built with the upper stories facing uphill while the lower stories faced downhill. Looking out of the window, I was fascinated by the landscape and I was getting excited. I was only minutes away from seeing my sister.

When the train pulled into the station, I quickly found a taxi that would take me to Bankfoot terrace, just a short distance away, but much too far to walk. Before I knew it, we were pulling up outside a stone cottage that looked like something out of a Dickens novel. I stepped out onto the cobblestone road and paused, unable to believe I had actually arrived then, I opened the gate and walked the few steps up to the front door, which was painted bright blue, and knocked. When I heard footsteps and the barking of a dog, my heart began to pound in my chest and, suddenly, the door opened and there was Maggie, my dear, sweet, Maggie. She looked exactly as I remembered her and not a day older. "Oh, my lord," she cried out, "you finally made it," and she threw her arms around me and started to cry.

I hugged her back and didn't want to let go. With tears running down my face, I managed to say, "Maggie, I can't believe I'm here. Did Beth phone you to tell you I was coming?"

She stepped back and took both of my hands in hers, "Yes, she did but she didn't know when you'd get here."

Just then I felt something brush against my leg and looked down to see a very shaggy, black and tan dog. "Who's this?" I asked.

Maggie smiled, "That's Jake; he likes a lot of attention."

I bent down to pat his head, "What kind of dog is he?"

"He's a Lakeland terrier. He was my sister's and I inherited him when she died. I never regretted it for a moment. He's been a great companion." She hesitated for a moment while I stood up, then picked my bag up from the floor where I'd dropped it, "Speaking of sisters, come on in. Portia's in the garden and she'll be so excited when she sees you."

I followed her into the hallway and then grabbed her arm, "How is she?" I asked.

Maggie sighed, "I think she's going to be fine but I'm going to let her tell you what's happened. She's been through a rough time."

I thought we were going straight out to the garden but Maggie led me up a staircase into a small bedroom with two single beds, an armoire and matching dresser. The hardwood floor was partially covered by a dark green rug, while the comforters and drapes were a paisley pattern, in colors of green and deep red. I stepped over to the window and looked

out over a field and a wooded hillside. "This is lovely," I
remarked turning back towards Maggie.

"Well, I hope you don't mind sharing a room with Portia
while you're here. I'm afraid this old cottage only has two
bedrooms."

"It's perfect and it will give us a chance to really catch up,"
I answered.

Maggie nodded, "You can put your things away later but
if you want to wash up before we go back downstairs, the
bathroom's right next door."

I shook my head, "No, I want to see Portia now. Do you
think she's still in the garden?"

Maggie started to leave the room and I followed her, "Oh,
I'm sure she is. She seems to be obsessed with planting every
kind of flower you can imagine. I think it takes her mind off
things."

I continued down the stairs behind her and then
continued along a short hallway to a door, which opened out
onto a stone courtyard with a small seating area. I could see
a grassy expanse and, beyond it, a single towering tree and a
high fence but no sign of Portia. Jake was a few steps ahead
of me and kept looking back, as though he was willing me
to keep going, then he ran off out of sight and I heard him
begin to bark. A moment later I heard Portia's voice, "What
is it, boy?" she called out. "Come here." I stopped dead in my
tracks, I had no idea why but I couldn't seem to move. Then
I heard her voice again, "Okay, okay, what's going on? Was
somebody at the door?"

I waited, sensing Maggie standing quietly behind me
then, suddenly, Portia appeared a few feet away and I gasped
out loud. The lovely blonde hair that used to tumble over
her shoulders was gone. Now her hair was styled in a blunt
cut, level with her chin, and a deep auburn color. Even more
startling, she had lost a lot of weight, to the point where she
looked almost anorexic. She was holding a trowel in one hand
and dropped it onto the grass then, a moment later, she was
screaming my name, "Sam, oh my god, Sam." Racing towards

me, she threw herself at me and practically knocked me over and we both started howling like a couple of babies.

Maggie stood and watched, while we continued to hold onto each other without speaking then, after a few moments, she placed a hand on each of our shoulders and said, "Come on inside to the living room and I'll make you both some coffee."

Chapter Thirty-Eight

Portia took my hand and led me down the hallway into a room with heavy chintz covered furniture and, in the center, a raised stone fireplace and an archway that opened up to the kitchen. I only had a moment to take it all in because Portia was dragging me down beside her onto a sofa and slowly shaking her head, "I can't believe you're really here. Beth told us you were coming but we didn't know when. How did you get here? Are you sure nobody followed you?"

I squeezed her hand, "I'm absolutely sure. I hid in the back of Aaron's car when he went to his office and then I stayed hidden until he came back out later and drove me to Newark. I took a flight from there so I can't imagine anyone following me but, by now, they probably know I'm not around and are looking for me. I didn't even tell the clinic where I work, I wouldn't be in, so Aaron was going to call them and tell them I was sick. Incidentally, I have to let him know I got here safely. I guess I should phone Beth and she can pass a message along."

Portia glanced at her watch, "Yes, I think it would be a good idea but it's only about three in the morning in Boston, so you should wait a while."

While she was talking, I was staring at her, "Now are you going to tell me what this is all about? What happened to your hair and how come you've lost so much weight? I've been worried sick about you."

She sighed, "I hardy know where to begin, Sam, but it didn't take me long to figure out you were right about Philip. He isn't the man he appears to be. Do you remember when I went to Cabo San Lucas and he didn't show up until the next day?"

"Yes, I remember you telling me you were taken to the guest bedroom the first night and I joked about him being gay."

"That's right, and then the next night, after he moved me into the master suite, he didn't come to bed at all."

"But you told me, once you'd slept with him, it was worth waiting for."

"What else was I going to say? I thought it would get better. I'd only ever been with Hayden and he hadn't been intimate with anyone before me, so neither one of us was exactly experienced."

"I see. So I gather it didn't get any better. Why did you marry him?"

"I've asked myself that question a million times. I think I was caught up in the lifestyle. I was traveling to places I never dreamed I would ever see, on a private plane no less. I was able to shop in the best stores and Philip was generous. He wanted to show me off to the world because it made him feel important but he never really loved me, Sam."

I slipped my arm around her shoulders, "I'm so sorry, Portia. When did you realize what you'd gotten yourself into?"

Just then, Maggie came in with a tray and set it on the table in front of us. "Here's your coffee," she said, "and a few cookies in case you're hungry. I'm just going to take Jake for a walk and I may pop into Annie's, so I'll be a while."

After she left, I asked, "Does Maggie know everything that happened?"

"Yes, and she's been a godsend. I don't know what I would have done if I hadn't had this place to come to."

"So what happened?"

She gave a deep sigh, "I knew things weren't right when he began leaving me alone for days at a time and then, when he did show up, he was cold and distant. The odd time when we were intimate, it was as though he was punishing me for something. I tried talking to him but he shut me out and I didn't know what to do or who to turn to. You were so far away and I was either in London, or France, or some strange place where I didn't know anybody, except the housekeeper. We had never had a serious talk about having children. I just assumed he would welcome a family to carry on his legacy and, when I got pregnant, I was excited. I thought he would be too and I couldn't wait to tell him."

"I gather he wasn't too pleased."

"He was furious. He screamed at me that he didn't want any kids around and he blamed me for not taking precautions. I tried to explain it must have been an accident but he wouldn't listen and the angrier he got, the more fearful I became. We were in the bedroom and, when he got so enraged that I thought he was going to strike me, I ran out of the room. He caught up with me at the top of the stairs and I turned, just before he pushed me. I saw the look in his eyes; he was like a mad man, Sam. I don't remember much after that. I woke up in the hospital and I'd lost the baby."

I'd been holding my breath as I listened, "My god, Portia. Why didn't you go to the police?"

She actually chuckled, "You're kidding. First of all, I was too afraid and with all of Philip's money, I wouldn't have had a chance bringing any charges against him. He couldn't hide the fact I'd been pregnant, because someone at the hospital leaked the news and then he played the grieving husband. When he took me home, he actually told me he was sorry and I thought he'd had a change of heart but it didn't take long before I realized it was all an act. He told everyone I'd tripped and fallen down the stairs and how upset we both were about the loss of the baby. I'm surprised you didn't see the photo of him escorting me out of the hospital; it was in the New York Times and one of the British papers. He had his arm around me and managed to look distraught, meanwhile I was shaking inside. I was almost on the verge of exposing him, in front of the press but, like I said, I was too afraid."

"I don't think I could have kept silent, Portia." I said softly.

"I know, Sam, but that's you. You've always stood up for yourself and everyone else too."

"What happened next?"

"After a few days, he took me to Menton. He seemed to be really remorseful about what he'd done. He showered me with gifts and promised things would change but he made every excuse not to sleep with me. I decided to forgive him even though I wasn't sure he was being sincere and then Serena arrived and everything changed."

"Was Lotti with her?"

"No, and when I asked her where Lotti was, she said that one of the dogs was sick and she wanted to stay in West Palm to look after him."

"I guess that sounded reasonable."

"I thought so too then, soon after Serena arrived, Philip insisted I stay home while they went out to dinner. I protested because I was tired of sitting around the house but he wouldn't listen. He suggested that I needed to rest and Colette would take good care of me. After they left, I told Colette I wasn't hungry and went for a walk. I stood at the top of the hill, overlooking the ocean, thinking about how much my life had changed and how much I missed you and Aaron and Beth. I imagined we were sitting together having lunch in one of those little cafes on the Upper East Side and I couldn't wait to get back to New York. I came to realize, what I really wanted was to settle down in one place; I was sick of traveling back and forth and I wanted a family. The longer I stood there, the more trapped I felt but I didn't know what to do. When I returned to the villa, it was getting dark and Colette was just leaving so I poured myself a glass of Chardonnay, made a sandwich, and sat in the kitchen considering my next move. I knew I needed some time alone and decided I'd tell Philip I wanted to go back to the States the next day. The more I thought about it, the more determined I became but, instinctively, I knew he'd try and stop me. I went to bed early and read for a while but my mind kept wandering and, eventually, I drifted off to sleep. I must have only slept for a couple of hours because, when I woke up, it was just past midnight. I hadn't heard Philip and Serena come in. I assumed they'd already gone to bed and it was obvious he was avoiding me again. After about fifteen minutes, I decided to get up and make myself a glass of warm milk. You remember, Sam, how Daddy always gave us warm milk when we had trouble sleeping?"

I nodded, "Go on. I get the feeling you're getting to the interesting part."

She frowned, "You could say that. As I walked along the hallway, I heard giggling coming from the guest room where I knew Serena was staying. I immediately thought she'd picked up someone at the restaurant, or maybe at a bar they might have gone to after dinner. It wouldn't have surprised me because I never saw her being that affectionate with Lotti and I didn't trust her. Anyway, I figured it was none of my business and I continued on down the hall and then, suddenly, I heard a man's voice coming from the same room but it was no stranger, it was Philip. I was puzzled as to what was going on so I went to the door and tried to hear what they were saying but I couldn't make it out. Suddenly, I heard Philip begin to moan and I stood there in shock for a moment. Then I threw open the door, instinctively knowing what I would find. They were both naked; her head between his legs and he was gasping for breath. Serena must have heard me because, briefly, she lifted her head, turned towards the door, and grinned. I wanted to smack her ugly face but I felt sick to my stomach, so I just started running and kept on running until I was out of the house."

I couldn't believe what I was hearing. I knew there was something strange about Serena and I'd always had my doubts about Philip but this was the last thing I expected to hear. "Oh, my god, Portia, what did you do next?"

She shrugged and let out a deep breath, "I didn't get a chance to do anything. I was thinking of running to a neighbor's but, just as I was getting my second wind, Philip caught up with me. He'd thrown on a pair of jeans but was still naked from the waist up and, when I tried to run; he wrestled me to the ground and whispered in my ear, 'You're not going anywhere.' I began pummeling his chest and screaming that he was a disgusting pig and to get away from me but, he clapped his hand over my mouth and dragged me back to the house. I didn't have the strength to resist him and, as soon as we got inside, Serena appeared and helped him carry me into the living room and throw me on the couch. The next thing I remember is Serena coming towards me with something in her hand. I was terrified because I thought it was a knife but it must have been some kind of hypodermic needle because, I woke up in bed in my room, and it was almost noon. I felt really woozy but managed to get out of bed and stagger over to the door, only to find it was locked. I started banging and banging until, eventually, I heard the key turning and, a minute later, Philip was standing there with a menacing look on his face. I yelled at him to let me go and I wouldn't tell anyone but he backed me into the room, closed the door behind him and grabbed both of my wrists. He told me I was to get dressed and pack up my things because I would be leaving within the hour, then he walked out of the room and, once again, I was locked in. You can imagine, Sam, all the thoughts going through my head. It was hard to believe my husband was in an incestuous relationship with his own sister. I wanted to think they'd both been so drunk, they hadn't known what they were doing but I knew, I was just trying to block out the ugly truth and wondered how long it had been going on. Anyway, after about an hour, Philip came back and announced that Serena was waiting for me in the car and we'd be flying back to London early that afternoon. He suggested what I'd seen was a figment of my imagination and warned me, if I decided to think otherwise and opened my mouth, I should think again. He also suggested I continue our sham of a marriage and divorce wasn't an option. He had no intention of honoring the prenuptial agreement our demanding father had insisted upon."

At that, I just had to interrupt, "The cheeky bastard. How dare he even mention Daddy's name."

"That's what I thought but it gets worse. What he said next made my blood curdle."

I was on the edge of my seat by now, "What did he say?"

"He said he'd already taken care of one wife and the second time around wouldn't be a problem."

I gasped, "Oh no, I just knew deep down there was something fishy about the way his first wife drowned but, if he did have something to do with it, how did he manage to cover it up?"

Portia sighed, "First of all it was off the coast of France and the authorities don't seem as thorough when it involves a foreigner. On top of that, maybe there was money involved. I'm sure Philip could buy his way out of any situation."

"Not if I have anything to say about it."

Portia glanced at me with a wry look on her face, "I figured you'd say something like that."

"What I want to know is; how did you manage to get away?"

For the first time, Portia grinned, "Well, I thought I'd pretend to be scared to death and totally powerless. On the drive to Nice, I never said a single word to Serena and the only time she spoke, was to the goon sitting in the back seat with me. I'd never seen the man before but he didn't look too savory. I guess Philip hired him to make sure I didn't run off. All the time, I was planning how I was going to escape and, when we got to Nice and I discovered we were flying commercial and not on the private jet, I figured I'd have a better chance. We took a British Airways flight to Heathrow and sat three seats across with me parked next to the window. I don't know where they think I was going to go and you know how I hate being hemmed in. The one time I got up to use the restroom, Serena followed me down the aisle and waited outside for me. It was almost laughable; maybe she thought I was going to tell the flight attendant they'd kidnapped me."

I giggled, "I'm glad you still have a sense of humor about all this."

"Well, it's easy to joke about it now but at the time my mind was in turmoil. When we arrived at Heathrow, I knew I had to make a move before we got back to the house. The goon vanished when we went to retrieve our luggage and I figured I now had my best chance. I'd been through the terminal two or three times before and I knew the restroom had two entrances. Serena would have trouble following me with all the suitcases so I told her I really needed to go and, although she grumbled and told me to hurry up, she waited outside the main entrance. I didn't waste a moment worrying about leaving all my belongings behind, I just took off out of the other entrance. When I glanced back over my shoulder I could see her looking at her watch. After that, it was easy, I just started running out of the airport, jumped onto a shuttle that was just leaving, and got off at the Sheraton where I checked in under a false name."

I didn't want to interrupt but I was really curious, "I'm dying to know what name you dreamed up."

"Sabrina Davis; she was a character in a book I'd read but, I forgot I couldn't use my credit card and I didn't have any luggage so I was praying I had sufficient cash on me to pay for one night. Lucky for me, I had enough in my wallet and was shown up to my room without any problem. I stayed there for almost two hours and then left the hotel and took a shuttle back to the airport. I figured nobody would expect me to be there after all this time, and it was the closest place I could think of where I could pick up some toiletries and a few clothes in the airport shops. First though, I needed to take a chance and withdraw money from an ATM and I knew this was a risk but I had to take it. As soon as I finished shopping, I returned to the hotel and, realizing I hadn't eaten for quite a while, and it was close to seven o'clock, I ordered an omelet and a pot of coffee from room service. Oh, and while I was in Boots, that's like Walgreens in the States, I bought some hair dye and a pair of scissors. I reckoned they'd have a harder time finding me if I was a brunette or a redhead. I still hadn't figured out where I was going to go, although I knew I couldn't come running to you because I might have put the whole family in danger."

"You know we would have protected you. One way or another we would have worked it out."

Portia shook her head, "I couldn't take that risk; I had to go someplace Philip knew nothing about. It was while I was coloring my hair that I suddenly had a brainwave and remembered Maggie lived somewhere in Lancashire or Yorkshire but I couldn't recall her last name. I didn't want to telephone you because I was pretty paranoid and thought your phone might be tapped, so using the hotel landline rather than my cell phone, I called Beth in Boston. I told her exactly what had happened and asked her to contact you and suggest you have lunch, but not to say a word about our conversation until she saw you in person. She then gave me Maggie's number and, first thing in the morning, I used the hotel landline again to call her. I didn't want to go into detail on the phone, I just told her I was in London and wanted to come up for a visit, if it was convenient. She didn't hesitate; in fact she was overjoyed to hear from me and invited me to come here right away. After she gave me directions, I got dressed, gathered up the few things I'd purchased and then checked myself in the mirror for the umpteenth time. I had discarded the outfit I'd been wearing, along with a pair of heels, and left them in the hotel closet. I was pretty sure one of the maids would appreciate them. Instead, I wore a pair of blue jeans, a grey hooded sweater, sneakers, and a baseball cap which partially covered my new hairdo. I hardly recognized myself but, for some reason I suddenly felt free. It's hard to explain but it was almost as though I had been playing a role for so long and now I was myself again, even though I looked so different."

I nodded, "I think I can understand what you must have felt."

"When Maggie opened the door and saw me standing there, she was shocked. She didn't even recognize me for a moment and then, when I smiled at her, she just gathered me in her arms and started to cry."

"Sounds like when I arrived!"

"Well, it was to be expected; she hadn't seen either of us for so long. Anyway, she knew immediately, I wasn't here for a nice visit and, after I told her everything, she said I could stay for as long as I needed to. She's been wonderful, Sam, and she's bound and determined to fatten me up before she lets me go."

"Well you have lost a lot of weight. What happened?"

"After I lost the baby, I just didn't feel like eating. I was pretty depressed and Philip's attitude didn't help but now, I've got my appetite back and I feel so much better. I just don't know what I'm going to do from here on in. Maybe you can help me figure it out."

Chapter Thirty-Nine

It didn't take me long to decide I needed to spend more time with Portia. I thought it would be safe to call Aaron at his office and let him know what was going on, and to tell him I'd be staying at Maggie's for two or three days. He wasn't exactly pleased but he knew any attempt to change my mind was a lost cause. When I got off the phone, I was feeling guilty about Vicky, not that Aaron had implied I was neglecting her, but deep down I knew she really missed me.

Portia and I spent the next two days being sisters again. We talked about so many things, sometimes far into the night, as we shared a room in Maggie's house. Meanwhile, Maggie left us alone most of the time except when she was trying to stuff all kinds of food down our throats and, the one time, when the three of us spent an evening reminiscing about Daddy and our house in Scarsdale. It was such a comforting feeling being together and I almost wished I could go back in time and live it all over again.

I envied Maggie living in Hebden Bridge. Portia and I took several walks with Jake, trotting happily ahead of us. We would stroll along by the river, in one of the wooded valleys, or climb uphill to the moorland. It was such a peaceful place and one

I wanted Aaron and Vicky to experience one day. We decided to take lots of photographs so they would have some idea what the place was like. For my sister, it was so different from the life she'd been leading and she knew she could never go back. Now, all she wanted was a normal family life with a husband who worked from nine to five and a couple of children. When I commented, while it had its positive side, it wasn't always perfect; she remarked that she still envied me. Apparently, traveling by private jet, visiting exotic places and being waited on hand and foot wasn't exactly fulfilling, especially if your husband didn't want you to work. Without something constructive to do, everything seemed pretty pointless. She thought having the baby would give her life some purpose and when she lost it, she lost all hope too. My heart went out to her when she talked about the baby. I couldn't begin to imagine how hard it must have been for her. The more I thought about it, the angrier I got and I was bound and determined to make Philip pay for his actions.

After spending two full days together, I realized Portia was deadly afraid to come back to New York and she felt certain Philip would eventually trace her to Maggie's. She had very little money left and I wasn't able to help her because I was running short myself and neither one of us wanted to use our credit cards. I thought I might ask Aaron to wire some funds to me but even that seemed risky. Then Maggie came up with a solution that seemed a little drastic but Portia needed to lie low for a while, or maybe just vanish from sight altogether. We were relaxing after a wonderful dinner of Lancashire hotpot and an apple cobbler when I mentioned I really needed to go home and was planning to leave the next day. "I hate to take off like this," I said, reaching across the table and grasping Portia's hand, "but I need to get back to Vicky. If it wasn't for her, I would stay a lot longer. Once I get there, I'll figure out how to get you some money and then I've decided to go after Philip and demand to know where you are. I might even threaten him with calling the police. Maybe that will stop him from any idea he may have about harming you."

Portia nodded, "You may be right but in the meantime he might come after you, Sam, just to stop you interfering."

"I'm not scared of him; I'm more worried about him finding you." I was distracted because Maggie was shaking her head and we both looked across at her. "What is it, Maggie?" I asked.

"I think it would be best if you moved from here, Portia. If your husband is determined to find you, he has all the resources to do so and I don't think it will take him long to track down anyone you've ever been connected to. He'll probably remember I worked for your father and, although he may have only known me as Maggie, it wouldn't take a rocket scientist to figure it out. All he'd have to do is check with our old neighbors in Scarsdale."

I couldn't help chuckling, "Sounds like you've been watching too much TV, Maggie."

Portia wasn't quite as amused, "Are you worried about what he'd do if he found me here. Oh god, I never even thought of that; I could be putting you in danger."

"You needn't bother yourself about that," Maggie replied, "because I've come up with a plan. First of all money isn't a problem, I have a lot of savings and I can go to the bank in the morning and get you at least five hundred pounds to tide you over. Now I know I've never mentioned her before but I have a niece, Erin, who lives in Northern Ireland. I called her yesterday and she wants to help. You can rent a car to drive to Stranraer in Scotland and then take the ferry to Larne; that's where she lives. It's only about twenty-two miles from Belfast, so you won't be stuck in the middle of nowhere, like you are here." Portia and I were sitting with our mouths open but she just ignored us and kept on talking. "She's in her late thirties and lives alone and she'd love some company. I think you'd get along well with her, Portia."

"This is incredible," I remarked. "What a fabulous idea. When did you last see this niece?"

"Two years ago. I went for a visit and stayed for almost three weeks. It was a bit of a drive to Stranraer, over four hours, but the scenery was lovely and I had Jake with me so I wasn't lonely."

"So am I just supposed to show up on her doorstep?" Portia asked.

"Absolutely," Maggie replied. "I told her that as soon as you left here, I would be calling to tell her you were on your way."

I turned to Portia, "I think this is a perfect idea and maybe I could come with you. That way, I can fly home from Belfast so it would be hard to trace me."

"Would you really come with me?" Portia asked.

I nodded, "Of course and I'd like to meet Erin and make sure you're in good hands."

Maggie scowled, "I can assure you she will be, Missy."

I patted her arm, "Sorry, Maggie, I know any relative of yours must be the salt of the earth."

Portia giggled and then we all broke down laughing. For the time being, I felt less anxious. Portia would be safe and I would soon be going home. We all slept well that night and it wasn't just from the effect of the brandy, Maggie insisted she serve as a nightcap.

The next morning, Maggie went into town to withdraw cash from her account and arrange for a rental car, while Portia and I packed up our belongings and spent a few minutes playing catch with Jake in the garden. It was upsetting enough to know I probably wouldn't see him again but saying goodbye to Maggie was really difficult. Portia couldn't have chosen anyone more loyal, when she decided to make her way to Hebden Bridge and we would be forever grateful for her generosity. Before we left the house, Maggie insisted Portia handwrite a letter detailing the incident that precipitated her abduction from Menton, her escape to London, and how she arrived at Hebden Bridge. In addition, she was to indicate, the authorities were to be contacted if anything should happen to her and that her husband, Philip Barrington, was most likely involved. When she handed Maggie the letter, to be kept in a safe place, they hugged and promised to stay in touch. It was a tearful scene as we left the house and I assured Maggie, once

I got home, I would arrange to repay her the money she had given Portia.

Minutes later we climbed into a bright red Vauxhall and drove away from the house, with tears still streaming down our faces. We had a long drive ahead of us but Maggie had packed us a lunch including a thermos of coffee and a whole bag of her favorite Lancashire cookies. It was a beautiful October morning, as we drove a few miles west to Preston and then began our long journey north to Stranraer. Maggie was right, the scenery was lovely; the trees were beginning to show their fall colors and we dipped in and out of valleys surrounded by hills, greener than I had ever seen before. When we reached Lake District National Park, it was almost noon and we decided to stop and eat our lunch by the side of the road and take some pictures. It was hard to imagine, in such perfect surroundings, that we were running away like two fugitives and we actually laughed about it but, underneath, we were still anxious. We had no idea what lay ahead.

Chapter Forty

We reached Stranraer at about three, turned the rental car in, and made our way to the ferry port which was close to the town center. We just made it in time for the four o'clock departure and were soon sailing through Loch Ryan and out into the Irish Sea. The trip took two hours and we spent a lot of time hanging over the railings, watching the coast of Scotland disappearing behind us. At one point, it got a bit choppy and I was feeling a little nauseous until a sweet lady, who must have been all of ninety, suggested I go inside and lie down on one of the benches so that I wouldn't feel as much motion. It certainly helped but when Portia came to tell me we were only fifteen minutes from Larne, I couldn't wait to get there.

Once we arrived at the port in Larne, we took a taxi to the address Maggie had given us on Edward Avenue. We pulled up in front of a terrace house which matched all the other houses on the street. Each one had a low stone wall surrounding a small garden, all of which were showing remnants of flowers, noticeably affected by the cooler weather. As we opened the front gate and walked up the short driveway, we noticed a curtain being pulled aside at one of the downstairs windows and a shadowy hand waving at us. It was hard to make out who the person was but, a moment later, before we even had a chance to ring the bell, the front door flew open and a woman came rushing out and threw her arms around us. We were a little stunned but then she took a step back and in a thick Irish accent said, "I just spoke to Maggie again. She said you'd be here soon and here you are. Welcome to my home."

Maggie was so small that I didn't expect her niece to tower over me but she was at least six feet tall and very slim, with shoulder length blonde hair and cornflower blue eyes. She wasn't exactly pretty but there was something about her that was uniquely different and I was sure many people found her attractive. Portia held back a little but I placed one hand on Erin's arm, "Thank you so much for helping my sister; this is so kind of you."

"You must be Sam, and this must be Portia," she said with a smile turning to Portia and reaching a hand out to her. "Do come inside, you must be tired and I'm sure you'd like a cup of tea."

We followed her inside, dropped our bags in the hallway, and walked into a small living area at the front of the house with oversize furniture covered in chintz, a round coffee table, matching end tables in a dark wood, a thick deep red carpet, and a giant flat screen television on one wall. "This looks really cozy," I remarked.

"Yes, I spend a lot of my time in here; maybe too much. I live alone, except for Daisy, so I usually eat in here in the evening and watch TV."

"Who's Daisy?" I asked.

"Oh, she's my cat. She's around here somewhere; probably upstairs sleeping on my bed. I'll take you up later and show you your room. Maggie told me you'd be going back to America almost immediately, Sam, but you're welcome to stay as long as you like if you don't mind sharing a double bed with your sister."

I smiled, "It would be perfect; thank you, Erin. I'll probably make arrangements to leave tomorrow if I can get a flight out of Belfast."

Erin nodded, "Well, make yourselves comfortable and you're welcome to use the telephone. There's a directory on the shelf over there and while you're doing that I'll go and make the tea, or would you prefer coffee?"

"Tea would be fine," I answered looking at Portia, knowing she was dying for a cup of coffee.

After Erin left the room, she said, "She seems really nice but I didn't expect her to be so tall."

I grinned, "I know, who would have thought it? Sorry about the tea but I didn't want to put her out."

"It's okay, but I hope she offers us something to eat soon because I'm starving."

"Me too, but we can't be rude and ask for anything."

Portia shrugged, "Maybe we can casually mention that we haven't eaten and we'd like to take her out to dinner."

I was just about to reply when Erin came back into the room, "The tea is just steeping so it will be a few minutes. I thought you'd be hungry so I made a shepherd's pie earlier and I just have to stick it back in the oven for a few minutes. There's also some rhubarb pie I picked up at the bakery."

Portia glanced over at me and I could almost see her sigh with relief, "It sounds lovely. Actually, I am a bit hungry."

"Good, then I'll be back in a moment with your tea and we can eat in the kitchen in about fifteen minutes."

While Erin went back to get the tea, I picked up the directory and found the phone number for British Airways. When I made the call, I discovered there were no direct flights to New York and the best way to get home was on a flight to London that left at 8.40 a.m. then via American Airlines to JFK which would get me in at 3.35 p.m. I realized I still had to get to Belfast International and just couldn't face getting up at the crack of dawn the next day, so I decided to stay over a day and leave the following morning. Portia was thrilled to hear I would be spending one whole day with her because, I could tell, she wasn't exactly comfortable in her surroundings.

Maggie assured me, before we left Hebden Bridge, she would be in touch with Beth to tell her where we were going. I knew I had to call Aaron and let him know what my plans were so, figuring it was around noon in New York, I decided to call him at his office. He was obviously pleased to hear my voice but also concerned, "Sam, I'm glad you called. Beth told me you were in Ireland. Are you and Portia okay?"

"We're fine, honey. Portia's going to be staying with Maggie's cousin, Erin, and I'll be staying one more day and then flying into JFK via London and arriving mid-afternoon. I still have to book with American but I'll let you know the flight number. I don't know if Erin has a computer but if she does, I'll e-mail you at your office with the details."

"Okay that sounds good. How long does Portia intend to stay?"

"We're not sure yet. I have so much to tell you, Aaron, and I'm not sure where we go from here but that bastard isn't getting away with this."

"Oh, Sam, I wish you hadn't gotten so involved."

"Well, I am and when I get back I'm going to decide what to do next."

Aaron sighed, "Okay, I guess there's no point in trying to dissuade you. I'll pick you up at JFK."

"Wait a minute! How's Vicky, is she all right? Has she been asking about me?"

"Of course and she'll be happy to hear you'll be home soon. I promised her that, when you got back, we'd all go to the zoo again."

"Oh, she'd love that. I can't wait to see you both again. I feel like I've been on the move for so long."

"Well you have and maybe now you'll spend some time at home."

There was no way I could assure him I wouldn't take off again so I decided to cut the conversation short. "Oh, I have to go, honey. Erin made us some tea and mine's getting cold. I'll let you know the flight number. I love you. Bye for now." I didn't even wait for him to answer. I just hung up the phone.

Chapter Forty-One

Portia and I were so hungry that we both had two portions of shepherd's pie and, after we'd eaten, Erin poured us each a rather large mug of Irish coffee. We were finally able to relax and tell her the whole story about how Portia came to arrive at Maggie's. She was a good listener and able to empathize because she had been through an abusive marriage herself. She was only nineteen when she got involved with a man she met at a local gym. At the time, she'd been living in Belfast with her father, her mother having died when she was only eleven. Ronan was twelve years older and a photographer for the Belfast Telegraph. He'd traveled throughout Europe and the Middle East and could charm the birds out of the trees. Not only that, but at six foot five, he towered over Erin and had movie star looks. It didn't take long for her to fall head over heels and, six months after their first date, they were married and moved into a small flat on Oxford Street close to the river. For the first year, everything went well, even though Ronan was away a good deal of the time. When he was home he seemed to be loving and attentive and full of fun and, when he was away, Erin kept herself occupied with her job at the Belfast City Council and spending time with her father and two or three friends she'd known since childhood. It was in the second year of their marriage when Erin began to notice a change in Ronan. He'd always enjoyed a drink or two, when he got home from work, but his drinking began to escalate to the point where he would slur his words and fall asleep on the couch, often remaining there all night. When she tried talking to him about it, he became angry and accused her of being a nag but she persisted and encouraged him to get some help. He finally joined AA and, for a while, attended the meetings regularly but, when Erin announced she was pregnant; he became enraged and started drinking again. He didn't want any children and demanded her to get rid of it. She refused and that's when he became physically abusive. It all sounded so much like Portia's story, but unlike Portia, Erin wasn't about to put up with the abuse, so she left and fled to Larne where she knew an old school chum who she could stay with for the time being. Unfortunately, a month later, she lost the baby and never saw Ronan again. It was another seven years before she obtained a divorce and bought the house she was now living in. She had never remarried, dated only casually, and was perfectly happy being alone.

As she was telling her story, I was thinking how lucky I was to have found Aaron. He was such a gentle and patient man but, at the same time, I know he was finding it difficult with me traipsing all over the place and making Portia my priority and, it was only a matter of time, before he insisted I come home and stay home. Erin must have sensed I was a little preoccupied, "Are you all right, Sam?" she asked.

I nodded, "I'm fine. Sorry, but I was thinking about my husband and daughter. I miss them a lot and I want to go home but I don't want to leave Portia."

My sister reached over and took my hand, "It's okay, Sam, I'll be all right and you can't stay here. You have to go home to your family."

I squeezed her hand, "But you can't stay here forever and what if Philip catches up with you?"

Erin cut in, "Portia can stay here for as long as she likes and I doubt that her husband will find her after the way you've covered your tracks."

"That's so kind of you, Erin, and as soon as I get back home, I'll wire you some money. After all, we can't expect you to let Portia stay here without repaying you."

"That really isn't necessary," she responded, then turned to Portia, "Do you know what you want to do? Will you file for divorce?"

Portia shook her head, "I don't know what I'm going to do. Philip will never go for a divorce. Frankly, Erin, I'm scared to death of him."

"And that's why I have to figure out how to stop him from hurting Portia," I said.

By eleven that night, both Portia and I were worn out. It had been a long day and, after wishing Erin goodnight, we crawled into the cozy double bed and fell asleep almost immediately.

The next day, Erin suggested we do a little sightseeing and she drove us to the Giant's Causeway, just over an hour away on the northeast coast. It was magnificent, a whole area made up of thousands of basalt interlocking columns that had resulted from a volcanic eruption millions of years ago. We spent a lot of time there, bought dozens of post-cards, and then doubled back to a town called Ballymena, where we had a late lunch at the Countryman. It was hard to imagine, that the very next day, I would be back in the States.

Portia seemed a bit subdued during the whole trip and I was worried about her. It was only when we arrived back at Erin's and she was relaxing, with Daisy curled up on her lap, that she looked up at me and smiled, "That was a lovely day. Ireland is such a beautiful place."

"Yes, it is," I replied. "I wish I could stay a few more days and do some more sightseeing but I think I'd be headed for divorce if I did that."

"Fat chance," she said. "Aaron is a keeper, that's for sure. You're so lucky, Sam."

I grinned, "Yes, I know but I don't want to push my luck. As for you, Portia, I really believe, one of these days, you'll find someone just like Aaron."

She shook her head, "I'm not so sure. I don't think I have very good judgment when it comes to men."

"Oh, I don't know about that. I always liked Hayden. It's too bad you didn't marry him instead of Philip."

Portia was quiet for a moment. "He was a good man and I hurt him badly."

"Did you ever hear from him after you broke it off?"

"Yes. He wrote me a long letter begging me to reconsider but I didn't answer it."

"Maybe, when this is all over, you can get back together."

Portia smiled as she stroked Daisy, "You are a hopeless romantic, Sam. I wouldn't have expected Hayden to wait for me and, in any case, it could be a long time before I get out of this mess."

"Not if I have anything to do with it," I said.

Chapter Forty-Two

The following day, I arrived at JFK at just after four in the afternoon. The American Airlines flight had been delayed for an hour in London and it had been a long and tiring journey. Aaron wanted to meet me but I discouraged him because I wasn't sure if Philip was having him followed. Needless to say he wasn't happy and commented that the whole situation was getting out of hand. I wasn't quite sure how much more he could take.

I took a cab back to the house and, the minute I pulled up outside, Vicky came running out to greet me. She was calling "Mommy, mommy," over and over again and threw her arms around my legs, when I stepped out of the cab. I picked her up and nuzzled my nose against her neck. She smelled of honeysuckle and I could feel my eyes beginning to tear up. I kissed her on the top of the head and that's when I saw Aaron walking towards me. He grinned, "The vagabond returns," he said. I lowered Vicky to the ground and held out my arms to embrace him. I was so happy to be home with my family again, but one little corner of my mind was still thinking about Portia.

Later that day, after Vicky was in bed, I decided to have a serious talk with Aaron to see if he had any ideas about stopping Philip from getting anywhere near my sister. At first, he was reluctant to talk about it but I persisted and, eventually, he commented that maybe Philip had no interest in finding her and I should just stay out of it altogether. I realized then that he wasn't going to be of any help and I would have to figure it out for myself.

In bed that night, we made love, and Aaron told me how much he missed me and begged me not to leave again. I wanted to make him a promise but I just couldn't do it. Afterwards, when he was sound asleep, I lay awake trying to figure out my next move.

The next morning, after he left for work, I dropped Vicky off at school and then made my way to the clinic to tell Bette I wasn't coming back. I needed to free up my time to help my sister and I couldn't just keep taking days off without any notice. Bette was upset but she understood and we promised to stay in touch and meet up once in a while for coffee or lunch. She hugged me as we said goodbye and then she suddenly remembered a telephone call she'd received a couple of days earlier. A man had asked for me and when she told him I wasn't available, he wanted to know where I was. Naturally, she didn't tell him anything and, when she asked who was calling, he hung up on her. I wasn't really surprised and it didn't scare me. I expected Philip to try tracking me down.

On the way back home, I picked up a copy of the New York Times and then decided to stop at Starbuck's and sit and relax for a while. I ordered a cappuccino and started flipping through the paper, discarding all the sections that didn't interest me, like sports and business. Then, a photograph caught my attention and I could hardly believe my eyes. It was a picture of Serena and Lotti attending an art exhibition at the Museum of Modern Art. When I realized they must be in New York, I suddenly had an idea. Maybe Lotti could help me.

I returned home to look up the number of Philip's place on Central Park West, assuming Lotti would be staying there, but then I wondered how I'd manage to get her on the phone. Maybe Serena would answer or, heaven forbid, Philip. Eventually I decided I'd take my chance and leave a note with the concierge, expressly marked private and confidential, for Lotti. It all seemed very cloak and dagger and, as I changed my clothes, for a drive into the city, I felt excited. If only Lotti could help.

Leaving the note with the concierge, who confirmed Miss Barrington and Miss Herczeg were staying there, was simple although I was more nervous than a cat on a hot tin roof wondering if Serena or Philip might come wandering through the lobby. I was adamant that the note only be given to Lotti but I couldn't be absolutely sure if that would happen. I'd asked Lotti to call me on a very private and serious matter and not to discuss it with anyone else. I figured it would get her attention. Now I just had to wait.

I returned home feeling restless and not sure what to do for the rest of the day, when a call came through on my land line. It was Beth. The minute I heard her voice, I sensed something was wrong. I told her I'd call her back on my cell phone as I was still convinced the phones in the house were tapped. In the next few minutes, I learned Portia was leaving on a British Airways flight at about three o'clock in the afternoon. She was headed for Boston. My heart leapt into my throat when I found out she was on her way back to the States and I was anxious to know what had happened to cause her to suddenly leave Ireland. Beth soon filled me in. A strange man had shown up the day before at Erin's house, at around dinner time. He claimed to be from the Census Office and began asking all kinds of questions. When Erin asked for identification, he produced a business card but she wasn't convinced it was genuine and, when he asked if he could come inside to use the loo, she told him she wasn't comfortable allowing any stranger into her house and he finally left. Through the front window, she watched him get into a green sedan and slowly drive away but, later that evening, she noticed the same car parked across the street and that's when she alerted Portia that she was sure they were being watched. In the early hours of the morning, leaving through a gate at the back of the house, Portia made her way to the main street in Larne and flagged down a cab to take her to Belfast International. When I asked how she managed to pay for her ticket, Beth told me Erin had let her use her credit card and Portia had promised to repay her. Beth had received a call from Portia asking her to let me know she was coming back home to New York. She had no alternative but to take a chance and return under her own name using her own passport. Beth was concerned about her being in New York and persuaded her to return to Boston instead. She said she would drive her to Cape Cod where she could stay in a cottage, belonging to her cousin, until the whole issue with Philip was sorted out. Portia was reluctant at first, but finally agreed. I breathed a sigh of relief and thanked Beth for her help. The idea of my sister being back in the States was bitter sweet. I loved the fact she would be only a short distance away but I was still concerned for her safety.

Ten minutes after the call from Beth, my cell phone rang. I didn't recognize the number but hoped it was Lotti, and it was. She was anxious to know what I wanted to talk to her about but I wasn't about to discuss it on the phone. I asked her to meet me at one o'clock at Lansky's Deli on Columbus, just a few minutes away from Philip's apartment. She wasn't sure she could make it but then she remembered Serena had an appointment at the Trump Spa and would probably be there most of the afternoon. When I asked where Philip was, I learned he was back in London and wouldn't be in New York for at least another week or two. She pressed me again, impatient to know why I needed to see her but I told her she just had to wait.

I decided to change into something a little more suitable for lunch in the city, even though it was certainly nowhere fancy, but I felt more comfortable in an ivory wrap dress, I hadn't worn for at least two years, and my favorite tan leather jacket. After slipping on a pair of three inch pumps, I looked in the mirror, nodded at my reflection and then left the house to drive into the city, for the second time that day.

It was almost one-thirty when Lotti arrived at the deli. I was beginning to think she had chickened out but, apparently, Serena was running late and didn't leave for the spa until just after one. Despite the fact Lotti was obviously nervous, after ordering a cup of coffee, she seemed to settle down. Whenever I had seen her in the past, she had made me think of Mia Farrow and today was no exception. With her long fair hair, elfin face and wearing the palest lavender, fine wool suit, she looked exquisite. "Do you want to order something to eat and then we can talk?" I asked.

She shook her head, "I don't think I can wait that long to hear what you have to say, Sam," she replied.

"All right, I'll just order another cup of coffee and we can eat later."

She nodded and I signaled to the waiter, who came over right away and, a few minutes later, returned with my coffee. I poured some cream into the cup and then looked across at Lotti, "I'm here about my sister," I said.

"I was sure this was about Portia," she said, "but what has it to do with me and why all the secrecy?"

I immediately felt her defenses go up but I had to continue. "You must be aware Portia's in hiding and Philip's been looking for her."

"Well I did hear they were no longer together and I know there hasn't been any contact lately but that's about all I know."

"I see, and do you know why she left him?"

"I thought they just agreed to part ways but I had no idea why. What is this all about?"

"Didn't Serena tell you why they split up? She must have talked to you about it."

"She just said Portia didn't fit in with Philip's lifestyle. I gather that isn't the way it is?"

I took a deep breath and decided, now was the time to tell her the truth. "Philip has been both mentally and physically abusive to my sister. The reason she lost the baby was because he pushed her down the stairs. Then she discovered something very disturbing and it's hard to tell you this because it affects you and I really don't want to hurt you."

Lotti held up a hand to stop me, "Wait, how could I possibly be involved in any of this?"

I reached over and grasped her hand, "You aren't involved directly but, let's just say, the collateral damage affects you a great deal."

She pulled her hand away, "You're beginning to frighten me, Sam."

"I'm so sorry but you need to know. Philip is carrying on an incestuous affair with Serena." I hesitated but Lotti's reaction surprised me. She lowered her head and I saw her eyes start to tear up. Suddenly I realized the truth, "You knew didn't you?" I whispered.

She took a tissue from her purse, dabbed at the corners of her eyes and nodded, "I've suspected it for a long time. How did Portia find out?"

"She actually caught them red handed when they were in Menton. After that, they drugged her and kept her locked up but she managed to escape at Heathrow, as they were attempting to take her back to London."

"Oh my god, where is she now?"

"I can't tell you that because we know Philip's been trying to find her and we don't know what he plans to do."

"Why would he want to hurt her?"

I sighed, "Because he wouldn't want a scandal or a divorce. There's too much money at stake, not that Portia wants any of his money but he will never believe that."

"What are you suggesting? Do you think he'd actually try to get rid of her?"

"He's done it before."

"What do you mean?"

"I talked to someone who was very close to his first wife and she suspects the drowning was no accident. She also believes his wife suffered a miscarriage because of Philip's abuse."

"Who is this person?"

I didn't want to tell Lotti, it was Rosemary Harte, after all she must have stayed at the Mayfair House on a number of occasions. "I'd prefer not to disclose that," I answered.

Lotti frowned, "Well, what can I do to help?"

"I need proof that Serena and Philip are having an affair."

"What are you saying? Do you expect me to watch their every move and catch them in the act just like Portia did?"

"I want more than that. I want proof in the form of photographs. Blackmail is the only way I can get my sister out of this mess."

Lotti shook her head again, "You're asking me to jeopardize my relationship with Serena."

"She's using you, Lotti. How can you stay with someone like that? She's a despicable individual and you deserve better. You're a beautiful young woman and I don't understand why you stay with her. Does she have some kind of hold over you?"

She dropped her head again and couldn't look me in the eyes, "She's abusive just like her brother and very controlling. I'm ashamed to say this, but I'm scared of her. If I ever tried to leave her, I'm not sure what she would do."

It was my turn to gasp, "Oh, my goodness, I had no idea. I'm so sorry, Lotti, but will you help me? If you do, I promise I'll help you to get out of your relationship unharmed."

Lottie looked flustered, "I don't know. I wouldn't even know where to begin."

I patted her hand, "Let's think about it. Right now I'm starving so I'd like to eat and I have to get back to pick Vicky up from school. Why don't you call me tomorrow and we can get together again after we come up with some plan."

She nodded, "Okay, but I'm not sure how I'm going to act normally around Serena when she gets back."

I smiled, "I know you can do it. Now let's order one of their famous sandwiches."

Chapter Forty-Three

I was surprised when Lotti called me early the next morning. I had planned to give her a couple of days to think over what we'd discussed and yet here she was anxious to meet me again, early that afternoon. "Can you get away without Serena asking a lot of questions?" I asked.

"She has a meeting with her lawyer. I don't know what it's about but I know they're having lunch at the Rainbow Room so she'll be gone quite a while. I told her I was going to do some shopping. What time can we get together?"

I suggested we meet at the Pine Tree Café in the Botanical Gardens. It meant I wouldn't have to drive all the way into the middle of the city again and we could be almost certain we wouldn't run into anyone we knew.

I was already seated at a table in the patio section, nursing a cup of coffee, when I saw Lotti approaching. It was easy to pick her out of a crowd even though she was so tiny. With all of that blond hair and wearing a mint green wrap dress, she was hard to miss. She looked a little lost until she caught my eye and I waved her over to the table. "I'm so sorry I'm late," she said.

I glanced at my watch, "It's not a problem. I've just been sitting here enjoying all the greenery. It's such a beautiful day and it's so nice to sit outside for a change."

Lotti nodded but I noticed she seemed uncomfortable. "Look, why don't we order and then we can discuss what we can do to help my sister."

She didn't answer directly but picked up the menu and sat staring at it for a long time. Then she looked up and asked, "What are you having?"

"I think I'm having the turkey club sandwich," I replied.

Lotti ordered a harvest salad, and while we were eating, she asked me about my family. She seemed particularly interested in Vicky and I couldn't help asking her if she'd ever wanted children. She said that, when she was married, her husband didn't want a family and after she met Serena it seemed out of the question. "What about adoption?" I asked.

She scoffed, "You have to be joking. There's no way Serena would want to bring up a child. She has enough of a problem dealing with the dogs, Max and Buddy, and they're so easy to take care of."

We continued to chat until we were both half way through our second cup of coffee and then Lotti said, "I think it's time we talked."

I nodded, "I agree. I'm actually surprised you got back to me so quickly. Did you come up with a plan?"

She dropped her head and I noticed her hands were trembling, "I need to tell you the truth," she whispered.

I reached over and patted her hand, "That might be a good idea, Lotti."

She looked up and then glanced around as though she was afraid someone would hear, "I've known about the relationship between Serena and Philip for a long time. They didn't even try to hide it and, on one occasion, they wanted me to join them."

I was shocked, "Oh, my lord. What did you do?"

"I refused and told Serena exactly what I thought about the whole business. I was disgusted and didn't want any part of it."

"But why did you stay with her knowing she was carrying on with her brother?"

Lotti got very quiet for a moment, "I had no choice. She warned me that if I told anyone or tried to leave her, I would suffer the consequences."

"So she threatened you but what with? What hold does she have over you?"

I saw the tears begin to form in the corners of her eyes, "My parents are both still alive. Serena paid for them to come here from Budapest and she set them up in a small house in Coral Gables. When, my father began to show the first signs of Alzheimer's and my mother was being crippled with arthritis, she moved them into a long term care facility in Miami. It costs a fortune, Sam, and I could never afford it. I know Serena would cut off funds and they'd be out on the street or in some awful place run by some charitable organization. I can't risk that happening, I love my parents too much and I would never be able to forgive myself."

I paused for a moment trying to take it all in, "What if I could guarantee that your parents wouldn't have to leave the facility?"

Lotti frowned, "How can you possibly guarantee that?"

"Well, if Portia gets a divorce, she'll come into a pile of money and I know she'd be willing to step in and provide the funds."

"But that could take time, even years. What would happen in the meantime?"

I decided to throw caution to the wind, "I have money my father left me. I could bridge the gap."

"I could never ask you to do that, Sam."

"You're not asking. I'm offering, Lotti. Serena sounds like a monster. How dare she hold you hostage like that? She and Philip make a good pair and I hope they both rot in hell." I said, my voice rising in anger.

Lotti began to tremble, "I'm scared, Sam. If I do anything to raise Serena's suspicion she may even become physically abusive."

I frowned, "Has she ever hurt you?"

She nodded, "Once when she caught me admiring the husband of a business acquaintance. He was one of the most handsome men I'd ever seen. She knew I'd been married and was heterosexual at one time and she felt threatened."

"What did she do?"

Lotti looked embarrassed, "She spanked me with a leather belt that cut into my flesh and I had trouble sitting down for almost a week."

"She sounds like a pervert. What on earth made you hook up with her in the first place?"

"I married very young and my husband, Kristof, was quite a bit older. I soon realized I didn't love him, even though he was a good man, and I was very unhappy. That's when I met Serena and we became friends. She was someone I could confide in and she was the one who persuaded me to leave Kristof and start a new life in America. When she said she would help relocate my parents when they retired, it was too much of a temptation. I'd always wanted to leave Hungary and I knew I wouldn't be alone in a new country. Back then, I had no idea my friendship with Serena would change but, soon after my divorce was final, we became intimate. Serena had come back to Budapest to see me and was leaving the next day so I was feeling very low. That night, she came into my room and climbed into bed with me. At first, I was nervous and I didn't know what to do. I'd never been with a woman and I had no idea what to expect. Serena knew exactly what to do and, afterwards, I felt more feminine and desirable than I'd ever felt with my husband."

I shook my head, "But didn't you realize that Serena was gay. You only have to look at her to be suspicious?"

Lotti shrugged, "I guess I was too naïve."

"Well now we know she's actually bi-sexual. Not only that, she's so depraved, she even sleeps with her own brother."

"What can we do, Sam?"

I frowned, "I'm not sure. I've been thinking about how we can catch them in the act but it would be dangerous. It would mean the need to set up cameras in Philip's apartment and how can we do that without being caught? Even if Serena and

Philip weren't on the premises, I expect there are a few staff members around at all times. Is that the case, Lotti?"

"Surely you're not suggesting we plant cameras here in New York? That won't work, Sam. Philip isn't even in town right now and I think Serena is planning for us to go back to West Palm in the next day or two. I have no idea when they'll be in the same location again, let alone the same place."

I mulled this over for a moment, "Why don't you try and find out what their schedules are? Until then, there isn't much we can do."

Chapter Forty-Four

After lunch, I went back home feeling rather despondent. It was difficult not having a concrete plan to catch Philip. I wanted my sister to be free and no longer living in fear. Thinking about Portia prompted me to call Beth to see if she'd heard from her. Luckily, I caught Beth just as she was about to go shopping. It was so good to hear her voice and I realized how much I missed her. She'd been a positive influence in my life and had made Daddy happy and, for that, I would always be grateful. "Have you spoken to Portia?" I asked after we'd exchanged a few pleasantries.

"Yes, I spoke to her earlier today. She's getting along well with my cousin, Emma, and she's fallen in love with Cape Cod. Why don't you call her yourself on your cell phone? I'm sure it will be safe."

I was excited thinking about talking to Portia but still nervous about calling from the house, even using my cell phone, so I decided to go into the garden and call from there. A woman with a distinct Boston accent answered after three rings, "You must be Emma," I said.

"I am," she answered rather tentatively, "who's this?"

"It's Sam," I replied, "Portia's sister. Is she there, please?"

"Hold on," she said rather abruptly and then I heard murmuring in the background.

Suddenly I heard Portia's voice, "Sam, is that you?"

"Yes, who did you think it was?"

She sighed, "Oh, thank heaven. Emma thought it might be someone pretending to be you."

"No, it's me all right. I hear you're loving Cape Cod."

"Oh, it's fabulous here, Sam. The cottage is almost on the beach and Emma has really made me welcome."

"Do you really feel safe there, Portia? I was so worried when I heard you left Ireland in such a hurry."

"That was so scary. We had no idea who the man was, who showed up at the door. I hope he didn't go back after I left. Have you spoken to Erin?"

"No, I planned to call her tonight and then I'll arrange to repay her for your airfare back to the States."

"I'm so sorry, Sam. This must be costing you a fortune but you know I'll pay you back as soon as I can."

"Don't worry about that now. I just want this all to be over so that you can come back home."

"Me too but I can't risk Philip finding me."

"I agree but you can't stay in hiding forever either. I had a meeting with Lotti today and she's going to try and help."

"Oh Sam, are you sure you can trust her? What if Serena finds out?"

"It's okay. I know what I'm doing. There's a lot you don't know about what's really going on in that relationship but I'll fill you in later. Right now, I just want you to relax and not to worry about anything. Philip isn't going to find you and when I do bring you back home, he won't be in a position to hurt you."

Portia sighed, "This all sounds rather dangerous. If you cross Philip, he'll come after you and I'll never forgive myself if that happens. You've got Vicky to think of too. Please be careful, Sam."

"I will, I promise. Now I'd better go, I'm still nervous about contacting you directly."

"When will I hear from you again?"

"Hopefully as soon as the plan I've cooked up with Lotti actually works. It could take some time though."

"I'll be on pins and needles worrying about what you're up to, Sam."

"Don't be. Everything will turn out okay. Now you go and relax and enjoy Cape Cod while you can. Before you know it, you'll be back in the city complaining about the pollution."

Portia sighed again, "I can't wait, pollution or not. I miss New York, Sam, and I miss you."

"I know but I'd better ring off now. Take care of yourself. I love you."

I barely heard Portia as her voice began to break, "I love you too," she whispered.

The very next morning, after Aaron had left for work and I'd just returned from dropping Vicky off at school, I was surprised to get a call from Lotti. She sounded panicked, so I walked back out to the garden with my cell phone, still paranoid about the house being bugged. "What's wrong, Lotti?" I asked, "You sound really upset."

"It's Serena, she knows I had lunch with you yesterday and she's furious," she replied.

I was stunned, "How on earth did she find out? Surely you didn't tell her, Lotti?"

"No, of course not," she answered, her voice rising. "An acquaintance of hers saw us together at the Pine Tree. At least, she thought it was me and decided to call Serena and tell her."

"Why didn't you deny it? You could have told her this person was mistaken."

"It's no use trying to lie to Serena, she's like a dog with a bone."

"So what did you tell her?"

"I told her you'd asked me to have lunch to find out if I knew where your sister was. Of course, she suggested you could have asked me that on the phone and why would I need to meet you in some out of the way place. She then suggested maybe I was having an affair and she got so angry, I thought she was going to get physically abusive again. I finally settled her down and apologized for not telling her I was meeting you but she warned me over and over about the consequences if I ever double crossed her."

"You mean the threat she made before about your parents?"

"Yes, and I can't help you now, Sam. It's too risky. I hope you understand."

I felt so let down but I knew I couldn't involve Lotti anymore, "Of course I understand," I said. "I'm so sorry about what happened and I won't bother you again. There is one thing I want you to promise though, Lotti. You mustn't tell Serena or Philip that I know where Portia is."

"You have my word," she whispered.

After speaking to Lotti, I spent the next several hours attempting to come up with a new plan. By mid-afternoon, I was exhausted and decided to take a drive, just to clear my head, but I couldn't get Portia off my mind. I was relieved when it was time to pick Vicky up because she was always a welcome distraction. She was anxious to show me a rather comical drawing she'd produced in art class. It was supposed to be a portrait of the family but Aaron and I resembled Fred and Wilma Flintstone, while Vicky looked like Tinkerbell. When I reacted with a chuckle, she didn't look too happy. "Don't you like it, Mommy," she asked.

I tried to look serious, "I like it very much," I replied. "You're such a clever girl."

She smiled and looked rather smug, "Mrs. Morgan told me it was very good and she gave me a gold star."

"Oh, wow," I remarked, 'that's wonderful, honey. Daddy will be so proud of you."

"I know," she said and I tried hard not to grin.

Aaron was late coming home from the office and I was getting impatient because I wanted to talk to him but I knew I still had to wait until Vicky was in bed. It was close to nine o'clock, by the time the dinner dishes were put away and Vicky had settled down for the night. By that time, Aaron was sprawled in his favorite chair watching the sports news on ESPN. I knew he'd had a difficult day and didn't want to disturb him but I just couldn't wait. "Can we talk," I asked?

He looked up at me, "I guess you want to tell me what happened with Lotti?"

I nodded and, reluctantly, he turned down the volume on the television. "My plan didn't work out." I admitted. "An acquaintance of Serena's saw us having lunch and she blew up. I can't involve Lotti anymore."

"So what are you going to do?"

"I'm going to expose Philip anyway."

Aaron chortled, "How are you going to manage that?"

"I'll write to the New York Times anonymously and tell them his wife is missing."

Aaron shook his head and laughed, "You have to be joking. Do you really think the New York Times is going to publish a letter from someone who doesn't even identify themselves and without any evidence to back up their accusation?"

"Well I'll write to one of the tabloids then. They're always putting out stories that have no basis in fact but people still read them and, maybe, someone will take it seriously and start investigating."

"But you can't suggest Portia is missing when you know where she is. You can get in a lot of trouble. What if there's an investigation and the authorities find out the truth?"

"I don't care, it's worth a try. I want to discredit Philip any way I can and maybe someone will bring up the issue of his first wife's death."

Aaron shrugged and turned back to the television, "Why wait for someone else to do it. You might as well bring up the subject yourself in your letter."

I knew he didn't want to talk about it anymore and obviously thought I was crazy but he had given me something to mull over.

Chapter Forty-Five

I was awake for hours that night composing a letter in my head. By the next morning, I couldn't wait to be alone and begin putting pen to paper. It was close to nine o'clock by the time I was satisfied with what I'd written and I was just reaching for an envelope when my cell phone rang. I immediately recognized Beth's number and my heart skipped a beat. I figured something had to be wrong and I was too anxious to even step out of the house to take the call. I picked up on the second ring, "Beth, what is it?" I asked, "Are you all right? Has something happened?"

"I hope you're sitting down, dear," she responded. "There's no easy way to tell you this but Portia's missing."

I gasped, "Oh no, did Emma call you?"

"Yes, just a few moments ago. She thought it was getting a little late so she went to check Portia's room to see if she was all right. The bed clothes were in a shambles and it looked like there'd been a bit of a struggle. Emma checked to make sure she wasn't anywhere else in the house and then she contacted me right away to see if she should call the police. What do you want her to do, Sam?"

"Did you try phoning Portia?"

"Yes but there was no answer and I asked Emma to check to see if she could find her cell phone but she couldn't. Whoever took Portia must have taken her phone too. Emma said her purse was still there and money was still in her wallet."

"Have her call the police right away. She has to tell them I have reason to believe she's been abducted by her husband. Clue her in on everything you know already, Beth, so that she can back up her story. Meanwhile I'm going to catch a flight out of JFK and I'll let you know what time I'll be arriving in Boston. Can you pick me up at Logan and drive me to Cape Cod?"

"Yes, of course, I'll do anything I can to help. Right now, I'll call Emma back and ask her to let me know what the police plan to do after she contacts them. I'll fill you in when you let me know your arrival time."

I was beginning to panic and I could feel my heart racing, "Okay, Beth, I'll call the airline right now and talk to you soon."

At just after 11 o'clock, I was on a Delta flight, due to arrive at Logan shortly after noon. My anxiety had spurred me into action and, after packing a small case, I arrived at JFK just half an hour prior to departure. That barely gave me enough time to call Aaron and I was dreading his reaction. Luckily for me he was in a meeting and, although I was aware he would have excused himself to take my call if he knew it was urgent, I decided to leave him a message. I knew he'd be angry, especially as I had no idea when I'd be back and he would have to take care of Vicky again. I just hoped, by the time I did speak to him, he would have calmed down.

Beth was waiting for me in the arrivals lounge at Logan and we practically fell into each other's arms. "Have you spoken to Emma?" I asked anxiously.

"Yes, she called the police and they were sending a couple of officers over to check out the house."

"Oh my god, I hope they believe what she's telling them."

"Well, you're going to have to fill them in on the details so let's get going. It will take just over an hour to get to Emma's, that's if the road is clear."

"Where does Emma live exactly?" I asked as we started to exit the terminal.

"In Sandwich; it's the oldest town on the Cape. I believe it was first settled early in the seventeenth century."

I wasn't really ready for a history lesson. "Is her house near the water?"

"Yes, it's only about a five minute walk to the marina."

I stopped and grabbed Beth's arm, "So she could have been abducted and taken away by boat?"

Beth grimaced, "You could be right, dear, but we shouldn't jump to conclusions. Let's see what the police have to say."

Chapter Forty-Six

As we passed through Plymouth and approached the Cape, at any other time I would have been enchanted with my surroundings. It was a bright, afternoon and the sun sparkled on the ocean but my thoughts kept bouncing back to Portia. Where on earth was she?

We arrived at Emma's house, a single story cottage-like home, surrounded on each side by groves of maple trees. I could hardly wait to make my way inside and see what was going on but, just as we were exiting the car, Beth's phone rang. She gestured for me to wait while she answered it. From what I overheard, it was obviously Emma and she was asking us to meet her somewhere else. When Beth rang off, she motioned me back into the car, "We have to meet her at the police station," she said.

"Where is it?" I asked impatiently.

"It's just back on the highway, less than a mile from here. Don't worry, Sam, we'll be there in no time."

I sighed as I got back in the passenger seat. My nerves were beginning to get the best of me.

When we reached the station, I couldn't help comparing it to the police headquarters in New Rochelle. It looked so insignificant by comparison; I didn't think, for one moment, they would be much help in finding my sister. I glanced over at Beth as we parked the car and shook my head. "I know what you're thinking," she said, "but let's see what's going on."

When we entered the building, we were greeted by a young officer who asked us to take a seat, while he informed the Chief of Police we had arrived. Minutes later, he was back and directed us to an office, where I finally came face to face with Emma. She looked like a younger version of Beth, a couple of inches shorter, slightly overweight with short, fair hair. She hugged Beth and then turned to me, "It's nice to meet you, Sam," she said. "I just wish it had been under different circumstances."

"Me too," I replied, gently rubbing her shoulder.

I spent the next half hour, relating every detail I could remember, starting with what led up to the original abduction from Menton, and Portia's escape at Heathrow airport. I knew it all sounded rather melodramatic and hard to believe but Chief Harris didn't interrupt me as I continued on with my story. Meanwhile a female officer, tapped away on a computer recording every word. It was only when I finished that he began asking me questions. "Why would your brother-in-law abduct your sister from this location when you were aware she was hiding out here? Surely, he'd realize you'd be contacting the police as soon as you knew she was missing?"

"But he didn't know I was aware of Portia's location. Through Lotti I gave the impression I had no idea where Portia was and I was looking for her myself."

He nodded his head slowly, "Mrs. Reynolds, do you have any concrete evidence to support your story?"

I was beginning to feel angry and was about to react, when I remembered the letter Portia had written and left with Maggie. "My sister wrote a letter in case something happened to her. She implicated her husband."

"Where is this letter?"

I sighed, "It's in safe keeping with Maggie in the north of England. I told you all about Portia staying with her before we went to Ireland. Maybe if I phone Maggie, she can get a copy of it to us."

Chief Harris paused, "I suggest you telephone her and have her fax it to us, but we'll eventually need the original to verify its authenticity." I nodded and he passed me a slip of paper with the station's fax number and e-mail address. "If she can send it by email, it would be even better."

Beth stood up, "Why don't I go call her now. Maybe she can find an internet café close by."

I looked over at the Chief and after he nodded, I passed the slip of paper to Beth and she left the room. As she was walking out the door, I remembered all the photos Portia and I had taken when we took walks with Jake in Hebden Bridge and the ones at Lake District National Park, on our way to Stranraer. All of these photos had been transferred to my computer, along with some I'd taken when I was in London. I realized they were all time stamped and I could get them transferred easily if I called Aaron to help. I relayed this to the Chief and he agreed they would be useful in supporting my story. "I suggest you get them transferred here right away and, once we've gathered all of the information and are convinced your concern is credible, we'll take it from there."

"How can you think for one moment it's not credible?" I asked raising my voice in frustration. "Didn't you go through the house? Wasn't it obvious my sister didn't leave of her own free will?"

Emma put her arm around me in an attempt to settle me down, "Chief," she said calmly, "shouldn't you be out there looking for her?"

"We already have the coast guard searching for any sign of suspicious activity off- shore but in order for my officers to begin patrolling throughout the Sandwich area, we will need a photograph of Mrs. Barrington. The sooner you can arrange to get those photos here the better."

I started scrambling through my purse and pulled out my wallet, "I have a picture of my sister here," I said as I passed it to the Chief.

He stared at it for a moment, "Is this a recent photo?" he asked.

I nodded, "It's only a couple of years old."

Emma stood up and leaned forward, "May I see it, please?" When Chief Harris handed it over, she shook her head, "She's not blond like this anymore and her hair's shorter. It's an auburn shade now."

I sighed, "Oh, I forgot about that but she still looks the same. She lost some weight but she gained most of it back. You shouldn't have any trouble recognizing her."

Emma handed back the photo and Chief Harris stood up, "Well ladies, I think we're finished here for now. If you'll leave me a number where I can contact you," he said, looking at Emma, "I can call you to let you know if we've made any progress but I will need that letter and the photos you mentioned before I can proceed any further."

"But shouldn't we call in the FBI?" I asked. "I thought that's what happened when someone was kidnapped."

The Chief smiled, "Mrs. Reynolds, let's not get ahead of ourselves. Now, the sooner you let me get on with my job and make some inquiries, the sooner we'll have some idea of where your sister might be."

I knew he was just trying to placate me, and I was seething inside, but I shook his hand and left his office with Emma trailing behind me. Beth was just getting off the phone when we found her waiting near the front door. She smiled at the two of us, "I talked to Maggie and she said she knew of an internet café in town and she'd go there right away. She was pretty upset Portia had gone missing again and it took me a while to convince her we'd find her and Philip would be held accountable." She hesitated for a moment, "I'm sorry, Sam," she continued, "but I think you should know, she isn't well. She had a mild heart attack and was in the hospital for a few days. Of course, she was more worried about Jake than herself but one of her neighbours stepped in to help."

I could feel myself tearing up, "Poor Maggie, is she going to be all right?"

"As long as she cuts down on meat and dairy products and tries to walk a little more, the doctor says she could live to be a hundred."

I couldn't help grinning, "I hope that's true although I can't imagine her giving up her hot pots."

It was already close to dinner time when we left the police station and Emma suggested we get a bite to eat at Seafood Sam's. I was reluctant to go anywhere other than Emma's place because I wanted Chief Harris to be able to contact me at any time of the day or night. It was only when I found out Emma had given him her cell phone number that I was able to relax, but not enough to really enjoy the lobster ravioli Beth suggested I try.

Emma insisted we stay at her house for as long as we needed to and, I had to admit, I was exhausted and didn't want to leave the area. It was only when we were settled in her cozy living room, with lots of dark wood and comfy furniture in calming neutral colors, when I suddenly remembered I hadn't called Aaron. "Oh heavens, I forgot about the photos," I said jumping up and pulling my phone from my purse. "How could I have done that? What's wrong with me?"

Beth was at my side within seconds and gathered me into her arms, "You're under a lot of stress, Sam," she said, "Why don't you let me call Aaron?"

"Would you mind?" I replied, "I know he's going to be so angry with me and I don't think I can deal with it right now. I'm afraid I may have stretched his patience to the limit."

"It's okay, I'll just tell him you needed to lie down for a while and I offered to make the call."

I nodded, and sat down again, then watched as Beth pulled her phone from her jacket pocket and began punching in the number at my house. As she waited for Aaron to answer, I was wondering if he might be upstairs and unable to hear it ringing in the kitchen and then, after what seemed like forever, I heard Beth say, "Aaron, its Beth and don't worry, Sam is perfectly fine." There was a pause while he answered and Beth gave me the thumbs up.

Aaron had received my message and had left his office early to pick up Vicky. He told Beth that although, angry at first, he was getting used to my chasing off all over the place and wasn't surprised at this latest incident. He just wanted me to get in touch with him as soon as we had any news of Portia's whereabouts. He promised to email the photos I needed right away and finally, he asked Beth to tell me he loved me. When she relayed the whole conversation to me I just burst into tears. I couldn't believe how lucky I was to have found someone who continued to put up with my erratic behavior. My husband was one in a million.

Chapter Forty-Seven

It was nine o'clock the next morning and the three of us were sitting around the kitchen table when Emma's cell phone rang. I held my breath as she answered and then turned to me, "It's Chief Harris, he wants to talk to you."

My hand shook as I took the phone from her. "It's, Samantha Reynolds, what have you found out, Chief?"

Without any preamble he announced, "Your sister has been located."

I suddenly felt faint. I immediately imagined her body being dumped somewhere. "Oh, no, please god no," I screamed. "He killed her didn't he?" Both Beth and Emma jumped up and tried to put their arms around me but I waved them away.

"Mrs. Reynolds, please calm down," the chief said, "Your sister is alive and, a far as I know, perfectly well."

"Thank god," I yelled, "Where has she been? Is she here?"

"I need you to come back to the station and I'll give you all the information."

"But why can't you tell me now?"

"Just get here as soon as you can. I'll be waiting for you."

I felt like every nerve in my body was on edge as Beth drove me back to the station and I was visibly shaking when we entered Chief Harris's office. I didn't even bother to shake his hand, "Where is she? Tell me, is she here?"

He motioned for us to sit down, "No she's not here; she's in London."

I gasped, "That's not possible; she was at the house two nights ago."

"Mrs. Reynolds, if you will allow me to continue I will tell you what I've discovered. This morning I attempted to contact your sister's husband through his New York office. I was advised by a Mrs. Lessing, he was in London and would be staying at his residence there for another week. When I requested his home number, she was unable to give it to me but suggested I call his London office, at which time it would be noon there, and I was to speak to a Miss Stamos. I then asked if Mrs. Barrington was also in London and was told that she arrived there last night. When I pressed for more details, I was advised she flew out of Boston on a private jet and was accompanied by her sister-in-law, Serena Barrington. Mrs. Lessing was very forthcoming but had no idea why your sister was in Boston."

"Did you make the call to London?" I asked impatiently.

He nodded, "I did and not only did I speak to Miss Stamos but I actually spoke to Philip Barrington."

I gasped, "My god, what did he say?"

"Well obviously he wanted to know exactly who I was and why I was calling."

"And what did you tell him?"

The chief scoffed, "I told him you had contacted us regarding your sister's whereabouts and suspected he was involved with her disappearance."

Beth chimed in, "Naturally he denied it."

The chief actually chuckled, "He claimed you were a nutcase, Mrs. Reynolds, and demanded to know what evidence you had to suggest his wife was even missing. He assured me she was safe and sound at their home in London." He paused, "I was not prepared to accept his word and it's not our normal procedure to conduct an investigation over the telephone. However, in this case, there didn't appear to be much choice. If I had more substantial indication a crime had been committed, I would have been obliged to contact the British authorities".

"But I gave you sufficient evidence. Did you tell him about the letter Portia wrote and all the photographs proving she was in northern England and Ireland with me?"

"I gave him all those details, Mrs. Reynolds, and he repeated that you were a nutcase, his words not mine, and you probably forged the letter yourself. As for the photographs, he claimed he was well aware you were in the U.K. recently on vacation with your sister."

I sighed, got up, and started pacing the room. "What was she doing in Boston? Did he give you an explanation for that too?"

"Yes, she was visiting a friend of his sister's and it appears that Serena Barrington accompanied her. He even gave me the name and contact number so I could follow up and confirm."

I turned, walked over to his desk, and glared down at him. "Don't you see it's all a set-up? He's a liar and he's dangerous. I think he even murdered his first wife."

His eyes widened in surprise, "Why would you say that?"

"She drowned in a so-called boating accident but she was an experienced sailor."

"Was Mr. Barrington charged?"

"Of course not," I answered angrily.

"Well, I suggest you stop throwing any more accusations about."

I shrugged and sat down, "What did he have to say about the first time she was abducted and what happened between them in France before that?"

"I didn't see any point in going into all that. He was obviously going to deny it and make even more disparaging remarks about you."

"Why didn't you ask to speak to my sister?"

"Because I didn't expect her to be at his office," he replied with a hint of sarcasm, "and I wouldn't know if it was really Mrs. Barrington who I was speaking to."

"Well, did you at least phone this supposed friend of Serena's in Boston?"

He looked down at his notes, "Yes, a Mariana Caroli. She actually lives in Cambridge and is a research assistant at Harvard Business School. Apparently, your sister drove down with Serena from New York and spent two days with her. They then drove to Logan airport to catch a flight to London."

"What happened to their car then? It would still be at the airport. This is all nonsense. He bought off this Mariana Caroli, or whatever her name is. She's a liar just like he is."

Chief Harris closed the folder he had open on his desk, "Mrs. Reynolds, why don't you just save yourself a lot of anxiety and just call your sister?"

I was furious and began to retaliate but Beth put her hand on my shoulder, "So you don't believe a word of what we've been telling you?"

He ignored Beth and leaned back in his chair, "I'm afraid, as far as I'm concerned, this case is closed. There's no real evidence your sister didn't leave of her own accord. Now, I suggest you contact her yourself or speak to her husband."

I stood up and scowled at him, "I may just do that. Thanks for nothing." Then I motioned to Beth, "Come on, let's get out of here. Maybe we can get someone more professional to listen to us."

Chief Harris didn't comment as I stormed out the door with Beth following a few feet behind me. Once outside, she caught up and grabbed my arm, "Sam, slow down. What are you going to do now?"

I stopped and turned towards her; my face beginning to crumple as I tried to hold back tears, "I'm going back to Emma's to pick up my bag and then, if you don't mind, I'd like you to drive me to the airport. Maybe we can pack up Portia's things while we're there and, if you don't mind, you can keep them at your place."

"Of course, dear, I gather you're anxious to go home."

"Yes, and once I get to New York; perhaps the police there will listen to me."

Beth sighed, "Oh, Sam, do you really think they're going to believe you? Why don't you just try calling Portia first? If she's there, maybe she can explain what happened and, if not, you might have a better chance of getting help."

"You're right, but first I need to get a flight back home and, once I get there, I'll try phoning her."

Beth put her arm around me, "I think that's the best thing to do. I'm sure Aaron will be happy to see you."

I shook my head, "Maybe, but I wouldn't be too sure."

Chapter Forty-Eight

I managed to get on a Delta flight at three-twenty that afternoon and arrived at JFK a few minutes before five. I then decided to call Aaron but he didn't pick up and I had to leave a message. I figured he was on his way back home, after picking Vicky up from school, and I couldn't wait to see them both.

When the taxi pulled up in front of the house, the door opened, and Vicky came racing down the driveway, "Mommy," she screamed, "look what I've got!"

I could see she was holding, what looked like, a small stuffed toy and she was obviously excited and anxious to show it to me. "Be careful," I called out, as I stepped onto the sidewalk, "Mommy's coming."

I might as well have saved my breath because, a few seconds later, she was almost on top of me and I realized the toy she was holding was actually a puppy and one of the most adorable puppies I'd ever seen, "Look what Daddy got me," she said thrusting it towards me, "isn't he sweet, Mommy?"

I held the puppy gently in my arms and noticed its curly black hair and dark eyes, "He's beautiful," I said, "what's his name?"

Vicky grinned, "Riley," she answered, "and guess what, Mommy, when he gets bigger he won't be black anymore."

I stared down at him, "Oh, what color will he be?"

"Daddy said he'd be a bluish grey and his face will get longer."

"That's amazing," I remarked, "and do you know what kind of dog he is? He looks a lot like the dog our old housekeeper, Maggie, owns." Just then I heard footsteps and saw Aaron approaching.

"He's a Kerry Blue terrier," he said. "Welcome home stranger."

I put Riley back in Vicky's arms and reached out to Aaron, "Hi, honey, I hope you got my message."

He looked annoyed but he returned my hug, "I guess you have a lot to tell me," he said.

I nodded and put my hand on Vicky's shoulder so that I could steer her back into the house, "What's with the dog?" I asked. "We've never seriously talked about getting another pet?"

Aaron scoffed, "How many times have you taken off without discussing it with me first? I figured our daughter needed a distraction from feeling abandoned, each time you leave like a thief in the night."

I stopped and glared at him, "Let's not do this now. Later, when we're alone, you can berate me all you like."

I was too tired to prepare dinner so we ordered in pizza and afterwards, because it was such a beautiful evening, I took Vicky and Riley for a walk in Davenport Park; just minutes away from our house. It took us almost an hour before we were home again. So many people out enjoying the warm weather, some with their own dogs, stopped to admire Riley. Vicky was like a proud mother showing off her new baby and, I had to admit, I was pleased Aaron had made the decision to get her a pet without even consulting me. Throughout our walk, I kept remembering Griffin and all the wonderful times we'd shared together especially after Erica, the miserable woman who was afraid of dogs, forced me to keep him in my room whenever she was around. I knew, one day I'd have to tell Vicky to beware of people who didn't like animals. In my opinion, they just couldn't be trusted.

After Vicky was tucked up in bed with Riley by her side, I was ready to tell Aaron what happened in Sandwich. He listened without interruption and, when I finally asked him what he thought had actually happened to Portia, he just shrugged and said, "Why don't you ask her yourself?"

I glared at him and then looked at my watch, "I will," I answered, "but it's after midnight in London. It will have to wait until morning."

He picked up the remote and turned on the television, "Good idea," he muttered.

I was so put out by his attitude that I grabbed the remote from his hand and turned the TV off. "You might show some interest. I need your support, Aaron, if I'm going to find out the truth about Portia."

"Sit down," he said; motioning to the chair opposite him, "we need to talk."

I hesitated and then sat down, "Go ahead," I said sarcastically, "I'm just dying to hear what you have to say."

He nodded, "This can't go on, Sam. I know you're worried about Portia but you can't keep going off on all these wild goose chases trying to save her from whatever you think is going on." I opened my mouth to interrupt but he put up his hand to stop me. "Let me finish and then you can have your say. If, there truly is a situation where Portia is being held against her will, there would have to be some way she could contact the authorities. Barrington Multinational is a Fortune 500 company. Philip's picture is in the New York Times and other papers on a regular basis. Questions would be raised about his wife if she wasn't seen in public for an extended period."

I couldn't help myself, I had to say something, "What about when she was abducted the first time and ended up with Maggie and then Erin in Ireland? Nobody else seemed to be looking for her then."

Aaron sighed, "How do you know that? Maybe somebody questioned not seeing her around and perhaps Philip had a plausible explanation. The only way you're going to know what's going on now, is to speak to Portia directly. You can do that tomorrow but, whatever the outcome, I'm not having you flying off to London. Enough is enough."

"Do you think I enjoy chasing around like I have been?" I said, my voice rising in anger. "It's exhausting and I worry all the time, not just about Portia but also about you and Vicky."

Aaron scoffed, "You've no need to worry about me but you should consider what you're doing to our daughter. Do you know how difficult it is trying to explain to her why her mommy isn't here? You have to stop this now, Sam."

"Are you forbidding me to go and see my sister?" I asked, standing up and scowling at him.

He shook his head, "You know I can't forbid you to do anything, Sam. You've always been headstrong and I understand your determination to do anything to protect Portia but not at the risk of affecting Vicky, not to mention our relationship."

I sat down again feeling deflated, "I thought you loved me no matter what."

"I do love you but you need to be here with us. Not only that, Sam, I worry that you might be putting yourself in danger if you're right about Philip."

"That's just it, I know I'm right but I'll call Portia tomorrow and maybe I'll be able to clear this all up."

The next day, being Saturday, I was busy in the morning making breakfast, taking Riley for a walk and shopping for groceries with Vicky. Aaron had gone to his office for a few hours and it was close to eleven when I finally had some time to myself. It was four in the afternoon in London.

I picked up the phone and tentatively called the house in Mayfair, hoping Mr. or Mrs. Harte would answer. I remembered them mentioning they would be retiring but I couldn't remember when. The phone rang several times before it was finally picked up but I didn't recognize the voice.

When I asked to speak to Mrs. Barrington, I was asked who was calling. When I said I was her sister, I was told to wait while she was being contacted. It seemed like forever, but suddenly I heard a man's voice and I knew immediately, it was Philip, "Hello, Sam," he said, "sorry but Portia's out at the moment."

I'd forgotten it was the weekend and he might be at home, "Where is she?" I asked. "What have you done with her?"

He had the gall to chuckle, "My, oh my, typical Sam. You don't waste any time getting to the point."

"You're damn right," I responded. "I know you took Portia from the house in Sandwich. She certainly didn't leave of her own accord."

I cringed when he laughed, "The police there didn't seem to believe a word of it. Let's face it, Sam, you're delusional."

"Oh, you think so? Well if you don't let me speak to her, I'll be calling the New York Times. See how you feel when you see your name plastered all over the front page accused of abducting your own wife."

I was so angry, I was almost hyperventilating but it didn't have any effect on Philip and he laughed even harder, "Pick up the paper tomorrow and you may see a photo of your precious sister. I hardly think anyone's going to believe anything you have to say."

I couldn't contain myself and screamed into the phone, "You bastard, you're not getting away with this. I have proof and soon everyone's going to know it. You may be able to control Portia, but you can't control me."

He wasn't laughing anymore and his voice took on a menacing tone, "If you start spreading these absurd rumors, you'll regret it. I'll sue your ass and you and your pathetic little family will end up on the street." Then I heard a click as he cut me off before I could respond.

I stood there shaking, for what seemed like several minutes, then I went to find Vicky. I thought, if I walked with her and Riley to the park, I'd find a peaceful spot where I could calm down and think rationally about what to do next.

When Aaron came home for lunch, I told him about the telephone call. He said he wasn't in the least surprised at Philip's reaction and perhaps now, I should drop the whole matter. The last thing we needed was a lawsuit and, despite his connections, nobody he knew in his profession would be a match for any lawyer Philip could afford. I listened and nodded my head but, deep down, I knew I couldn't ignore my gut feeling that, if I didn't intervene, Portia would be in danger. I decided not to say any more on the subject but I wasn't sure if he thought he'd convinced me to stop making waves and just stay home like a good wife. He should have known by now, that just wasn't my style.

Chapter Forty-Nine

On Sunday morning, I couldn't wait to get out of the house to pick up the New York Times. I made an excuse that we'd run out of cheese, which I needed to make a lasagne, and drove to the nearest convenience store. I didn't want Aaron to know I had the paper, so I parked at the end of our street and searched for the society news. It didn't take me long to find what I was looking for. There was no doubt; the woman in the photograph was Portia.

My heart skipped a beat when I saw her face, still as stunning as ever and with her hair restored to its beautiful pale golden color. She was wearing a sapphire blue, strapless gown which appeared to be chiffon and was smiling up at the man by her side; the man I hated most in this world, her husband, Philip Barrington. They were surrounded by photographers as they left the Royal Opera House after a performance of Carmen. It was all so surreal. I must have sat there for at least ten minutes trying to take it in. None of it made any sense.

I didn't know whether to show the paper to Aaron but, after a few minutes of indecision, I decided I'd leave it in my car and would only show it to him if he brought up the subject. I started towards the house but suddenly remembered the cheese, I supposedly needed, and headed back to the supermarket just a few blocks away. Aaron never did ask me why it took me so long.

The next day, after a sleepless night, I was thankful it was Monday. I had some time to myself and attempted to catch up on some household chores but my heart wasn't in it. I kept thinking about Portia and I was already plotting how I could get to see her, but I knew Aaron wouldn't accept my flying off to London again.

Just after lunch, when I was getting ready to take Riley for a run, I got a call on my cell phone. My heart raced when I saw it had to be an overseas call and my voice cracked as I answered, "Hello." At first, I could hardly hear the person on the other end of the line. "Who's there?" I asked, "I can hardly hear you."

My sister's voice was unmistakable even though she was whispering, "Sam, it's me."

I gasped, "Oh my god, Portia, where are you?"

She continued to whisper and I had to strain to hear her, "I'm at a restaurant with Serena and a friend of hers. I told her I had to go to the loo but I'm near the entrance, just out of sight. I can see her from here but I've only got a minute because she might come looking for me."

"What happened in Sandwich? Beth and I called the police but you were gone. Are you all right? We tried calling you but there was no answer."

"Lotti lent me her phone this morning. I just needed to tell you, you have to stop interfering, Sam. Everything's fine now."

I couldn't believe what I was hearing, "You expect me to believe everything's fine when you suddenly disappear from Emma's and there was obviously a struggle. You have to tell me the truth, Portia, what's going on? Does Philip have some kind of hold on you? Whatever it is, you need to expose him."

"Please, Sam," she begged, "leave it alone".

"How can I? You're my sister and I'll do anything I can to help you."

"I know and I love you for saying that but we can't even see each other. You have to stay away." I was just about to respond when I heard a rustling noise and she sounded in a panic as she whispered, "I have to go, I can see Serena's friend coming my way." Then she was gone.

I was so disturbed after I got off the phone; I knew I just couldn't sit around and do nothing. I had to go to London but, before I had a chance to think about checking flights and packing a bag, I heard the ring tone of my landline coming from the kitchen. I raced down the hall to answer it and was relieved when I heard Beth's voice. I told her about my conversation with Philip, the photo in the New York Times, and the call from Portia. She pleaded with me not to do anything rash. "You don't know what you might be getting into," she said. "Philip could be dangerous."

"I can't just sit around and do nothing," I responded.

There was a pause, "Why don't I drive up and stay for a few days? I can bring Portia's things with me although I'm not sure she'll really want them. Maybe together we can decide what to do."

My father had always taught me, two heads were better than one, "When can you be here?" I asked.

"Well I have to sort out a couple of things here but I should be able to leave in an hour or so. It will take me three hours to get there, if the traffic isn't too bad, so I should be there between six and seven."

I breathed a sigh of relief, "Oh, that's wonderful, Beth. I can't wait to see you but I have to warn you, Aaron is losing his patience with me over this whole business. I told him about the conversation with Philip but he doesn't know about the photo in the paper and I'm not going to mention Portia's call this morning."

"Oh dear, it's going to be difficult not being able to discuss the situation when he's around."

"I know but he'll be at the office all day tomorrow and we'll have lots of time to talk. It will be nice having you here to support me."

"I just want to make sure you curb that impulsive nature of yours. Chances are you'd arrive in London and the whole Barrington clan will have flown off to France or somewhere else on the planet."

I chuckled, "You're right, Beth. I love you, you know."

"Yes, I know and I love you too but I'd better get going so that I can get on the road."

"Okay, drive safely," I responded.

I spent the rest of the afternoon, before picking Vicky up, running to the store to get the ingredients I needed and then preparing a Lancashire hot pot, just like Maggie used to make. When Aaron arrived home, he was surprised to find me surrounded by pots and pans in the kitchen, "What's going on?" he asked, "Something smells really good."

"It's a surprise," I answered, kissing him on the cheek. "Beth should be arriving soon. She'll be staying for a few days."

He looked surprised, "When did you arrange all this?"

I shrugged, "Today. It was a spur of the moment, sort of thing."

He looked skeptical, "What's really going on, Sam?"

I frowned at him, "Nothing's going on. Can't I invite my stepmother for a visit without getting the third degree?"

He put up his hands in resignation, "Okay, just asking; that's all. You know I've always liked Beth. I think it will be good for you to have some company for a while."

I started to turn my back on him, "Dinner won't be served until she arrives so why don't you relax or, better yet, take Riley for a run."

"Yes, ma'am," he answered as he walked out the door.

A few minutes before seven, I heard a car pull up and ran to open the front door. Beth waved as she stepped out onto the driveway and I called out, "Wait and I'll help you with your luggage."

Aaron appeared right behind me and laid a hand on my arm, "I'll do it," he said.

There were lots of hugs and kisses, and then Beth saw Vicky standing shyly in the open doorway. "Oh my," she said teasingly, "who's that pretty little girl?"

Vicky continued sucking her thumb, "Say hello to your grandma," I said.

Beth walked towards her and was just about to speak when Riley came rushing past Vicky, almost crashing into Beth. She managed to catch him and scooped him up in her arms, "Oh, heavens, who's this?"

Vicky suddenly lost her shyness, "It's Riley," she said, coming forward and reaching up to stroke his back. "He's my dog; Daddy got him for me so I wouldn't be lonely when Mommy is away."

Beth glanced over at me and I shook my head slightly, warning her not to say any more. "He's very sweet," she said. "What kind of dog is he?"

Vicky looked up at Aaron, who replied, "He's a Kerry Blue terrier. His fur will turn grey when he gets a bit older."

Beth placed Riley gently on the ground then looked at Vicky, "Maybe we can take him for a walk together. Would you like that?"

Vicky shrugged, "I suppose so," she said nonchalantly. "He likes to go to the park where all the other dogs are."

Beth smiled, "All right, the park it is."

"Let's go inside," Aaron suggested, "I'll take your bags upstairs and put them in the guest room."

As we trooped into the house I grabbed Beth's hand and squeezed it. It felt so good to have her there, not only because she was family but she was there to support me and I no longer felt alone.

Chapter Fifty

On Tuesday, I decided to keep Vicky home from school so that she could spend the day with us. I wanted her to really get to know Beth and love her as much as I did. Beth was delighted but also a little surprised. She had suspected I'd want to spend the whole day mapping out a strategy for dealing with Philip and getting access to Portia.

Right after breakfast we were on our way to the Beardsley Zoo, just an hour away near Bridgeport in Connecticut. Vicky was upset about leaving Riley behind but, once we were on our way, she got excited about seeing all the animals. When we arrived, we found out there was a scavenger hunt. This involved answering questions and then searching for animals on the endangered species list. Even though the zoo is nowhere near as big as the Bronx Zoo, it took us well over two hours before we gave up, although we managed to find all but one of the animals. Afterwards, we visited the Carousel Museum, housing a genuine antique carousel, which Vicky got to ride. I thought we'd never get her off of there. Her favorite animal was the two-toed sloth because he was so slow and looked so gentle. She asked if we could get one for a pet and then it could keep Riley company when we weren't there. I had to explain; he was a wild animal and needed to live in the rain forest. Naturally, she had to point out, he wasn't living in a rain forest in the zoo and I was lost for words. Thankfully, Beth came to my rescue when she spotted a café and cut in, "Oh, there's a place to eat. Let's go, I'm starving."

We munched on chicken sandwiches and French fries, while contemplating what to do next, but I noticed Vicky was getting very quiet. She was obviously worn out and needed a nap so, right after lunch, we made our way home. I think Beth was beginning to feel a little weary too and I encouraged her to spend the rest of the afternoon relaxing in the garden while I pottered around the house and made a call to Emily. I hadn't spoken to her since the whole situation with Portia had begun. I felt badly about not keeping in touch with her, especially as she was the only true friend I'd ever had. We'd always exchanged Christmas and birthday cards and I knew nothing major had happened in her life but I suddenly felt the need to reach out to her. She was surprised and delighted when she heard my voice and, strangely enough, she'd been planning to telephone me that very evening. I began to wonder if there was such a thing as telepathy. She had some exciting news; she was pregnant and due in August. She and Larry had been trying for a baby for years and were beginning to talk about adoption, when the miracle happened. I was so thrilled for her and didn't want to spoil the mood so I decided not to tell her about Portia. Naturally she asked about her and I lied and said she was very happy and enjoying her life but I felt like choking. We talked for almost an hour and promised each other we wouldn't lose touch again and we'd email or phone, at least every other week, even if we didn't have any news. I was so elated when our conversation ended; I couldn't resist racing out to Beth and telling her all about it.

Just before dinner, Beth and I were in the kitchen when Aaron arrived home from the office. He kissed me on the cheek, gave Beth a hug, and then tossed a folded up newspaper onto the kitchen table. "I think you ladies might be interested in the news today," he said, and grinned as he walked out the door.

I immediately grabbed the paper and saw it was the New York Times. I had no idea what I was looking for so I gave some of the sections to Beth, "Look and see if you can find anything," I said. Then, as I began to shuffle through my sections, I muttered, "Damn that man, couldn't he just show us."

Less than a minute later Beth announced, "Here it is, I've found it."

"What is it?" I asked, leaning over her shoulder.

"It's about Philip, he's in New York."

I snatched the paper out of her hand and read the article. It was very brief and there was no photo but it told me all I needed to know. Philip was to speak at the Entrepreneur Conference at the Manhattan Center the following morning. My hand began to shake as I looked at Beth, "You know what this means? Portia must be in New York too."

Beth patted my shoulder, "You may be jumping to conclusions, dear."

I shook my head, "No, I have to be right. She's here, I just know it and I'm determined to see her. If Philip's going to be at the conference, then he won't be at the apartment. We can go there in the morning and, if anyone tries to stop us, I'm going to kick up such a fuss, they'll have to call the police to get rid of me."

Beth looked a little uncomfortable, "I'm not sure that's a good idea."

I sat down and looked at the article again. "Perhaps Lotti will help. When Portia called me from the restaurant, she told me she had Lotti's phone. She lent it to her so, even though she told me she couldn't help me anymore, it looks like she might have changed her mind. Maybe we can get to Portia through Lotti."

Our conversation was cut short by Vicky racing through the kitchen, with Riley at her heels, and Aaron returning to enquire when dinner would be ready. He never asked what, if anything, we had found in the paper and we didn't bring it up. I just didn't want to get into an argument with him, especially in front of Beth.

The next morning, as Aaron was leaving for the office and Beth and I were having breakfast in the kitchen, he popped in and said, "Have a good day, ladies, and good luck with whatever you're plotting to do today."

I frowned at him, "What do you mean by that?"

He smiled, "Oh, sorry, did I say plotting, I meant planning? See you both later." And before I could respond, he'd gone.

"He's trying to humor me," I said angrily, "and I'm not finding it very funny."

"That's because he doesn't believe Portia is in any danger. I wouldn't rock the boat if I were you, Sam. Aaron's doing the best he can considering what's happened. He's been more than patient and supported you all along."

I felt a little guilty, "Yes, I know. He's been amazing but there may be a limit to what he'll put up with."

"Well, let's not worry about that now," Beth remarked as she got up and started clearing up the dishes, "As soon as we get finished here and drop Vicky off, we'd better be on our way. The conference starts in an hour and we'll probably have to fight traffic most of the way."

I jumped up to help her, "You're right, let's get a move on."

Less than an hour later, we pulled into a parking garage on West 93rd. It cost a fortune but we didn't want to risk parking illegally and it was just a few minutes' walk to Philip's building.

I was surprised, when we entered the lobby, to find the concierge on duty was a rather attractive young woman. I introduced myself and asked if she would contact Mrs. Barrington and see if it would be convenient for us to visit. She politely requested we have a seat while she called upstairs. I gathered she wanted us far enough from the front desk so that we couldn't hear her conversation. She waited until Beth and I were seated and then picked up the telephone. I sat there with baited breath attempting to read her lips, but she was too far away and it felt like several minutes before she finally put the phone down and came around from behind her desk. I noticed, as she walked towards me, she had a distinct limp and as she got closer, I stood up, "Is my sister able to see us?" I asked.

"I'm afraid Mrs. Barrington is indisposed," she replied, "but Miss Herczeg will be coming down shortly to speak with you."

I thanked her and then turned to Beth, "It's Lotti, I wonder what's going on?"

"Well I guess we'll soon find out," Beth answered.

Beth and I sat waiting in silence and, each time we heard the elevator doors open, we looked up in anticipation. Finally, we saw Lotti emerge and make her way towards us but I was shocked by her appearance. She looked white as a ghost and her hair was hanging limply about her shoulders. Wearing jeans, a pale blue sweater and a pair of sneakers, this was not the Lotti I was used to seeing. She nodded at the concierge as she passed the desk and then quickly crossed over to me and grabbed my hand. Without preamble she asked, "Where's your car?"

I glanced at Beth and replied, "It's down the street in a parking garage."

She then took hold of Beth's arm with her other hand and pulled us out onto the street, "Take me to it," she said.

I sensed this was not the time to question her and the three of us scurried along the sidewalk until we reached the garage. "Do you want to sit in the car or do you want me to drive somewhere?" I asked.

"Let's just drive around," she answered.

Beth sat in the front with me while Lotti insisted she wanted to sit in the back. I got the impression she was hiding from something, or someone. We pulled out of the garage and I began to drive west towards the Hudson River; then Beth looked back at Lotti and said, "What's going on? You need to tell us or are we going to keep driving around all morning?"

I was a bit shocked at Beth's direct approach but it paid off, "I'm sorry," Lotti said," I just needed to get away from the building in case somebody saw me with you."

"Where's Portia," I asked, "Is she here in New York?"

"Yes she's here but you can't see her. Philip won't allow it."

I was incensed, "Nobody can stop me from seeing my own sister. Why don't we go back there now and you can take us to her."

"You don't understand, he practically keeps her under lock and key."

"But we know he's not there right now and that's why we came. He's at some conference."

"Yes, and Serena's with him. I'm supposed to be making sure Portia doesn't slip off somewhere."

Beth shook her head, "I don't understand, Lotti, why would you go along with this? I know Serena has a hold over you but why won't you allow Portia to leave?"

Lotti started to cry, "She doesn't want to go."

I pulled into a parking area adjacent to the Holy Trinity Church and stopped the car. "What on earth do you mean?" I asked angrily. She continued to sob so I got out of the car and slipped into the back seat beside her. I pulled her towards me and stroked her hair, "Lotti, you have to tell me what's going on."

She pulled a tissue from her pocket and dried her eyes, "Philip's threatened that, if she ever tries to leave him, there will be dire consequences. He told her he wouldn't be responsible if anything happened to her family."

I gasped, "Her family? We're her only family."

"Yes, I know," Lotti whispered, "and he's always taunting her about what a sweet little niece she has and how awful it would be if she had some kind of accident."

Right then I felt sick to my stomach. I was so infuriated but, at the same time, a little afraid, "You're saying he'd actually harm Vicky if she tried to leave?"

"He's a sick, sick man," Beth interjected. "Why on earth does he want to stay in this marriage?"

"Because he's found someone he can blackmail into going along with his perverted lifestyle."

"I hope you're not telling me he and Serena have drawn Portia into their devious incestuous world?"

"Not yet, but she's well aware of what's going on. While he's got this hold on her, she isn't going to risk publicizing it."

I sat for a moment trying to take it all in and then Lotti looked at her watch, "Are you anxious about getting back?" I asked.

She nodded, "Yes, if I'm not there when the conference is over, we'll all be in a heap of trouble."

I hugged her and then stepped out to return to the driver's seat, "We'll drop you off close to the building and you can run inside. What about the concierge? Are you sure she won't tell Philip we were here?"

"Monica? No, she won't say a word; she hates Philip."

I began to drive back to Central Park West, "How do you know that?"

"Her father used to work for him. He held a senior position in one of Philip's companies and then, out of the blue, he let him go. I won't go into the details but, a year later after a bout of depression, he died and Monica blames Philip."

"Is it just a coincidence that she works in the building where he lives?" Beth asked.

Lotti scoffed, "If it were only that simple. He was attracted to her but she wasn't interested in having anything to do with a married man. Philip's not used to being rejected so he recommended her for the concierge position in the hope he could win her over, but it didn't work. I'm surprised he hasn't got her fired by now. Don't worry, I'll tell her not to mention seeing you and I guarantee she won't say a word."

"I don't understand," Beth said. "Why doesn't she just quit if she hates him so much? Surely an attractive young lady like her could get a far better job."

"Again, it's not that simple. She has Parkinson's and she could never get the kind of insurance Barrington offers anywhere else. It's so sad because she's so young."

"So is that why she's limping? I couldn't help noticing."

"Yes, I'm afraid so."

As we got closer to Philip's building, I asked Lotti to tell Portia how much I loved her and how determined I was to get her out of the situation she was in. Lotti reached over and grasped both Beth and me by the shoulder, "I'll be in touch somehow. Don't do anything rash."

I reached back and grasped her hand, "One more thing, Lotti, what made you change your mind about helping me?"

She sighed, "I just couldn't stand seeing Portia so miserable." Then she leapt out of the car and we watched as she raced along the sidewalk and disappeared from sight.

Both Beth and I were silent until we got onto I-95 and then she asked, "Well, what do you propose to do now?"

I hesitated before answering, "I'm going to see Philip."

Beth gasped, "You can't be serious. I hope you're not considering threatening him with exposure. He's a dangerous man, Sam, and you need to think about what Lotti said about Vicky."

I reached over and patted her hand, "It's okay. I'm not planning to threaten him. I'm planning to seduce him."

She actually started to laugh. "Now I know you're just pulling my leg." I paused and turned towards her and she noticed the look on my face. "Oh, my god, you really are serious. What on earth would possess you to do such a thing and what do you hope to achieve. You can't do this, Sam, I absolutely forbid it."

I scoffed, "You can't forbid it, I'm a grown up and I can make my own decisions."

She sighed, "I know, I know, but why would you even consider it?"

"Because, if my plan works; I might be able to get him in a compromising position and then I'll have the upper hand."

"And what is your plan exactly?"

I hesitated, "I haven't worked it out exactly but I'll think of something in the next few days. Just don't tell Aaron what I'm up to."

"As if I ever would," she responded.

Chapter Fifty-One

I decided, even before we reached the house that, from now on, it would be best if I kept Beth out of the picture. She was too concerned for my safety and might even decide to tell Aaron. On Friday afternoon, she told me she was leaving to go back to Boston the following morning. She felt I needed to spend the weekend with Aaron and Vicky and she would just be in the way. She was also under the impression I had second thoughts about my plan to meet with Philip because I'd made every effort to distract her every time the subject came up. What she didn't realize was, while she was taking her morning walk, a routine that had been part of her life for the past few years, I was surfing the internet searching for any mention of Philip. In particular, I was checking for any upcoming event which he might be attending. It was a frustrating task, especially as there were dozens of other Philip Barrington's in existence and by the time Beth left on Saturday morning, I had failed to come up with any useful information.

On Sunday, as it was such a beautiful June day, Aaron suggested we take Vicky to Playland. It was only a short twenty minute drive away in Rye and a really fun place for families.

We wore our bathing suits under our clothes, in case we decided to go for a swim in the Sound, and packed our own lunch, rather than eating in any of the fast food restaurants available. Vicky was excited and wanted to go on every ride in Kiddyland and Aaron and I were having trouble keeping up. We put our foot down when she demanded to go into the Zombie Castle, but we did take her into the Hall of Mirrors and all laughed ourselves silly. It was a good feeling.

We eventually made our way to the beach, had a picnic lunch, and then decided to strip down to our bathing suits and dip our toes in the Sound. It only took a few seconds to discover the water was freezing and there would be no swimming for us although, some brave souls were happily splashing about a few yards from shore.

By the time we got home we were exhausted but happy and then Aaron decided he would take us out to dinner at Fratelli's, a gem of a place we'd been to on several occasions. It was a wonderful way to end the day even though Vicky kept complaining that Riley would be lonely, left all by himself again.

In spite of the enjoyable weekend, I was happy when Monday rolled around. I couldn't wait to be alone so that I could continue surfing the internet but, after hours of sitting in front of the computer, I finally gave up. Then I decided to try a different approach. First, I had to make sure Philip was still in town and see if I could somehow trick him into meeting me. I spent most of the afternoon coming up with a plan and finally had a brainwave. I began practicing a Hungarian accent which I'd picked up from Lotti. I just hoped it sounded authentic. The only other accents I'd really had any exposure to were Maggie's which, being from the north of England didn't sound too exotic and there was Erin's, but she was Irish and it just wouldn't do. I needed to sound mysterious and I had to chuckle at what I was about to do.

When I finally got up enough courage, I placed a call to Philip's office and was put through to his personal assistant, Pamela Lessing, who I had spoken to before. "May I please speak with Mr. Barrington?" I asked, trying desperately to maintain the Hungarian accent.

"May I ask who's calling, please?"

"Yes, my name is Petra Kovacs. I'm an old friend of Philip's."

She hesitated and then responded, "My apologies, Miss Kovacs, but Mr. Barrington is away from the office until later this afternoon but I can give him a message."

I hadn't, for one minute expected to be put through to Philip and I was relieved because it wasn't part of my plan. "That's very kind of you. I was wondering if he could meet me for lunch either tomorrow or Wednesday. I will be available at noon on either day."

"Well, I can certainly pass your message on to him. May I have your phone number so that he can call you back?"

"Oh dear, I'm afraid he won't be able to reach me by phone. Perhaps if I called back early in the morning you could let me know if he's available for lunch."

"Yes, I can certainly do that, Miss Kovacs. I should be able to get you an answer by then."

"Thank you, I'll call back tomorrow. Oh, and please tell Philip I'm looking forward to seeing him again."

I got off the phone feeling elated. I had managed to pull it off and now I could just imagine Philip trying to remember who on earth Petra Kovacs was and where he had met her before. Of course, there was no Petra, I just got the name off the internet. I had no doubt he'd be too curious not to follow through and now I had to figure out what I was going to wear for the upcoming lunch date. I chuckled again thinking about his reaction when he saw it was me.

That evening, I was so engrossed in thinking about seeing Philip that Aaron wondered why I was so quiet. "What are you up to now?" he asked.

"I'm not up to anything," I answered defensively.

"I know you better than that, Sam," he said. "I hope you're not still plotting to rescue your sister from the clutches of the evil Philip Barrington."

I was annoyed, "It's not a joke, Aaron, and I wish you wouldn't treat it like one, but to put your mind at rest, I'm not plotting anything."

"Then why are you so quiet? You've hardly said a word since I got home."

"I was busy getting dinner ready and you were gone for almost an hour walking Riley. I've hardly even seen you."

"That's not true, we've been here stuck in front of the TV for a couple of hours and you're not even watching the program. You've just been staring into space most of the time."

I stood up, "What do you expect? I'm not interested in watching a bunch of zombies taking over some fictitious town in the middle of nowhere. I'm going to bed."

He shrugged, "Suit yourself," he said and turned his attention back to the TV.

I was angry but glad for the excuse to get away. I just wanted to be alone and the bedroom was the perfect place.

I didn't hear Aaron come to bed that night. Strangely enough I slept soundly considering how much I had on my mind and, when morning came, I was feeling wide awake and ready for the day.

The first two hours, getting breakfast for everyone; dressing Vicky and taking her to school, seemed never ending. It was a routine we went through every weekday but on this particular morning it seemed to drag on and on. I finally breathed a sigh of relief when I closed the front door and called Riley in from the back yard.

At exactly fifteen minutes after nine, I called Philip's office and was again put through to Pamela Lessing. "Good morning," I said, "This is Petra Kovacs, Mrs. Lessing."

"Ah, good morning," she answered. "I'm pleased you contacted me so early. I gave Mr. Barrington your message and he said he could meet you for lunch today at one o'clock."

My heart skipped a beat, "Did he suggest a place?" I asked.

"Yes, Les Halles. Do you know it?"

"Yes, I do," I lied trying to sound sophisticated. "I'll be there at one. Thank you so much for your help."

"My pleasure," she answered. "I hope you enjoy your lunch."

I couldn't wait to get off the phone because now I was in panic mode. I'd already figured out what to wear but I needed to shower and wash my hair, and I still needed to drive into the city. Suddenly I realized I had almost four hours before I was to meet Philip and I flopped down onto a kitchen chair and waited for my heartbeat to stop hammering in my chest.

Chapter Fifty-Two

At exactly fifteen minutes after one, I walked through the doors of Les Halles. I had deliberately arrived late hoping Philip would already be seated and, I wanted to make an entrance. I was wearing a dress I'd bought on a whim years earlier and never worn. It was a brilliant shade of crimson with cap sleeves, a low scoop neck, nipped in at the waist and had a flirty a-line skirt. Along with my five inch ivory sandals and matching clutch I was sure to attract some attention.

I saw Philip almost immediately. He was seated at a table in the center of the room and looking down at his cell phone. I hesitated but waved away the hostess as she came towards me, "It's okay, my lunch date is already here," I said and sailed past her. Suddenly the room seemed to go quiet and I was aware of people looking up at me as I literally sashayed between the tables. It was then that Philip glanced in my direction and, with a shocked expression on his face, rose to meet me. When I reached him, I merely smiled and, in my newly acquired Hungarian accent, said, "Hello, how are you, Philip?"

At that moment, his face changed and he actually grinned, "So you are the mysterious Petra Kovacs," he said.

Dropping the accent, I replied, "Yes, are you disappointed?"

"On the contrary," he remarked as he pulled out a chair for me "I'm pleased to see you, Sam. Please sit down." He returned to his side of the table and, after putting his cell phone in his pocket, asked, "So why the charade? Did you think I wouldn't want to have lunch with you?"

"Seriously? I thought you'd avoid me like the plague. You must know why I'm here."

"Obviously you want to talk about Portia. Go ahead; I'd like nothing more than to clear up this whole business. I've got nothing to hide."

I looked around, "Could I please get a glass of wine or something and then we can talk?"

"Of course," he replied beckoning to a waiter who was just passing by.

It was only a few moments before the waiter returned with a bottle of Riesling and filled our glasses but, in those few moments; Philip had been staring at me and making me feel a little uncomfortable. Alone again, he leaned back in his chair and said, "You look absolutely stunning, Sam. I'd forgotten just how attractive you were."

I ignored his remark, "I want the truth about Portia, Philip."

"You mean about me abducting her and all that nonsense? Yes, I picked her up a couple of times when she ran off. Your sister is a little unstable, Sam, but I'm sure you already know that."

I knew what I was about to say was a betrayal but it was all part of my plan to gain his trust, "Portia's always been a little unstable but after what you've done, I can't blame her for running away from you."

He frowned, "I suppose she told you some outlandish stories about me but they're not true."

"Why would she make them up?" I asked, knowing full well Lotti had confirmed everything I'd heard.

"You'll have to ask her yourself," he replied.

"That would be a little difficult considering she refuses to see me or even speak to me."

He smirked, "And why would that be, Sam?"

I stared him straight in the eyes, "Maybe because you've threatened to hurt my family if I interfere."

"What utter nonsense, if you want to see your sister, I won't stand in your way."

I was about to respond when a man approached our table and Philip immediately jumped to his feet. "Arthur," he said, extending his hand, "good to see you."

The man, who looked to be in his seventies and extremely well dressed, shook Philip's hand, "You too, my boy," he said and then glanced down at me.

Philip followed his gaze, "Petra," he said, "I'd like you to meet Arthur Grayson, one of my father's closest friends." Then, looking back at the man, he continued, "Arthur, this is Petra Kovacs. She's visiting from Hungary."

I was stunned at his audacity and it was a few seconds before I managed to respond, once again assuming an accent. "It's a pleasure to meet you."

"You too," he replied bowing slightly from the waist.

"Will you excuse us for a moment?" Philip asked, and I nodded as he stepped away from the table and led Arthur Grayson to the side of the room. I watched them wondering if they were talking about me but neither one of them looked in my direction. I glanced at the other diners around me and then looked back at Philip; there was no doubt, he was the most handsome man in the room and impeccably dressed, as usual, in a charcoal grey suit and striped tie. After just a few minutes he returned to the table and apologized for the interruption.

"Why on earth did you tell him I was Petra Kovacs?" I asked.

He grinned, "Why not? I thought you were enjoying playing a mysterious foreigner."

I shook my head, "How about we order now, I'm hungry."

I studied the menu and ended up ordering the grilled salmon with asparagus, while Philip ordered the beef tenderloin. That done, I felt awkward, not sure what to say next. I thought I had it all worked out but I didn't expect Philip to be so amenable. Suddenly he broke into my thoughts, "Speaking of your family," he said, "how is Aaron and what about Vicky? I bet she's quite a young lady."

"Hardly," I replied, "but she's growing up fast."

He nodded, "And Aaron?"

I decided to go ahead with my plan and let Philip think my marriage was not all hearts and roses. "He's well, but I don't see too much of him because he's been working such long hours."

Philip frowned, "That must be difficult for you with Vicky at school all day too. Have you considered getting a job?"

"I had a job but I got so busy chasing after Portia, I had to quit."

"I'm sorry to hear that, Sam. Perhaps now you know the truth you can look for employment again."

I knew he was playing a game with me and maybe he suspected I was playing a game too but I couldn't stop now, "I'm not sure I do know the truth but I need to think about myself now. I'm tired of spending all my time trying to protect my sister. She's always been the center of attention."

"I'm surprised to hear you say that. I always got the impression you were very close."

I nodded, "We are, in a way, but I felt like I always took a back seat to her. She was the one who always got the compliments. People constantly commented about how beautiful she was. It made me feel like the ugly duckling."

He chuckled, "Well, that ugly duckling had grown into a swan. Don't you realize how attractive you are, Sam?"

I shrugged, "I may have improved with age but I could never compete with Portia."

"Why on earth would you want to? You're a beautiful woman and not only that, you're an interesting woman. I can't really say the same for Portia."

I felt my anger start to rise and hesitated for a moment to suppress the feeling, "Why did you marry her then?"

He sighed, "I guess I was just infatuated but, after the wedding, that soon wore off. I need someone who can be my equal. Someone I can actually share my life with."

"Then why don't you just divorce her?"

He actually grinned, "You're father was a very smart man. He made sure she had an iron clad pre-nup; it would cost me a fortune."

"But wouldn't it be worth it? From what I hear, you could certainly afford it."

"Would that make you happy, Sam? Come to think of it, what would make you happy; you seem rather discontent?"

"I don't really know. Maybe I'll go back to work if Aaron doesn't object."

"Why on earth would he object?"

I smirked, "He never likes it when I'm away from home; it puts too much pressure on him."

"In what way?"

"Having to help with chores, stuff like that. He doesn't understand what it's like to be home all day and have nothing to do but cooking, laundry and walking the dog."

"Ah, so you have a dog now!"

"Yes, he's just a puppy. We got him for Vicky."

Just then our lunch arrived and we sat in silence until the waiter refilled our wine glasses and left the table. "I hope you enjoy your salmon. The food here is excellent."

I looked around again, "I've never been here before; it's very elegant."

He smiled, "Just like you," he remarked.

I laughed, "Elegant is not the way I've ever thought of myself. Portia was always the one who had an innate sense for fashion. Daddy used to tell me I was a bit of a tomboy."

"Well, you must have grown out of that stage because, now, you are every bit as lovely and fashionable as your sister."

I knew he was lying but decided to go along with it, "Thank you for saying that. It's hard always living in someone's shadow but don't get me wrong, I love Portia."

He nodded and picked up his fork, "Why don't we eat before our lunch gets cold and then we can talk some more."

Again, we sat in relative silence, only commenting on our meals then, when finished, he asked, "Would you like some dessert, they have wonderful Crème Brulee here."

I put my hand over my stomach, "No thank you but I would like some coffee, just regular will do."

"Very well," he said looking around for the waiter.

Once coffee was served I leaned back in my chair and said, "I'm glad I got to see you today."

He smiled, "It's been delightful, Sam. I know you have a lot of unanswered questions but maybe we can clear them up some time."

"I'd like that because I'm very confused about my sister and I want to be sure she's where she wants to be, and happy."

"Look, I'll talk to her tonight. I'll find out why she doesn't want to see or speak to you. This issue about me threatening your family is absurd."

I reached across the table and grasped his hand, "Would you do that for me please, Philip?"

He looked down at my hand and then back into my eyes, "Of course I will and I'll either call you tomorrow or have Portia call you herself."

I drew back my hand and looked at my watch, "I'm sorry but I really need to leave in a few minutes. I have to pick Vicky up and I can't be late."

"I understand," he responded, reaching in his pocket for his wallet. "I'll just settle this while you're finishing your coffee and then I'll walk you out."

He took my arm as we exited the restaurant onto the sidewalk. "Where are you parked?" he asked.

"Just down the street. There's a parking garage; it's only a few minutes away."

"Well I guess I'll be leaving you here. I'm walking back to the office."

"Thank you for lunch. I'll be waiting to hear from you tomorrow."

"It was my absolute pleasure," he responded. "Do I get a hug?"

I was a little surprised but I moved a little closer and he folded his arms around me. "We'll have to get together again soon," he whispered.

I hesitated for a moment and then drew back, "I'd like that," I said.

Chapter Fifty-Three

On the way home, I was elated. My plan was working. I could tell he was attracted to me and so, like a spider, I was drawing him into my web. I knew I was playing a dangerous game but I was determined to take Philip down. I hadn't quite put my plan together because I needed to get Lotti involved and I didn't even know if that would be possible. However, my immediate problem was the fact that I was running late to pick up Vicky, and I knew I'd stick out like a sore thumb in my red dress, among all the other mothers.

When I climbed out of the car outside of the school, there were only two or three children still waiting accompanied by their teacher. Vicky broke loose and started running towards me as soon as she saw me pull up, but she stopped dead in her tracks when she got a good look at me. "Oh, Mommy," she called out, "you look so pretty."

I smiled and held out my arms, "Come here, honey, give Mommy a hug."

On the way home, she must have asked me a dozen questions. "Why was I all dressed up? Where did I go? Who was I with? What did I have for lunch?" I hated lying to her but I had no choice and merely said I'd met an old school friend from out of town who was just here for the day. I hoped I'd satisfied her curiosity but, at the same time, I was sure Aaron would soon hear all about it. I didn't have to wait too long to find out I was right.

I'd just finished preparing dinner when I heard Aaron's key in the door and Vicky's footsteps as she ran down the hall to meet him. "Daddy," she called out. "Guess what's for dinner? Sgetti and meat balls."

"Mmm," I heard him reply, "Sgetti, eh? That's my favorite."

"Yes, and you should have seen Mommy today; she looked bootiful."

Aaron appeared in the doorway to the kitchen, blew me a kiss, and then turned back to Vicky. "Tell me all about it, honey."

I gave Vicky a slight shake of my head but it was hopeless, "She had on this red dress and it was so pretty and she wore her shoes with the big heels."

"I see, and where was this?"

Vicky was starting to lose interest as Riley crawled out from under the kitchen table, "When she picked me up from school."

Aaron patted her on the head, "Okay, why don't you take Riley up to your room for a while and we'll call you when it's time to eat."

Without hesitation, she took off down the hall with Riley behind her. "Don't forget to call me when sgetti's ready," she called out.

Aaron put his brief case down on the kitchen table, "So what was the occasion today?" he asked.

I kept my back to him while I began slicing a baguette at the counter, "Lunch with an old school friend."

"What old school friend?"

"You don't know her. I haven't seen her for years. She lives in Vermont now and was in New York for a few days."

"What's this friend's name?"

I hesitated, "Eh, Janet Moss."

"Funny, I've never heard you mention her before. I assume you had lunch together; where did you go?"

I couldn't think fast enough so I had to tell the truth, "Les Halles."

I turned to see the stunned look on Aaron's face, "Wow, that's a bit high end isn't it?"

I frowned, "Don't worry, it was her treat."

"Well that's a relief," he responded with a hint of sarcasm. "I guess spaghetti is a bit of a come down?"

I waved my hand at him, "Why don't you just go and get changed. Dinner will be ready in about fifteen minutes."

He nodded very slowly as though he was considering continuing his interrogation but, he picked up his brief case and left the room.

It was three days before I heard from Philip and, although I'd been confident he would get in touch, I was beginning to wonder if my plan had a remote chance of working. He told me he'd spoken to Portia and she was adamant that I stay away and stop interfering in her life. I knew he was lying through his teeth but I responded by telling him I'd had enough and couldn't go on wasting my time worrying about my sister. As I'd hoped, he suggested I not give up and perhaps it would be a good idea if we met again to discuss the situation. He was so transparent that it was almost laughable. I agreed to meet him as long as it was in a public place and he agreed. We made a date for the following Thursday evening when I knew Aaron would be attending a business dinner and likely to be home late.

On Wednesday evening, I told Aaron I was going into the city the next day to have dinner with Emily and Larry, who had driven up from Philadelphia. "I thought you just spoke to her on the phone," he remarked.

"I did, but I'm dying to see her. She's about four months pregnant now."

"What about Vicky?"

"I'll get Jen from next door to babysit. She could do with the extra money."

I'm not sure whether he believed my story or not but, the next morning before he left for the office, he told me to say hi to Emily and hoped I had a nice evening.

Philip and I had arranged to meet for a drink in the rooftop lounge at the Peninsula Hotel on 5th Avenue. He apologized for not suggesting dinner but, he had a prior engagement with a business acquaintance in the hotel's Clement restaurant. He hoped to get away by eight and proposed that we meet at eight thirty.

I decided to wear a simple form-fitting black dress with a boat neckline and long lace sleeves. It was a little shorter than the dresses I was accustomed to wearing but it was still elegant and sexy at the same time. In my four-inch black sandals and a pair of gorgeous silver drop earrings Portia had given me, when I surveyed myself in the mirror, I was pleased with what I saw. I knew I could fit in with any of Philip's crowd, not that I wanted any of them to see me. It was important that I kept my meetings with Philip a secret if my plan was going to work but, at the same time, I wasn't ready to meet him anywhere where he could take advantage of me. At least, not yet.

At eight thirty, when I entered the lounge, Philip was already there. It was a beautiful summer evening and he was seated at a table in the outdoor area. As soon as he saw me, he rose from his seat and, when I got within arm's length, he leaned forward and kissed me on the cheek. "Hi, Sam," he whispered, "great to see you and you're looking lovely as usual."

I smiled as he pulled out my chair and I sat down, "Good to see you too, Philip," I replied. "What are you drinking?"

He looked down at the rather exotic looking cocktail, "It's a Ning Sling. Would you like one?"

"I'm not sure, I usually only drink wine."

He grinned and handed me the glass, "Here, live a little, see if you like it."

I took a sip and recognized the taste of gin, obviously mixed with some type of fruit. It was pleasant and I decided to go for it, "Mmm, it's nice. I think I'll have one."

"So what do you think of the view?" he asked as he signaled for the waiter.

It was early July and the sun had only just set but the view over Central Park was awesome. We were on the top floor of the hotel, some thirty floors above 5th Avenue and the perfect place for a rendezvous. "It's wonderful," I remarked, "I'm glad I came here tonight."

Once the waiter had served my cocktail, Philip asked if I'd like something to eat but I declined. I'd made Vicky a hot dog and French fries for dinner, not a very healthy choice, but she loved them and I was too anxious about the upcoming evening to get too creative. I'd nibbled on a few French fries myself but really had no appetite and, sitting across from Philip, I couldn't begin to think about food; I had other things on my mind. I needed to address the reason I was there and we couldn't avoid talking about Portia. I listened as Philip described several incidents he claimed had occurred in the last year, where he made it look like my sister was becoming more and more unstable. I'm not sure how I maintained my composure because I knew it was all a pack of lies and he was just trying to widen the gap between Portia and me. I shook my head over and over as he rambled on and on and even managed to get teary eyed at one point. I should have tried out for the theater instead of Portia! My response to all of this, when he'd finished speaking, was one of sympathy. I told him how sorry I was I'd been so taken in by Portia and I felt like a fool for believing all the stories she'd told me. Then to add to the deception, I reached across the table for his hand and said, "I know it must be really difficult for you dealing with all the drama. I guess we both got the short end of the stick," then I released his hand and lowered my eyes.

He picked up on what I was trying to say immediately. "You're not talking about your relationship with Portia now are you?"

I shook my head and looked back at him, "I only have myself to blame. I was never overly ambitious and now I have the life to show for it. Every time I come into the city, I feel myself come alive. It's vibrant and exciting and there's so much to do here."

Philip frowned, "You're beginning to sound like a bored housewife."

I nodded, "I guess that's because I am. If it wasn't for Vicky....."

I hesitated and Philip cut in, "If it wasn't for Vicky, you'd leave. Is that what you were going to say?"

"I don't know," I replied with a sigh. "Don't get me wrong, Aaron's a good man but I was far too young when we got married. If I'd stayed single, I would have been able to travel and experience other places and other cultures. Maybe, one day, I'll have the opportunity to do that but I'll probably be an old lady by then."

He grinned, "I can't imagine you as an old lady but, tell me, what does your husband think of the way you feel?"

"Aaron? He has no idea and, in any case, I hardly ever see him. He's always working and even on weekends, he often spends time at his office."

"I'm sorry, Sam. It's hard to understand how any man would treat you that way." He reached across and covered my hand with his, "I know if I were your husband, I would never neglect you."

I looked down at his hand and then stared into his eyes, "Thank you for making me feel desirable," I said, with all the sincerity I could muster.

"No need to thank me. You are desirable and would be to any man worth his salt. You're a beautiful woman and you deserve better."

I suddenly pulled my hand away and reached for my purse, "I really think I should go," I said.

He shook his head, "There's no need for that, Sam. Please stay a while longer, you only just got here."

I stood up, "No, this isn't a good idea. I need to go home."

He insisted on walking me to my car which was parked in a lot on W54th, just a couple of blocks away. As we left the hotel, he put his arm around my waist and I didn't stop him. As much as I despised him, I had to admit he was one of the most attractive men I'd ever met and I noticed several women staring at him as we passed by. They were probably envious of me but they had no idea what I was up to. When we got to my car, I opened the door to get in but he took me by the elbow and gently turned me around so that I was facing him, and only inches away. "I'd like to see you again," he said.

"It's been lovely," I responded, "but I don't think this can happen again. I......."

I didn't get the chance to say anymore because he pulled me towards him and kissed me hard on the lips. My head was telling me to stop him but I needed to give in to his advances if my plan was going to work. Eventually, after what seemed like forever, he let me go and whispered, "Now will you see me again?"

I began to slide into the driver's seat, "I'll call you," I answered.

Chapter Fifty-Four

On Friday morning, after dropping Vicky off at school, I noticed a voice message on my cell phone. It was Philip thanking me for a wonderful evening and hoping we could get together soon. I smiled to myself, now I had to come up with the next part of my plan.

The weekend was uneventful and, once again, I couldn't wait for Monday to come around. I knew Aaron would be working late that night and I only had a short period of time to act. The sun set at about eight-thirty and I needed it to be dark. At exactly eight-forty-five, after Vicky was in bed, I opened the back door, pushed Riley out into the garden and then stood back in the doorway and threw his favorite chew toy as far as I could. He reacted the way I'd hoped, racing to find it and barking with excitement. I whispered to him to bring it back to me and then I threw it again. There was such a commotion, I was sure the neighbors could hear him and, after the fourth throw, I called out, "Riley come in, boy."

Minutes later, I contacted the police and reported that someone had been in my back yard and had been looking in the window but my dog chased him off. I guess it was a slow night because they sent an officer out right away to take my statement. I did my best to show how fearful I was and even mentioned I'd seen a strange car going past the house two or three times, earlier in the evening. When I was asked to describe the car, I said it looked very expensive, maybe a Bentley and it was a light color. The officer completed his notes and advised me he'd be checking with my neighbors to see if they'd noticed anything unusual. Then he advised me to be sure my doors and windows were locked. When he left I smiled to myself but I knew the hard part was ahead of me. Meanwhile, I decided not to tell Aaron the police had been to the house. The less he knew the better.

On Tuesday morning, I telephoned Beth and asked if Emma might be up for a visit from my whole family. I knew Aaron had the following Monday off and I had every intention of asking him if we could go away for the weekend. Beth said she would call Emma and ask her but pointed out it was about a four hour drive to Cape Cod from where we were. When I remarked, "The further away the better," she was immediately suspicious.

I had made up my mind Beth would be a much better person than Lotti to be my accomplice. Lotti was much too fragile and had a lot to lose if my plan failed. So, when Beth asked, "What are you up to now, Sam?" It gave me the opening I needed.

"Well, I have no intention of going to Emma's and once Aaron and Vicky have left I want you to come here. I need your help."

I told her what I'd dreamed up and, needless to say, she was skeptical, thought I was crazy, and was also concerned for my safety. It took some convincing on my part but she finally agreed to contact Emma and go along with my plan. By the afternoon, she had already returned my call and told me Emma would be delighted to see me again and was looking forward to meeting my family. She had no idea I wouldn't be there but I didn't want to involve her at this point. Now I had to convince Aaron.

I was more than a little surprised when Aaron thought it would be a great idea to go to the Cape, even though it was a long drive, and a bit of an ordeal with Vicky being stuck in the car for hours on end. I couldn't believe how everything was falling into place but I still had to draw Philip into my trap.

On Wednesday morning, I called Emma to make arrangements for our visit and, I'd only just finished speaking to her, when my cell phone rang. The voice was unmistakable; it was Philip. "Good morning, beautiful lady," he said, "I was hoping to hear from you by now."

"Good morning," I replied, "I was actually just thinking about you."

"Well, I hope you were having good thoughts because you've been on my mind a lot since I saw you. I decided I couldn't wait any longer for you to call me."

"I'm sorry Philip, but I can't see you again. I just feel I'd be betraying my own sister. I know we're estranged at the moment, but I just can't do this."

There was a moment of silence. "What about your husband? Has your conscience been telling you, you might be betraying him too?"

I sighed, "Aaron really doesn't pay much attention to anything I do. He even suggested taking Vicky away next weekend for a special father and daughter visit to Cape Cod. He didn't even consider that I might want to go with them."

There was a pause before I heard the words I'd been waiting for. "Does that mean you'll be home alone all weekend?"

"Not necessarily, I may just take off myself and visit Beth or I might even drive down to Philadelphia to see my friend, Emily."

"Don't do that, Sam," he said rather abruptly.

"Why wouldn't I?" I countered. "I don't want to spend the whole week-end alone."

"You wouldn't have to," he said softly, "I could be there with you."

I hesitated, "No, Philip, I can't let you come here. I've already told you, this isn't going to work. What if somebody sees you? How would I ever explain a strange man visiting me with Aaron away?"

"I can be very discreet, Sam. Nobody will know I'm there and I guarantee you won't regret it."

I kept my composure, even though my heart was racing. "I need to think about it, Philip. Please try to understand, I need more time. I'll call you back tomorrow, I promise."

"Aah, Sam," he responded, "you need to live a little. I told you that before. You want this, you know you do and I want it too. I'll wait but I don't have a lot of patience so a promise is a promise. I'll expect to hear from you tomorrow. Goodbye, lovely lady." And he hung up.

I looked at the phone in my hand and muttered, "Bastard," under my breath.

The following morning, my hand was shaking as I called Philip's number. I was almost relieved when he didn't answer and I had to leave a message. I merely asked him to call me back, when he had a moment, and then just sat motionless for the longest time. I was beginning to have second thoughts. Was it too late to stop this charade?

I didn't have long to wait to hear from Philip, he called me back within a half-hour. "Sam, I was hoping you'd contact me this morning. I have to go out of town later and I won't be back until early on Saturday. I'll be extremely busy so you might have trouble getting in touch with me. I hope you've reconsidered."

I was a little taken aback by his tone. It almost sounded as though he was talking to a business associate and I was annoyed, but managed not to show it. "I'm glad you called me back, Philip," I said. "I've been awake most of the night thinking about you. I do want to see you again but we have to be discreet. If you come here on Saturday, it will have to be after dark. I can't risk any of my neighbors seeing you."

He chuckled, "It all sounds very clandestine. Do you want me to wear a disguise?"

"I'm not joking, Philip. I don't want you coming to the front door, I need you to come around the back of the house and come in the back door. Oh, and by the way, what kind of car are you driving?"

"Why are you asking, Sam?"

"Please, I just need to know and what color is it?"

"It's a Chrysler, cream or beige, I don't know. This is getting a bit ridiculous," he answered, sounding a little impatient.

"That kind of car would be a bit conspicuous near the house," I responded. "You'll have to park at the end of the street, right at the corner under the Davenport Road sign."

"You have to be kidding," he said. "I'm not used to following a lot of rules and regulations, Sam."

"Take it or leave it," I said abruptly and then wished I could take it back. My voice softened, "I'm sorry, I'm just nervous, I've never done anything like this before."

He paused before answering, "I understand," he said gently, "but you have no need to worry and I promise it will all be worth it."

"Thank you, "I responded. "I can't wait to see you."

"I'll be there at about ten, lovely lady," he whispered and, once again, just hung up.

I was trembling as I put the phone down. I couldn't believe I'd pulled it off but I had all of the next day to get through, attempting to behave like a normal wife and mother. Aaron must never know or I might lose him forever.

Chapter Fifty-Five

On Friday night, after dinner, I behaved as though I was feeling a bit under the weather and decided to go to bed early. Aaron commented, "I hope you'll be okay by the morning so you'll be okay to travel."

I gave him a peck on the cheek and answered, "Oh, I'm sure I will be, honey," and I left him in the family room watching a documentary about basketball. A sport I was not particularly interested in.

I got up early on Saturday morning and started packing for the trip but, when Aaron woke up and saw the state I was in, he was more than a little concerned. My normal routine was to take a shower, get dressed and make myself presentable before breakfast but, on this particular morning, I was still in my robe with my hair uncombed and looking pale faced, due to the application of some very light make-up. "My goodness, Sam," he said. "You look awful. How are you feeling?"

I shrugged and shook my head, "Not good. My stomach's really upset. I've already thrown up twice this morning."

"Well it can't be anything you ate because we all had the same thing. I feel fine and Vicky's okay. I just looked in on her and she's still sleeping."

I sighed, "Thank goodness for that. I'm not sure what this can be other than stomach flu."

"Mmm, well the doctor's office is closed today but we could go to the walk-in clinic on Heathcote."

"No, it's okay. I'm sure I'll be fine after I get cleaned up. Anyway, we need to be on the road by about eleven if we're to be at Emma's by mid-afternoon. Will you go and wake Vicky up now and I'll let Riley in. I can hear him scratching at the back door."

Aaron took hold of my arm and pulled me towards him, "You're not seriously suggesting we still go away when you're not feeling well?"

"I'll be fine; we can't disappoint Vicky. She's so excited about this trip."

"I know, honey," he said, "but she'll get over it. What if there's something seriously wrong with you? We can't risk it, Sam."

I pulled away from him and sat down, "Then go without me. I'll just stay home and rest up."

He shook his head, "No way. I can't leave you here alone and, in any case, I've never even met Emma. I don't think she'd appreciate me showing up without you."

"Emma won't mind," I protested. "I'll call her and explain what's happened. Please, Aaron, I want you to go. Vicky's going to love it there. The cottage is so close to the beach and I know she'll like Emma, she's such a lovely person."

He threw up his hands in frustration, "What if I don't want to go without you?" he asked.

I stood up and put my arms around him, "Please, honey, do this for Vicky. I promise I'll be all right. If I get any worse, I'll just go to the clinic."

He hugged me and kissed me lightly on the lips, "Okay, you win. Why don't you go and wake Vicky up and I'll make us some breakfast."

"That sounds like a good idea," I replied, "but don't make me anything. Maybe I'll have something a little later."

He pulled away from me and turned to go up the stairs, then suddenly stopped. "What about Riley? I'd rather he stayed here with you."

I'd already planned to keep Riley with me and was surprised when Aaron suggested it, "Yes, I think it would be best although Vicky won't be too happy about it."

He shrugged, "Life is full of little disappointments," he muttered and proceeded upstairs.

It was already after eleven, when they finally pulled out of the driveway. I thought they were never going to leave. Vicky kicked up a fuss when she found out I wouldn't be going with them and she had a major temper tantrum when she discovered Riley wouldn't be going either. Aaron was so annoyed at her behavior, he threatened to cancel the whole trip and, for a few scary moments, I thought my whole plan was going to fall through.

When I was finally alone, I took a well overdue soak in the tub and then got dressed in a pair of chinos and a t-shirt. I'd washed my hair the night before and let it air dry so it fell naturally in a mass of curls and, without any make-up, I could almost pass as a teenager. I grinned at myself in the mirror, imagining how surprised Philip would be when he saw me. He probably expected me to be waiting for him, posed in a black teddy with smoky eyes and scarlet lips!

At one, I made myself a sandwich and then decided to take Riley for a walk. It was a beautiful day with just one solitary cloud in the sky. It had rained heavily on Friday evening and now, wherever I looked, the grass was greener and everything looked and smelled so fresh. Rather than go to the park, we just walked around the neighborhood and, on the way, ran into a number of people also walking their dogs. One elderly gentleman, the owner of two French bulldogs, was a delight to talk to and one of his dogs, Mimi, took a particular interest in Riley. It was a pleasant distraction on the day I'd been planning, and somewhat dreading. I just hoped it would end up the way I wanted it to.

I made sure we were back at the house by three because I expected Beth to arrive in about a half-hour. I got more than a little anxious when four o'clock came around but, a few minutes later, I heard her pull into the driveway. I was so pleased to see her that, as she stepped out of the car, I ran towards her and threw my arms around her, "Oh, thank goodness you're here," I said, "I've been a bundle of nerves waiting for you."

"Sorry, Sam," she responded returning my embrace, "there was an accident at New Haven and we got held up for a while. I guess I should have messaged you but I didn't even think of it until I was almost here."

After we went into the house, Beth took her overnight case up to the guest room and I went to the kitchen to pour us both a glass of wine. I heard her footsteps a few minutes later and turned to see her in the doorway, "You must be hungry." I said. "Would you like something to eat now or will you wait for dinner?"

She smiled, "I'll wait," she said and sat down at the kitchen table. "So, obviously you managed to convince Aaron you were too sick to go to Emma's."

I nodded, "Yes, but he didn't want to go without me. I told him he couldn't disappoint Vicky and he finally, but reluctantly, decided to go ahead."

Just then Riley came bounding into the kitchen but stopped in his tracks when he saw Beth. "Hey boy," she called out. "Come here." He crawled forward on his tummy and then draped himself over her feet. She looked down and smiled, "I thought Aaron was taking him to Emma's."

"No, I decided to keep him here. Maybe he'll help to scare Philip."

Beth started to laugh, "I hardly think so. Look at him; he's as docile as a lamb."

I had to laugh too, "I suppose you're right. Maybe I should keep him out of the way tonight."

"I think that's a good idea. Now, why don't we go over this plan of yours step by step? I still think you're playing with fire but I'm willing to help. Please god, it works."

"It has to work, Beth. I want my sister back."

"I know you do and there's nothing more I'd like either. Tell me, did you find that old tape recorder you mentioned?"

"Yes, and it still works perfectly. I just haven't worked out where I'm going to hide it."

We continued talking about what we expected to happen that evening. There was no way I could be certain how Philip would react but, I believed he would want to protect his reputation. Up until now, his public image had been stellar and he couldn't afford for that to change. My attempt to tarnish his image by reporting his activities to the Sandwich police had failed. I couldn't afford to fail again.

By six o'clock, we were both getting hungry but weren't in the mood for cooking so we drove over to McDonald's on Main Street and picked up two cheeseburgers and some fries. Rather than return to the house, we drove to the Municipal Marina where we could see across to Sedge Island. Up until then I'd been feeling anxious but, sitting in the car with Beth munching on fast food like a couple of teenagers, I began to relax.

After we got home, I realized I'd forgotten to feed Riley and I made sure he'd cleaned out his bowl of kibble before I took him upstairs and locked him in Vicky's room. I didn't want him around when the fun began. Then, at eight o'clock, there was a call on the landline in the kitchen. It was Aaron and I felt a little guilty because I hadn't really thought about him since they'd left. "Hi, honey," he said, "just thought I'd let you know we arrived in one piece. Vicky was really good on the way here. After the long drive and running on the beach already, she finally wore herself out. I just tucked her into bed."

"Oh, I'm so pleased, Aaron. What do you think of Emma? Are you two getting along all right?"

"She's great, Sam. She was so welcoming and Vicky took to her right away. She insisted on taking us out to dinner at a place called Seafood Sam's. Fortunately they had a special kid's menu. You know Vicky isn't a great fan of fish."

I laughed, "Yes, I do know. That's so generous of Emma. I knew you'd be comfortable there and it's only for a couple of days."

"Actually, we've only got one full day left. Anyway, how are you doing? You sound a lot better than when I left this morning?"

I almost forgot I was supposed to be sick and I decided not to tell him Beth was with me. "I'm feeling a lot better and I'm sorry I didn't come with you."

"Well I'm glad to hear you're okay. I was worried about leaving you alone."

"There's no need to worry. I'm fine here by myself and if I feel up to it tomorrow, I may just drive up to Oakland Beach and just lie in the sun for a few hours. I need to work on my tan."

"Don't overdo it, Sam. Make sure you put on a lot of sun screen."

I chuckled, "Okay sir, will do."

"Just want to make sure you look after yourself. I miss you, honey."

"I miss you too but I want you to enjoy yourself while you're there. What are your plans for this evening?"

"Emma's invited some neighbors over and we're just going to sit around and have a few beers."

"Well I was about to go soak in the bath so you have a good evening, honey, and I'll talk to you tomorrow."

"Okay, Sam, I'll call you at about the same time. I love you."

"Love you too. Bye, honey and give Vicky a big hug for me."

After hanging up the phone, Beth, who'd been listening to my end of the conversation asked, "Are you really going for a soak now?"

"No," I answered, "but I didn't know how else to get him off the phone. I'm not exactly thrilled about having to constantly lie to him."

She reached over and stroked my shoulder, "It will all be over soon, dear."

"Will it?" I responded somberly. "As long as I'm able to keep all this from Aaron, I'll always feel as though I'm deceiving him."

"Maybe one day you'll feel secure enough to tell him the truth."

I shrugged, "Maybe, maybe not." I looked at my watch, "Let's go over things one more time, Beth. I'm especially concerned about you getting back here in time. The second we suspect Philip is coming through the back door, you're going to have to run like mad to the corner to get that photo and then run right back. I'm worried you won't be able to make it."

Beth grinned, "We've been over this a number of times already. I may be no spring chicken but I'm still pretty fast on my feet. Stop worrying, Sam; I'll be there and back before he has time to know what hit him."

"I hope you don't mean that literally. I'd like to avoid any violence."

"I know, but you'd better be sure you have that baseball bat handy just in case."

By nine-forty-five, we were both a bundle of nerves; our relaxing respite at the marina long forgotten. Five minutes later, I was in the hallway at the foot of the stairs and facing the back door. The tape recorder was sitting on a small table on the first floor landing and all the lights in the house were out, except for a lamp in the living room which gave off just enough light so that I could see anyone entering the house. Meanwhile, Beth was stationed just inside the front door ready to sprint out the moment I gave her the signal, which was a clearing of my throat.

After what seemed like forever, I glanced at my watch. I could just make out, it was exactly ten o'clock and my heart was pounding. Minutes more passed and I was beginning to wonder just how long we were going to have to stand there when, suddenly, I heard the back door open. I hardly had time to signal Beth before Philip appeared, just a few feet away from me. He paused before closing the door and then called out, "Sam, is that you?"

I lifted the baseball bat I'd been grasping in my right hand and called out, "Philip, what are you doing here?"

He took a few steps forward and I backed up in the direction of the front door. He was all in black and I couldn't help thinking how appropriately he'd dressed for the occasion. When he saw the bat in my hand he laughed, "Is this a joke or some kind of kinky sex game you're playing?"

I lifted the bat higher, "Get out of my house before I call the police," I yelled out in a shaky voice.

He hesitated, "Seriously, Sam, what's going on?"

I repeated, "I warned you. If you don't leave I'm calling the police."

He stayed where he was but his voice was menacing, "You little bitch," he hissed. "You tricked me into coming here. I don't know what you're up to but I'm not sticking around to find out."

He turned to go out the way he came in but stopped when I yelled, "If my sister isn't here by three o'clock tomorrow, the tabloids are going to have a field day."

He swung around to face me, "You fucking cow," he spat out, "are you threatening me?"

Suddenly, for some reason, I no longer felt nervous. "Yes, I'll make sure everything I reported to the police in Sandwich will soon be public knowledge. They may not have thought I had a case but I have enough evidence to expose you."

He took a step towards me and I backed up again praying for Beth to come through the front door. "You're bluffing," he said. "You can't prove anything. Your sister is my wife and she'll do exactly what I tell her to do. No woman has ever controlled me. Is your husband such a wimp that he lets you call all the shots? Maybe you should consider what Aaron will have to say when he finds out how you lured me here? You wanted me just as much as I wanted you."

"Ha!" I scoffed, "I never wanted you. You're a despicable pig. You abused my sister and think you can get away with it;

well think again because she's not going to end up like your first wife."

I knew I had enraged him but, just as he rushed towards me screaming, "You can't prove anything you little slut," I heard the door behind me open and suddenly there was a flash as Beth captured the scene on her cell phone. It stopped Philip in his tracks, as he tried to adjust his eyes to see who was standing there, and I slowly lowered the baseball bat.

"Call the police, Beth," I said. "We want to report an intruder."

"Wwwait," Philip stammered holding up both hands, "you can't prove anything. I'll tell them you invited me here."

"I don't think so," I said quietly. "You see, Philip, we've been taping every word you've said."

His eyes darted from side to side then he started to back up. "You've got nothing incriminating on me," he said.

"I have the tape," I responded, "and a photo. Beth also took a photo of your car parked right under the street sign. It proves you were here."

"So this whole thing was a set up," he said quietly looking from me to Beth.

"Yes, and not only that, we have a police report from a few days ago about a car, similar to yours, going up and down the road and a prowler in the back garden. If that isn't incriminating, I don't know what is."

He actually smiled, "You seem to have thought of everything haven't you, Sam, but what if you're wrong. What if I call your bluff and I make sure you never see Portia again."

My heart caught in my throat as I caught the implication of what he was saying, "If you harm my sister, I'll make sure you go to hell even if I have to send you there myself."

He nodded at Beth then turned to walk out the back door, "I warned you not to threaten me, Sam," he said.

"Three o'clock tomorrow," I called out, "don't forget."

After he left, we were both shaking so we locked all the doors and I ran upstairs to let Riley out of the bedroom. Just having him with us made everything seem more normal. Even though it was a warm night, I made us some hot chocolate and we munched on shortbreads as we listened to the tape. Beth was optimistic about how Philip would react to my threat and excited about having Portia back with us. I wasn't quite so sure. My plan had worked out well, but not exactly the way I would have liked it. I was hoping to provoke Philip to the point where he would show exactly the kind of abusive individual he was, but that didn't really happen. Had I failed? It would be a long night and several hours before I found out.

Chapter Fifty-Six

By midnight, both Beth and I were exhausted but we didn't expect to get too much sleep. I was still unsure as to how Philip would react. Maybe he would be so enraged that he'd resort to violence and attempt to break into the house in the middle of the night. I was so nervous; I suggested Beth sleep with me in the master bedroom. Once we were settled, with Riley at the foot of the bed and the baseball bat handy, I felt a little more secure but my mind was in overdrive. What if my plan hadn't worked? What if Aaron found out? What if I had put Portia in danger? I knew I would be getting very little sleep that night.

Beth was an early riser and when I glanced at the clock, I saw it was just after six. "How did you sleep?" I muttered.

She had her back to me, putting on her robe, and turned around in surprise, "Oh, sorry dear," she said, "I didn't mean to wake you."

"It's all right," I responded, "I wasn't really sleeping, I feel like I've been awake most of the night."

She sat down on the edge of the bed, "I'm sorry to hear that. I hope I didn't disturb you."

I reached over and grasped her hand, "No, Beth, you hardly moved. Thank you for staying with me."

"My pleasure," she said releasing her hand and motioning towards Riley who was just beginning to wake up. "I'll let Riley out and then put the coffee pot on. You don't have to get up. Try and get some more sleep."

I shook my head, "No, I'll get up now and have a quick shower. I think it will make me feel better."

"Okay, dear, maybe when you come downstairs, I can make us some breakfast."

I watched her as she left the room, with Riley trailing after her, and couldn't help thinking how normal everything seemed. It was hard to envision what the day would bring.

Beth insisted we just take our time and have a nice relaxing breakfast so, we sat in the kitchen enjoying banana French toast and then took our coffee out into the garden. It was a glorious morning and the perfect time to enjoy the day. Late in the day, the temperature was expected to climb into the high eighties but I had never been a sun worshipper. I wondered if Portia would be back with us by then.

The morning seemed to drag on, despite getting the guest room ready, walking Riley and shopping at the local A & P and, every minute we were out of the house, I was afraid Portia would show up and we wouldn't be there.

At last, it was one o'clock and time for lunch. Beth and I were both hungry because we hadn't eaten anything since breakfast. We decided to go all out and busied ourselves making Reuben sandwiches and heating up some wonderful tomato basil soup I'd found at the supermarket and, for a while, it took my mind off of Portia.

By two o'clock we'd already finished lunch and cleared away the dishes and we were both at loose ends. I really wanted to be alone but didn't have the heart to tell Beth. Oddly enough she seemed to sense I needed some time to myself, so she suggested taking Riley for another walk and said she'd be back before three. Once they left the house, I went upstairs to the master bedroom, which overlooked the driveway, and gazed out of the window. What would I do if Portia didn't come?

At two forty-five, I saw Beth and Riley approaching the house and, when I heard the front door open, I went back downstairs to greet them. "Has anything happened?" Beth asked.

I shook my head and looked at my watch for the umpteenth time. "No, but it's not three o'clock yet. I suspect Philip will drag this out until the last minute."

Beth sighed, "I hope you're right, dear," she responded.

A half hour later, I was pacing the hallway while Beth tried to placate me, "Maybe they got delayed in traffic," she suggested, "or maybe the car broke down."

I shook my head and was just about to answer when I thought I heard a noise and ran to look out of the living room window. My heart leapt into my mouth when I saw a black limousine inching into the driveway and I immediately took off for the front door screaming at Beth, "She's here."

I only waited a few seconds before I was running towards the car and then, suddenly, the back door opened and my sister stepped out. Her arms reached out to me and I fell into them, sobbing, and burying my face against her shoulder. She rubbed my back and then gently pushed me away so that she could see my face, "I'm okay, Sam," she said.

I stared at her and saw she'd lost weight again and had dark circles under her eyes but, even so, she was still beautiful. I took her hand and said, "Come inside; Beth's here and dying to see you."

She looked over at the man in chauffeur's uniform who'd been driving the car, and who was removing suitcases from the trunk, "Leonard, would you please take my luggage into the house."

"Yes, of course, Mrs. Barrington," he replied.

Five minutes later, the suitcases were in the hallway and Portia and Beth had their arms around each other watching the limo pull away. "It's over," Beth said.

"Yes," Portia said, breaking away and turning to look at me, "and now I want to hear how you managed to convince Philip to let me go."

I smiled, "How much time do you have?" I asked.

We took Portia's luggage up to the guest room and I left her to catch her breath while she changed out of the dress she was wearing into a pair of shorts and a tank top. When she came back downstairs to the family room, she looked even thinner and I was concerned. "Haven't you been eating?" I asked.

She shrugged, "I haven't much felt like it," she answered.

"Well, we'll have to do something about that," I remarked. "How would you like one of those hotpots Maggie used to make? We could have it for dinner with a little salad."

"I think it's a bit too warm for that," Beth said.

"Maybe you're right; what would you like, Portia?"

"Just a salad would be fine but right now I could do with a cup of coffee."

"Coming right up," Beth said as she exited the room.

Portia sat down opposite me in one of the wing chairs, "So what did you do, Sam? I had no idea anything was going on until just after noon today. I was having lunch with Lotti when Serena showed up and informed me my bags were packed and I should be ready to leave the premises within the hour. When I asked why, she told me Philip no longer wanted me there and had made alternative arrangements for me. I had no idea what they had planned so I protested and insisted on staying. Then she told me I was being brought here to you and, when I asked if you were expecting me, she got very huffy and said it had all been settled between you and Philip. I had no idea how I was going to get here until Serena escorted me outside and Leonard pulled up. Even as we drove onto the ramp at I-95 I still didn't believe I was coming here. It even crossed my mind that something really bad had been planned for me."

"Oh my god, Portia, you must have been terrified. What did Lotti think about what was happening."

"She started grilling Serena but she was told to mind her own business. I honestly don't know why she stays in that relationship."

"I know why but we'll talk about that later. Did you see Philip before you left?"

Portia frowned, "No, and I didn't want to. I hardly ever saw him, in fact, the only times I'd get to see him was when he wanted to have sex with me and, when I wouldn't come across, he'd get abusive. I grew to hate him, Sam. He was a different person than the man I fell in love with."

I sneered, "I doubt anyone could change that much. I know it's hard to accept but I think he was probably just using you, right from the beginning. He wanted a trophy to show off and then he found out you weren't into his kinky lifestyle and you suddenly became excess baggage."

I saw tears come into her eyes, "Wow, you sure know how to tell it like it is, Sam. I feel like such a fool now for believing he'd hurt you or Vicky if I ever left him."

I shook my head, "He wasn't fooling; he meant every word of it."

"How do you know that?"

"I'll explain everything when Beth comes back. She played a big part in getting him to let you go."

Portia sighed just as Beth entered the room with a pot of coffee, three mugs and a plate of petit-fours. "Here we are," she said. "Does anyone want cream or sugar?"

We both shook our heads and, while she poured the coffee, I began to tell Portia every detail of my plan from the moment I decided to seduce Philip.

Chapter Fifty-Seven

By dinner time, Portia had heard everything she needed to know and she was dumbfounded. She chided me for taking such a risk but said she would be forever grateful for what Beth and I had done. She was still convinced Philip would retaliate in some way and I tried to allay her fears. I suggested that, on Tuesday we call Elliot Abramson, the lawyer who drew up Portia's prenuptial agreement, and file for divorce. Of course, I had no real idea what it would entail but I knew the sooner we made the situation public, the safer we would all be. Portia was reluctant to move ahead so quickly and said she didn't want Philip's money. I couldn't believe how naïve she was and got a little annoyed. Daddy had gone to a lot of trouble to ensure she would be well taken care of in the event of the marriage breaking down. She got very quiet when I reminded her, she deserved what was coming to her and then I decided to drop the subject and let it all sink in.

While I was preparing a Greek salad with lots of olives and feta cheese, Portia was sitting at the kitchen table watching me. Suddenly she gasped and I asked what was wrong. "I just thought of something," she said, "what on earth does Aaron think about all this?'

I turned to look at her, "He doesn't know a single thing about it," I answered, "and he's not going to know. That's why I had to be sure he wouldn't be here this weekend, I already told you that."

"That's right, you did but didn't you speak to him earlier today? Didn't you tell him then what had happened?"

"No and I never will. When he gets home tomorrow and finds you here, we'll tell him you walked out on Philip and you'll be staying with us for a while. Of course, you can stay for as long as you like but it's pretty quiet in New Rochelle and you might want to move back to the city at some point."

"I understand," she responded looking around. "By the way, where's Beth?"

"She's out walking Riley. You haven't met him yet. He's Vicky's dog really but we all love him; he's the perfect pet."

She nodded, "How long will Beth be staying?"

"Just for tonight," I replied. "She'll be leaving before Aaron gets home. I don't want him to know she's been here."

"Wouldn't Emma have told him she was visiting you?"

"Emma doesn't even know."

She grinned, "Boy, I didn't realize what a devious little sister I had."

"There's a lot you don't know about me," I teased.

That evening we just sat around drinking wine and catching up. Beth and I had so much more to learn about the life Portia had endured since she married Philip. Meanwhile Riley had taken to Portia right away and was curled up with his head resting on her feet.

Much later, we wandered out to the garden and breathed in the cooler night air. It was a gorgeous night and we ended up just hugging each other. We were so happy to all be together again.

Beth left right after lunch on Monday and Portia and I decided to drive to Hudson Park with Riley, take a stroll, and just sit and look out over Long Island Sound. We didn't expect

Aaron and Vicky back until five and we needed to take some time to relax before we had to face them, and literally lie through our teeth.

Aaron called soon after we got back to the house. They had stopped in Branford for a quick bite to eat and expected to be home in just over an hour. It gave Portia and me just enough time to make sure we were on the same page. We decided it would be best if she told Aaron she'd walked out on Philip but didn't really want to talk about it. Knowing my husband, I was convinced he wouldn't pressure her. He'd always respected an individual's privacy.

When I heard him drive up, I ran outside and, as soon as she saw me, Vicky jumped out of the car and came running towards me, "Mommy, we had so much fun," she called out and threw her arms around my legs.

I picked her up and kissed her on the cheek, "You'll have to tell me all about it, honey."

She struggled to be let go when she saw Riley scamper down the driveway, "Come here, boy," she yelled and then squeezed him so hard, he actually yelped.

I turned as Aaron came up behind me, "How's my girl?" he asked. "Are you really feeling better?"

"I feel wonderful now that you're here," I answered giving him a hug, "and I've got a surprise for you."

"Oh?" he responded taking my hand. "Where is this surprise?"

I grinned, "In the house. Just leave you bags in the car for now and grab Vicky for me."

He frowned and then, with Vicky in tow, followed me through the front door and into the living room. Portia was standing in front of the fireplace, wearing a sky blue maxi dress that brought out the color of her eyes. Her golden hair tumbled over her shoulders and she looked a little frail but, in some obscure way, even more beautiful. I glanced at Aaron wondering how any man could resist her but the smile on his face was open and genuine, "Portia," he said, walking towards her and then embracing her. "How wonderful to see you; Sam's been so worried about you. How are you?"

She smiled back at him and then lifted one hand to stroke his cheek, "Dear Aaron," she replied, "I'm so happy to be here but I'm afraid I have some unfortunate news. I've left Philip."

Aaron shook his head, "I'm sorry to hear that but I'm not surprised after some of the things Sam's been telling me. Here, come and sit down," he said, motioning to the couch. "Tell me what finally made you decide to leave?"

I held my breath as Portia sat down, "I really don't want to talk about it, if you don't mind, Aaron," she answered.

I decided to intervene, "Portia's feeling a bit under the weather, honey. I've told her she can stay here until she feels up to finding a place of her own."

"She's welcome to stay as long as she likes," he responded.

At that moment, I heard a noise and Vicky appeared in the doorway. She stared at Portia and then looked up at me, "Who's that lady, Mommy?" she asked.

"You don't remember your Auntie Portia, do you?"

She shook her head and then walked over to where Portia was sitting, "Are you staying for dinner?" she asked.

Portia smiled and reached out to hold Vicky's hands, "Yes, darling and Mommy and Daddy said I can stay here with you for a few days; or maybe a little longer."

"You're very pretty," Vicky remarked.

"Thank you but you're pretty too. I think you're going to look like Mommy when you grow up."

Vicky looked over her shoulder at me and then back at Portia, "No, Mommy's got dark hair. I want angel hair like yours," she announced emphatically.

Portia laughed, "You're so adorable. I can't believe how much you've grown since I last saw you."

"When did you see me?"

"When you were a little munchkin," Portia replied tickling her under her chin. Vicky giggled and pulled away, "Come and play with Riley," she said.

Portia got up and, holding onto Vicky's hand, walked out of the room, "See you later folks," she said looking back at us and grinning.

"Well that went well," Aaron remarked.

"Yes it did. I think those two are going to get along like a house on fire."

"What happened, Sam, with her and Philip?"

I shrugged my shoulders, "She doesn't want to talk about it, not even to me. I think she needs a little more time and then maybe she'll open up."

Chapter Fifty-Eight

Early on Tuesday morning, after Aaron left for work, Vicky was protesting about having to go to school. I'd considered keeping her home for a few weeks during the summer months, but the school had a special summer program and we thought she would benefit from being with other children. We were just finishing breakfast when she whined, "Why can't I stay home with you and Auntie Portia?"

"Because you already had a day off yesterday," I answered.

"It's not fair," she said, crossing her arms on her chest. "You get to stay home."

I chuckled, "That's because I have lots of things to do, like making sure the house is clean and your clothes get washed, and there's enough food for dinner when you get home."

"Alice's mommy doesn't stay home; she goes to work like Daddy."

Alice was her closest friend, "Yes I know and I used to go to work too,"

She looked puzzled, "How did you do all that stuff at home if you weren't here?"

"Well, I had to do chores at night and Daddy used to help out more."

She shrugged, went back to nibbling on her toast, and then got down from the table, "It's still not fair," she mumbled.

I finally dropped Vicky off at school and returned home to find Portia in the kitchen making coffee, "How did you sleep?" I asked.

"Like a baby," she answered smiling.

It was only on Sunday that Beth and I had learned the whole truth about Philip's demands on her; the times she lay awake, on alert, just waiting for another assault in the middle of the night. "I'm so pleased to hear that," I said. "He's not going to hurt you anymore. You're safe now and, as soon as you've had some breakfast, we'll phone the lawyer."

We made an appointment to meet with Elliot Abramson the next day. I'd suggested Portia go alone but she begged me to go with her. I think, deep down, she was still nervous and thought Philip was having her followed. She was obviously afraid of what he might do when she filed for divorce.

Elliot advised us there would be a mountain of paper work to be filed with the county clerk's office, before Philip could be served. He suggested Portia file for an uncontested divorce based on irretrievable breakdown of the marriage and, provided Philip agreed, there shouldn't be any issue. There weren't any children to consider and the prenuptial, he'd originally drawn up, was airtight. When I asked how long it would take, he told us, if everything went smoothly, it would probably be about three months before everything was finalized and Portia would be a free woman. I reached over and squeezed her hand, "Everything's going to be okay," I whispered.

That night, in the privacy of our bedroom, I told Aaron about our visit to the lawyer. Up until then, he hadn't asked any further questions about the reason for Portia's separation from Philip but, now, he was curious to know more. I told him, everything I'd told him before was true and perhaps, now, he could understand why I'd made every effort to rescue my sister from an abusive relationship. I didn't tell him about how I'd deceived Philip and my threat to expose him. I merely said Portia had finally gathered the strength to leave and, with nowhere to go, had landed on our doorstep. He looked at me rather skeptically, "Are you sure you had nothing to do with this?" he asked. "I find it rather odd that he hasn't come after her."

I shrugged my shoulders and turned away because I couldn't meet his eyes, "It was Portia's decision," I answered. "Perhaps Philip realized he couldn't hang on to her anymore."

Aaron reached over and spun me around so that I faced him, "Is that the truth, Sam? Are you sure you haven't done anything I need to know about? I thought we agreed there wouldn't be any secrets between us."

I don't know how I kept a straight face but I guess I'd become pretty adept at lying. "I had nothing to do with Portia leaving. You have to believe me."

He slowly shook his head, "I just hope you're being honest with me," he said, walking away into the bathroom and shutting the door.

It was almost three weeks before we heard back from Elliot. All the necessary papers had been filed with the county clerk and Philip was about to be served. We hadn't heard a peep out of him but I was almost certain he wouldn't contest it, because he had too much to lose. I still had more than enough evidence to ruin his reputation.

A day later, Aaron brought home a copy of the New York Times and we were surprised to find the story had already leaked. In the business section, there was a photo of Philip and Portia attending a fund raiser at the Pierre Hotel. The article accompanying the photo read that Portia Barrington, nee Lawrence, had filed for divorce from Philip Barrington, head of Barrington Multinational. Irretrievable breakdown was cited as grounds for the divorce. It went on to say this was the second marriage for Philip, after the death of his wife in a drowning accident, and the first for Portia. There was even mention of the fact that Portia was now residing with her sister in New Rochelle. I have to admit, I was astounded at how the press managed to latch on to these stories so quickly and assumed they must have had some spy permanently hidden away in the county clerk's office.

The following Monday, Elliot advised us, Philip would not be contesting the divorce, however, there were some small details to be worked out before the case could go before the court. He mentioned that Philip's lawyers had questioned the validity of the prenuptial agreement but Philip insisted he had no issue with it. Elliot assured us, once again, the agreement was airtight and, once the divorce was granted, Portia would have immediate access to the amount agreed upon. Portia was nervous about having to appear in court and was surprised to learn, providing both parties agreed on all aspects of the divorce, neither she nor Philip would have to face each other in front of a judge. The lawyers would take care of everything.

I had been waiting for this news for a long time and felt it was the opportune moment to approach Portia about my concern. Since she'd been with us, we'd talked about Lotti, on several occasions and Portia was well aware of the way Serena treated her. However, she wasn't aware of the hold Serena had over her and I wanted to make sure she was in a position to help before I pleaded my case. It was only a few minutes after Elliot called when I mentioned I had something important to discuss with her. "What is it, Sam?" she asked, "You look worried."

"I need to talk to you about Lotti," I answered.

"Lotti? Is she okay?"

I sighed, "Yes. Well, she's not sick or anything like that, if that's what you mean. You already know the way Serena treats her but you don't know why she puts up with it. Haven't you ever wondered why she just doesn't walk out?"

Portia frowned, "I asked her once and she said she had nowhere else to go. Then she just left the room as though she didn't want to talk about it. I didn't want to pressure her, so I never brought it up again."

We were standing in the living room and I suggested we sit down. Then I told her about Serena's threat to abandon Lotti's parents, if she ever decided to leave. I explained that she didn't have sufficient funds to look after them and there was no way she would see them put in a home run by some charitable organization. She had read so many horror stories about such places and she would never forgive herself if they ended up there. Portia was horrified and, before I could even continue, she broke in, "I can help her, Sam. She won't ever have to worry about her parents again. They can stay at the facility and I'll see that the expenses are covered. Lotti stood by me all the time I was with Philip and the least I can do is repay her."

"That's really generous of you," I said, "but it will probably cost a fortune."

She laughed, "I'll be getting a fortune, Daddy saw to that. You know, Sam, I said I didn't want Philip's money but I've changed my mind. I realize I can do a lot of good for other people."

"What about you? You deserve to think about spending some on yourself too."

She shook her head, "I really don't need much. I've learned material things can't buy you happiness. I'd just like a comfortable place to call home, but nothing too grand. I've had enough of the kind of life I've been forced to live, never wearing the same thing twice, always having to look presentable. I think I'll stick to jeans and a tee from now on and, there's something else, I'd like something constructive to do. Being a lady of leisure is not my cup of tea."

"It's so good hearing you talk like this," I remarked, "you seem to be getting your confidence back."

"Thanks, Sam. Hey, why don't we call Lotti and ask her to meet us for lunch? We can tell her the good news and see what she says."

"Okay, let's not tell her anything on the phone. I'll call this afternoon and see if she can sneak away tomorrow."

Chapter Fifty-Nine

Rather than meeting for lunch in the city, Lotti agreed to drive to New Rochelle early the next morning. Luckily, Serena had recently been appointed director of a foundation associated with the performing arts, and would be tied up at a board meeting for most of the day. When Lotti arrived at the house and saw Portia waiting on the front step to greet her, she rushed into her arms and immediately began to cry. "I didn't think I'd ever see you again," she burst out. Everything had happened so quickly when Portia was forced to leave. Her bags had already been packed and she never got the chance to really say goodbye to Lotti.

Once we were settled in the family room, we filled her in about how I'd seduced Philip and what happened when he showed up at the house. Like Portia, she was astounded but actually laughed and said she wished she'd been there to see it. "I'll miss you," she said, reaching for Portia's hand, "but I'm happy for you. You deserve so much better than the life you had with Philip."

Portia nodded, "And you deserve so much better than the life you're living with Serena. I saw how sadistic she could be and it's time you left too."

She shook her head vehemently, "I can't do that," she protested, glancing over at me.

"It's okay," I said, "I've told Portia about the circumstances with your parents and she wants to help."

She looked back at Portia, "I can't let you do that, it's my problem and I have to deal with it."

Portia smiled, "I want to do it. Leave Serena, Lotti, and you'll never have to worry about your parents again. I'll take care of them for as long as they live."

Lotti began to cry again, "But how am I ever going to repay you?"

Portia squeezed her hand, "I don't want to be repaid. I'm going to be a very wealthy woman once the divorce is finalized. You were the only person I could turn to when I felt like a prisoner in that house and I treasure your friendship. I want you to leave, Lotti. Please do this for me."

Lotti began to calm down and wiped her eyes, "I feel relieved already," she said. "I've been like a rat trapped in a cage for so long, I had visions of having to put up with Serena's cruelty until the day she no longer had any hold over me. Sometimes, I even prayed for my parents to die so that I could be free but then, I'd feel so guilty and I'd beg God to forgive me."

"It's all right, Lotti, we understand," I said.

She looked at Portia and whispered, "I'm scared but I'll do it. I'll leave Serena."

Portia threw her arms around Lotti's shoulders, "Atta girl! You won't regret it, I promise you."

She sighed, "But I have nowhere to go."

Portia glanced across at me, "I think Sam will let you stay here until we sort things out."

I was a bit surprised at this turn of events and immediately thought of Aaron's reaction but I nodded, "Of course, you'd be welcome here, Lotti."

That night at the dinner table, I told Aaron that Lotti would be staying with us for a short time. I'd decided to bring it up while Portia was there because I figured I might need her support. He frowned, "What's going on? Are we taking in strays now?"

I looked over at Portia but she just rolled her eyes, "What do you mean by that remark?" I asked.

He sighed, "Sorry, that didn't come out right. I assume, from what you've told me in the past, that she's leaving Serena."

I nodded, "Yes, and it's about time. She just needs a place to stay for a week or two until she finds somewhere else."

Vicky had been fidgeting in her chair, her eyes darting back and forth between me and her father, "Who's Lotti?" she blurted out.

Portia smiled, "She's a very good friend of mine and your Mom's. I think you'll like her."

"I hope she likes dogs," she responded.

"She likes them very much," I said. "At her house in Florida, they have two dogs, Max and Buddy."

Her eyes opened wide, "Can we go see them?" she asked.

Aaron cut in, "Florida's a long way away, honey. Maybe Lotti will have some photos to show you."

Vicky shrugged, "Okay, but it's not the same as seeing them for real."

"Lotti will be leaving on Friday," I said. "She has to wait until Serena's out of the house before she can even pack any of her belongings. Thank goodness she has an ally to help cart her luggage down to her car. Leonard, the chauffeur, can't stand Serena and, now both Lotti and Portia will be gone, he's talking about giving in his notice."

"Serena doesn't sound too popular," Aaron remarked.

"Well, you've met her and I don't think you were exactly a fan," I said.

"I didn't take too much notice of her, actually," he replied.

Portia cut in, "She's a monster."

Vicky's eyes widened, "What kind of a monster? Is she like the Cookie Monster?"

We all looked at each other and began to laugh. My sweet daughter was so naïve and so lovable.

Lotti arrived, as expected, on Friday afternoon. She had walked out of the house without any interference and left Serena a brief note to let her know she would not be coming back. She didn't explain why and she didn't mention where she was going. She could only imagine Serena's rage when she read it. I just hoped she realized, if she tried to make trouble, it would bring Philip into the picture and he still had his reputation to worry about. As for her threat to no longer support Lotti's parents, it was too late for her to retaliate; Portia had already made arrangements with the facility to provide whatever funds were necessary.

Portia offered to pick Vicky up from school while I helped Lotti to settle in. Our guest room had twin beds and Portia was more than happy to share the space with Lotti. My only problem was finding room for all of their belongings but I knew it wouldn't be for long. We were just coming down from the second floor when Vicky came bursting through the front door. She stopped dead and stared when she saw Lotti and even Riley, who'd run down the hallway to greet her, couldn't get her attention. I really wasn't surprised at her reaction. Lotti was wearing a white, peasant style dress, and espadrilles and her hair, even lighter now from being out in the sun, fell well below her shoulders overwhelming her slight frame. She looked almost childlike although she was already in her mid-thirties. Vicky finally managed to speak, "Are you Lotti?" she asked.

Lotti continued down the stairs and bent down so that she was at eye-level with Vicky. She then held out her hand expecting Vicky to take it, "Yes, I am," she answered, "and you're Vicky and I'm very pleased to meet you."

Vicky frowned, "You talk funny," she said ignoring Lotti's hand.

"That's rather rude, honey," I said.

Lotti chuckled, "It's okay, lots of people tell me that."

Vicky looked up at me, "Why does she talk like that Mommy?" she asked.

"Because Lotti comes from another country and in other countries people speak in all different kinds of languages."

Vicky frowned, "There's a boy in my class who talks funny too. Everyone calls him Bo but I don't think that's his real name."

Lotti was distracted by Riley who was rubbing the side of his head against her thigh, "I've already met Riley," she said, petting him and then standing up. "He's a beautiful dog."

Vicky put her hand on the top of Riley's head, "Mommy told me you had two dogs but they're a long way away. Daddy said you might have photos of them."

Lotti smiled and bent down again, "I think I do have some photos. I'll have a look after dinner."

Vicky pushed Riley away and reached out to touch Lotti's hair, "I like your hair," she said. "I want mine to be as long as yours when I grow up."

Portia had come through the door and was observing the scene, "I don't think you'll have to wait that long," she remarked.

I have to admit, having two guests in the house was a bit stressful and I think it was beginning to take a toll on Aaron. Two weeks after Lotti arrived, he asked me how much longer they would be staying and all I could tell him was that Portia was looking at houses for sale in the area. He was just as surprised as I was that she'd decided to settle in New Rochelle and even more surprised to learn she'd persuaded Lottie to move in with her. "What on earth is she going to do here?" he asked. "I know she doesn't need to work but she doesn't have a family to look after. She'll need to do something to occupy her time."

"I know she's been thinking about that a lot and even mentioned starting her own business."

"What kind of business?"

"I don't know. We haven't really talked about it. She's concentrating on finding a house at the moment."

A week later, when Portia and Lotti were out, being shepherded around by the real estate agent, the telephone rang in the kitchen. After I answered it, I heard a man's voice that sounded vaguely familiar. "Is this Sam?" he asked.

"Yes," I answered rather tentatively, "who's this?"

"It's Hayden, Sam. How are you?"

"Oh my god, Hayden, how great to hear from you. How did you find us?"

"It was pretty simple. There aren't too many Aaron Reynolds in the New York area. I found you on the internet."

"I assume you heard about Portia's divorce?"

There was a pause before he answered, "Yes, I read about it in the Times but I thought I should wait a while before I called. I read she was staying with you. Is she okay, Sam?"

"Yes, she's fine and she's still here with us but not for much longer. She's out right now looking for a house in the area."

"Where are you exactly?" he asked.

"New Rochelle, do you know it?"

"Yes, I know it well. I've been living in Poughkeepsie for the last two years."

"Really? That must have been quite a change for you. What have you been up to? Are you still single?"

He sighed, "Not exactly. Unfortunately, I made the mistake of marrying someone I met soon after Portia and I split up. To make a long story short, my wife got pregnant right away and we decided to move out of the city. That's how we ended up here. I tried my best to be a decent husband but Sherry had a lot of anxiety issues and we just couldn't make a go of it. She walked out with my daughter when she was just a year old."

I was surprised he'd been so forthcoming, "I'm so sorry, Hayden. Do you get to see your daughter? What's her name?"

"Her name's Josie and I have joint custody but I only manage to see her every other weekend because they live in Syracuse, with Sherry's parents. It's about three and a half hours away so I usually have to drive up and spend the night in a hotel. It's not an ideal situation but, at least, we can be civil to each other. I gather the same applies to Portia and Philip. I read the divorce was uncontested so it must have been an amicable separation."

I almost choked but decided it wasn't my place to tell him the truth, "I'd rather Portia told you all about it. I'm assuming that's why you got in touch. Did you want to talk to her?"

"There's nothing I'd like more, Sam, but she may not want to talk to me. What if I give you my number and then we can leave it up to her. I don't want to put any pressure on her."

"I think that's a great idea," I answered but, after I finally put the phone down, I thought it was more than great; it was excellent. I'd always liked Hayden and I was disappointed when Portia gave him up for Philip. He said he didn't want to put pressure on her, but I did. She needed a man back in her life and I couldn't think of anyone better. I couldn't wait for her to get home.

Chapter Sixty

It was Christmas Day and we were celebrating at Portia's new house. It was a magnificent waterfront home with panoramic views of Long Island Sound, access to a private beach, and a large landscaped, terraced plot. The rooms were light and airy and almost gave one the sense of being outdoors. It was a much larger house than Portia had intended to purchase, even though she could well afford it after the divorce went through, but she fell in love with it on sight. A lot had happened since the end of October, when she and Lotti moved in. Furnishing the house and overseeing some minor renovations took up a lot of their time, but Portia insisted they also found time to relax and enjoy themselves.

After recovering from the shock of hearing Hayden had telephoned, Portia decided to call him back the next day. They must have talked for over an hour and agreed to meet two days later, at the Crown Plaza in Danbury. I remember how flustered she was and how long it took her to decide what to wear. Eventually she chose a simple white top with a pale green peasant skirt and strappy white sandals and she looked exceptionally young, and as lovely as ever.

The meeting was obviously a success and she met him a number of times after that. I wasn't surprised when, eventually, she asked if she could invite him to dinner. Naturally, I was delighted; things were going exactly the way I'd hoped and I couldn't wait to see him. When Saturday evening rolled around and he arrived on our doorstep, it was almost as though time had stood still. He still had the same mop of light brown hair, the boyish face and those remarkable green eyes. He handed me a large bouquet of white roses and, grinning from ear to ear, said, "Hi, Sam, you haven't changed a bit."

"I was just thinking the same about you," I responded and, reaching out with my one free hand, I pulled him inside.

The evening was a great success. Aaron greeted Hayden like a long lost buddy and I couldn't help noticing the little glances passing back and forth between Hayden and Portia. It was evident their relationship had become more intimate. Meanwhile, Lotti spent most of the evening interacting with Vicky, who insisted on staying up past her bedtime. She didn't want to miss anything and repeatedly snuck table scraps to Riley, who was already content enough, allowing Lotti to use him as a foot rest.

The celebration on Christmas day included Hayden and Lotti's new friend, Joe. Portia had mentioned Lotti had been struggling with her sexuality. Her experience with Serena had made her think long and hard about the path she'd taken, and she wondered what it would be like to be with a man again. It seemed like fate intervened when one of the contractors, hired to do the renovations, showed up at the house for the first time. Joe Ferris, was not only attractive but obviously very fit. He was a large man but muscular, at least six feet tall, and had the rugged look of someone who spent a lot of time outdoors. I could never have imagined Lotti being attracted to him, mainly because she was so slight and only a little over five feet, but I was wrong. Maybe it was his easy going manner and the way he treated her with such respect that made her fall for him and, before the renovation was complete, they were having an affair. Joe had married his high school sweetheart when he was twenty three.

They'd spent an amazing four years together before she was diagnosed with cervical cancer and died, less than six months later. They never had children and Joe wasn't interested in pursuing another serious relationship, until he met Lotti. He was thirty-five now and knew it was time to move on.

Portia and I were disappointed Beth couldn't be with us. She was supposed to arrive on Christmas Eve and planned to stay at Portia's for a few days but, due to a severe storm throughout the whole of the northeastern states, driving down from Boston wasn't an option. We did manage to have a lengthy telephone conversation with her on Christmas morning and, right after lunch, when we figured it was around dinner time in Hebden Bridge, we called Maggie. We had so much to tell her and begged her to come for a visit in the summer. I hadn't realized how much I missed her until I heard her voice, with that marvelous northern accent.

As both Hayden and Joe weren't due to arrive until mid-afternoon, Portia suggested we wait for them and open our presents just before dinner. Vicky was not happy. She had been eyeing the gaily wrapped packages, piled under the ornately decorated tree, since we got there shortly after breakfast. When Portia finally announced it was time, she let out a whoop, which startled Riley, and grabbed for the pettiest package, oblong in shape, covered in bright pink paper and topped with an enormous silver bow. Fortunately, the package was for her and contained one of the most beautiful dolls I'd ever seen. Lotti had found it in a vintage shop in Manhattan and thought it was the perfect gift for Vicky. She immediately christened it Rose.

We spent almost an hour opening the rest of the gifts but I began to notice that, other than one each for Aaron and Hayden, there were no other gifts from Portia. She was grinning, as we began to clear up all the wrappings, then she looked over at Lotti and me and said, "I suppose you think I've forgotten you both."

"Me too, Auntie," Vicky called out.

Portia walked towards her and reached out to take her hand, "Oh that's right," she said, "I did almost forget you but now it's your turn. Why don't you come with me?"

Vicky turned to look at me as they left the room and I wondered what on earth was going on but I didn't have to wait long to find out. A few minutes later the door opened and Vicky was standing there holding a ball of white fluff in her arms. I glanced up at Portia, who was standing behind her, "Tell me you didn't," I said.

She just grinned back at me and Vicky came further into the room. "Look Mommy," she said, "isn't she sweet. Auntie Portia says she's mine now."

I got up, walked over to her, and stroked the tiny kitten on the head, "She's beautiful, honey. What are you going to call her?"

Vicky shrugged, "I don't know. Maybe I'll just call her Kitty."

"That's not very original," Aaron remarked. "Why don't you wait a little while before you pick a name for her?"

Vicky nodded, "Okay, Daddy," she answered, bringing the kitten over for Riley to sniff at. "You've got a friend now," she said, "but you have to be careful because she's so little."

I looked over at Portia and smiled, "Thank you. You've made your niece a very happy little girl today."

Portia smiled back, "Well, I hope I can make you happy too. I actually have some rather surprising news to tell everyone." It got silent for a few moments before she continued. "Sam, do you remember when I worked at the boutique in the West Village?"

"Yes, of course," I answered, "it was called Veronique's."

"That's right. Well, I dropped in there two weeks ago just to say hello and I couldn't have picked a more opportune time."

"Don't tell me you're thinking of going back to work there," I said, shaking my head.

She smiled, "Not exactly. Veronique is almost eighty now and she wants to sell up, so I'm going to take over the business."

I gasped, "Oh, what a great idea, Portia. I know you've been thinking about starting up something on your own and this would be perfect for you."

She glanced at Lotti and then back at me, "Not only for me," she said grinning, "I want you both to be my partners. This will be my Christmas gift to you, we'll each own one third of the business."

Lotti's mouth dropped open and Joe put his arm around her. "That's really generous of you, Portia," he remarked.

"It's more than generous," I said. "It's too much. We can't let you do this, Portia, and I don't want to sound ungrateful but it would mean all three of us commuting every day. I can't speak for you and Lotti but I'm not sure I can manage it with Vicky's schedule."

Aaron cut in, "I'm certain we can work something out, honey."

"You won't have to," Portia said. "I'm going to manage the shop and keep the staff that's already there. Then, after about three months, I plan to open up another shop here in New Rochelle. We'll have to find the right location and there will be a lot of planning to do but I want you both to be involved."

Lotti finally found her voice and clapped her hands together excitedly, "Oh, this is wonderful. How can I ever thank you, Portia?"

"No need for thanks," Portia replied, "I could never do this on my own and I really need you and Sam."

I walked over and gave her a hug, "This seems too good to be true."

Vicky, who'd been too engrossed with her new kitten to pay any attention to the conversation, suddenly called out, "What's too good to be true, Mommy?"

I turned and smiled at her, "I'll tell you all about it later, honey."

We left Portia's at a little after ten o'clock. The trunk of our car was packed with gifts and an assortment of supplies for the kitten. Portia had thought of everything. Vicky was strapped into the back seat, with her new doll in her lap and her arm draped across the top of the brand new pet carrier; while Riley was cooped up in one corner. I was hoping Vicky would stay awake during the short drive home and I glanced back at her a couple of times, but she was staring out of the window. I looked over at Aaron and suddenly remembered something Portia told me earlier that day. On Christmas Eve, Hayden had picked up a copy of the New York Post and seen a picture of Philip descending from his private jet at Luton airport in London. He was accompanied by a striking brunette, one of Europe's top models and by his sister, Serena, with her new partner, a slim figured blond who resembled Lotti. "So, I guess everybody's moved on," Aaron remarked.

I was about to answer when Vicky called out, "Look out the window, Mommy."

"What is it, honey, what do you see?"

"It's a star. It's so big and bright. Can you see it?"

I glanced out of the passenger window and noticed the star way overhead. It seemed to be the only one in the sky. "Yes, it's awfully bright. I think that's because there aren't any clouds tonight." Suddenly, I had a thought and twisted around so that I faced her. "That gives me an idea, honey. Why don't you call your new kitten, Star?

A big smile came over her face, "Yes, Mommy. I love it," and she leaned over so that she could see inside the carrier. "Hello, Star," she whispered.

Aaron and I finally got to bed just before midnight. We were tired but not too tired to make love and, when it was over, he held me in his arms and said, "Today was a good day, Sam. I guess you're pretty happy, honey."

I snuggled up even closer to him, "I couldn't be happier. I've got the best husband in the world, an amazing daughter and my sister's back in my life."

He poked me in the ribs, "About Portia, you made it happen didn't you, Sam? I don't know how you did it but maybe now you'll let me in on the secret."

"I don't know what you're talking about," I responded trying to get away from him.

He actually chuckled, "Okay, I'll let you go but I'll get it out of you one of these days."

"Yeah, when hell freezes over," I muttered under my breath.